QUEEN OF FIRE

To Ken,
With thanks.
Regine Haensel

Regine Haensel

SERIMUSE

QUEEN OF FIRE

Book One of the Leather Book Tales

ISBN-13: 978-1495909511
ISBN-10: 1495909514
Cover design by Meshon Cantrill
Cover photo Regine Haensel
Printed by CreateSpace

Thanks

The Saskatchewan writing community (many supportive writers over the years) and the Saskatchewan Writers Guild have been important fixtures in my development as a writer. For this book in particular, I need to acknowledge the usefulness of the SWG's Manuscript Reading Service.

My writing group, Visible Ink, saw and commented on early and later drafts of the book – a helpful and awesomely talented bunch.

My son, who is multi-talented, both literary and graphically, performed a read through and edit during a late stage of the rewrite and also designed the cover and interior.

For Meshon

Queen of Fire

Prologue

He came upon the cave in the mountains years ago, seeking shelter during a rain storm. The downpour sent him to crouch under a ledge where a depression filled with sand and rubble gave way under his weight and tumbled him onto a sandy floor. He lay there, winded, looking about in the dimness, trying to penetrate shadows with his gaze. There were no footprints or other marks on the ground, no smells of animals, so he assumed the place was uninhabited. Luckily, once he got his breath back and the rain stopped, he was able to find enough rocky protrusions to climb out.

It didn't occur to him, even at the beginning, to share his discovery with anyone. He had no one that he called a friend among the young men of his father's castle or its surroundings. And as for his young step brother, they never had taken to each other.

Later he brought rope and torches and discovered that the cave held secrets that would take months, even years, as well as perseverance and skill to unravel. The first fragments of parchment he found lay in a niche just off the main chamber; most were too small and faded for him to read, and difficult to piece together. So he explored side passages and stumbled over a partially deteriorated scroll wrapped in a cracked piece of hide. This old and faded writing also gave him much toil and trouble, but words like "sorcery" and "power" grabbed his attention. He craved both. Afraid that others would learn his secret, he wrapped the fragments and his translations in soft hide, then placed them in a locked metal box hidden behind stones.

A first incantation deciphered, he tried speaking it immediately. Cracking and rumbling sent several small rocks to batter his shoulders. Caution suggested that he take his reading and reciting outside. The fall of a scrubby tree an arm's length away scared him enough that he stuck to written translations and silent reading for a while.

Often he wondered about who had left these secrets in the cave. Had someone lived here and meant to return? How far did the passages go and what might he discover in the future if he had the time? He didn't like to be away from home for too long in case someone became suspicious and followed him.

As he pieced together more fragments of scrolls, he began to understand that timing, location and intention all combined for success or failure. Perhaps other elements mattered, too, such as the alignment of stars and moon. He determined to find out. Worked on developing patience, though now and then he couldn't resist reciting one of the spells. A rabbit died, then came briefly back to life. A gust of wind knocked over a tree that almost hit him. These incidents reinforced the need for caution.

From waves of elation he plunged into troughs of despair. At times he went months without visiting the cave, and then for a period of time he would go every few days, taking great care, however, that no one followed him. He grew older and became ever more cautious and patient.

Raven and Eagle

Chapter I
Rowan

I'm kneeling in dirt, grubbing around the strawberries, weeding between herbs, and whispering encouragement to make our garden grow. Mother always says that plants do better if you talk to them, and she must be right because we produce some of the best food around. Of course, she has traded for seeds from far away, and has plants that no one else in the area has seen before, like lettuce. She's also been able to transplant wild things such as onions and make them grow bigger.

These are probably some of the reasons why people mutter about Mother and me – a woman in the village turns away as we pass, or talks behind her hands to a neighbour. A couple of children might follow us, then run when I swivel to look at them. I've never heard the word 'witch' uttered; though I'm sure they gossip out of our hearing. Still, even the ones who look at us askance don't hesitate to buy our vegetables or to take advantage of Mother's herbal lore.

I yank at a weed which refuses to budge. A weed is any plant that grows where you don't want it. Like me stuck here in this clearing in the woods. I wonder what it would take to release our roots, propel us out of this place where I've lived all my life. These days I find our three-room cottage nestled into a low hill too cramped, though I used to love it.

"Rowan! Rowan!"

Mother's voice carries over the sound of leaves rustling in the aspens nearby, bird song and a faint rush of water. She is using tones of persuasion, but I manage to ignore her for the moment. She knows where I am and could easily take the few steps from the house to the garden. As I finish and stand up, her call comes again.

This time there is an undercurrent of temptation, like a lure to a hungry fish in the river. I want to resist that coaxing tone, be like the girl I saw the other day in the village who stamped her foot, turned her back on her mother and ran away down the street. I'm too old for tantrums, but can make a small rebellion by staying here.

"Rowan!" Her voice commands me now. I've heard her use that tone on a trader who tried to cheat her and know it's not to be resisted.

I throw a last weed on the pile, brush dirt off my hands and skirt. "Yes, Mother?"

She sits on a stool by the door of our cottage as she often does, finger weaving grass and twigs with lengths of spun wool. In this pose she appears gentle and innocuous, one of the many guises she uses. Various shapes and sizes of her creations hang from roof, rafters and trees – triangles, star shapes and hexagons, the shades of tree, leaf, earth, sky and cloud. Their intricate interlacing and knots capture and hold the eye, are meant to snare evil intentions and keep them imprisoned, but I wonder if that's just superstition. Mother taught me to make them when I was small; I liked them because they were pretty. Now and then the wind blows a few away, but even with that we have a surfeit of them, and I wish she'd stop.

"Have you seen Thea?" Mother asks, tilting her head in the way that is so familiar and as irritating as a pebble in my shoe. Many things about her annoy me these days, and I swallow a sigh.

"The goat is gone again?" I brush at the strand of black hair tickling my nose, then notice that there's mud on the back of my hand, probably transferred to my face now. "No, I haven't seen her."

"I don't know what's the matter with her the last few days. She's continually wandering off." Mother shoos at the chickens pecking the ground around her feet.

I rest my back against a tree, not ready to give her reasons why the goat may have disappeared. It could tell her too much about my own thoughts, though Mother probably knows that I'm increasingly discontent. My friend Lynx and his family passed through a few weeks ago heading north as they always do at the beginning of summer. They left us some of last years' wild grain, which grows in shallow lakes. It's delicious with meat and vegetables or with milk. I suggested to Mother that we travel with Lynx's family for a couple of days. We could have harvested herbs and other plants as we went. Mother didn't agree. I considered running away then, but this year they were fourteen with the new baby and on thinking it over, I wasn't sure I could stand the crowd. When Lynx and I first met, he couldn't believe that my mother and I lived alone.

"Only two of you?" he said. "Where's the rest of your family?"

A good question, but I changed the subject by asking him about the land to the north of us. Where the trees stop is beautiful in a different way than the forest, Lynx told me – you can see all the way to the place where earth meets sky. I try to imagine long stretches of flat land where a person can see nearly to forever and wonder where animals find places to hide. Lynx says there are vast herds of a kind of huge deer, myriads of birds and small creatures. He spoke of a sky crammed with stars at night, and circular sunsets, as well as a time when the sun barely dips to the horizon at all.

"Thea may have gone looking for excitement," I say.

"Hmm?" Mother glances at me and puts down her weaving. "I'm going after that goat."

Purplish-grey clouds are massing over the trees to the west. "Storm coming," I say.

Mother gathers her white-streaked red hair in both hands, twists it into a knot at her neck. I wonder whether my father had black hair and that's where I got mine from. Mother never talks about him anymore, though when I was small she used to say that he'd gone on a long journey. I remember nagging her to describe him and asking what games he played with me; she would start talking about something else or snap at me to stop pestering her. I think he must be dead, must have been dead all this time and Mother didn't know how to tell a child that he wasn't coming back.

"I'm going to find that stupid goat before she falls in the river and is swept away," Mother snaps. "You shut her kids into the shed with the donkey, and close the chickens in there, too." She frowns. "Pay close attention to what needs to be done. You've been abstracted lately."

I feel a sudden lurch of guilt, my stomach roils. "Wait," I say and dash into the cottage. Mother's green-dyed leather cloak hangs on a hook beside mine just inside the door. I bring it to her. "In case you're caught in the rain."

A smile lights her grey eyes and she touches my cheek in thanks, then briefly the necklace of leather, wooden beads and a sapphire at my throat. She made it for my fifteenth birthday, just a fortnight ago, and I love it. I have a sudden impulse to hug her, but she has already stepped away.

"Are you sure you don't want me to come along?" I call as she starts off.

She turns. "No. Keep the stew warm and stir it once in a while so it doesn't burn."

I'm not that bad of a cook I want to shout, but she's already disappeared down the path that leads into the trees. I head for the shed that leans against the far wall of the house, and the donkey standing half in and half out of it, placidly munching hay. After I've finished with the animals I enter the cottage and notice that the fire is almost out. We don't need it to keep us warm at this time of year except occasionally, so I add only a little wood to keep the stew simmering, then begin to set the table.

A bright flash lights the darkening room; a crack of thunder follows almost immediately. I drop a spoon. The pair of doves in the rafters flutters at the clatter, then settles down again, cooing soothingly to each other. They can be messy now and then, but Mother says she likes to see them nestle there and she's been trying to teach them to carry messages, though without success so far. The fledglings are well hidden near the hole at the peak; we hear them cheep sometimes. I cross to the front window as rain begins to flow down the wavy glass. The path is already a churning of mud.

"Hurry up, Mother!" I whisper.

Behind me a log snaps. I pull a stool close to the fire and grab the poker. Tending to the partially burned logs and adding more pieces takes time and concentration, helps keep thoughts away. I pick up the long-handled spoon lying on the hearth, wipe it on my apron, and stir the cauldron of stew. Usually at this time of day Mother and I drink a cup or two of a special tisane that she has mixed from various herbs. She hasn't told me the ingredients yet, but says that she will one day. A pottery jar of the mixture sits on the counter nearby and I think about heating water, then decide to wait for Mother.

Flames flicker, rise and fall, red and yellow, a dash of blue. Shapes of wood and fire flow and change. As a child I would spend hours staring at the flames, imagining people and places from the stories Mother read to me out of the big leather-covered book that was kept in the chest in her room. It's the only book we own. The Fire Queen was one of my favourites. She had the ability to take the form of fire as well as to shape it, sending forth sparks that became birds or dragons. None could stand against her for fire consumes everything. As her lust for power and destruction grew, the people of the land searched for a hero to save them. A young man, an orphan cast up on the beach in a small boat, offered his services. Of course, it turned out that his father was a god of the sea and so the young man defeated the Fire Queen with a tidal wave. I was sad at that and imagined other endings where the Queen survived and became a better person. There were always villains and heroes in the stories, sometimes monsters. Mostly the heroes were boys or men, but now and then a girl saved a kingdom. Some of these set off on quests and had amazing adventures along the way. When I was small I thought that my father had gone off on just such a journey and I wished I could be riding at his side. After I learned to read Mother let me keep the book in my room, but I haven't opened it for a long time. I'm not so interested now in made up stories; life is generally much duller than what you read in books. A sigh escapes me. I rest my chin on my hand, yawn.

After a while it seems to me that fire shapes eyes, a nose, a man's square face and a boy beside him. They look familiar, but of course I don't know them, they're only imaginary. Mother's face takes their place. She opens her mouth to speak to me, but the fire crackles and snaps too loudly. I lean forward to hear better. A baby cries, and I search the fire for it, but there are only flames flowing like red and orange water over black logs.

I wake to glowing coals and a dark room. Someone taps on glass, a baby bleats again. The glass in our two windows is another thing that I've heard others discuss when they think we don't hear. Most people use wooden shutters or animal hide. I don't actually know where Mother got the glass. Rubbing sleep out of my eyes, I stand creakily to straighten my back. Sleeping hunched on a stool is not good for a person. The tapping again.

"Coming."

I stumble against furniture until I am able to find a couple of candles and light them from the embers, throw a few sticks on. There is no sign of Mother in the house, so hopefully she has found shelter, but perhaps she's been hurt and having trouble opening the door. I want it to be Mother, even if she shouts at me for falling asleep, but it's most likely some village or farm woman who needs herbs for a sick child. I can deal with that. Ever since I could walk and talk my mother has been teaching me all she knows of the lore of plants and healing.

I approach the window wondering why whoever is there didn't come to the door – perhaps it's too dark outside to see properly. My fingers fumble at the latch. Darkness flutters on the other side of the glass and there's another knock. I wrench open the casement. In hops Mord, wet-feathered and stained with mud. The raven squawks at me and lets a few reddish filaments that resemble mother's hair fall from his beak. I try to catch them, but they slip through my fingers and disappear.

"Mord! What's happened, what have you been doing?"

The raven hops to my shoulder, dragging it down, and squawks in my ear. Mother and I have had this bird since he was a nestling. He's part of the family, like the goats, the donkey, the chickens and the doves, though to my mind he's the smartest of our menagerie. I think he likes me better than Mother, has always stayed closer to me than to her. Lynx says that raven, along with bear, rabbit and a few others were the first inhabitants of this land. Some of them were powerful spirits who could take other shapes, even that of people. Mord nibbles at my ear. He wouldn't come knocking at the window for a trivial reason. From the front door comes a thump.

"Be right there!" I shout.

Outside stars glitter and a gibbous moon floats just over the trees. I have no idea how long I slept, but it's not raining anymore. Thea, the nanny goat, butts my knees and bleats again. She too is soaking. I can't see Mother anywhere, and push Thea away.

"Where is she?" I shout to the goat, the bird, the trees.

Mord leaps into the air and flies to the lowest branch of an evergreen near the path into the forest. He calls twice, with a harsh croak, furls and unfurls his wings, then screeches again.

"Yes," I call, holding on to the frame of the door to steady myself. My heart thumps in my chest and I'm having difficulty catching my breath. "I'm coming."

Thoughts whirl through my head – Mother would want me to shut the goat in the shed so she doesn't run away again; would expect me to make sure the fire is not in danger of getting out of control, the stew safe from burning. What has Mord seen? Cold night air sends shivers down my neck and raises the hair on my arms. Best concentrate on what I have to do. There is no sense in letting worry rise up like a dark shadow to envelop and blind me.

I finish with the goat, then run back to the cottage, grab my cloak. Mord still calls outside, and I worry that he'll leave without me. Cast a glance at the fire, set the cauldron of congealed stew aside on the hearth and cover it. Light the lantern, blow out the candles in the room, slam the door and run.

The raven flies ahead, sometimes landing on a tree or bush, now and then walking on the muddy path. I don't try to search for Mother's footprints – the rain will have washed them away. My wooden sabots splash through puddles, but I ignore the increasing dampness of my feet. If only I could run faster, or had wings. I'm afraid Mother is hurt, otherwise she would have come home long before this. I shouldn't have fallen asleep. Perhaps she has slipped into one of the pits that hunters use to catch large game; I should have brought rope. Water drips from the leaves of trees, some of it spatters on my head and rolls down my neck. I pull up the hood of my cloak, stop to catch my breath. Mord circles, calls impatiently. My chest aches and I try to breathe evenly and slowly, though I want to swallow air in great gulps and tear along the forest path.

A pale slash cuts across the trail – a tree, split by lightning, uprooted by the storm. I clamber over it, take time to search beneath and around. Nothing and no one lies entangled there, though I find one smudged footprint. Not from a sabot, but a paw of some fairly large animal. It worries me and I hurry on.

At last we reach the river swollen with rain, almost overflowing its banks. It surges and rages like a great sinuous monster, leaves and pieces of trees tossed in the wake of its passing. The path splits to both sides. The left leads toward a neighbour's farm and then to the village. Mord alights on a tree to the right. Pale moonlight filters through the trees, glinting off turgid water. A darker area lies just under the bank, a snarl of branches and weeds, a shadowy mass.

I am a tree blasted by lightning on the river bank; my feet are rooted to the ground, my legs like dead stumps. Mord croaks loudly and the sound breaks my paralysis. There's a sick churning in my stomach. I step forward, lean over the slippery edge and grasp sodden cloth.

At first I have hope because there seems to be nothing but leather and cloth, though it's heavy and waterlogged. A sudden flash of white makes me bite my lips to bleeding and I heave harder. The roots of a huge broken tree have a tenacious hold. In the struggle, I catch glimpses of a face, distorted, but still recognizable – Mother. Now and then a hand floats up as if trying to help. My own fingers are numb from the biting water.

After I have dragged her onto the bank, I kneel weeping, stroking her hair. Her hands are like ice and her body feels so stiff. I can't feel a pulse or heartbeat, but maybe that's because I'm shaking too much. I must move her to warmth, but how will get her home? She is too heavy for me to carry that distance and I won't drag her through mud. There is only one thing possible, but I'm reluctant to leave her alone while I fetch the donkey and the cart, because I've noticed more paw prints on the bank, some animal that came sniffing about after the rain perhaps, but couldn't get to Mother in the river. Mord, who all this time has perched in a tree, flutters down to my shoulder and rubs his head against my cheek. He hops to the ground by Mother's head and caws quietly twice. I understand that he will stay and watch. I take off my cloak and wrap it around Mother.

One moment I'm looking down at Mord, the next my feet race along the path, arms fending off branches of trees. I stand in front of the cottage, a faint glimmer of light from the fire shining through the windows. I have no memory of the time between. The cart stands beside the shed – inside are the warm and dozing animals.

The donkey is reluctant to move at first, but finally I get him fastened into the traces. Once we reach the forest path, he actually begins to trot. Scraped and bleeding hands wrestle with the fallen tree on the path. Pale moon and my mother's face shine equally white, as if all of her blood has drained away, though I can see no wound on her. Skeletal tree trunks and branches reach down as if to pluck us from the ground as the donkey labours to drag the cart, and dark water drips from a cloak. The rosy glow of fire flares up as I add more wood and gives colour to Mother's cheeks. How did I get back to the cottage, and did I remember to unhitch the cart and shut the donkey in the shed? My memories are like shards of glass, sharp but fragmented.

Is it my imagination or do I see her lips start to curve in a smile as if she is ready to wake? Perhaps she wasn't in the water too long. The snap and crackle of the fire reminds me of the creak of the cart, Mord's raw cry. I shiver with wet and cold, and something else that I am not ready to name. My hands and feet do what needs to be done and my head feels as if it has floated upward to hang with the moon, above everything.

***

I'm lying on a rug trying to stay awake by watching the flames, looking for pictures that will give hope to the night. I see a girl weeping. She is waiting for her mother to come and comfort her. I know that she waits in vain and I try to reach out to her, but the child is gone and the fire is hot. I pull back, look again. Perhaps the Fire Queen will come and give courage to the girl, for the Queen wasn't always evil, was she? No one comes; it's up to me to do what is necessary. Did I get Mother to bed? I shiver and exhaustion drags down my eyelids. A soft hand touches my cheek, smooths my hair. I smell lavender and cinnamon.

"Mother," I whisper, "are you going to bake cinnamon bread?"

"Thea," a voice answers.

"No." I struggle against sleep, though my eyes remain shut. "The goat is in the shed, Mother, I'm Rowan. I'm glad you're back. I had such a terrible dream."

The hand soothes. "Rest my dear."

I smile and whisper, "Tell me a story."

The tale is about a woman who can take goat shape. No one must find out. I like secrets, but want to know who is keeping this one and for what reasons. It's between the mother and the goat, meant to keep the girl safe. I don't understand why the child can't be given the secret, she wouldn't tell. I imagine that the mother is going out to meet the goat, but they miss each other in the downpour. How can that be when Mother said the goat had run away? The goat speaks about the unnatural storm with much more rain and wind than usual.

"I wonder if your mother's protections have been breached," the goat says. "I'm not certain, but we should be careful none the less."

A kiss soothes my forehead; the light weight of a blanket surrounds my shoulders. I snuggle into warmth and safety without opening my eyes.

I sigh. "Tell me more of the story."

Mother walks with me along the ridge of hills behind our cottage. The sun has just crept over the horizon and I can see the forest with its clearings for small farms, the river winding away to the south, and part way along, the smudge of smoke that marks the nearest village. I've never travelled beyond that village, never used to think much about the rest of the world except when we read the stories in the leather bound book.

"I'm sorry," Mother says.

Why, I wonder, is Mother sorry, when it's I who should apologize for wanting to leave her?

"I should have told you more," she continues. "I was going to soon, but now you'll have to find out for yourself."

I turn away from the view to look at her and ask what she means, but she is gone like mist dissolving over the river. I search everywhere and call loud and long. Finally I give up and return to the cottage. I enter, then stop as I notice someone lying in front of the fireplace under the blanket from my bed. Mother and I wove it several years ago of goat's hair, and sheep's wool that we got from a neighbouring farmer. Who has dared to take it? My next step sinks through the wooden boards of the floor. The cottage shivers and tilts as my head whirls.

Warmth and light creep across my face like a caress. I smile and stretch without opening my eyes. Soon Mother will come to wake me and we can eat together, our morning gruel with wild honey, goat's milk, and berries. Or perhaps she did make that cinnamon bread. I draw in a deep breath, but smell only dust and ashes. My arms ache and the bed has too many hard lumps.

I open my eyes to morning and no gruel cooking, no baking. In the rafters, the doves' coo sounds sad to me, and in spite of their presence the cottage feels empty as a hollow log. The blanket slips from my shoulders and I remember someone putting it over me. I believed it was Mother, but she said her name was Thea. No, impossible, just a strange dream. The door to Mother's room is shut. Last night, did I help her to bed or was that a dream, too?

I stand in front of the bedroom door and stare first at it, and then at the heap of dirty cloak lying on the floor. Did I leave it so or did Mother? There are great gaps in my memory of last night. I can't take the next step and open the door, not yet. Besides, if Mother is sleeping, she won't like me waking her. I convince myself that there are things that need doing outside.

In the shed the donkey, the chickens, the two kids, and the nanny goat greet me – clucking, bawling, bleating, butting, stamping, swarming round my feet, crowding toward the door. I glance out at the trees and see that many of Mother's weavings have blown away in the storm. I suppose I should start replacing them, but I don't feel like it. Chickens flutter past and begin scratching for worms and bugs; the donkey kicks up his heels and heads for the water trough. The two kids butt at their mother's belly, but she ignores them.

I stare at the goat. Thea looks back at me, holding my eyes, and I can almost hear her whisper: I'm sorry, it's my fault. I drew her out into the storm, and she drowned.

I shake my head and turn away. Goats can't speak. This is not some story out of a book or one of Lynx's tales from long ago. A gust of wind rattles the branches of a nearby tree; their scraping sounds like dead fingers. I wrap my arms tightly around myself, wishing it was Mother standing behind me, pulling me into a hug, using her gifts of language to convince me everything is all right.

Reluctantly I re-enter the cottage, which feels too large. I clear my throat and the only sound that greets me is a sort of faint echo. I wish Lynx and his whole family were here, crowded into this one room, chattering, moving about. Even the doves have flown from the rafters, perhaps to find food. I could follow their lead and cook myself some gruel, but instead I just stand in the middle of the room.

The green wooden door gapes open behind me. I painted that door a year ago, over Mother's initial objections – she wanted brown, but she gave in eventually. To my left the large window is closed, unusual for this late in the morning. Nearby on the scrubbed wooden table a heel of bread lies on a cutting board; a couple of plates, goblets, and cutlery are spread around – no one tidied last night. To my right, under the small window a vase of wilted flowers sits on the large chest; Mother would scold if she saw that. Beyond the chest, a torn, partially mended skirt is thrown over one arm of the well-padded arm chair. Mother's footstool is nearby, as if she had just this moment stepped away. She does often go out early in the day to gather herbs or to tend a sick child.

I ignore the mess, including the blanket heaped on the floor near the fireplace and the stool lying on its side. Grab the dry bread and nibble it while I built up the fire; I'm so cold. I refuse to think about Mother's bedroom.

Once I've warmed up, I begin to set things to rights, as if Mother has merely gone away, and expecting her back at any moment, I want the room to look its best so that she will have nothing to complain about. I should shake and brush her cloak, so that everything will be perfect when she returns.

The cloak is stained with mud and smells of the river. A few red and white hairs cling to the hood. I pick them off carefully, holding them tightly between my fingers. Why did I let her set out alone when I knew a storm was coming? Why had she not paid attention to the dark clouds and the river rising and returned home? She could have left the goat to her own devices.

I drop the cloak and push open the door to Mother's bedroom. The room is silent, with a scent of lavender hanging in the air, also cinnamon and a bitter smell that reminds me of yarrow. This is odd because cinnamon is expensive and Mother would never scatter it around her room. She always has bunches of lavender hanging on the pegs with her clothes and in the chest at the foot of her bed though, but not yarrow. It, as far as I know, is used for treating digestive problems. The clothes are still there, of course, and so is the shape on the bed that could be someone sleeping, except there is no sound of breathing.

"Mother," I whisper.

There's no answer. An aching emptiness stabs my stomach. Silence surrounds me, as loud as thunder on a stormy night. I cover my ears and run from the room and the cottage, slamming doors behind me.

Outside there is more silence, the day still, the leaves on the trees unmoving. A quiet bleat turns me toward the shed. Thea is curled there, while her kids frolic nearby. It's her fault that Mother went out into the storm. I squat beside her, stare at her goat face. Is there human intelligence? Did she really come to me last night as a woman? If I have stumbled into an old tale or legend the goat might be able to help.

"Thea," I say urgently, tapping her nose, "there must be herbs, or other things for Mother."

Her dark blue eyes lift to my face. Briefly, her head moves from side to side. She bleats once and it sounds like 'no.'

I bend lower. "Listen," I hiss, "she went out because of you. You have to make it right."

Her voice is as muted as mine, but the words are unmistakable. "I would help you if I could. I know of no way to bring someone back from the dead."

***

Sun blazes into the clearing, glints off the windows of the cottage, shoots sparkles from the water trough. Chickens scratch in the dirt near the shed; the donkey stands in the shade, lazily flicking his tail. Everything as usual, quite normal, except that the most important person is missing. I notice that the kids are in the garden, heads down in the lettuce. Mother would want me to chase them away and close the gate, but today I can't be bothered, merely stand, staring at everything and nothing. My mind wanders into memory.

It rains all morning; Mother snaps at me because I don't stop racing around the cottage and knocking into things. When the clouds finally clear I rush outside to play, partly to get away from her. A huge puddle covers the low spot in the centre of the clearing. Mother is calling, but I pay no attention, run full tilt into the water, splash and laugh, slipping and sliding. Fall into mud and get up again. Mother stands in the door of the cottage shaking her head and smiling.

Another day Mother relaxes under a tree, sorting through seeds. It's a quiet kind of work and picky, needing no interruptions so she has set me to sorting stones nearby. I look up now and then, wanting her to finish and play with me. A butterfly lands on her hand. Mother stops moving and I hold my breath until the brown and orange wings flutter into the sky.

One afternoon a woman clutching a baby hunches on a bench by the cottage. The child screams with pain. The woman pats the baby, croons to it, rocks back and forth, but nothing soothes it. Mother comes out of the door, administers a few drops of liquid, lifts the child, rubs its belly. The screams quiet to sobs. Mother puts the baby over her shoulder, pats its back. I watch from the window.

We are at the table, just the two of us, sipping a tisane. It's dark outside, but inside the fire and candles create a warm glow. Mother has laid out bunches of dried herbs on the table and is asking me to identify each and explain its use. When I get them all correct, she smiles.

I don't know how long I've been standing lost in thought when a shout brings me back. At the opening of the path into the forest stands a large man. The sun is behind him throwing the front of his body and face into shadow. For a moment I am terrified, can't move. Who is this interloper and what does he want? The man takes a couple of steps forward and I am able to recognize Olwin, our nearest neighbour.

"You took no damage from the storm?" he asks, looking around. "That's lucky. We lost two chickens when a tree crushed the coop, though they'll make a fine meal."

I stare at him. I've forgotten how talkative some people can be.

"And the babe tumbled out of her crib, so the wife sent me for a poultice. Where's your mother?"

I shake my head. Don't have the words to tell him.

"Gone gathering? I didn't see her in the forest as I came along."

He takes several more steps in my direction. "What ails you, Rowan? Are you hurt?"

I shudder and my legs give way. Olwin holds me up. Suddenly the dam of control that has been holding my feelings back breaks. Sobs shake me, tears flow. He pats my back, leads me slowly to the bench by the door. Stands nearby, shifting from foot to foot, waiting for my weeping to abate, I suppose. I could use a shoulder to cry on, but it's not his I want.

"Tell, me child. Is it that your mother has been hurt?"

I nod, staring at his feet in muddy sabots. My feet are bare because I forgot to put my shoes on when I came outside, can't remember where I left them. They must be muddy, too. I know that normally people answer questions, speak to each other, have conversations, but I can't remember how to do that.

"Where is she?"

I shake my head and point at the cottage door, quickly lowering my eyelids because I am afraid of breaking down again if I see sympathy in his face. His feet turn and move away from me. I hear the creak of the cottage door, and then everything goes quiet. I could follow him with my mind, imagine what he will see when he opens the door to Mother's bedroom, but I push those thoughts away. Better to just wait, sitting in the centre of silence, staring at my dirty toes. There is no wind, no cry of bird or animal, no motion. Finally I have to take a breath, and Olwin's feet are beside me. I catch a hint of cinnamon.

"I'm so sorry," he says, crouching down and touching my shoulder briefly. "Rowan my dear, this is terrible!"

I nod, wondering whether I'll ever be able to shape words again.

He has left my side and I glance up to see him pacing. "What happened, was it the storm? Was she struck by lightning?"

He comes back to stand beside the bench. I'm sure he is trying to see my face, attempting to catch my eye. A few moments before it had been a comfort to have him there; now he is an irritant, like a burr caught in my clothes. I will have to make the effort and find words to give him, or perhaps he will imagine me driven mad and take me away. There was a girl once who wouldn't talk. Her parents brought her to Mother, but none of the herbs worked. The girl started shouting wordlessly and flailing about with her arms. They had to tie her to the wagon when they drove away. I manage a deep breath, am able to raise my head and look not at Olwin, but at the trees.

"River," I whisper. I shiver, though I can feel the heat of the sun on my face.

"We'll help you," he says. "Come with me now, you can stay the night. I'll send Medwin to see to your animals."

"No!" I nearly shout the word. Swallow, move my tongue back and forth to start saliva flowing. "Staying here." I turn my eyes to his face, try to look calm. I take a deep shuddering breath and clasp my hands together behind my back, the nails biting into my palms. The slight pain steadies me. "I'm all right." I know it's not true, but I have to convince him.

He narrows his eyes and gazes at me, wringing his hands. "The wife would never forgive me if I didn't bring you home. This is no place for a girl alone."

A gust of wind whips the hair round my face, making my eyes sting. I shake my head. "Not a girl anymore," I say.

For a long moment he studies me. I'm glad he hasn't attempted to touch me again. I realize that he's waiting for me to say more. I close my eyes for a moment, see the words written there, as if on a fragment of parchment.

"Please." I open my eyes, make myself stare at his face, his pale blue eyes. "It's what I want. Tell . . ." I can't remember her name . . . "your wife I said so."

"You truly would be welcome with us."

I take another shuddering breath, continue to hold his eyes, trying to put as much conviction and persuasion into my voice as I can. "Thank you. I'm used to it here." He blinks so I rush on before he can speak. "Tomorrow you can come and help me . . . do what's necessary."

He stops protesting. Walks over to shoo the kids out of the garden and fasten the gate securely. Next he scatters grain for the chickens and puts fresh hay out for the goats and donkey. While he is doing all that I slip indoors and make up the poultice he's requested. It's a simple recipe that I've mixed many times. When I hand it to him, he stares stupidly.

"For the babe," I say.

He frowns.

"The tumble out of the crib?"

"Oh, yes!" he says. "To think that with all your troubles you remembered that!" He pats my shoulder and I grit my teeth. "Are you sure you won't come with me?"

"Thank you, no," I say firmly.

"We'll be over in the morning, then. If you change your mind this evening get on that donkey and ride to us."

I nod and watch thankfully as he strides away. I'm actually surprised that he left, wasn't sure I could convince him that I'm all right when I'm not. Though I really don't want anyone else here, so maybe that got through. When the trees hide Olwin, I sigh deeply, then wait a little longer in case he decides to return. I become aware of the hollow feeling in my belly. It comes to me that except for a dry crust of bread, I haven't eaten since the previous mid-day and by the sun, it is nearly that again.

Familiar actions soothe and I let them, pushing other thoughts away. I get water from the well, set it to heat, add wild grain, get out a bowl and spoon. Sit at the table and eat the gruel with milk and honey. It's lumpy, but I don't care, want only a few mouthfuls anyway, and the chickens will enjoy the leftovers. In the rafters the doves coo, returned again to their favourite perch, though I haven't noticed them arriving. I haven't seen Mord since the night before. No matter how much we delude ourselves that we've domesticated him, he's still a wild bird. That's what Mother always says, but I worry about him.

There is no sign of the raven anywhere outside. The goats are asleep in the shade of the shed; I watch them. Do I really believe that a goat can talk? I tug one of her ears. She opens her eyes, raises her head, and looks mournfully at me.

"Thea, have you seen Mord?" I glance quickly around, but of

course no one is there to see me talking to a goat. When I turn back, she is still looking at me. I tug her ear again.

"You mustn't keep doing this," she whispers softly.

"What?"

"You should not keep speaking to me."

She's not really talking back, I'm just imagining it. I know this isn't a wise thing to do, but who else is there?

"You must treat me like a goat," Thea continues, "the way you used to. Something or someone could be watching. That might mean danger for you."

I glare. "Explain yourself!"

The goat bares her teeth. "I know hardly anything."

I bury my fingers in the pelt of her neck and twist. "Tell me whatever you can."

"Tonight, when it's dark I'll come to you." She closes her eyes, lowers her head to the ground.

No matter how I coax and plead the goat has gone mute. And I still don't know what has happened to Mord. I consider leaving the clearing to search for him, but he could be anywhere. Besides, the trees surrounding me look dark and forbidding now, though I've always considered them friendly before. A breeze rattles a few leaves and seems to whisper words I can't quite make out. I can't let myself get spooked. There's weeding to finish and herbs to gather – sage and parsley for adding to meat and vegetables, horehound for coughs, chamomile and mint for soothing the mind and stomach.

Gradually, behind the clouds, the sun moves toward setting. I tidy the kitchen. All day I have avoided looking at the closed door of Mother's bedroom, but I'm always aware of it. Finally, I can think of nothing else that needs doing and find myself standing in front of that door. I simply stare at it, studying the grain, the swirls and knots, attempting to see faces or scenes from stories, finding only a wooden barrier separating me from the truth.

At last I light the lantern. Slowly I open the door, take a few steps forward and hold the light so I can see the bed. Her face looks washed out, but tranquil, eyes closed. I set the lantern on the small table beside the bed. Light puts a gold and silver glow into her hair. Tentatively, I reach out a hand to tuck a few stray waves into place. My fingers encounter the clammy skin of her cheek, causing me to shiver and draw back. How cold her hands were when I pulled her out of the river. I bite my lip and touch her again, laying a warm palm against the side of her face.

"She was proud of you."

I jerk at the voice, turn and see a woman in a faded grey dress standing in the doorway. She is about the height of my mother and has a similar face though her hair is brown, and her eyes are dark blue. We stare at each other.

"Rowan," my name on her lips is soft and tentative.

"You're a dream or vision."

I feel pain in my hands and realize that I am clenching my fingers so hard the nails have left marks. When I look at her again tears are overflowing her eyes.

"No," she says, "I'm real enough." Reaches out a hand, but doesn't touch me. "Breathe, Rowan."

The floor moves under my feet, tilting, and I know that I'm falling. I wait for the thump and bang, but her arms are strong and hold me up. I sigh and let myself sink against her. Close my eyes and imagine Mother, but she doesn't smell right. Instead of lavender, there's a scent of hay and milk.

"Are you truly a goat that can change shape?" I ask. A soft chuckle like Mother's. Slowly I lift my eyelids.

"It's true, Rowan. I'm sorry that I couldn't tell you before."

I frown. "Mother knew."

"Of course she did. We're cousins."

"No." I shake my head and pull away from her. I turn to the shape on the bed. Shout, "What else didn't you tell me?"

"Rowan." The woman takes a step toward me.

"Is your name really Thea?"

"Yes."

My head begins to pound. I press the heels of my hands against my eyes. A hand pulls them away.

"Don't do that, Rowan. If your eyes are sore, bathe them."

"What do you know about it?" I shout. "What are you doing here? I want Mother!"

Thea takes my hand and pulls me to the bedside. "It's time for us to say goodbye. I know it's hard, but it has to be done. We can't leave her lying like this much longer. I scattered tansy and yarrow to preserve, and a little cinnamon, but . . ." She shakes her head.

Thea coaxes me to one side of the bed, sits on the other. She takes one of my mother's hands and reaches for one of mine. Slowly, I do the same; Mother's hand and fingers are limp now, not rigid as they were last night. Thea begins to hum. The tune is familiar, a lullaby Mother used to sing when I was small; the words come back to me. *Do you know how many stars are in the dark night sky? No one can count them all. Every child can choose a star, though unlike birds and stars, children can't fly. Only in dreams, only in dreams can we join the stars in that far distant hall.*

A slight breeze stirs my hair. I'd like to believe that it's part of Mother hovering in the room with us. Want to feel the warmth of her hand in mine, want her to speak. We come to the end of the song, and my hair is still. Mother's hand remains unresponsive and her face immobile. Thea pulls the covers up to Mother's shoulders and gives her a hug. I lean over and kiss the pale forehead, shiver. We leave the room and I don't look back.

Collapsing into the arm chair, I sigh. Thea stirs up the fire. This is my house now, I should be doing that.

"Would you like food or a hot tisane?" I ask. "There's a special kind that Mother used to make. Not much of it left now, but we could drink it in her memory."

She shakes her head and perches on the stool. "The reason she gave it to you was so that you wouldn't remember the things she didn't want you to remember."

"What do you mean?" I whisper.

"It's complicated." She clears her throat. "Your mother and I grew up in a city far from here in sight of the mountains and we were close as sisters. Both of us lost our parents to illness so our grandparents brought us up together."

"Are they still there?" I ask. "My great grandparents?"

Thea shakes her head. "They died some time ago. Your mother and I," she continues, "come from a family with special gifts. I could shape small things, turn a walnut into a beetle, or a twig into a worm; I was told my mother could do the same. Your mother, learned about herbs and healing from our grandmother."

Thea stares into the fire and I wonder what she's seeing there. Sadness has hold of me. Why did Mother never tell me about her childhood? Why did I never ask?

"Life was good," Thea continues, "and then Zarmine met a man. I only saw her with him a few times; he was dark, tall and handsome." A brief laugh turns into a sob. Thea shakes her head and bites her lip. After a while she continues. "The kind of thing you read about in one of the old tales. The handsome young prince comes and woos the princess, except she wasn't a princess, though I don't know what he was. Perhaps he told your mother where he came from, who his people were, but if so, she never confided it to me. Before that, we used to tell each other everything." She sighs, covers her face. "And now she'll never tell me anything again." I wait, not knowing what to say. Eventually, she continues. "At any rate, they decided to travel with a trade caravan. Your mother said they wanted to see the world. I cautioned her, asked what she really knew about him. She only laughed and said she knew enough. After they were gone, she sent messages now and then, telling me of strange lands and customs, and that they were happy. Then nothing for more than four years. I feared her dead." Thea buries her face in her hands. "And now she is."

I touch her arm. "Was he my father?"

"I think so, though by the time she sent for me, he'd left her. You were about four years old, and both of you were living here. She said she needed me, spoke of danger, said we had to create protections. That was when I learned how to be a goat and hide in that shape when anyone came."

I wait for more, but Thea is staring into the flames, as if she can see the past flickering there. A man's square face, perhaps. I frown.

"Would I remember my father?"

Thea looks at me, clears her throat. "Not likely. Zarmine fed you the forgetting tisane regularly. I tried to persuade her not to do that, suggested that you should know about your father, but she disagreed."

I want to keep her talking; it helps me not to think about other things. "The night she . . . Two nights ago? I saw a face in the flames – a man. I hadn't drunk the herbal mixture that evening. Could I have been recalling my father?"

She shrugs. "Your mother told me so little. Said he'd gone, that was all she'd disclose. I don't know why or when." She touches my hand. "Perhaps memories are coming back to you."

"But what was the danger she spoke of? Does it still threaten?"

"There was risk, she told me, but no details. She wasn't so secretive before she met him, and I wondered whether she had grown afraid of him. Perhaps he'd turned into someone she could no longer live with, who had been cruel to her. I begged her to tell me more, but she wouldn't. And later when you were older, I wanted her to tell you."

"She was going to. Soon."

"What? She said something to you?"

"In a dream or vision." I stare at Thea. "Are you a dream or vision, too?"

She pinches my cheek lightly. "No."

"Why did she keep you a secret from me? Perhaps when I was a child and likely to mention your abilities in company, it made sense. But later? Why wouldn't she let me know you?"

"I'm sorry, Rowan, I haven't answers for those questions."

"If my father wasn't the threat," I say slowly, "maybe she was so upset when he left that… do you think?"

"She imagined things, saw perils where there were none? Did she seem like that kind of person to you?"

I sigh. "No. But did you ever see any signs of this danger she spoke of?"

"Maybe. Now and then, walking in the woods as a goat, the hair on my neck would rise as if a strange wind ruffled it. I know that sounds silly, but I've learned to trust my feelings over the years. Lately, your mother kept telling me she saw wolf tracks in the forest. It made her uneasy. I didn't see any, but I've been feeling on edge, that's why I went away just before the storm. I looked for tracks, any sign of strangers."

"Did you find anything?"

Thea shakes her head. "No, but then the storm came and the rain could have washed the signs away."

I think about telling her of the tracks I saw, but decide not to for now; after all, I was upset and could have been mistaken. "So what do we do now?"

"Bury your mother."

"And then?"

"Learn how to go on with life."

I pick up a piece of wood and throw it into the fireplace. It smashes into a partially burned log, sending sparks flying. A large one lands on Thea's foot.

"Ow! What are you doing?"

"I don't know," I snap. "Are you going to keep being a goat?"

"For now. Let's just watch and wait."

I grind my teeth in frustration, but can think of nothing better.

***

Mid morning the next day I look out of the window to see Olwin and his family arrive. I've barely gotten out of bed, forgot that I told them to come. They have brought food, a cartload of boards, and a cleric.

The cleric asks if I've chosen a place for the grave. His hands are tucked into wide sleeves, and he wears a self-satisfied look. Once in the village he approached Mother and me, asked why we never came to the temple. Mother said it was none of his business and walked away. Afterwards I wanted to know why she'd been rude to him; it wasn't like her. She told me that he'd tried to discourage people from coming to see her for healing herbs and medicines. I'm sure Mother would not have wanted him at her burial, but I don't know how to tell him to leave. I look around for Thea in hopes that she might butt the man, but can't see her. I have no idea what the burial customs of Mother's people are, and I can't leave her lying in that bedroom any longer.

Without speaking I turn and lead the way around the garden to the green ash tree. "There," I say, "beneath the shelter of its branches."

I wander off and leave them to it. Behind the shed is a path that winds over the hill in back of the cottage. I take it, ducking behind bushes, hoping no one has seen me go. Even if someone does notice, perhaps they'll reason I'm grieving, and leave me be.

On top of the hill in a slight hollow rises a great stone, a sacred spot of the ancients, Mother told me. That's one reason why she said she chose this cottage; she thought the stone would watch over us. It didn't help Mother in the storm, though. Lynx said that certain animals gathered here to scratch, though I've never seen any. I sigh, and sink to the mossy ground, leaning my back against the rough surface that has been warmed by the sun. Its light shines through my lowered lids, making a rosy glow.

I find myself on top of the old rock, though I don't remember climbing it, and look out over forests, villages, towns, rivers, lakes, cities, deserts. It seems as if I can see to the ends of the world and back again. Far away stands a tall man with shoulder-length black hair. He appears to be in a garden and there's a bush nearby where a boy with red hair crouches. I can't see either of their faces clearly and I wonder whether they can see me.

The man raises his arms, speaks; I hear his husky voice plainly. "I know where you are."

A raven screeches and I'm sitting on the ground in front of the stone with the goats around me, Mord flying above. My head feels oddly light and slightly dizzy. I suppose that I must have fallen asleep and dreamed. Below in the clearing people have gathered. It looks as if much of the village and many neighbours have come to pay their respects or to satisfy their curiosity. The cleric is wandering among them. He peers into the shed, then walks over to examine the garden. I wonder if he's estimating the worth of the place. I let out a long breath and Mord lands on my shoulder.

"Where have you been?" I scold.

He merely mutters into my ear before taking off again to fly in circles. As I watch him I imagine that dark-haired man as my father. Perhaps he knows what has happened to Mother, and might be on his way to me now. On the other hand, if Mother was right about danger threatening us, the dream could have been a warning. Later, when everyone has gone I will tell Thea and ask her advice.

I go reluctantly toward the cottage where faces with mouths moving surround me, and disembodied hands pat me on the shoulder. I distinguish the odd word, know that they are attempting to be kind. There are too many people, but I can't run away again. Olwin and three other men carry a long wooden box out of the cottage, and the cleric leads the way to the grave.

I don't listen to the words of the cleric; he didn't know Mother, can't say things that will mean anything to me. But the flowers, sweet smelling herbs, and the branches of evergreen trees laid on top of the box that hold her body bring a lump to my throat. Each person who comes forward with their gift has a few words to say. One she cured of a boil, another a broken arm, still another speaks of a baby saved from fever. Most of them are women – men rarely came for advice from the witches in the wood. I have a hard time holding back tears, but I don't want to break down in front of everyone. So I bite my lips and remember the secrets Mother kept from me, until anger rises and burns away the lumps in my throat.

Parna, Olwin's wife, pulls me gently away as some men start filling in the hole. In front of the cottage a makeshift table groans with food – roast chickens, bowls of boiled potatoes, vegetables, salads, round loaves of bread, a wheel of cheese, butter, milk, cakes and pastries.

People come to me. Some shake their heads in disbelief that this could have happened. Others merely clasp my hands wordlessly. I observe that the cleric is eating steadily, though now and then he glances at me. I hope that he's not going to approach me, for I have nothing to say to him and no inclination to hear anything he might say. After a while he goes back for seconds; perhaps he came for the food. He's probably a terrible cook and has no one to make meals for him, so he eats as much as he can whenever he's asked to officiate at any kind of ceremony. I start to giggle, and stifle it by stuffing half a potato in my mouth, though I'm not actually hungry.

Eventually the crowd begins to thin and I notice the cleric wander into the cottage with his plate. I am about to follow and ask what he is doing, when a woman touches my arm and expresses her sympathy. When she is done I see that the cleric is at the food again. Casually, I wander toward the cottage door. I want to see if anything has been touched within, but I don't want the cleric to see me.

Dishes of food fill the table and the counters. A cupboard door is ajar. I know the women have been in and out of the kitchen so it's hard to tell if anyone has poked about unnecessarily. Nothing appears to be missing. The door of mother's bedroom is open. Thea's goat head pokes out. I reach her and kneel down.

"He was in here," she whispers. "The cleric. I don't know what he was looking for, but I followed and butted him." A soft chuckle. "That drove him out."

"Stay here," I whisper.

Outside, the women have started cleaning up. I search for the cleric and see him at the edge of the clearing. As I head in his direction he takes the path to the village and slips behind the trees. I decide not to follow and confront him. The men are taking down the tables. Finally only Olwen and his family are left. I lean against the cottage door and watch Medwin hitch their ox to the cart.

"Are you sure you don't want to come with us?" Parna asks, hoisting the toddler onto her hip.

I shake my head.

"You shouldn't be alone."

Olwen walks over to stand beside her. "You're more than welcome," he adds.

I recall their cottage, which is no bigger than mine, and wonder where they would put me. In Medwin's room perhaps, and he'd be relegated to the barn. There would be little privacy and people around me all the time. Parna would probably expect me to talk.

"Thank you so much for all you've done, today," I say. "I really will be fine on my own. After all, I might as well get used to it."

Parna and Olwen exchange glances. Then Olwen looks at Medwin, who is putting a few boards into their ox cart. I know what they're thinking, but thankfully they say nothing, know it's too soon after Mother's death. I'm sure that when what they would consider a decent mourning period has passed, one of them will come to me with a proposition. It's to their advantage after all. Their land and Mother's – mine now – would make a very good-sized farm.

Olwen shakes my hand. Parna gives me a one-sided hug. Medwin waves and smiles. I wonder how much he knows about his father's plans for us. He's never said anything to me, but they must have discussed it. I watch them clamber into the cart, wave good-bye. Sigh with relief when they've disappeared behind the trees.

I go in to look for Thea, but she must have left the house while I was saying good-bye to the stragglers. She isn't in the shed or the garden. I sit on the bench outside the door until the first star comes out, listen to the quiet, and breathe the cooling air. I keep hoping that Thea will return, but she doesn't. Perhaps I should go and search for her, but I feel so tired, that I can just manage to make it to my bed to lie down before I fall asleep.

***

I sleep well into the next day and no dreams or visions trouble my rest. On waking, I immediately go out to check on Thea. She is asleep in the shed while her kids gambol nearby; what a relief. I was worried that I'd lost her too.

I sit on the bench by the front door and think over the life Mother and I have lived here, trying to come up with anything that might help me get the smallest inkling of what danger Mother feared. Was it, as Thea suspects, to do with the man who was my father? Or are there other secrets that Thea knows nothing about? I need to find out.

Mother's room is dim and quiet. Someone has tidied the bed. I open the shutters to let in the late afternoon sun. The most obvious places – under the bed, among her clothes on shelves or hanging on pegs, the wooden chest – yield nothing. I shake out the bedding. Feel inside sleeves of dresses and blouses, bury my nose in them, wipe away tears; I check the toes of her sabots. I lift the lid of the chest, take out the stack of parchment that has her recipes inscribed, untie the faded ribbon holding it together, read a few. No answers there. I move the chest around the room, climb it, and search the rafters. Dust falls on my head and few spiders scuttle away as I disturb their webs.

In the main room I move pots and dishes off shelves, open jars and packages. The chest by the window holds only a couple of spare blankets and a shawl. I look in corners, feel around the edges of the arm chair, search the wood box. I know it's ridiculous that she would hide anything there, but I'm determined not to leave out any likely spot. I find nothing out of place. There's a lot of left-over food from the neighbours that I'm sure I won't be able to eat, but maybe Thea can.

I try my own room next, though it doesn't make sense that she would hide anything there that she wanted to keep from me. One of the first things I come across is the leather bound book. I turn pages, enjoying the coloured drawings, remembering more of the stories: a princess who saved her city from a dragon, a younger son who left home to seek his fortune, evil sorcerers, wicked and good queens. Tales for children who haven't yet seen the real tragedies of the world. The rest of my search yields nothing important except too much dust. The room needs a good cleaning and I do that, scrubbing harder than necessary, remembering how exasperating Mother could be sometimes. Like when she'd held back information about a healing concoction because she said it was too complicated.

"I'll tell you when you're older," had been a common phrase with her.

The day gets away from me and I feel as if I haven't accomplished anything. When I go to check on the animals, Thea whispers to me, "I'll come when the younglings are asleep."

I throw out the special tisane that Mother used to make – now is no time for forgetting – and instead, I drink a tisane of mint and chamomile, a relaxing mix. Thea enters as a woman, wearing a loose green gown that looks like one of Mother's. It jars me for a moment, but I shake that thought away.

"Was it hard to learn to change?"

"I didn't want to do it at first, didn't believe I could, but your Mother was persuasive. She had learned a lot of strange things in her travels."

I lean forward. "You mean, Mother knew how to transform, too?"

Thea gets a cup from a shelf and pours from the pot. "No. Though she did try, it just wasn't in her. But she had recipes for herbal mixtures that would help."

"Do you have to drink them each time?"

"Drink and bathe at first, but eventually, I learned to do it without. Your mother said the herbs were just helping my natural abilities come to the fore."

"I can hardly believe this. If I hadn't seen you as a goat and then as a woman . . ."

She shrugs. "I told you, your mother and I were born into a family with special gifts."

I sip thoughtfully on my tisane. "So, I should have some of those gifts, too."

"You do," Thea says impatiently. "You have your mother's gift with herbs and healing."

"But that's nothing special! Just another kind of learning."

"Really?" Thea thumps her cup on the table. "Then why aren't more people doing it? Why did so many come to your mother with their hurts and problems?"

"Oh, I know she was good, but . . ."

"It's a gift, Rowan, believe me." Thea looks sad.

"Did she ever try to change me? Could I become a goat?"

"We never tried. Do you want to? It takes time and hard work."

"Maybe in a few days. Did she ever explain why she ignored you for so long? And why did you come when she sent for you? Weren't you angry with her?"

"No. Because I was lonely and missed her. And yes, I was angry with her. Your mother had powers of persuasion beyond the ordinary, Rowan. It was one of the abilities that made her a good healer. I sometimes thought that she willed people into health."

Thea doesn't have any suggestions for where Mother may have hidden secrets. In fact, she is certain there won't be anything to find. My mother, she tells me, knew how to keep things to herself. I have no argument with that, but I'm not ready to give up. At the end of the passage at the back of the cottage where it meets the hill is a sort of dirt cave for keeping root vegetables, dried herbs and a few odds and ends. Both of us were always in and out of that room and I've never seen anything unusual. Still, I'm not going to take the chance of missing something.

I disturb more spiders and other insects, find dust and the smell of earth. There's a sack of wrinkled carrots that I put aside for compost. Dried marjoram and foxglove are in short supply; I'll need to harvest more soon. A few potatoes are sprouting so I break off the white bits and decide to shift the whole pile to another corner. Perhaps it is damp on this side. Half way through the pile my fingernails scrape against wood and a splinter lodges in one finger. I pull it out, then push away the rest of the potatoes. A small wooden box inlaid with coloured stones is revealed. I've never seen it before. A metal clasp holds the lid fast.

In the main room I wipe dust off the box. It's made of some kind of pale aromatic wood with patterns of blue and red inlaid flowers and spirals of green leaves. In my book there was a story of a boy who opened a jar that he'd been warned to leave alone. When he pried out the cork, black clouds billowed forth – sickness and pain that could never be put back and afflicted the world for evermore. The clasp fits over a curve of metal with a pin to hold it closed – rusty. It's too late for me to put back the pain and anger that have come into my life. I fetch a jar of wild beeswax and a cloth to loosen the rust.

When the box opens a faint scent of roses spills out. Dried red, pink and white petals are scattered over two small leather bags and several sheets of parchment. One bag holds four curls of hair tied with thread. Two are coarse, one black, the other red. Two are softer, like young children's hair, one black, the other light red. I guess that the red could be Mother's; perhaps the others are mine. The second bag holds only a silver circlet, a narrow bracelet shaped of interlocking ivy leaves, which I never saw Mother wear. I turn it in my hands; wonder whether my father gave it to her. As I slip it over my wrist it's cool, but it soon warms to body temperature, lying bright against my tanned skin. Setting the bags aside, I take out the sheets of parchment, expecting recipes for herbal remedies.

Dearest Zarmine, I miss you dreadfully already and I haven't even left yet. Am sitting on the hill by the stone you love so much, looking over the place where you and Rowan will live, and finding it good. There's work to do here, but you say that you'll manage. I wish we didn't have to do things this way, but you've persuaded me that it's the best way to keep the children safe.

I hold the lantern closer to the parchment, peer at the word. It is 'children' not 'child.'

They are so small still, and vulnerable. Pretty Rowan, and sturdy little Samel.

Carefully I set the lantern down, then the parchment. Slowly I rise and move away from the table. Wordlessly, I scream, pouring out my anger. She kept my father from me and my brother, then died without telling me about them? How could she, how dare she! If she were in the room I would rush at her, hit her with my fists.

"Rowan!"

Thea grasps one of my flailing arms. I hit her with the other, then step back, anger checked for the moment. She touches her nose gingerly. It's bleeding.

"Did you know?" I shout. "I've got a brother."

She gasps. "What?"

"There." I gesture at the box and its contents. "A letter. I haven't read all of it yet." Quickly I thump onto the bench, Thea beside me.

Ah, Zarmine, how will I bear being away from you and Rowan? It feels as if I'm tearing my heart into pieces. I would rather talk to you, but you've made it clear that there's no more to be discussed between us. We've made our decision. So I write all the important things for you to remember. We fear the danger to our children if we do not do this. You as well as I saw when the wolf came out of the forest, heading for the little ones that day of our picnic. You were gathering blueberries; I had started to climb a hill. Neither of us could have gotten to the children in time. Do you remember how Rowan reached out and took Samel's hand? I held my breath, expecting to see my children ripped to bleeding shreds in front of my eyes. Then, there was a flash of light and the wolf ran away, yelping. I could smell the odour of singed fur. The children were quite calm and only began to cry when we ran up and made a fuss. They were each wearing one of the bracelets.

We discussed it so many times – how on earth had they got hold of them? You thought the wolf might have been a test to trap us, to show the children's talents. I thought it had been meant to flush us out of hiding. After all, we'd come to the village precisely to get away. We debated whether someone or something had found us; there's been nothing further, no watchers that we could detect, no hint of evil power.

We've moved out of the village to this cottage, set all the protections that we can, but it may not be enough. The forest that seemed so safe once now looks to me as if it's looming over us. I know you don't feel the same for you've decided to stay here with our daughter, even though I've argued with you, pleaded, tried to convince you to go somewhere else. Is there nothing I can write or say to change your mind? You say that the cottage is out of the way, and you'll be fine. I wonder if you have plans that you're not telling me about. I know it's better that we not be together, that we separate the children, but I'm not sure this is the place for you. Still, I've agreed to abide by your decision.

Thea and I stare at each other.

"This," she shakes her head as if having difficulty finding the words, "why didn't she tell me any of this?"

"Or me." I turn over the sheet of parchment. "I want to know what happened to my brother."

I've spent a lot of time thinking about him lately. None of it good. Do you know I wonder at times whether he brought us together? It seemed only chance at the time, wonderful chance. I'd joined that troupe of travelling players because they begged and pleaded: their musician had died from a fever and they heard me playing my flute on a street corner. They weren't even heading in the direction of your city when I started off with them, but a storm came up and we lost our way.

I have years more to tell you about and only these scant pages of parchment to do it on. Only a few more days to spend with you and both our children.

You remember that first performance of the troupe in the square? You told me later that you'd come on a whim of your cousin's. I saw you immediately, your red hair blowing like flames in the wind. You felt the connection between us, too, I know. My music and talent were stronger because of you, and you discovered soon that your ability to heal was greater near me. At first that merely convinced us that we were meant to be together, and so we decided to go off and see the world. Your cousin tried to warn you about me, didn't she? Given what we know now, I'm sure she was right. I led you into danger.

There were times I started to feel an odd prickling when we were together, like the air before a thunderstorm. Perhaps I should have discussed these feelings with you. I didn't pay too much attention, thought it only more of the attraction between us. Then we decided to have those identical bracelets made, a way to show our commitment to each other, we said. He seemed a proper silversmith, nothing strange or evil about him, and he made them exactly to our specifications – beautiful.

"Here," I say, showing Thea the circlet.

"She didn't have this when she left home. And I never saw her wear it."

I slip it off my wrist, heft it in the palm of my hand. "I never saw her wear it either." I put it down and pick up the next sheet.

We'd decided to do without a cleric, because you said you didn't like them – some family antipathy – just you and I making our vows by the light of the full moon. Was that our mistake? When we chimed the metal together and held hands, it was as if our bracelets joined too, caught the moonlight and turned it into a circle of pale fire around us. Cold, like a silver cage, trapping us. The noises of the night were suddenly muted as if the light held back sound, but I thought I could hear distant laughter. We had celebrated with wine earlier, and so I wondered if I was drunk and having visions. You tightened your clasp on my hand.

"What if we step into the light," you said, always braver than I. "No," I pulled you back and held you tightly.

Then a cloud covered the moon, the circle of light disappeared and so did the laughter. But the bracelets held power. We both knew it, for I saw you take yours off that night and put it on a cord around your neck, hide it under your dress. I tucked mine into a pouch beneath my tunic.

Though we were careful with everything we did after that I think the bracelets still influenced us. I played my flute more quietly; you took more time testing every new recipe for a poultice or medicine mixture. But our work seemed better, easier, stronger. So we searched for tales, spoken and written about bracelets, or other jewellery. Anything that might explain what was happening to us. I have all the scrolls of our notes up here on the hill with me. As I promised I'm going to burn them because they might pose a danger to the children. Each of us is going to have to decide how much, if anything, we tell Rowan and Samel when they're older. Perhaps you'll burn this letter, too.

At any rate, we hid successfully in the nearby village, and the memories of that time will always be with me. We used our talents for small things and never together because I believe it's the doubling of power that draws him. That's the danger now for our two children. They've each inherited some of our abilities and if they ever jointly use the bracelets it might call him, the way it seemed to that time for us. You don't agree, but then you never met him. Just be careful.

Too soon Samel and I will have to go. I'll think of you here in the north when I'm in that southern city.

My love to you and Rowan forever,

Yarvan.

"Yarvan," Thea nods, "was the name of the man she went away with."

"My father."

"I can see you're angry," Thea says. "I'm not very happy myself."

"How could he leave one of his children; why did she let him?" I feel the heat of anger on my face.

"She was persuasive, remember?"

"You mean she may have compelled him in some way."

Thea touches my cheek. "There's a lot here that needs reflection. I'm going to the shed for the night, back to being a goat. The children are used to me that way and they might get restless if I'm not there. Get some sleep yourself, don't make any rash decisions."

I can't sleep – too much emotion, too many thoughts cram my head. The woman I called Mother was someone I never knew at all. I can't understand how she could live such an enormous lie. How – I want to scream it, but remember that it's the middle of the night and my yells would certainly disturb Thea and the animals – how could she give up her son and never speak of him? How could she deny me a brother and father? After tossing and turning so much that my bedclothes are twisted into thick ropes about me, I disentangle myself and get out of bed. Moonlight, entering through the windows of the cottage, lays the lines of the crossbars onto the floor. I don't need to light any candles.

I take the bracelet out of the box that's still sitting on the table carry it to the window. The bracelet looks like a pretty bangle, nothing more. Could it really have power to call some evil? It seems impossible. A finger of moonlight touches my hands. Gradually the circlet warms and I think that I see a faint glow around it. The facets and edges of the leaves as well as the rim catch light so that a second silver circle appears to rest in my hands, but this one is weightless, insubstantial. Nothing else happens; more lies perhaps in my father's letter, or delusions. I sigh and put Mother's bracelet away.

As I start back to my bed, the open door of her room pulls at me. I stand looking in. There's not even a faint scent of lavender. I pace through the cottage, back and forth and around. It feels much too small. My movements disturb the doves until they rustle and coo uneasily. I asked her once why we'd always had doves roosting in the rafters.

"It makes us a family," she'd said.

What about my father and brother, I want to shout, didn't they make us a family? It's as if I've discovered the doves lying dead on the floor gutted by some wild animal that found its way into the house.

The floor feels uneven, my legs shaky. I grab the back of a chair and hold on. I want to know what it's like to have a real family, but I'm not sure that I want to find my father, because he was as much a part of creating this web of lies as my mother. Except that he's probably got my brother with him.

I whisper the word, "Samel," and it's like a soothing swallow of mint tisane on my tongue.

Chapter II

Samel

It's still dark when I wake to a groan and a shout from the next room. "Papa?" I call. "Anything wrong?"

Silence.

I hold my breath, lie perfectly still so as not to rustle the sheets, but I don't hear anything more. Quietly I get up, tiptoe across the chilly hall floor, lean against the doorway. Can barely make out the humped shape of Papa on the bed.

"Zarm mumble mumble sorry," I hear. Then, "No! Zarmine!"

I kneel by his bed, grab his shoulder. He pulls away, rolls, tangles in the sheet, slips out the other side of the bed, thumps on the floor. A muffled curse.

"Papa."

"Samel?" His head and shoulders rise. "What are you doing out of bed?"

"Heard you call out. What's wrong?"

He shakes himself like a dog stepping out of water. "Nightmare."

"Who's Zarmine?" I ask, standing up.

"What?"

I know he's heard me, is just stalling for time. After thirteen years

I know his ways. He's keeping secrets, which isn't surprising, because I don't tell him everything either, though he probably guesses most things about me.

"Zarmine," I repeat. "Sounds like a woman's name."

"Go back to bed," Papa says. "It's the middle of the night."

"I wouldn't be up if it wasn't for your shouts."

"Samel!" Louder and snarly.

Oh, yes I know that voice and it means I'd better do what he says. Even though I've grown in the last year he's still bigger than me, could squash me like a bug if he wanted, though he never does, hasn't hit me since I was about four – a slap on the rump for lying to him. He can make me do all the dirtiest chores around the house, or keep me inside when I'd rather be out. So I go back to my room and lie awake listening to his bed creak as he tosses and turns.

***

Sun blazes into my eyes. I fell asleep again and forgot to close the shutters all the way last night. The house is quiet, which probably means that Papa has gone out. Sure enough his room is empty and very tidy, bed made as an example to me. Papa isn't the kind to pester me about keeping my room clean, and he doesn't snoop if I close my door, so I usually don't root around in his stuff either, but this is different. I'm worried about him; he's not the kind to have nightmares.

His bed is smooth and tight as the skin of the drums that the Lord's militia uses to beat out the marching rhythm. There's nothing under the pillow. On the chest beside the bed only the stub of a candle. I lift that and raise the lid. Underwear, robes, a belt. I try to be careful, because what if Papa finds out I've been looking through his things? He could walk into the room right now. I duck under the bed even though I haven't heard a thing. It's dusty down there; even Papa misses spots, so a few times a year he gets in a woman who gives everything a good going over. She washes windows, floors and walls, sweeps under beds and cupboards. Her name is Anna.

There's a shiny thing underneath the head of the bed, by the wall. I stretch out an arm, stirring up bits of fluff. I always wonder where this stuff comes from because you never see it anywhere but under things. When I was small I thought there was some kind of creature that lived under beds and cupboards. Its fur was made of fluff and would fall out. I'd try to sneak up on it, but never managed to see it. I get a fingertip on the shiny object. It slides away, toward the other side and out from under the bed so I follow, cleaning the floor with my shirt front.

I sit on the far side of Papa's bed holding a silver bracelet in my hand. It's warm, which is odd because even though Papa's shutters are open, no sunlight reaches under the bed. I wonder who the bracelet belongs to. The woman whose name he mumbled last night perhaps or a present he's going to give her. Most of the women I've seen with Papa are other musicians or neighbours, and none of them is called Zarmine. He's never talked about any woman that he might give gifts to. Unless the bracelet is meant to be for the Lady Domitilla, which doesn't make sense because, although Papa works for the Lord, that doesn't mean he walks in the Lady's circles. I just hope that if he's going to present me with a new mother, he'll give me some warning.

I stand and brush dust off my clothes, blow as much of it as possible back under the bed. Look over the room, move to the other side and shift the candle on the trunk just a finger's width. Good, everything looks the way it did when I first walked in. At the head of the stairs I listen for a moment, but hear no sounds of movement downstairs.

Back in my own room I shut the door, then open the shutters all the way. Sit on my still unmade bed and examine the bracelet, a circlet fashioned of leaves linked together. I don't know much about metal work, though I'm interested in this sort of thing, how objects are made. Why one drum sounds different from another, and why wheels sometimes fall off chariots.

I shift to get the bracelet into the light coming from the window so I can see better. A blaze of reflected brightness spears my eyes making them water. The room is blurry, and my head spins as if I've been turning in circles. A woman's pale face framed by hair as red as mine floats there in the air. I blink, fumble, drop the circlet, hear it clink on the floor. I rub my eyes to get them clear. The room looks ordinary again, but chills are moving up and down my back. Nothing like this has ever happened before. The circlet lies by my right foot. I nudge it gingerly. Nothing happens except that it slides. I get up, walk carefully around the bracelet and close the shutters almost all the way. When I swivel, I see a faint glow. I return and squat, cautiously slide one finger toward the glow. There's no flash of light, no visions. I take a deep breath, and move my finger to actually touch the silver. It feels slightly warm. Taking a deep breath, I pick up the bracelet, ready to throw it back down immediately. Nothing happens. Did I just have a vision or is it lack of sleep making me imagine things? I don't want to ask Papa because he'd not only be angry that I poked around in his room, but also furious that I was talking about visions.

I ought to take the bracelet back to Papa's room and put it away, under the bed or on it, as if it fell there accidentally. Probably a trunk would be better. If I don't put it back Papa might miss it and ask me about it.

I don't want to give it up.

There's a bunch of long leather lacing in the trunk at the foot of my bed. I've been planning to make a braided belt for a small drum, but haven't started yet. I take the longest piece and completely wrap the bracelet, leaving two ends that I can knot together. It takes a while, and when I've finished it looks like a sort of braided leather amulet. I tighten the knots, then slip it over my head and tuck it under my shirt.

My stomach's really noisy because I haven't eaten. In the kitchen there's a note on the table from Papa. I tear off a hunk of bread and stuff it into my mouth while reading.

Samel. I've gone to the palace and should be back for our evening meal. Bread, cheese and fruit? Please can you clean and polish my flutes. Papa.

I've finished most of the bread and there isn't much cheese left either. I sigh and find the wooden box in the back of the cupboard. There are enough coins.

The street outside our house is busy as usual. It's actually a side street, but because it's so near the palace a lot of people use it instead of one of the wider ones. They imagine it's a short cut, and they're going to avoid the crowds. It's too narrow for chariots or carts, though you can see donkeys and the occasional horse, and of course people on foot.

For a few moments I stand in our doorway, looking across the street at the huge mural painted on the artists' house. It's an ocean scene – sand and water, fish jumping, boats, a row of twisted trees. You can almost hear waves brush against sand, and wind sighing in leaves. To the right is a collage of clay tiles showing a desert oasis. More sand, a few palm trees but only a small pool of water. I always get thirsty looking at that.

I set off, threading my way through the crowds. There's an eagle soaring overhead. The great birds are guardians of the city of Aquila. Our city motto is, 'An eagle does not catch flies.' It means we don't bother with trivial things. Keep our dignity always.

As I get closer to the market the street fills with people – men and women dressed plainly in cream or beige coloured robes and baggy trousers, others wearing gaudy colours like orange or pink, along with gold and silver bangles, earrings or other jewellery. All shades of skin from pale milk to dusky night. Aquila is a trading city so people from all over come here. Quite soon I hear the racket of the market: shopkeepers calling out their wares, chickens clucking, a rooster crowing, a donkey braying. A child screams. More colours hit my eyes – red and white striped awnings, streamers of blue and yellow fluttering, stalls of fruit and vegetables, multi-coloured rugs. There are smells of fresh bread and other baking, roasting meat. Unpleasant stinks, too, like camel and goat poop. I'm careful to avoid stepping in any of that. A knot of people clogs the market entrance where a stall keeper is giving out free samples of a new cheese he's brought. I think about getting in line, but don't want to wait; there are other cheese sellers. I shove through, get a few elbows in the ribs in return and my toes stepped on a couple of times.

The bakery I like is a small store squeezed in between larger buildings half way down the square. Jammed with customers, of course, but they've got several people serving behind the counter so it doesn't take long for me to move up.

"Haven't seen you for a few days, Samel," the girl behind the counter says. She's the baker's cousin, recently moved here, but I can't remember her name.

I smile. "Been busy. Could I have two loaves of that bread, a meat pie and a poppy seed cake?" I stuff everything into my string bag.

I want a fruit stall next. The nearest doesn't have much left except bruised bananas, mashed berries, a few coconuts, some dusty dates. I carry my bag carefully – don't want anything to get squashed – and squeeze through another line of people around a corner and into an alley. Not such a crowd here at this fruit seller.

Pasha smiles at me as I pick out a couple of nicely ripe bananas and a basket of plump strawberries. "What about a melon?" he asks. "Just came, fresh and juicy."

I count my money. "All right." I pay and turn to leave.

"Ouch! You stepped on my toes!"

A laughing face, brown hair sleeked back into a braid. A dark red dress and sandals. I lift my big foot.

"Sorry, Magenta. Any damage?"

She wriggles her toes. "I don't think so. Maybe I've lost a little skin."

"Nothing lasting?" I tilt my head. "Your future husband won't come looking for me?"

A peal of laughter. "I think you're safe."

I glance around. "Anyone else with you?"

"One of my sisters you mean? One particular sister?"

My neck and face get hot. I know I'm turning red, but I can't help it. Magenta watches me, smiling broadly. Then she takes pity.

"Ali's at home painting. You can come see her later if you like."

Ali, short for Alizarine. Mère and Père have named each of their three daughters after a colour. Magenta is seventeen and soon to be married. Ivoire, the youngest, is ten. Ali is thirteen and a half.

"I still have to get cheese."

"There's a new stall with the best cheese. Wait until I buy some fruit and I'll show you."

We wander through the market stopping at a stall here and there. Magenta wants to look at cloth because she has a wedding dress to make. It always amazes me how one piece of cloth can be so different from another both in colour and texture. The weavers' and dyers' arts are mysteries to me. Then my eyes are caught by a nearby stall of musical instruments – flutes, drums, a harp, and a box zither. I look them over critically. They're all quite good, but apprentice work, I think. Next we have to stop at a vendor of pigments. Following in their parents' footsteps all three girls of the family paint, work in clay, and carve.

"What's Ali painting?" I ask.

"The walls of her bedroom."

Magenta studies a mixing apparatus. The vendor says he uses it to combine dry pigments with oil, water or other media. The technical discussion goes over my head. Magenta hasn't answered my question, but I don't want to interrupt. As we walk away I try again.

"I meant what design is she painting?"

"Hmm?" Magenta shrugs. "She won't say. Keeps the door of her room locked."

I try to come up with other questions to get Magenta to talk more about Ali, but we've reached the cheese stall. Only a couple of people are shopping here. A plate of fragrant samples is set out. I try a pale cheese with large holes. Lick my lips and smile.

"Was I right?" Magenta says, taking a piece of dense yellow cheese.

"Mmmmm!"

She laughs. "I have to leave you here, Samel."

I wave her off and try another cheese. I'm going to have a hard time making up my mind. In the end I buy two kinds – the one with holes and a spreadable white cheese. My bag is full and heavy. I don't have to be quite so careful of it though. The crowd has thinned.

After lunch I get out beeswax, polishing cloths and thin long handled brushes, take them upstairs to my room and set them on a small table by the window. The three flutes are in a special case in Papa's room. Cleaning and polishing the flutes is one of my favourite things; he's let me do it since forever. I can play the smallest, the soprano, adequately. The alto makes only a barely audible sound when I blow it, but the bass doesn't even wheeze for me. Papa, of course, can make all of them sing. That's the secret of his flutes: no one else can play them unless he wants them to. When I was small I thought I just didn't have a big enough chest. Now I know it's something else, but it's not anything Papa will talk about.

He has always avoided discussions about what he dubs hocus-pocus. It's my belief he calls it that to make me think it's trivial stuff, not worth bothering about. Except that he's also warned me to keep away from folk magic. There are always old women in the market who sell charms and love potions. Some people believe in them and others laugh. With Papa, it was like the warnings parents give children about looking both ways crossing the street; they remind you every time. A good thing when you live in a city where horse and chariots can come hurtling at you. I've never figured out why Papa seems so tied up in knots about anything to do with conjuring and spellcraft, though he'd hate me to call it that, even to myself.

I finish with the soprano flute and set it back into its slot. Pick it up again, look out the window. Our house is two stories; the house across the street is only one, so I can look over into their courtyard. That's another reason why I like sitting here. The yard is a peaceful place of stone paths and greenery with a small fountain, a fig tree, flowers and vegetables, as well as a sundial. There's no one in it at the moment. Maybe if I play the flute the sound will carry over and Ali will come out. She follows her curiosity just as I do.

My fingers slide into place. A simple air I decide, 'Summer has Come.' I start softly as flowers edging up through the earth. Blow harder as the leaves spread. Then louder as all the blossoms unfurl. A swirl of dust dances on the window sill, almost in time to my tune. The cloths lying on the table stir in the breeze. One of the brushes rolls and falls to the floor. I stop playing and the dust settles, cloths lie still. After a moment, I put the flute to my lips again. When the sound comes out things begin to move once more: dust whirls, cloths lift and twist. A second brush rolls off the table. I stop blowing and everything else stops, too.

I'm shaking slightly, both excited and scared. Nothing like this has ever happened to me before. I ought to test it again, see if blowing causes the same effects each time. There's a clatter on the cobblestones outside – a rider making his way toward the palace. Quickly I put the flute into the case; I don't want anyone to catch me doing odd things. Once at the market a young man got beaten because he danced to the music in his head. I lean down and pick up the two brushes, start cleaning the alto flute. When I'm done, I put it to my lips, but get only a wheeze. I put the alto into its slot and reach for the bass. What if I could get a sound out of it? Would a great wind come up that rattles the shutters, maybe blows down trees?

When all the flutes are in their places, the box closed and locked, I return everything to Papa's room and hang up the key. Back in my room I decide to make the bed and put away clothes, clean up in general. I glance out of the window once or twice, but there's no sign of Ali. I'd like to talk to her about the flutes and the bracelet. For now I'll just let them be. The sun is touching the western horizon when I hear Papa downstairs.

I beat as much dust out of my clothes as I can and smooth my hair. The bracelet is hidden in its braided nest and tucked into my shirt. A quick look in the small mirror near my bed shows my normal slightly freckled face, so I take a deep breath and walk downstairs.

"Samel," Papa says. "You're here and dressed. Good."

"I've cleaned the flutes. And I bought food for supper."

Papa gives me a light punch in the shoulder. It's one of his ways of showing he's pleased with me.

"Anything new at the palace?" I ask as we put plates and cutlery on the table.

"All the musicians have been asked to work on a special composition and performance for the Lord's twenty-fifth wedding anniversary."

Papa is one of the primary musicians for the Lord. He's asked to play once or twice a week for small dinners, a few times a year in the great hall for public concerts. It's a great honour for him. He gets paid a stipend for this and that's what we live on. It also gives prestige to the Lord and the city, because Papa is a distinguished flute player.

As for the Lord, he's the ruler of the city of Aquila and the lands around, the lands of Ameer. There are other Lords of Ameer, brothers, sons, cousins, but when we speak of 'the Lord' we always mean Lord Davus, the current ruler.

***

The next few days Papa has a lot of meetings with musicians. When he's at home he spends most of the time in his room writing music or playing his flutes. Being so preoccupied probably means he hasn't noticed the bracelet is missing, which is a good thing. I take it out now and then when I'm alone in my room, but nothing strange happens. During the days I make sure we eat regularly and I clean the house. I'm Papa's apprentice officially. It's somewhat unusual for a son to apprentice to a father, but I wanted to and the Lord agreed. Part of the agreement, though, was that I'd also spend time with other musicians and with musical instrument makers. At present I'm working with two – a man who both crafts and plays drums, as well as a harpist.

Tamtan is tall and broad in the shoulders, though not fat. He makes and plays drums of all sizes; the biggest carved from a single huge tree. I'm only one of four apprentices; the others are full time with him. Also, he leads two groups – his youth band and an ensemble of senior drummers. I know it's a privilege to be taken on by him, even for a couple of afternoons a week.

When I get to the workshop today there's an argument going on. Two of the apprentices bicker about who's made the better drum. While they're shouting at each other I go over and tap each of the small drums in turn. The boys pivot at the sound and stare at me, as if I'm an interloper, which I am in a way. At the same time, I belong here, too, and I don't like their attitude.

"So," sneers one, "give us your expert opinion."

"Yes," grins the other, "tell us which is the better drum."

I've just opened my mouth, when Tamtan strides into the room.

"Neither," he says. "They're both crap. Start again." He turns to me. "Samel, I've got wood that needs shifting. Come."

I follow him without a backward glance; would rather do any amount of scut work with Tamtan than stay with those two. There's a yard at the rear of the house, nothing like the artist's courtyard. This one is filled with wood, leather – camel, goat, cowhide – on stretchers, metal, tools, odds and ends. Tamtan leads me to a far corner, pulls out a couple of half barrels. Sits on one, gestures to the other.

"Now," he says when I'm seated, "you were going to say the same thing I did to those two bone heads."

I nod.

"Do you know why I stopped you?" He pierces me with his blue eyes.

"Maybe."

"Out with it." He wags an admonitory finger. "And think before you speak!"

This is typical Tamtan. Telling you two seemingly opposite things and expecting you to put them together the right way. So I go over it in my head. See the gleam in his eyes. I grin and spit it out.

"If I'd said that they would have hated it, hated me. Even more than they do."

He lifts an eyebrow. "And now?"

"They hope I'm in trouble, too. Because you spoke gruffly to me and gave me work they don't like."

"What work?" He looks around.

"Better get me started in case they glance out."

Tamtan laughs softly. "There is some lumber over there," he points, "that I want you to re-stack. Otherwise it'll warp. But before you get to it, there's one more lesson."

I wait.

"Do you know why they dislike you?"

"I'm not sure." Raise one shoulder. "Because my father's a musician? And theirs aren't. So they imagine I have special privileges?"

He purses his lips. "Partly right. They also envy you because they know you're a better musician than they'll ever be." He slaps me on the shoulder. "Don't let it go to your head. There's gloves over there.

Get to it."

The whole time I'm working I can't stop smiling. I'm extra careful with the lumber. Wouldn't want Tamtan to yell at me for real. Besides, I respect him. He's the best drummer in the whole of Ameer; I've heard Papa say so. Tamtan never gives you work that you can't learn from, so I study the wood I'm rearranging. There's all kinds – mahogany, birch, ash – a few I don't recognize. I know Tamtan uses local trees, but he also gets wood from traders, and not just any wood. He uses dead trees when he can, and buys from reputable dealers who guarantee sound practices, like not taking too much at any one time, and replanting. I'll have to ask Tamtan to identify the wood I don't know. I inhale the different scents.

To make one kind of drum planks are steamed and bent into shape. That takes time so you don't end up with a cracked or warped instrument. In the yard there are also piles of logs for carved drums. I've learned to make both and have one of each at home. Small ones, one of ash, the other mahogany. They're the best of a whole bunch I discarded. There's no shame in making mistakes, Tamtan says, as long as you admit your mistakes and learn from them. Papa's like that too. He says practise makes perfect, but mistakes can be creative. So play those scales, Samel, go over that song again. And listen to yourself, hear and feel the music. Let your heart lead you.

When I've finish with the lumber Tamtan sends me to the palace. He wants me to pick up a drum that needs repairs which belongs to one of the young princes, a grandson of the Lord. The boy has been getting lessons from Tamtan's oldest apprentice. I know the two apprentices who were bickering will be jealous because going to the palace is a special treat for them, though not for me. I've been in and out of it all my life, with Papa.

Tamtan gives me a copper medallion on a chain to put around my neck. That's my pass. Most of the guards know me by now and would probably let me in anyhow. I don't dawdle on the way as I might ordinarily do. This is business after all.

The first thing you notice as you approach the palace is the trees all around it: elm and cypress, also palms. Walls and towers rise out of the trees as if they've grown up together. Papa says that's literally true because the first Lord started bringing in seedlings as soon as they'd started constructing the outer walls. The main gate is closed and barred, used only for chariots on special occasions. There's a smaller side entrance to the left. The guard barely glances at my medallion and waves me through with a grin.

Once you're in it's the sounds and smells that get you. Fountains and flowing streams are everywhere. Some of the buildings look as if they're floating on water. The scent of roses, and all kinds of other flowers, like orange blossoms, saturates the air. It's almost like magic, though I don't ever say that to Papa.

Because the city of Aquila is right on the edge of a desert, water is especially precious to us. Though we have the river to the south, everyone knows that rivers can dry up and so we don't waste water. All of the fountains and streams in the palace re-use their water. I don't know how that works, but someday I'll ask Papa to explain it. And there's the architecture – columns and courtyards, space and light. Rich colours, pale grey, warm rose. It's a good thing I've been here so often or I'd be paralysed with amazement.

I hurry along, taking a short cut to the west tower where someone is to be waiting for me with the drum. An old man I haven't met before is seated on a bench nearby. There's a parcel at his feet. He smiles and nods.

"Yarvan's son," he says.

I bow respectfully. When you're not sure of someone's rank or status it's best to err on the side of deference. When my head comes up, I see there's a calculating look in his eyes.

"Wisdom in one so young," he says.

My face heats and I stutter. "Sir . . . you . . . I."

"Yes?"

"A drum. I'm supposed to take it to Tamtan."

He gestures to the parcel at his feet. I don't know whether I'm to pick it up or wait for him to hand it to me. Papa has always impressed on me that in the palace the slightest act can have political consequences. I've never been really sure what that means, except to be careful, so I wait. The old man gestures again and I bend down. He nods. I pick up the package with both hands.

"Nicely done."

He claps once. A young man appears, gives the old one an arm and shoulder to lean on. The old man inclines his head to me. I bow again.

"Give my greetings to Tamtan," the old man says. He lets the young one guide him into the shadow of a doorway.

I carry the wrapped drum carefully, making my way out of this courtyard and into another. In one of the smaller towers nearby Papa has an office and studio. Sometimes he spends the day there; I might see him on my way by. There's a small garden with a fountain at the centre where a man stands, his back to me. Then I realize it's Papa. I'm just about to call him when he raises his head to stare over the adjacent roofs and walls.

"I know where you are," he says.

A few moments later there's a scream as an eagle pounces to the ground. Its wingspan is immense. Papa turns and I duck behind a rose bush because I don't want him to think I'm spying on him. The eagle hops toward Papa who bends down. I can't see clearly through the bush and am afraid to move in case they hear me. Could Papa be talking to the eagle? There's another scream as the bird rises. Papa walks to the tower. I wait until he's inside and has closed the door, then sneak over to the spot where they met, looking around to make sure no one is watching. Some of the plants are flattened and I try to lift them back into place. I'm sure that a man talking to an eagle is not a common sight and I don't want people to gossip about Papa. Under a tuft of grass lies a dark brown and white feather. I pick it up and hide it in my shirt, then leave quickly. I am so absorbed in my thoughts I almost forget to show my medallion to the guard at the gate to let him know I'm leaving.

When I get back to Tamtan's workshop with the drum, it's nearly time for the evening meal. The regular apprentices take it there while I get to go home. Another strike against me, I guess, though I wouldn't mind eating someone else's cooking for a change and

Tamtan's wife is a very good cook. Now and then, if I look hungry enough, Tamtan invites me to stay and eat with them. Today he takes the drum and tells me to go home.

Because Papa isn't there yet, I sit by my window and watch the street. It's quiet this time of day with only a few people out. Ivoire is in the courtyard across the way, climbing a tree. She sees me and waves. I wave back and wish it were Ali; I could really use someone to talk to. Briefly I consider going over to the artists' house. They'd invite me to eat with them, but it's not polite to visit right at meal time and I might miss Papa. It's really him I want to talk to.

There's half a cold cooked chicken in the larder, also a round of bread and a bunch of dates. Papa must have gone shopping today. I get so hungry I can't wait any longer and have finished a drumstick, a wing, and a quarter of the bread by the time Papa comes in.

"Sorry I'm late," he says, "one of the musicians wanted to talk about the anniversary concert. I couldn't get away."

He goes to wash, then comes and sits down. I'm gnawing on bones trying to think of the right words to say to him. He tears off a hunk of bread, cuts chicken. Chews. I bite into a date.

"You're quiet," Papa says. "Anything wrong? How was your afternoon with Tamtan?"

It's the best opening I'm going to get. "He sent me up to the palace."

"Oh?" He sounds only mildly interested.

"To pick up a damaged drum from one of the princes. I met an old man who knows you."

Papa waves a hand for me to continue.

"He didn't tell me his name."

A smile. "But you can describe him of course."

"Grey hair and beard, stooped, needs help to walk."

Papa frowns. "That could be any of a number of old men at the palace."

"He knew I was your son, too."

"Never mind, it doesn't matter."

I nod. "It's odd what a person remembers and doesn't. And what they imagine they see," I add. "As I was leaving I thought I saw an eagle come down."

Papa is taking a gulp of water and nearly chokes. "Really?"

"Hmm." I can't decide whether to tell him the truth or lie and say I didn't see where the eagle landed. Decide to say nothing else for now. Eat another date.

We sit without speaking, chew, drink. Papa drums on the table with his fingers. It could be just a nervous gesture, but I decide to play. Rap my knuckles against my half-full goblet. Papa grins, increases the tempo and adds a slight creak from his chair. We've played this game often. The trick is to add something new each time, but not the same thing as the other person. Also, keep doing what you did before. I start clicking my tongue. Papa snaps the fingers of his other hand. Quickly I come in with a tap of my foot against the table leg. A heel and toe on the floor from Papa. I grab a knife and rap it on my head. Papa can hardly keep from laughing. His chair rocks harder, there's a loud crack and the chair collapses. Both of us roar.

Finally I take a deep breath. "Guess I won." Add quickly, "That means you have to pay a forfeit, answer a question. Who's Zarmine and why were you talking to an eagle?"

Papa's still sitting on the floor. He rises, looming over me. "That's two questions."

"All right answer one of them. Your choice."

He leans down to pick up two pieces of the chair. Throws them down again. "Some things can't be mended."

I stand, too, and face him. I'm nearly as tall as he is now. Am searching desperately for the right words, the ones that will make him talk.

"You're almost a man."

Did I say it out loud, or did he read my mind? A shiver rattles me. No, it's Papa giving me a shake.

"I should have told you before now, I suppose, but I didn't want to blight your childhood." He lets me go. "Zarmine is your mother. Was your mother. I think she might be dead."

There's a rushing sound in my ears and although I'm standing still, it feels as if the floor is moving me backwards away from Papa. I shake my head and take a steadying breath. "The way I remember it, you told me years ago that my mother was dead."

He pulls out another chair, sinks into it. I stay standing though I feel as if the floor is shaking, a slight tremor, like an earthquake just beginning. A tear trickles down Papa's cheek.

I don't know what to do, so I sit down. "You never talked about her, never even told me her name until now. I thought she'd died of some horrible disease. Was that a lie?"

Finally Papa lifts his head; his eyes and nose are red. "She wasn't dead. We parted when you were only a baby."

"Wonderful, my mother abandoned me."

I start to get up and he puts a hand on my arm to stop me. "It wasn't like that. We did it to keep you safe."

I jerk away. "How could that possibly make sense?"

He sighs and puts his head in his hands. "Maybe I never told you because I didn't know how to make you understand."

"And now you're having nightmares about her?"

"What?" His head lifts. "Oh, yes. You came into my room that night."

"You were yelling!" I shout. "What was I supposed to do? Roll over and say, just my father having a nightmare, nothing to worry about?"

"Oh, Samel, I'm sorry. I haven't been a good father to you lately."

"You've been a perfectly fine father all my life!" I shout. "Except for not telling me the truth," I add more quietly. "I suppose that's a strike against you. But don't change the subject!" I jump up and start pacing. "It's my mother we're talking about. She hasn't been a good parent at all!"

"Stop shouting, son. I can hear you without that."

"Oh, you can, can you?" I move to face him head on, fists clenched. "Then tell me the truth. Why did my mother leave?" I put up a hand to stop him interrupting. "All right, why did you part?"

"Could we go into the other room? More comfortable chairs. Light the brazier? This might take time."

"NO!" My voice gets quieter. "We're staying right here until you tell me."

"Fine. I'll explain if you sit down and promise not to interrupt."

I fling myself into a chair. "Start."

"Your mother liked my music." His eyes get a distant look. "She was so stunning with that red hair, just like yours, and grey eyes, pale, creamy skin."

He stops to swallow several times, but I don't say a word.

"We met in a town on the edge of the mountains – Schönespitze it was called, means beautiful peak – on a lake with a high mountain behind it. I was there with a band of travelling actors, playing my flute between scenes. I had only one at that time. Your mother and I decided to travel, set off on our own." His voice cracks. "It was a special time."

He just sits there until I clear my throat. That's not really an interruption, especially when the other person isn't talking.

Papa shakes his head. "We decided on a life partnership, and agreed to have bracelets made to mark our decision in the tradition of her people. The silversmith was a dark little man in a tiny shop in a town in the northern forest. I didn't fancy his looks, but Zarmine liked the samples of his work he had laid out, and so we ordered the bracelets."

This time when he stops I get up and fetch a couple of goblets for wine. It might smooth the way and keep his tongue loose. From the barrel in the corner, I fill one goblet full for Papa. Half that much for myself, and I add an equal amount of water. He doesn't notice, merely takes the goblet when I hand it to him. Drains half.

"The trouble started with those bracelets, though we didn't realize it at first. My music improved even more; Zarmine's success with healing herbs increased." He takes another gulp of wine. "Did I tell you she was a healer? A good one. Anyway, I bought another couple of flutes, and one day when I was playing the bass in a market square in some backwater town a wind came up that blew dust and debris everywhere. People could barely stand it was so strong. I couldn't keep playing, and as soon as I stopped the wind died."

I've just taken a sip of my wine and nearly choke on it. Set the goblet down with a thunk. He doesn't notice. "It's cold in here," I burst out. "You were right; we should go into the other room. Light the brazier."

Papa looks at me blankly, as if he's been far away and can't quite remember who I am.

"Sorry to interrupt," I say. "Come on, into the other room."

After I get the fire going, I fuss around with chairs and blankets. Papa is in a sort of trance, doing what I tell him, sitting and staring into the flames. I'm in two minds about pushing him to go on with his story.

"So," Papa clears his throat, "what was I saying?"

"About your flute and, um, wind?"

"Yes. We didn't connect any of those things with the bracelets at first, but I found I could call up wind at other times with my music. Zarmine could heal ordinary maladies like colds and coughs and even fevers more quickly than before. Also with serious ailments like pneumonia, her methods gave quicker results than anyone else."

I'm staring into the brazier now. Gradually a girl's face emerges among the coals; it's similar to the one I saw the other day. Is this my mother? She seems much too young. Perhaps that's the way she looked when I was a baby.

"Papa?"

He's staring toward the wall, as if trying to see through it to the past. When I glance back at the brazier, there are no faces or other images. I take a deep breath. "What does any of this, what you've told me, have to do with Mother leaving?"

"We decided together. For your welfare and . . . to keep you safe." He sighs. "We thought someone, probably the silversmith, had enchanted the bracelets, and so we put them away. For a while that seemed to fix things." He scratches his head. "I don't know where mine is now, maybe lost. I can't decide whether that's good or bad."

I clutch at my neck. Wonder if he has noticed the braided leather there, but he's not looking at me. I suppose this is the time I could tell him that I've got the bracelet, but the words stay stuck in my throat.

"We lived quite happily for a time, until one day," he stops to take a deep breath. "It's hard to explain, but we had a manifestation, a message that you were in danger. That we all were in danger if we stayed together. Somehow the combination of your mother and me, and you . . ." He shakes his head. "I'm sorry, it probably sounds ridiculous, but we very clearly saw that for your safety we had to split up. I took you, came here. Zarmine stayed in the north."

"All this is very vague, Papa. What danger, and why did you put the bracelets away?"

"We saw, that is a wolf came out of the forest, after you and . . . well there were a lot of things and we just knew it was dangerous."

"You never had any messages from her? Or sent any? She never wanted to know about me?"

He raises his palms to me as if in supplication. "I told you, it was dangerous. What if there's evil just waiting to use us and the bracelets are a way to force us to do its will? I'd hoped all that was over for good."

"Farfetched." Still, because I've seen evidence of what the flutes and maybe the bracelet can do, I'm more than half way to beliving what he's telling me.

"I tried to keep you away from spellcraft and arcane arts of any kind. Was afraid of the power you might have."

"Power I have? Like what?"

He shakes his head. "I'm not sure; have been afraid to test it. I haven't even tried to use my own abilities with the flutes recently."

"Sounds as if you can control it. Deciding to use it or not."

"When I brought the wind . . . if I could choose whether to make it weak or strong, that would mean I'm master of my own ability."

I lean forward eagerly. "Of course! The way you're in control when you play the flutes in concerts. The way Tamtan masters the drums. It takes time, practise and patience."

"No! It's not the same thing. You don't know how dangerous these powers can be."

"But have you ever really tried them out? How do you know unless you do it over and over? You always say that practise makes perfect and mistakes are creative."

"Samel, I beg you, don't even make the smallest attempt to play with this! You have no idea what you're dealing with. You're much too young to go up against this . . . whatever it is. I couldn't bear to lose you!"

He beats one fist into the palm of the other hand, squashing my ideas and enthusiasm. This isn't like the father I remember all my life. He always encouraged me to try new things. Except, of course, anything to do with folk magic. There's one thing he hasn't explained.

"Papa, you said that you thought my mother was dead. Why? Have you had some kind of message after all?"

He scrubs at his face and yawns. "That night you came into my room I said I'd had a nightmare. Well, I had a dream about Zarmine. She was floating in a river, and I was certain she had drowned."

"Since when have you started putting your faith in dreams? Hocus-pocus you call it."

"Get this through your head once and for all. Things we can't explain – premonitions, dreams, visions, flutes that cause wind – I've always believed in them. I just didn't want you dabbling in them. That's like poking a caged leopard with a stick and then letting it out."

"All right!" I rub my itching eyes. "Do you really think Mother is dead?"

He gets up and comes over to me. Kneels beside my chair and takes one of my hands. I almost pull back, don't want to hear what he has to say. I've just found out that the mother I thought was dead all these years had actually been alive. And now, if she is dead, I'll never get to see her. It confuses me.

"There's a hollowness around my heart," he says, "a strong feeling that she's gone from me for good." He rocks back on his heels, lets go of me. "And then there's the bracelet. It's left me I think. The bond between us is broken."

No, I want to shout, the bracelet is still here. I've got it, found it, stole it. But I don't say a word because I know what will happen. He'll take it from me.

Papa sighs and yawns. "It's late Samel. I need to sleep, and so do you. Have I answered enough questions?"

"Yes," I say, and add in my head, *for now.*

Chapter III

Rowan

The pale light of dawn spills through the windows as a raven calls. When I answer a thump at the door , a woman hunches there, hugging a cloak around herself. She was at the burial and I've seen her previously in the village, though I'm fairly certain she lives on a farm. I must look the way I feel – rumpled, hair tangled, wild-eyed – because she takes a step back.

"Oh," she whispers, "forgive, it's so early. I didn't think." She turns to walk away.

I clamp a hand on her arm knowing she wouldn't have come if there isn't a remedy she desperately needs for a sick child, a husband, or herself. Her startled eyes turn back to my face. She shakes her head.

"I can come again."

"Tell me what you need."

I guess I'm persuasive, because she tells me that she hasn't been able to sleep for several nights, and this evening went for a walk in hopes of wearing herself out. But it only made her wider awake, so she kept walking and decided to come to me. I almost burst out laughing; it's so ludicrous. One woman who can't sleep asking for help from a woman who's been awake all night.

I beckon her into the cottage and seat her in the armchair; pull up another chair and ask a few questions. She's of the age when women go through what people call 'the change.' I know the herbs to use for that. Four of her children are living, two dead in infancy. Her eldest son is married and lives with his parents in a small addition to the house. His wife is with child and can't help much around the farm. The woman's eldest daughter is to be married soon to a neighbour's son, and spends all her time with him or planning her wedding. The woman's husband cleared more land this spring and that makes more work for everyone. It's not surprising she's worn out. She doesn't understand why she can't sleep, then. I try to explain as I heard Mother do many times.

"Remember when your children were babes?" I ask. "Sometimes they wouldn't want to go to bed though they were tired, and the struggle made things worse. So when they finally were put to bed, all they could do was lie awake and cry. It's like that. You have years of tiredness behind you. Women get to a certain age when they can no longer bear children, and sometimes their bodies crave rest, but can't seem to get it."

She stares at me. "So what do I do?"

I'm amazed that she looks to me for answers. At a third or less of her age, I've never experienced the symptoms she's described to me, can only pass on the wisdom my mother gave to me and hope that it's sufficient. At the same time I know that what I'm about to tell and give her will indeed make her feel better. Self-confidence or mother's persuasive abilities? No time to sort this out, she's waiting.

"There are herbs that will help. I'll make you a tisane first and while you're drinking that, I'll put together a couple of mixtures for you to take home."

I put the stool under her feet and get her settled with the pot of chamomile and a cup. She smiles in thanks and leans back against the chair. As I move quietly around the cottage gathering the ingredients I need, I glance at her now and then. As often happens, when a person believes help is on its way, she can relax. I slip over to her and take the cup out of her hands just before it falls. Her eyes are closed and she's breathing evenly.

I go back to mixing the tonic to help build up her strength. If only there were herbs to give courage, which is what I need now, because I know that I must find my brother. As I heat wild honey and berry juice, adding ground poppy seeds for sleep, as well as a few other ingredients, I think of herbs I should take on a journey in case of aches and pains, wounds, insect bites. I fill a jar, set it and a package of herbs on the table. The woman still sleeps peacefully so I put a pot of water on to heat and get out the makings for gruel. When that's cooked, I touch her shoulder.

She wakes with a smile on her face, immediately frowns and wants to rush home, saying her family will be needing breakfast. I persuade her to eat a few spoonfuls. She leaves with her packages, believing in miracles. I sit at the table staring into space realizing how dependent on my mother and me the people in the area have become. What will they do if I leave? The day continues as it began – more people with various ailments or complaints. I'm kept busy, and I suppose that's a good thing, because it doesn't allow me to brood. At the same time, I know that I won't be doing this sort of thing for much longer.

That evening Thea comes to me again as a woman, her proper shape. I'm sitting at the table sorting through clothes. She glances at the things I've laid out – bunches of herbs, a knife and a wooden bowl, a small cooking pot, Mother's bracelet, a loaf of bread, carrots, cheese, and a leather satchel.

"Where were you all day?" I ask before she can comment on what I'm doing. "I didn't see you."

"I wandered the forest looking for anything unusual. Saw a few broken branches, some flattened plants, but otherwise nothing untoward. The branches and plants could have been from animals."

"Thank you for keeping watch," I say.

She sits across from me. "I'll come with you."

"Thea, you can't. What about your children? Are they really goats? How did you get them? I mean suddenly you were pregnant. Who or what . . .?"

"Their father was a travelling peddler. I met him in the woods during my wanderings almost three years ago. No matter how much your mother worried about danger, sometimes I got tired of being a goat. And despite our worries and cautions, I trusted him. Anyway, I told him I was on my way to visit my cousin a long distance away. It was just a short liaison and he didn't know about the twins. He's never been back this way."

"Our family isn't good with men, are we?" I say.

She shrugs. "It doesn't matter now. But yes, the twins are real babies. Your mother helped me change them. We thought it best, but now . . . I don't know."

I thump the table. "She controlled us all."

"Rowan," Thea reaches out to touch my hand, "please don't hate your mother. It looks to you as if she did terrible things, but I knew her for a long time. She was a good person."

"I don't want to talk about her. What about your children? Can you change them back? They're not stuck permanently as goats are they? Thea, I don't have the skill . . ."

"Don't worry. Your mother made up a herbal mixture and told me what to do with it." Thea smiles at me. "See, I told you she wasn't so terrible. But why did she keep so much to herself instead of sharing the burden?"

I sigh. "I wish I knew."

"So," Thea says, "I could change them back and we could all travel together. Or do you think it best that we stay as goats for now? Do you want to take the time to try to learn to be a goat as well?"

I look around the cottage as if for an answer, mainly to give myself time to find the words. I can't be burdened with children, have to be able to move quickly. Besides, although several days ago I thought of travelling as an adventure, now I'm thinking of the perils that may lie in wait, and I'm not taking two babies. On the other hand, I've just lost my mother and found a second cousin. Perhaps I should take time to get to know these new members of my family.

"We've just met," Thea says as if she's reading my thoughts or perhaps my face is an open book. "You may never find your father and brother, so let's not lose each other."

In many ways she reminds me of Mother – her looks, her manner, the things she says. I could stay here, slip back into the old life. But somewhere there's a young boy who might look like me. I have to make sure he's all right. And I don't want constant reminders of Mother dragging along behind me, and I don't want to try to do things the way she might have. Mother is dead.

"Listen," I say, turning back to Thea, "people will need someone to take over here."

"Me?"She shakes her head. "I learned a few things from your mother about how to use herbs, but for taking over? I don't have the knowledge."

"Mother wrote a lot of it down," I tap the packet of parchment notes. "You'll be able to take care of most things. Besides," I glance round the room again, "this place needs looking after, and it's been your home for several years."

"Rowan, you can't be planning to set off on your own to find your father. It's not safe!"

Already she's trying to take over, just like Mother would have. "I'll find people to travel with, Thea. A caravan or a peddler."

She shakes her head. "I'm sure your mother wouldn't want me to let you go."

"My mother has nothing to say about this!"

Thea reaches for my hand again. I pull back. Shake my head.

"Change the babes back, Thea. They should learn to be what they really are. Any danger that threatens was for Mother and me, and my father and brother. It will leave you in peace."

"You don't know that!" she exclaims. "And even if it's true, that's no comfort to me, and doesn't change what I think."

"You can't stop me going," I say gently. "And your children will be safer here."

Thea glowers at me. I look steadily back; hope that she will give in.

"I don't want to quarrel with you," I say. "I've just found you and it's hard leaving, but I know that's what I have to do."

Finally she hugs me. I feel the wetness on my shoulder from her tears, and sigh deeply. Thea holds me at arm's length.

"Oh, darling Rowan, I wish I could do more to help."

Thea must have spent a lot of time ruminating overnight, because the next day she comes to me with more arguments as to why I can't go. At least not alone. I have no way of knowing exactly where to go, except south, which is true. How can I possibly recognize my father and brother, she asks. Again she's right, I could walk right by them and not know them. There is the possibility that I may never find them at all. If there is danger, I shouldn't be out in the world alone at such a young age. Which we've already discussed. I listen to all of it without arguing. I'm not going to tell her I've had those same discussions with myself. I don't want to give her any encouragement, don't want to let her see my doubts, no cracks in my determination. Don't want to give her any power over me. When she finally stops talking, I take her hands.

"We've been over all this. I haven't changed my mind. No matter what, I have to go and try to find them, Thea. You'd do the same in my place. Remember how you came running when Mother sent for you? So you know what it's like. The village isn't far and I'll find someone from there to travel with to the next large town beyond that. Then I'll see. I promise to be careful."

She groans and pounds the table, but finally gives in. Then I mention that I'm leaving the next day, and she starts in again. Finally, I put my hand over her mouth.

"Go and get your children. Let's change them tonight. I want to get to know them before I leave."

We have to bathe the kids in a mixture of herbs in a tin tub. They don't like the water, even though it's warm near the fire. Maybe they're frightened of the flames and of the unfamiliar room. Thea has to be in woman shape to do it, as I can't handle the two kicking, squirming creatures by myself. She probably smells right but looks wrong to them. Finally we're done, both of us soaking, our clothes plastered to us. Each of us holds a naked boy, howling loudly, copious tears flowing. We wrap them in towels and blankets, sing lullabies to them until they quiet. Then we feed them on gruel and milk, reasoning that's the closest we can come to what is familiar. Finally, they doze in our arms.

"You can sleep in my bed with them," I say. "I've put on fresh sheets. They'll feel most comfortable close to you. I can curl up out here." Neither of us suggests using Mother's bed. It's too soon.

Thea takes them to bed while I clean up. She comes back sighing.

"I haven't any proper clothes for them."

"There's a chest in Mother's room where she kept some of my old things. There should be garments you can use."

She nods and sighs again. "They're going to be odd, poor little ones. How can I comfort them, explain what's happening?"

"You'll manage, Thea, give it time. The neighbours can help. Olwin and Medwin will cut wood for you, and I'm sure Parna would love to bring her daughter over to play."

"You're still leaving tomorrow?"

"I have to go." She shakes her head, but I ignore that. "We'll go to Olwin's farm and I'll tell them you're a relative, come to look after the place while I go on a journey. Now go to bed."

"You sound like Zarmine," Thea says. She rubs at her eyes. "I miss her."

***

The next morning we reach our neighbours' clearing just as Medwin is carrying a load of wood to the outdoor stove. Mother and I never built one, but in summer Parna does all of her baking there and she often makes enough crusty bread and other delights to sell in the village. Medwin spies Thea and me walking beside the donkey cart, which holds the two children, and he drops the wood on his feet.

"Rowan," he gasps, hopping about from the pain, "you've come to stay with us?"

"No," I shake my head, trying not to giggle at his antics. "This is my mother's cousin Thea and her two boys." I point to the cart where only the children's heads and tiny hands show.

We decided to bring the cart because the boys can't walk yet without assistance. Thea is going to tell everyone that they are recovering from a bad fever that has left them unsteady and muddled in the head. This will explain why they make odd noises rather than talking. I have spent time teaching them to say 'mama' and that's what they come out with just then, staring open-mouthed at Medwin. He gapes back, equally stunned.

"Thea arrived late last night with a peddler," I say. "She brought word of my grandmother's ill health. I need to go."

Thea and I agreed on this story in order to keep as much distance from the real truth as possible, while still presenting a plausible explanation for my journey.

"I'm meeting the peddler in the village," I lie. "I'll travel on with him from there."

Parna appears with two loaves of bread on a long-handled wooden tray. She nods at us but doesn't stop. Bread takes precedence over visitors. Medwin is still speechless when Parna comes back.

"Rowan, I'm glad to see you," she says.

I introduce Thea and reiterate my story.

"There's fresh bread and jam if you'd like to come into the cottage," Parna invites. "We can talk about things."

I shake my head and start to unhitch the donkey. Nothing is going to delay me now. The need to leave is like a raging thirst that won't be quenched until I'm on the road.

"Can you take Thea and her children back to my cottage later with your ox?"

Unfortunately Medwin finds his voice just then. "I'll come into the village with you."

"No, it's all right," I say, shaking my head vigorously.

At the same time, Parna says, "That's a good plan."

They are watching me, so no one notices Thea crouch down behind the cart, race to the trees at the edge of the clearing and dash back. I've been expecting her to create some kind of diversion, but don't know what it will be. A roar from the forest makes all our heads turn.

"Olwin!" Parna exclaims.

"What," Thea gasps from behind the cart, "no, is your husband over there?"

"He's cutting wood," Parna moans biting her lip. "What could that noise be?"

"I'll go look," Medwin offers. He runs to the chopping block, picks up an axe and races toward the trees.

Parna glances at Thea and me. "Please, look after my daughter, she's in the house." She runs after her son.

"Go," Thea says. "Everything will be all right. The change I did, it won't last long."

"What was it?"

"A dragonfly enlarged to about the size of a dog. It might startle someone, rather." She gives me a push.

I mount the donkey, chortling at the thought of Olwin and a gigantic dragon fly. I hope they won't hurt it. The last I see of Thea, she is leading the two boys to the cottage, trying to keep them from crawling in the dirt. I wave, she waves back and then has to grab at one of the boys.

A deep breath, a nudge of the donkey with my knees, and I'm on my way. The donkey likes to amble, but I get him to move faster, until we're out of sight of the house. Then he slows again, even stopping periodically to nibble at a clump of grass beside the path. At this rate, Medwin or one of the others could catch up and try to stop me. I jump off the old slow poke and rig up a long stick with a clump of grass tied to one end. That works as he keeps trying to catch hold of it and I dangle it just ahead of his nose.

I remember stories in the leather book about younger sons going out to seek their fortunes, and one about a stepmother who sent her three stepdaughters away, ostensibly to seek for a stone of power, but she really wanted to get rid of the girls. All of them had to improvise, to think of solutions to problems as they came up. I determine to be like that, to succeed in my own quest.

Soon I reach the village; no one has followed me. Thea and I agreed the best plan was to look for a peddler, just to confirm the story we'd told. The inn is the place for that, and anyway I'm hungry. There's food in my pack, but I want to save it for later. I have no idea how far the next town or village is. Mother had a good stash of coins hidden and I've taken half, distributing them throughout my clothes, sewing some into seams, knotting others inside sleeves, and so on. A few nestle in a small pouch on a belt around my waist. I will buy my mid-day meal.

The innkeeper and his younger wife greet me like a daughter. Fuss over me, ask how I've been doing, tell me how much they'll miss Mother. They've always been customers, but today their assumption of intimacy is unwanted, and feels like bindweed in the garden, choking new plants. They want to know if I have wild honey for sale or perhaps mint leaves. They are running low on both. I shake my head.

"I'm off on a journey," I say. "A cousin of my mother's is looking after things at home, so I'm sure she'll be in the village soon. Meanwhile, I'd like to buy a bowl of whatever you have for mid-day."

They send their stable boy to look after my donkey, then lead me into the kitchen. A plate of roast chicken with potatoes and carrots is set in front of me, along with a glass of watered ale. They refuse payment for any of it. When I ask about peddlers or anyone else I could travel with, the innkeeper looks thoughtful.

"There's two strangers been staying here. They've paid until tomorrow," he says, "but I don't particularly like the looks of either one. At least not as travelling companions for you."

His wife nods. "Karl and Karolina would be better."

"My sister and her husband," the innkeeper adds. "They've been in the village all day selling cloth, though I know they want to leave again by nightfall. They can take you to their farm."

"I'd hoped to leave before then."

The innkeeper's wife pats my shoulder. "You go into our bedroom and rest. It's what you need after all your trouble."

"That's kind of you. Um, I'd like to keep it quiet that I'm travelling."

"Don't worry," the innkeeper assures me. "We won't tell anyone you're here."

The bed is soft, shutters keep out the light. I think of Mother's dark room, empty now, and wonder whether Thea will take it over. The innkeeper and his wife are friendlier than I'd expected. Have I seen the people of the village and surrounding area in a negative way because Mother wanted to keep her distance and instilled that in me? My life has changed irrevocably, in ways I never expected. Perhaps life is like that, changing at whim and there'll be more changes to come. A couple of weeks ago I was still a child; now I feel like a bird on its first flight, rising high above the tree tops to take a look around, both excited and terrified by the experience. I know that I have to go south, but have no idea what I'll find when I get there. Unlike a migrating bird, I have no flock.

Eventually I sleep until the innkeeper's wife wakes me. She brings food, and water to wash with. Karl and Karolina are shorter, rounder versions of the innkeeper. They accept me without so much as a blink, and again I have to revise my view of people. They invite me to ride in their ox-drawn cart with them, as my donkey ambles along, tied behind.

"Sorry it's not more comfortable," Karolina apologizes. "We sold all the padding."

Karl chuckles and nods. "Except for what we carry under our own skins. Not much use to you, unless you want to sit on my lap." He wiggles his eyebrows suggestively.

Karolina punches him lightly on the shoulder. "Pay no attention," she says. "He's only teasing. Does it with our daughters all the time, but they expect it and know how to retaliate. Behave yourself, Karl!"

A father with daughters; a family with two parents and children. I watch Karl and Karolina surreptitiously, wondering if my parents had been like this together: loving, funny, caring. So much that I've missed having – someone to play with as a child, a father to tease me. I'm angry all over again, try to imagine reasons that would cause parents to break up a family. War perhaps, if one of them had to go and fight. But then the children would stay with the other parent and be told the truth. Karl hums to himself while Karolina sways to the tune.

Just as we're nearing the edge of the village, I catch a glimpse of a familiar figure in robes. It's the cleric, standing in the shadow of a doorway. In the dusk, I can't see his face, so I don't have any idea whether he's happy or annoyed to see me leaving. I wonder if I've seen him the wrong way round as well as others. Too late to find out.

The path we travel winds through dense forest, lit only by the moon. I peer around, wondering whether there are dangerous animals watching us, like the wolf my father wrote about. I've lived in this country all my life and have never been attacked by any creature except the odd insect. Mother taught me to walk carefully in the woods, and Lynx said not to be afraid of the forest or its creatures. If you treat them with respect he told me, they will do the same for you.

"Your mother and I," Karolina's voice is soft, "traded cloth now and then for herbs and other plants. Many years ago when you were small, she helped us perfect the dyes that make our cloth so sought after. We'll do all we can to help you."

And yet my mother never introduced me to these two people. What harm could it have done? "Did you know my father, too?" I can't help asking. Such a simple question gives nothing away. If I don't ask questions, how will I find things out?

Karolina sighs and pats my hand with her rough one. Spinning, weaving and dying is not kind to the skin. "I met him only once, briefly. Your mother never spoke of him after he left."

I almost grab her hands in my excitement. "What was he like?"

"It was years ago." She screws up her face and closes her eyes. "Tall . . ."

"Dark and handsome," I put in. "I know that much. Anything else?"

Karolina opens her eyes to glance at me. "He seemed nice enough, friendly."

Does she know about my brother? I dare not ask. Trees crowd close to the path, seeming to lean over us. I may have said too much already. What if Mother was right about the danger, and someone is following and listening? In the darkness we wouldn't know.

Karl clears his throat. "Your mother was a fine woman."

"Yes," his wife nods. "And she spoke of you with pride whenever I met her in the village."

I stifle a sigh and a retort. Mother's pride in me does me no good at all; a little knowledge about her past and mine would have helped. I wonder how Thea is faring, wonder how late it is and how long it will take us to reach our destination. I could ask, but the motion of the cart is soothing, almost like a cradle, the creak of wood as Mother rocks me back and forth.

Do I dream? If so, it's about the past, memories of childhood when I felt safe and happy. My world was small and known, the dangers simple – a fall from a tree I'd climbed, a bruise or two, a scratch.

***

"It's a shame to wake you," Karolina says, "but we're home, and you're too heavy to carry."

I'm at a celebration of some kind, a party with laughter and a lot of talking. People hug each other, unhitch the ox and my donkey, chatter. Karl supports me into a warm and lighted house where food fills a long table. Eventually the crowd resolves itself into three females and a shy young man who hangs back, silent. Karolina introduces them.

"Our unruly daughters and our son."

Laughter erupts again and it's so infectious I can't help but join in. It must be very late, but none of them act sleepy. I doze over my bread and cheese until finally Karolina tells one of her daughters to show me a bed. I follow, unable to remember the girl's name. We climb a ladder to an upstairs room that is half filled with shadowy bundles. Several mattresses lie on the floor.

"I'm Katja," she smiles. "My family can be overwhelming sometimes, I know. Here's a mattress for you and blankets. All the girls sleep up here. I promise we'll be quiet when we come to bed. Sleep as long as you like in the morning."

I drop off almost immediately and don't hear a thing until late morning, when a loud clang and the sun blazing into the round window wake me. There is no one else up here, and all the mattresses except mine are neatly stacked with the bedding in a corner. The shadowy piles from the night before resolve themselves into rolls of cloth, skeins of thread, bags of raw wool. They bring to mind a tale of a girl who was shut up in a room to spin straw into gold. I don`t remember all the details, though it seems to me things ended badly for someone.

I think of the night before and all the people who live in this house. I have to get up and see them again. It shouldn't be onerous; I've met people before, but even Lynx's family can be daunting at times. If I`m going to continue this journey, this search, I will need to get used to new places and people. I listen and don't hear sounds of chatter or laughter; perhaps they're all outside.

Downstairs, one of the girls, not Katja, scrubs the long table. "Ma told us to let you sleep." She motions me to a bench. "Have some bread and butter to hold you over till our mid-day meal."

I rub at my face. "I didn't mean to sleep so long." It worries me that I seem to require more sleep than usual, but perhaps it has to do with the upsets of the last few days. My body needs time to recover.

"Never mind. You can spend the day with us, get an early start tomorrow. Pa has a plan for you, he'll explain later."

"Umm," I mumble, trying to remember her name.

She grins. "Kelda, that's me, the eldest. It can be confusing, especially since our parents decided to give us all names starting with 'K'. The others are Kimi, the youngest, and . . ."

"Katja, I know."

"She's about your age. And our brother's Keenan. He's the shy one in the family, so we have to take care not to overlook him."

Kelda gives me tasks like chopping vegetables and gathering eggs. It's a busy and hardworking household, though they laugh and sing over their work, tease each other and their parents. Rather overwhelming for me. Perhaps they pick up on my uneasiness because after a while Karolina sends me off to get firewood alone, though I'm sure they're used to doing it at least in pairs.

I've noticed how gently they speak to their brother, touching him often. He looks to be a year or two older than Kelda, but when I see him building houses out of sticks near the edge of the garden I think he must be younger, or maybe he is what some would call simple. I can tell that this family would never allow anyone to speak so about their brother, however. He's a valued and important part of the group, can carry big loads and handle fragile eggs. When I smile at him he rewards me with a slow, shy grin which lights up his whole face.

Watching Keenan makes me try to picture my own brother. Samel would be about thirteen years old and he might have red hair like Mother's. I held my brother's hand when we were small and don't remember it. Can't recall anything about him at all, and that's horrible to think of. I wonder if he felt safe with his hand in mine, the way Keenan is protected.

It's difficult for me to imagine what life would have been like if I'd been part of a family like this. Would you ever have time to yourself? Would you miss it? I notice that if Karolina is too busy the sisters help each other with tasks. Do they ever quarrel? Today there's so much joy and laughter it makes me want to cry because it doesn't belong to me.

I'm gathering an armload of firewood when a low moan causes me to turn. Keenan crouches nearby, hands clamped around one foot, rocking back and forth. A small hatchet lies nearby. Bright blood oozes through his fingers. I drop the wood, rip a strip of cloth from my camisole and pull the boy's hands away. A deep cut, but short. I bind it tightly. Blood still seeps. I tear another strip to create a tourniquet higher up.

Two of the sisters arrive and one touches my shoulder. "We'll carry him to the house."

By the time we reach the kitchen, the whole family is gathered, the message of their bother's need passed quickly. An armchair is pulled forward and a footstool for the injured limb. One sister strokes her brother's forehead, another clasps his hand.

"It's a deep cut," I say. "Needs to be sewn." They all look at me. I start to shake my head, stop. I've watched Mother do this kind of thing plenty of times, but have never been asked to do it myself. Still, who else is there?

I open the pouch at my belt, rummage for the small packet of needles and thread. The bracelet is in the way, so I take it out, slip it onto my wrist; it feels warm. "I'm going to need boiling water to clean the needle and thread. Also, my pack from upstairs. There's a tincture that will help the healing."

Everyone moves swiftly and purposefully. The youngest sister, Kimi, continues to sit holding Keenan's hand.

"You might want to turn his head away," I say.

The first stitch makes me bite my lip, however, Keenan doesn't flinch nor make a sound. I try to think of mending a tear in a shirt. There's no room for squeamishness or indecisiveness here. Soon I'm done and bandage the wound with a clean cloth that Karolina has brought.

"Thank you," she says. "If you give me your camisole, I'll hem it properly, and Katja will give you one of hers to wear."

Later I help Karolina and her daughters with the evening meal – a savoury stew of meat and vegetables – while Keenan dozes in a chair. I'm thinking about how I helped Keenan and that the skills Mother taught me are useful. I can't try to leave them behind just because I'm angry at Mother and want a different life. I sigh and decide to pay more attention to what I'm doing. One of the herbs Katja is chopping is unfamiliar to me. I crumble it between my fingers and inhale its scent.

"What is it?" I ask.

"Rosemary," Katja says. "Don't you know it?"

"Rosemary for remembrance," Kimi adds.

"What do you mean?" I say slowly, thinking that Mother had never had this herb in our garden or our house.

"Well, herbs have their different uses, don't they?" Kimi smiles at me. "You would know that better than we do."

I go back to chopping carrots, thinking so hard that I nearly slice into one of my fingers. Kelda takes the knife from me and sends me to lay the table. Spoons, bowls, goblets get set down haphazardly. My hands are trembling with the anger I dare not show, not here, not to these people who have been nothing but kind to me. It's my mother I want to shout at, her I want to have between my hands. What if I find my father, and he is like my mother? Would he prevent me from seeing my brother?

Gradually, the smiles and chatter of the family bring me calm and I am able to pay attention when Karl begins to speak at the end of the meal.

"None of us know where you're going, but Karolina and I remember that your mother came from the south. You're probably heading in that direction." He smiles and shrugs, as if in apology for presuming so much. "We have a friend who lives in a large town, called Timberton, where this forest meets the grasslands. From there many caravans and other travellers could help you. Edana will take good care of you and send you safely on your way."

Karolina adds, "Karl will take you to Timberton in the ox cart tomorrow."

"Oh," I say, "I didn't expect . . ."

"We'll provision you properly for a long journey," Kelda interjects.

One by one they lay their gifts in front of me. A tightly woven blanket to keep me warm, easy to roll up and tie onto the donkey. A pair of soft leather boots that will be much nicer to my feet than wooden sabots. A leather water skin. Several loaves of unleavened flatbread, wrapped in cloth. And a carved wooden spoon.

"Keenan made that," Karolina says.

I smile at the boy, and manage to speak past the tightness in my throat. "Thank you."

***

They wake me as the first rays of the sun begin to light the land. After breakfast Karl hitches up the ox, while the girls load my possessions into the cart. Karl ties the donkey to the back, then the rest wave as Karl and I roll away.

"With such an early start and luck," Karl says, "we should be able to reach Edana's town late this evening."

The morning is fine though cool and there are a few clouds. I'm wearing my cloak and have the blanket under me. This is a much more comfortable way to go than riding a donkey. I glance back where he is tied to the cart, ambling along, munching on hay that Keenan tucked into the back for him. The boy hardly limped at all this morning, so I guess my surgery was successful.

When we reach the place where this path joins the main track through the forest, Karl turns the ox to the left. North was home; south is the unknown. It's like jumping into the river and letting yourself go to be taken by currents. But I mustn't think of the river now.

"Karl," I say brightly, "tell me of Timberton."

"What would you like to know?"

"Anything!" I say desperately.

He glances at me. "You could stay with us longer if you like, you know. Unless you're in that much of a hurry? We'd all enjoy having you with us."

A place with people I like. They'd probably welcome Thea and her boys, too. But then I wouldn't find out about the rest of my own family, my brother. The road ahead might be long and lonely. It would be a relief to confide in someone besides Thea, but I don't dare. Although Karl and his family have been good to me, I'm still not willing to trust them that much. Besides, there could be watchers and listeners hidden among the trees.

"It's family," I say, to give him something. "I have to visit family."

Karl clears his throat. "Is it your father?" he asks. "Now that your mother is gone, you're going to look for him?"

When I frown, he gives a slight shrug. "Not hard to figure," he says. "Especially after hearing a couple of your questions yesterday."

"It's complicated," I mutter. "I can't go into details, but I'd rather you didn't say anything to anyone else."

"Of course. But are you certain you want to do this? You don't have to answer me, just think about it. If you don't know where your father might be, if you haven't heard from him . . ." He shakes his head. "This is where your friends are, Rowan. And there's plenty of people who care about you."

"You know something," I say, "about my father."

"I don't know why he left. Only ever met him once. He and your mother had come to market and we were there, too. He seemed friendly enough. But then the next thing we knew he'd left, and your mother wouldn't talk about it."

"Were they alone?" I ask. "I mean was . . . I with them?"

"You and your brother were with them."

I collapse over the sudden pain in my stomach. Karl drops the reins and grabs hold of my shoulders. The cart sways, but the ox continues on down the road.

"I'm sorry. Is it a shock? Did you not know you had a brother?"

I manage to sit up. Brush the hair out of my face.

"I've known for a few days, but not until after Mother . . . I found out after she was gone. It was a shock then."

Karl still has hold of me; if he didn't I might jump off the cart. Do anything just to be doing something.

"Why didn't she tell me?" I wail.

Karl pats me on the back. "My dear, I don't know. Your mother kept to herself after he left, moved out of the village into the forest. She never mentioned his name, never spoke of your brother. I suppose the people who knew her best just did what she seemed to want. We tried to forget about the past and concentrate on the present. I'm sorry."

I take deep breaths to calm myself, pull away from Karl. He picks up the reins again, but I catch glimpses of him watching me out of the corner of his eye. I concentrate on the trees and the road, the ox clumping along in front. I can't afford to break down, have to keep my wits about me. It should be easier soon when I'm with people who didn't know my mother.

"This woman, this friend of yours where we're going, did she know my mother?"

"No, I don't think so. Unless Zarmine met her before."

"Let me be the one to tell your friend about myself. I'd appreciate it if you would do that."

Karl shrugs. "Whatever you want."

As we rumble along, I watch the trees, and catch sight now and then of the river. It's wider here than near our cottage, and in places it has overflowed its banks, forming marshy areas near the road. Karl starts to hum the way he did last night. Maybe it's an unconscious habit of his, but it soothes me. The tune is vaguely familiar, but elusive. Or is it bits of songs that he is combining to make his own tune? My eyes close.

I dream about a man and a boy in a tower. Loud voices argue about over whether they will look for something or someone and I wonder what they've lost. They can't agree on what to do; the man keeps talking about danger, but the boy doesn't believe him. There's a crack and a rumble and the tower breaks apart, collapses. I want to yell at them to run, but my voice won't work.

"Rowan!" Karl yells.

Rain pours down, thunder mutters. The ox lumbers along, the cart sways. Karl tries to get things under control by pulling back hard on the harness leathers. A loud crack of thunder and the ox increases speed. I look back to see that the donkey is still tied to the cart, hustling for all he's worth. The cart slips and slides now as the road turns to mud.

"Here," Karl shouts, "you take the reins. I'm going to jump out, attempt to stop us that way."

I'm reaching for the reins when the cart lurches. A great bump as I see a wheel come off and go rolling to the side. The cart tips as we slide along on one wheel. Karl clutches the reins in one fist, grabs for me with the other. It's too hard for the ox to pull, though and that helps to stop us. We are half turned in the middle of the road.

Beside me, Karl wipes at his face. "Are you all right?"

"Yes, I'm fine. But your cart isn't."

Karl unhitches the ox and ties him to a nearby tree; I do the same with the donkey, who is tired, but otherwise unhurt. Mud sticks to my sabots, and I'm glad I didn't wear my new boots.

"We'll have to unload," Karl says. "Better put all your things on the donkey so they don't get muddy."

Rain continues to gush down, pounding the road which is getting more liquid by the minute. I watch Karl struggle with the wheel; it's going to take time for him to fix the cart. Can't tell how late it is, but my stomach says it's time for a meal. We likely won't make it to Timberton tonight. The most sensible thing might be to move the cart off to the side, take the ox and donkey and go back. I don't feel like being sensible. My donkey is piled with my possessions, and I have my green cloak, which will keep off most of the rain. I'd rather be moving, particularly after that dream.

"Karl," I call. He stops heaving at the cart. "Let's have something to eat. The trees over there will keep most of the rain off."

Karl looks bedraggled and morose, mumbling swear words between bites of bread and cheese. "This will delay you."

"Listen," I say, "I appreciate everything you've done, but I'm not much use to you here. You should ride the ox home and I'll go on with the donkey."

"You could come back with me."

"I'd rather keep going."

He thinks, then nods. Helps me get on the donkey. Squeezes my shoulder. "Just keep riding," he says. "It'll be late, but you can still make it by tonight."

I glance back once and see him setting off on the ox. He looks none too secure, and I hope he doesn't fall into the mud. I appreciate that he didn't spend time arguing and attempting to persuade me not to go off alone; perhaps it's because he has older children of his own and knows that a time comes when they have to be let go.

The road turns and he's out of sight. Perversely enough, not long after that the rain stops and sun breaks through the clouds. Suddenly wings beat about my shoulders, and a great shrieking assaults my ears. I nearly fall off the donkey as that ornery beast begins to run. The brouhaha resolves into a familiar form.

"Mord!" I scream. "Stop it!"

Both donkey and raven take me at my word. I land on the ground, shaken, battered and muddy. The donkey hunches at the side of the road, bawling. Mord flutters to my knees and perches, peering out of first one eye and then the other. If I wasn't so angry I could laugh. I groan and try to stand, but Mord digs his claws into my knee. At that point I notice that one of his legs looks rather odd, thickened. He holds still as I examine him and unwrap a piece of parchment.

The writing is tiny with a drawing of a goat's head at the bottom: *The cleric brought strangers to ask for you. Didn't like their looks. Go fast and carefully.*

I read it over twice, wonder who the strangers could be. What if they carry a message from my father or some other relatives neither Thea nor I know about? Surely they would have told her. Do I trust Thea's intuition? I stagger upright and limp toward the donkey. Thankfully, he remains in one place while I mount and Mord flaps up to roost in a tree. I consider sending a message back to let Thea know I'm all right, but decide against it.

Mord takes off and begins flying ahead of me down the forest track, as if to say, come on let's move. My bottom aches, there's a sore spot on my left knee and a scrape on my right wrist. The disagreeable beast of a donkey chooses this time to run again. He kicks up his heels like a young thing, jouncing every bruise in my body and my teeth clack together on my tongue. I don't stop him though.

Eventually the donkey tires and halts close to a crossroad. I get off and try to lead him without success; he prefers to eat grass. So I sit on a moss covered log and refreshed myself with an apple and a few sips of water. The donkey scents the water and saunters over; I give him some in my cupped hand. It's pleasant sitting there with butterflies flitting and bees humming. Mord lands on my shoulder.

"I wish you could talk."

We go in stops and starts, occasional gallops, and lots of slow walking. We see no other people. The sun moves past mid-afternoon and the heat beats on us, even in the shade of the trees. Now and then we pass the entrance of another path and I suppose we might find a farm or two where they would give me at least a corner or a pile of hay to nap on, but I prefer not to nap yet.

Abruptly the raven angles down to land on my shoulder and at the same time I hear the distant sound of horses' hooves moving swiftly.

Instinctively, I turn the donkey off the path into a thicket of bushes. Crouch down and wait. Donkey munches contentedly on leaves.

They come from the direction of home, two men riding slowly, glancing right and left. Are they looking for me and if so, should I reveal myself? Could my father have sent them to find me? But in that case they should be coming from the other direction. On the other hand, they are probably the men Thea wrote about and she didn't like them. I notice a hooked nose, a mane of white hair, two grey horses. There are other tracks on the road besides mine, so they probably won't notice that someone has left the road. I hold my breath and they're gone, leaving only dust hanging in the air. I wait in case there are others or they decide to come back. There is no way of knowing for certain if these are the men Thea wrote about or the innkeeper mentioned, and whether they carry danger or useful information.

I am about to get moving again, when a rustling in the bushes just down the road stops me. Then comes the neigh of a horse abruptly cut off. They haven't gone far. Did they see me and are creeping up? Or have they decided merely to take a break? I wait for a little while and nothing else happens except there's more rustling. I can't stand just sitting here. I tie the donkey to a small tree and creep carefully along on my side of the road until I think that I'm opposite the rustling. A horse steps out onto the road and I duck down behind a rock.

"I told you there was nothing," a voice rumbles.

"Had to check that glint I saw," a second voice responds. "Lucky anyway it was water. The horses needed a drink."

"She's probably in Timberton by now."

"Yes, but you never know. Might have decided to stop along the way, like with those weavers."

I hold my breath. They've been checking with Karl and Karolina?

"We should have asked if they'd seen her instead of skulking around."

"No one else except that cleric has been helpful, and besides we didn't see a thing out of the ordinary there this morning. Stop wasting time and let's get going."

I don't move until the sound of their hooves is gone. When I lift my head, Mord is circling just overhead so I feel it's safe to go fetch the donkey, though I don`t move too quickly. I don't want to catch up to the riders. I wonder who they are and whether they're connected to that danger Mother spoke of to Thea. If they are heading for Timberton maybe I should go somewhere else, but I don't know where. Once again anger flares, heating my body, but there's nothing I can think of to do except keep going.

Towards late afternoon, a few drops of rain wet my head and I observe dark clouds gathering. The path in front of me looks much the same as it has all day, with no sign of habitation to either side. I have no way of knowing how much longer to the town of Timberton, but I don't feel like riding through drenching rain again.

"Donkey," I say, "we're going to find shelter."

As if he knows what that means, he nods his head, and begins to trot.

Chapter IV

Samel

The next morning neither of us speaks about Mother or the bracelets. Papa has business at the palace again, but I have no apprentice duties with anyone, so after he's left I walk across the street. Ivoire opens the door to my knock. Her hair is in a multitude of braids sticking out all over and she has a smudge of yellow paint on one cheek.

"What's that supposed to be?" I exclaim, pointing at her head.

She grins and twirls so I can get the full effect. "Like it? I'm trying hair for Magenta's wedding."

"That doesn't look like a wedding hairstyle."

Ivoire pouts. "You better be nice or I'll shut the door in your face."

I swallow a laugh. "It's an amazingly artistic hairstyle. I'm too witless to really appreciate it."

She gives me a small, dignified nod. "Right. Now what do you want?"

"Who's being rude this time?"

She is just about to swing the door shut when a shout stops her. "Ivoire! Whoever's at the door let them in!"

Magenta pokes her head around the corner at the end of the hall.

Ivoire pulls the front door all the way open and I enter. Magenta comes forward wearing a stained smock and holding out clay-covered hands. Ivoire scurries away.

"Are you here to see Alizarine?"

I nod.

"She's in her room painting again. You can try knocking and see if she'll deign to receive you." Magenta pokes an elbow. "You know the way."

The artists' house is built around a rectangular garden and the quickest way to get to Ali is down the hall into the courtyard, then straight across. I've always liked the flexibility of the many rooms. The girls regularly exchange bedrooms and redecorate. Our house, with a small entry, kitchen and living room on the main floor, and two bedrooms upstairs, is dull by comparison. This house also has art everywhere – paintings, tile mosaics and textile hangings in the hallways, also a couple of wood carvings in the courtyard.

Today I get distracted by an odd contraption of wire and ropes. It's near the fig tree, and I wonder if it's some kind of climbing apparatus. The leaves on the tree shake and Ivoire's face looks down at me.

"Is that yours?" I say with the proper expression, I hope.

Ivoire sticks out her tongue and shakes her head. "Père's been experimenting again. Says he needs a break from painting. Don't ask me what it is."

I continue on my way. The door to Ali's room is closed and the windows are curtained. I knock. No response.

"Ali? Are you in there?"

The door opens wide enough for a paint-stained hand to poke out. The hand beckons. I pull at the door until I can squeeze through. Ali grins, a smudge of green on her nose, and quickly closes the door again. Many flickering candles make the images on the walls appear to move. The wall I'm facing is painted in shades of brown and sand, a desert containing indistinct figures in the middle of a sandstorm – a couple of horses I think, and people. On the wall to the right looms a partially completed set of mountains. To the left of the desert are the walls and towers of Aquila, an eagle soaring above. I turn. The wall with the door and windows shows forest surrounding a clearing with a small cottage in it. There are chickens and a donkey. A raven perches in a tree.

"What do you think?" Ali asks, brown eyes and hair glowing in the candle light.

"It's amazing. Ambitious, too. Must have taken days."

"And more days to go." Ali shrugs. "Don't get near me or the walls though. Lots of wet paint."

"Won't it be strange to sleep in?"

"I have been sleeping in it." She gestures at the mattress near one corner. "Anyway the dreams started before I ever put the first paint on the walls."

"What dreams?" I wave a hand. "Sorry, none of my business."

She rubs at her nose with the back of one hand so that a brown smudge joins the green. "None of the family have seen what I'm doing. Though, of course, Ivoire has done all she can to find out. I'm surprised she didn't stick to your heels."

"She was in the fig tree." I turn again to look at each of the walls. "What made you decide to do this?"

"I dreamt it."

I look back at Ali who appears much the same as usual. Hasn't sprouted a wart on her nose or grown a hunch back. Those are what witches and wizards are supposed to look like. One or two of the old women who sell amulets and charms in the market do look like that, but I'm sure they're not witches or wizards.

"Samel?" Ali says tentatively.

I can't figure out what to say. It's not that I don't have the words. Questions are crowding my head and pushing past my throat to teeth and tongue.

"Bllirp," I say.

Ali giggles. I grin, start to laugh, too. And pretty soon the two of us are sitting on the floor because we can't stand up any more. Our guffaws echo round the room.

"Ali!" comes a shout from outside. "Samel! What are you doing? I can hear you."

"Ivoire," Ali whispers. "Come on."

She walks across the room, puts a finger on a particular spot and part of the wall opens. Ali told me that one of the reasons she chose this room and won't switch with her sisters is this secret door, though the rest of the family probably knows about it. We come out into the back hallway, turn left. Go through a normal door into the store room, across the room and out into the courtyard.

"Hello, Sis."

Ivoire gives a jump. Turns around slowly. "Why were you laughing?"

"A joke," Ali says.

"Tell."

Ali sits on a nearby bench. "Well," she begins, "it's quite a long one so go ahead and get comfortable."

I grin and sink to the grass. Scowling, Ivoire takes the other end of the bench.

"There was this old woman with a wooden leg," Ali begins. "She used to like to go dancing at parties and festivals."

Ivoire starts to fidget.

"But whenever she danced with a man her wooden leg always got in the way. Sometimes the man tripped over it. Other times it stomped on his toes."

"Never mind." Ivoire jumps up. "Too boring. Gonna see what's for lunch."

We watch her skip across the courtyard. When I glance at Ali, she raises an eyebrow. "That worked exactly as I meant it to," she says.

"Do I get to hear the end of the story?"

Ali shakes her head. "I was making it up as I went along and have no idea where it was going."

"So you were just trying to bore Ivoire?"

"Exactly."

I grin. "The three of you always amaze me. Are all sisters like this?"

Ali puffs up her face and puts her hands on her hips. Trying to look offended, but there's a twinkle in her eyes and a quirk to her lips.

"No," I say before she can answer, "you're unique. This whole family is. I'm glad I know you."

Ali jumps up. "Back to work. You can help me paint, if you like. I'll find you an old shirt of Père's so you don't get your clothes messed."

I enjoy painting though I'm not very good at it. Ali gives me a section of mountain to work on. The sketch is there; all I have to do is fill in various areas with the colours as Ali directs. We've been working for a while when I recall what we were talking about earlier.

"Dreams," I say.

"Do you have them, too?" Ali asks.

"Everybody has dreams."

"I didn't mean that." She is crouched at the bottom of the wall with the desert scene.

I lift my brush from the wall and watch her. Whitish cream streaks are taking shape under her hand. "What's that?"

"I meant do you have dreams that are so real you have to paint them. Or maybe hear music in them that you have to play, in your case."

"Bones?"

Ali turns her head. "Samel, you're not making sense."

"Sorry. I did hear what you said, but I got caught up in what you're painting. Did you actually dream all this?" I gesture around the room. Forget I'm still holding a brush and fling a line of grey blobs across green trees. "Oh, no! I'm sorry!"

"Don't worry, we can paint over."

Ali puts her brush down and I do the same. She sits on one end of the mattress, the only piece of furniture in there at the moment. I take the other end.

"I haven't talked about these dreams to anyone else," she says. "They've been amazing. You were in the last one."

"I was? Were you in it too?"

"That's what's so strange. Mostly when you have a dream, at least when I do, I'm in it. You know?"

"Mmm."

"So these dreams were like I was reading a story with really vivid pictures. They were so strong I just had to paint them. The one you were in, I haven't actually finished yet. Over there." She points at the view of Aquila. "In the dream I saw you and your Papa on one of the walls looking out. An eagle was flying overhead."

"So some of your dreams are about places you know."

"Hmm."

I gesture at the walls. "Those are about things happening in other places, places you've never seen."

"Some people have true dreams don't they?" she asks. "The Lord's soothsayer is supposed to have dreamt of the future."

I shrug one shoulder. "But every day people? Like you and me or our parents."

"Have you had a dream like that?" Ali studies me again, shakes her head once. "Your Papa had one, didn't he?"

"He says he dreamt about my mother."

"But she's dead."

"That's just it. She isn't. Or wasn't and is now." I scratch my head. "It's all so complicated. Ali you have to promise not to tell anyone what I'm going to say."

"Never," she says and curves her fingers. "I swear on the talons of the first eagle."

That's the most solemn vow a person can make in Aquila, so I'm impressed. I can tell by Ali's face that she is totally serious.

I start with the night Papa woke me with his shouts. Tell her everything Papa told me about my mother. I even talk about playing the soprano flute and say what I believe happened then. Ali sits like a statue except I can see her breathing. This is one of the things I like about her: she can really pay attention. I finish and spread my hands.

"All these years your father taught you not to trust in dreams and charms and hocus-pocus."

"Exactly! And now he wants me to do the opposite."

Ali shakes her head. "It's not about what your father wants, not at all." She takes a deep breath. "See, these dreams and paintings of mine, they're about what I see and what I choose to do about it. That's what you have to decide. What do you want to believe, to do?"

I close my eyes. Imagine the soprano flute in my hands. "I want to play the flute again, see if I can bring the wind."

When I open my eyes I see a big grin on Ali's face. "Can I be there when you do?"

"Why not?"

"I know the perfect place – the grounds of the Sand Shrine. We can go this afternoon." Ali stands. "Now we clean up and then you can eat with us."

A meal at the artists' house is a noisy experience because all three sisters talk all the time. The cook throws in a comment or two while serving each dish. Mère interrupts the girls when they get out of hand, responds to the cook now and then, or asks Père a question. He grunts an occasional few words. I don't have to say much at all, which is fine with me because the food tastes wonderful as always. Today there is spicy baked chicken, vegetables with garlic, chilled mint tea, and cheese to finish. Plenty of wine, of course, although watered for us younger ones.

Afterwards Ali says that she is going for a walk with me. Ivoire makes lip smacking noises. Mère shuts her up by reminding the younger girl that it's her turn to help with the dishes. Magenta merely smiles. Père waves us off.

"I like your family," I say to Ali as we cross the street.

"And I like the quietness of your house," she tells me as I open the door.

I call out, but there's no answer; Papa is still away. I run up to his room hoping that he hasn't taken the soprano flute. It's in the box. I wrap it in a piece of leather and stuff it into a narrow sack for the purpose. This I hang over my shoulder under my shirt. I want as few curious looks or questions as possible.

The Sand Shrine is near the northwest corner of the city, so we have quite a walk, but the day is fine and both of us have our white cotton knotted head scarves to keep off the sun. Ali has brought a water skin. No one remembers the name of the god or goddess that the Sand Shrine was dedicated to. The buildings are of dried mud bricks, now half ruined. There's a caretaker, because a few people still come now and then to leave offerings and say whatever prayers they wish. On the whole it's a quiet place and has large, mostly empty grounds. The produce from a grove of olive trees helps with the upkeep. Ali and I make our way through shade until we reach the far side, and settle under a particularly old tree filled with holes. I wonder what animals live in them. Butterflies flutter and beetles crawl. The ground is soft for sitting and no one else is visible.

I draw out the flute, polish it. Then I put it to my lips and begin to play, softly at first. A leaf flutters from the tree and revolves in front of me before dropping to the ground. I blow harder. The leaf rises again, dances, then drops. Into my head comes a picture of a puff of dust, rising, circling so I play the tune that the picture brings to mind. Dust and leaves rise around us, our headscarves flap as above us leaves flutter on the branches. Ali claps her hands, laughs and I stop playing. The wind dies, leaves and dust settle.

Ali says, "Let me try."

I show her the fingering for a simple tune and how to blow. No matter how many times or how hard she plays nothing happens with dust or leaves or wind. She hands the flute back to me. I clean it, wipe it dry.

"Aren't you going to play again?" Ali asks.

"I'm a little scared. What if it works?"

"Then you'll know. And you'll go on to the next thing."

We test the flute and my abilities several times in different places and ways around the grove. I get better and better at calling up wind, though Ali is never able to do it. By the time we decide to leave it's late afternoon.

"Are you going to say anything to your papa?" Ali asks.

"No," I answer immediately. "At least not today. I need to think. You remember your promise? You won't tell anyone about this?"

"I won't. But I will tell you if I dream about you again."

Ali and I separate on the street in front of our houses. Papa hasn't returned, which is good because it gives me time to get a meal ready, and to reflect. First I put the soprano flute away, stand in the doorway of Papa's room for a look around to make sure the room is as it was. Downstairs I get out bread and cheese, set it on the table.

I wonder what might happen if I play the flute with the bracelet out right beside me or hanging uncovered around my neck. What I need is to make some kind of thing to keep the bracelet hidden, but also easy to take out. I get plates and cutlery and am placing them when I hear the front door open.

"You're just in time, Papa," I call. "Supper is almost ready."

"Good," he says coming to the kitchen door. "I'm ravenous."

He doesn't ask what I've been doing all day and I don't tell him. Instead, I ask about the composition he's working on. That keeps us occupied for the evening.

***

The following day I'm up early because we're almost out of food. After visiting the market I'm planning to fiddle around with the bracelet, see what I can discover. However, it turns out Papa is feeling guilty that he hasn't spent more time with me, both as a father and as a master to an apprentice, so he joins me for the shopping. Then when we get back home he suggests we play a few tunes together. That takes up most of the morning. He also gives me some sheets of music to transcribe, for when I have spare time. That isn't immediately since it's my afternoon for other apprentice duties.

Xylea plays and teaches harp, though she doesn't build them. My work with her is mostly cleaning, tuning, and learning the art of making music. She also collects harps and has one room dedicated to storing all the different sizes and kinds. Because Xylea is getting older and walks with a cane she expects her apprentices to do any heavy lifting. When I arrive she is directing two young ones in re-arranging the store room. Neither of them can be more than ten years old.

"Wait," I call and rush across the floor.

A huge harp, the largest in Xylea's collection, has started to tip. The boys are right in its path. I catch it in time though it nearly knocks me down and the strings let out a discordant twang. I push it gently back into position. The boys look scared, Xylea merely impatient.

"You should have waited for me," I say. "Just think of the damage that could have done. To itself, to you, to the other instruments."

"You were late," Xylea snaps. "I wanted it moved."

"Fine," I snap back. "Where?"

She points with her cane. I find the wheeled trolley and a thick blanket, wrap the harp protectively. Get one of the boys to hold the trolley steady while the other helps me shift the big instrument onto it. Then all three of us carefully move the harp to its new location. I give one boy the blanket and the other the trolley to put away.

"Anything else you want moved?" I say to Xylea.

She shakes her head, waves us all out of the room. The two young ones stick close to me.

"An old eagle might scream a lot," I whisper to the boys, "though she no longer bites very often."

Just ahead of us Xylea thumps her cane on the floor. "I heard that," she grumbles. "Just because I'm old doesn't mean I'm deaf."

I shrug and grin at the boys. Their eyes are quite round, mouths slightly open. I haven't seen them here before, so they must be new and still in awe of the master harpist.

When we reach the main teaching room, Xylea sends the boys to sit on stools in a corner. She gives each of them a tiny harp and tells them to play, make up tunes, do whatever they like for a time. She believes it's important to let children explore before putting them to the serious business of learning notes and scales. I follow her to a big easy chair and footstool in an alcove. Help her to get settled, take another chair for myself.

"Now," Xylea says, "what'll it be today?"

Recently, when I've done whatever mundane chores she requires, she lets me decide what I want to learn, do, or ask. All morning I've been going over this in my mind, have thought of different ways of broaching the subject. In the end I decide to be fairly direct.

"Xylea, do you know any old tales about magical instruments? A drum that could summon wind for instance."

She doesn't ask why I want to know or what prompted this question. Just narrows her eyes and peers at me. Those eyes may be old, but they're still sharp as a young eagle's, as is the mind behind them.

"There are always tales of conjuring and enchantment. Told to children by old women."

There's a glint in her eyes and I know she's getting back at me for my earlier cheek. I nod once to show her I've got the point. Fold my hands together and try to put on a look of pleading.

She snorts, shakes her head. "I don't know about drums," she says, "or other instruments. Harps are my specialty, as you are aware." Another piercing look. "There are old tales of harps that could put people to sleep for years at a time."

"Do you believe them? I mean could the stories be true?"

"I've known people put to sleep by music, though not for years, or even days. Perhaps they were merely bored. Music is magical when it's properly played on a first-rate instrument. People can be brought to tears or laughter by a master musician."

"Yes," I say slowly, "but I mean more than that. An instrument that can affect the things around us like wind or clouds. Leaves. Dust."

Xylea wags a finger at me. "Something like that could be dangerous."

"A person can be injured by a falling harp," I say. "Tumble down stairs and break his neck. Danger is all around."

Xylea leans forward. "If you really see that and aren't merely saying it to make a point, good. Now and then I give a lecture. You haven't had one in a long time. So listen carefully."

She clears her throat and stares at the ceiling. The two boys are playing softly on their harps, making tunes, creating harmony. Nothing complicated, but pleasant. I close my eyes and drift into a sort of half dream state as Xylea begins to speak again.

"When children are small their parents do everything they can to protect them, to keep them safe. Hold their hands when crossing the street; shoo them away from knives and boiling water. Feed them, clothe them, and give them rules. Tell them stories to warn them of dangers. Some parents keep on with that for too long, but children have to grow and explore, have to become adults. The only way to do that is by trying new things. When I give a child a harp I hope that she will make many mistakes. The first sounds may be horrible or she may break a string. If the child asks, I help him. If not, I let him work it out on his own. Even an eagle will push the young from the nest when it's time to fly. Remember, Samel, though adults can help you they don't know everything."

I remember Papa holding my hand when I was small as we walked to the market. When people crowd around us he lifts me onto his shoulders so I can see. And he never lets go of me. I listen to him play his flutes and then he moves my small fingers on the holes of the soprano flute. He nods as I blow. At night, he tucks me into bed and tells me stories about brave boys who help their fathers. When I ask for stories about dragons and wizards, he tells them reluctantly. There are always boys in the stories; boys who learn that they should listen to their fathers and stay away from arcane arts if they can.

Xylea has stopped speaking. It's very quiet. I open my eyes and find that her chair is empty. The boys are gone, too. I go to the kitchen. Xylea sits at the table talking to the girl who cooks for her.

"Sorry," I say, "must have fallen asleep."

"Enchanted by a magical harp?" Xylea teases.

"And your voice."

Xylea shakes her head. "I don't think I'll ever teach you to be properly deferential to an old woman."

I grin. "I don't think the old woman minds."

***

The next day Papa invites me to come to the palace with him, and though I usually love going, I've got other things on my mind. I tell him I want to stay and copy out the compositions he gave me. He looks disappointed and surprised, but heads off on his own.

I do work on the copying in my room, but after a while I stop, take off the bracelet and unpick the braiding. You can't play a bracelet the way you do a flute, drum or harp so I put it down on a sheet of paper. The sun shines on the circlet making it sparkle, no, spark! The paper underneath starts to smoke. I knock the bracelet away from the light, beat out the fire with my palm. As I'm doing this I hear the clink of metal on the floor. I go scrambling after the bracelet.

It's under my bed, in the farthest corner, shining brightly, but thankfully it isn't making the floor smoulder. I slide under and touch it gingerly. It feels warmer to my hand than before, but not much. I realize that I'm breathing hard, as if I've been running. Grasping the circlet tightly in my fist I go down to the kitchen to put some salve on my reddened hand and to fetch a pottery plate. Surely that won't catch fire.

Back in my room I clear away the paper. I'm going to have to recopy the page that got scorched, burn this sheet before Papa sees it and starts asking questions. I set the plate on the table in the sun, then put the bracelet in the middle of the plate. Nothing happens for a couple of minutes, but gradually the bracelet begins to glow and a circle of light expands around it. I can't take my eyes away from that circle. It forms a sort of frame for a picture that gradually appears. There's lots of green, a background of trees. I see a road and a black-haired girl on a donkey; she has a raven on her shoulder. Suddenly the picture winks out. I look out of my window to see a cloud over the sun. I'm down the stairs, into the street and across it in a couple of breaths. Pound on the door. Ali stands there.

"Samel!" she exclaims. "I was just coming over to your house."

"I have to see your room. The paintings."

Ali must have been working steadily, because there is quite a bit more to see. I turn to the forest scene and there's the raven in the tree and a donkey that Ali had painted before. Both as I saw them through the bracelet, too, though that could happen, just something I remembered. Then I see the figure standing at the edge of the clearing in the forest, a figure that must have been painted recently. She has black hair and looks just like the girl in my vision.

I grab Ali's arm. "When did you paint that girl?"

"Just this morning, from a dream I had last night. Do you see it too? That's why I was coming to get you."

"I see a raven, a donkey, and a girl that I saw a few minutes ago. In a vision from the bracelet."

Ali opens her mouth. Shuts it. Stares at me. "Look carefully at the girl. Does she remind you of anyone?"

Dark hair, grey eyes, a small nose, high cheekbones, and familiar, yes. Ali picks up a candle and holds it near the wall so I can see better.

"The face in the flames," I whisper. "Could it be my mother? Except I thought Papa said she had red hair like me. Ali, why would she look familiar to you? You never knew my mother."

"She looks like you," Ali says. "Never mind the hair, but her face, nose and cheekbones. Though her eyes are grey, not gold-flecked like you and your Papa's."

"So it must be my mother."

Ali shakes her head. "She's far too young. Closer to Magenta's age."

"My mother when she was young, when she first met my father. Except the hair's wrong." I step closer to the wall. My fingers hover over the face, but I don't touch it. The paint is still wet and might smear.

"Think," Ali says. "Why would we be having dreams or visions of your mother from so long ago?"

I raise my hands. Shout, "I don't know!"

"Don't yell. Let's think about this."

We sit on the mattress staring at the painting on the wall. I'm so confused and frustrated that I want to tear my hair out by the roots. What can it mean?

"Imagine if you had met me, but didn't know the rest of my family. Then you saw Ivoire and Magenta in the street. What would you think?"

I close my eyes and picture the other two girls. Magenta and Ali both have dark brown hair. Ivoire is blonde. But all three of them have the same nose and mouth, high cheekbones, similar ways of moving.

"I'd think you were related."

"Exactly!" Ali slaps her hand on the mattress. "When I finished painting this girl I stared at her for quite a while. I thought she looked like you. Samel, your Papa told you that he and your mother parted when you were quite small. What if . . ." Ali stops and swallows. "I don't know how to say this."

I've seen where she's going. "What if I have a sister?"

"Sorry, it's the first thing I thought of."

"He neglected to tell me everything. Was so careful of the words he chose when he told me about the past. Why didn't I see it before?"

"What are you going to do?"

"I'm going to go and ask him. Straight out. I won't stop asking questions until I know it all."

Ali is saying something, but I don't hear the words. I'm out of her room, down the hall and out the door. Into the street. Collide with someone.

Chapter V

Rowan

Walls of green rise on either side, more rain drips. When a faint indentation shows in the trees and bushes, I turn the donkey, stop and get off. There is an overgrown path leading into the forest. I can barely walk, am not used to this kind of riding and besides, took that fall earlier. In my pack is an herbal salve that I can rub on to ease the aches, but I want a fire, too, and something hot to eat and drink. I lead the donkey between overhanging trees, doubting that anyone lives at the end of this path now, it's too overgrown, but perhaps there will be an old barn or some other shelter. Several cold drops slip down my neck and I shiver, moving faster. The donkey speeds up too, almost treading on my heels.

The path opens onto an area of low shrubs and tiny trees. There's a heap of wood rubbish at one side that might once have been a barn – little use to me now. Just beyond that stand two partial walls of stone. The donkey breaks away from me to stop at what looks like another heap of stones. Upon reaching it I see that it's an old well with a warped bucket and a fraying rope.

"We can but try," I mutter.

The bucket descends into the dark and eventually I hear a splash.

Amid much creaking I turn the winch to raise it. The old wood leaks severely, but as soon as I set the bucket on the ground the donkey plunges in his nose and drinks. I leave him to it.

By cutting some low hanging branches from an evergreen tree and laying them over the corner of the two walls with a few small stones to hold them down, I make a roof. There is a pit filled with ashes, which I clean out. Then I winch up more water to fill my pot and replenish my water skin. Old wood from the ruined barn will do to build a fire. I wonder why the people left here, whether they were driven away, died out, or chose to move. Rain is falling more steadily and the donkey crowds into the shelter with me. He'll provide additional warmth and company, so I don't chase him out. I build a fire and with dried meat and herbs, concoct a savoury stew. Once I've eaten that, I put on more water for a herbal drink and while it's heating, I rub salve on my aching limbs. Bank the fire, stack more wood close by, roll myself into my blanket and cloak.

I haven't seen Mord, but hope that he's found a good tree to roost in, and hasn't flown back to Thea. Despite all the noises of a forest – rain, rustling leaves, creak of branches – I'm very aware that I'm alone in the middle of nowhere. I have no idea how close any habitation may be and if those men were to appear and ask me to go with them, I would have no defence, except a small knife. I suppose I should have thought of this before, but when I left home, I didn't imagine that men might be asking about me. I resent that Mother didn't take me into her confidence.

I shiver and throw more wood on the fire. It flares, a small wall of flame protecting my front. The partial walls shelter my back. If I were the Queen of Fire, I could burn down this whole forest, but what would that accomplish? It's knowledge I need, not destruction. I listen hard and look all around, but there's nothing unusual. Trees crowd the small clearing and I think of them stretching forever in all directions. I'm a speck in the middle of all that green. Insignificant. Who am I really? I mutter my name over and over until it becomes a meaningless jumble of sounds. What was I thinking leaving the place I knew, Thea and the twins, my neighbours and friends? I'm just like my father, leaving it all behind. But I have to do this, have to find him and my brother, no matter how long it takes. I yawn.

Smoke puffs from the fire, and I think that I should probably put it out – either its light or smoke might draw unwanted attention. But I crave the warmth and the light. As I'm thinking about the pros and cons, rain makes soothing music, and my eyes droop.

I wander in a dark wood, barefoot and cold. Water drips down my neck, but the cold and wet isn't as bad as the knowledge that something stalks me, has sniffed out my scent in spite of the rain I have called to wash it away. I rub strong-smelling herbs on my feet and all over my body to disguise my odour. Suddenly I come to a break in the trees and eyes look at me out of the darkness. They seem to be staring right at me, but can't see me. I hear the creature draw in a breath, but it can't smell me either. I am encircled and protected by light. There comes a sharp barking call.

Moonlight lies across my eyes; the rain has stopped. The donkey leans against one of the walls, probably asleep. I'm cold, and glance at the glowing coals. Stretch out an arm to reach for more wood and freeze as I spot a pair of shining eyes in a nearby bush. Branches rustle slightly and a black nose followed by a long muzzle emerges. For a moment I think it's a dog, and wonder if there's a farm nearby after all.

There's an odour, though, not the smell of a dog, but something wild. What if it's a wolf, the one that Father wrote about; but a wolf wouldn't live that long. Perhaps its the one Mother feared. Why would wolves hang about our family? Another rustle and the creature moves forward. It's a fox – sleek red-brown fur, white-tipped bushy tail. I'm barely breathing, avoiding any movement that might startle it. Is it looking for food? Would it attack me? I think I could beat it away; it's not that big, but would the bite of a fox cause much damage? The animal simply sits there and the two of us regard each other. I wonder what it thinks of me. The forest is quiet except for the occasional drip, drip of water. Eventually the fox fades back into the bushes. Perhaps I've merely been inspected and found harmless. On the other hand, if this were an old tale, the fox might be a messenger, but if so I don't understand the loll of a tongue, the sniff of a nose, the tilt of a head or the twitch of a tail.

Early morning finds me stiff, but wearing a smile because I've made it through a night in the forest all by myself. It gives me confidence that I'll manage all right on the journey ahead. When I untie him the donkey dashes to the well, kicking up his heels and I hurry to give him water. Leftover cold stew and unleavened bread make a good, if chewy, breakfast. I drench what remains of the fire and pack. Mord flutters down to take a few crumbs from my hand, then wheels off.

At first I proceed cautiously, watching for any sign of pursuit or men on horseback ahead of me. After a while, when nothing and no one appears, I hum under my breath, something about a happy wanderer, though I can't recall any other words. Rain-washed air invigorates and I inhale deeply. A dragonfly flutters in front of my nose, then lands on my head; I can feel tiny feet in my hair. I move carefully so as not to scare it prematurely, and wish I could have seen the dragonfly that Thea enlarged.

After a while, I reach another crossroad and from the right comes an ox pulling a cart. I have no time to hide, but these are merely a farmer and his son, off to sell chickens and eggs in the town. When they ask my destination, I tell them I'm going to visit my aunt Edana.

"Horse lady, Da!" the boy says.

"You know her?" I ask.

The farmer nods. "Know of her. Everybody knows the horse lady."

"Good, you can show me her house."

The boy turns and gazes at me, mouth open. His father gives him a nudge and the boy clears his throat. "Don't know where your own auntie lives?" the boy asks.

I shrug. "Never been to visit her until now."

They mull this over as their ox and my donkey plod along through the afternoon. I don't mind their silence. Far above a raven circles and I hope it's Mord. When I glance at the forest beside us I catch a glimpse of a dark shape among the trees, but it's gone too quickly for me to identify.

Soon other people join us, and I take comfort in their presence.

I wonder if it's market day, but the farmer tells me that Timberton is large enough that people can sell or buy every day. A burly, hairy man nods at us and strides by carrying a large axe and a huge hammer over his shoulder. Perhaps he's going to look for work. He passes a family in another ox cart ahead of us. Children are hanging over the edges so that I fear one will fall under the wheels, but a hand always pulls the precarious child back in time. The children wave at me so I smile and wave back. What had been a track through the forest becomes wider, a busy roadway, with carts going both ways, people on foot and horseback.

The forest ends abruptly. A swathe of trees has been cut down, and to either side I see many stumps. Just ahead a wall – wooden poles set on an earthen dike – rises to three times the height of a person. A wide double gate stands open, guards with spears on both sides. Perhaps there are lawless men or fierce animals in the forest around here. We pass through slowly, as just inside, two more guards ask each individual or group what their purpose is. Some, obviously regulars, move ahead with a nod.

"I'm going to visit my aunt Edana, the horse lady," I say when it's my turn.

The guard waves me along and I kick the donkey in order to catch up to the farmer and his son. People swarm everywhere like bees. Houses are of all sizes, including some that have four and five levels, which I've never seen before, and streets lead every direction.

"How will I ever find Edana?" I mutter.

"Easy!" the boy chortles. He points ahead. "Go to the end, turn before the gate."

I can't see a gate ahead, and the street curves so that I can't discern its end, either.

"I'll get lost for certain."

The farmer clarifies. "We're on the widest and longest street. Goes right through the town to the gate at the other end. Just before that gate another street goes right. Turn there and follow it. Can't miss the house and stable."

I thank him and wave good-bye to the two of them at the central square where all kinds of carts and booths are set up. I've never seen so many people or buildings in one place and it all fascinates me, but also makes me cautious. I scrutinize the men on horseback, a closed coach, two women fingering bright swatches of cloth, but see no one I recognize. Children dash through the crowd, people shout and argue. Heaps of fruit and vegetables mound carts, plucked chickens and skinned rabbits hang on hooks. The donkey tosses his head, walking more and more slowly until finally he stops, nose against the side of a house. I sigh and get down. He won't budge until I splash water into my cupped hands and let him drink. Poor donkey, I've certainly worked him much harder than he's ever been worked before.

"Soon you'll be able to rest," I soothe.

I hope Edana will be hospitable. I can pay her, but don't want to spend too much money as I have no idea how much farther I'll have to go and what expenses I might incur. So far I've been very lucky. Perhaps I should try to find work.

My legs ache, and now that those pains come to my notice, others make themselves felt, too. The scrapes on my arms, a sore place on my back, and of course my numb rear, which, like the donkey, isn't used to this kind of travel. I sigh and plod along no longer paying attention to the houses and people; all I want is a soft place to lie down.

What if Edana shuts the door in my face, or worse, she isn't at home and I'll have to find an inn. That could cost a lot of money and there will be people who ask questions, strangers I don't trust. Gloom settles over me like a cloak; why on earth did I ever start this journey. I almost overlook the side street, which is narrower than, and not as busy as, the main one.

The donkey gives a sudden bray and I nearly jump out of my skin. Barely have time to turn, trying see what's the matter, when he lunges past me tearing the reins out of my slack hands. He races down the street as I limp along unable to catch hold. Ahead is a two-storey house with a fenced area at the side. A horse raises its head over the fence and for a moment it seems that's where donkey is headed. I'm just off the mark. It's the pail of grain beside the horse that interests my beast and he plunges his nose in. The horse whinnies as if in greeting.

"Sorry, horse," I say. "This donkey has no manners at the best of times and they're worse when he's hungry."

A low chuckle sounds from my right. A tall man dressed in leather breeches and shirt walks around the corner of the house. Then I realize by the rounded shape that though the hair is short enough for a man and the clothing is what a man would wear, this is a woman.

"Edana?" I blurt.

She inclines her head and slaps my donkey on the rump. He doesn't budge. She laughs again.

"Karl and Karolina," I start.

"Oh," she taps me on the shoulder much the way she hit the donkey and I get a strong whiff of horse, "they sent you. Welcome. Let's get the baggage off this beast and get him a rub down. Boy!" she yells, cupping both hands around her mouth.

A tow-head pokes out of a window in the barn beyond the fenced enclosure.

"Get a move on," Edana yells, "this donkey needs caring for. As do you," she adds in a quieter voice giving me a push in the direction of the house. "We'll get you a bath and food."

It's as if I've acquired a rough older sister. She turns me over to her housekeeper, Ma Parnell, and leaves me with another push. I stand in the middle of the stone-floored kitchen like a chick nudged out of the egg, slightly damp, dishevelled. There is warmth here, and good smells.

"Come," Ma Parnell smiles. "We have a wash house just outside the back door where there's always hot water. We need it, with three perpetually dirty boys."

Mother and I bathed in a small tin tub in front of our fireplace or in a calm part of the river during the summer. I've never seen such place to wash in as the one that the woman leads me to. The tub is made of fitted stones sunk into the earth. Nearby hunches an odd metal contraption with a pipe that hangs over the tub. When Ma

Parnell opens a metal door and throws in a few pieces of wood I see it's a closed fireplace. Then she takes a plug out of the metal pipe and hot water gushes. She points to a couple of pails.

"Cold water there if you need it. Soap, a scrub brush, sponge, towels."

I can hardly wait to get my clothes off. There's even a hook to hang them on. Absolutely the best thing is the steaming hot water which soaks the aches out of my body. The soap scents my hair and body with lavender and a lump rises in my throat. Don't think about her, I tell myself, scrub, soak some more. Nearly fall asleep, my head pillowed on the stone edge.

"Clean clothes." Ma Parnell brings in a chair with a folded pile on it, takes my clothes away.

Underclothes and a faded shirt, slightly large for me. Breeches. I hold them up, put them against me. They are about the right size, but I haven't worn boys' clothes since I was small. Still if they've taken my clothes off to wash, I have to wear something, and one of Ma Parnell's dresses would be much too large. It's possible Edana doesn't even own a dress, though hers would be too long on me. I laugh at myself; what does it matter? I've fallen into a dream where all my needs are taken care of and I feel safe. Pull up the breeches, slip on my boots.

In the kitchen Ma Parnell motions me to a bench at the table and sets a bowl in front of me. The smell of garlic and onion makes my mouth water. "Lentils," she says, "with vegetables. I hope you're not fussy. A couple of the lads want nothing but meat. Edana says just like horses, humans need variety in food."

I spoon some of the colourful mess into my mouth and nod. Savoury. Ma Parnell goes back to her work and I concentrate on the food. When I've finished I want to lay my head on the table and go right to sleep, but a great deal of light is still spilling into the kitchen through a window so it can't be close to night yet.

Ma Parnell smiles, taking my empty dish. "She told me to take you up to your room, said you'd come a long way."

She leads me out of the kitchen into a hallway up some stairs to the left. A bed, blankets. I fall into softness. Ma Parnell pulls curtains over the window. I smile and close my eyes. Wake to the fragrance of fresh bread and roasting chicken.

Edana leans against the doorway. "We're about to eat our evening meal. By the way, you didn't tell me your name."

"Rowan," I say. "Sorry, I've been a terrible guest. Thank you for taking me in, and the bath, the food, clean clothes . . ."

She chuckles. "You'll have to pay." And she is gone.

I hurry into my clothes. How much will Edana want? In the kitchen several people have gathered around the table. Edana and the boy I'd glimpsed before, and two more boys, all slightly damp about hair and face. All are younger than I, though I'm not sure of exact ages.

Ma Parnell sets down dishes of food and slaps away grabbing hands. "We wait for our guest."

As I enter Edana waves casually. "Boy one, boy two, boy three."

They grin.

Ma Parnell is more enlightening, and points. "Corky." Red hair. "Dow." Black hair. "Benny." The light-haired one I'd seen in the barn window.

I bob my head. "Rowan."

During supper I learn that none of the boys is related to Edana, rather they are orphans that she has taken in over several years. They share a room in the loft of the barn, but eat all their meals as a family. I watch them and think of my brother Samel. The boys nudge and tease each other. Edana punches one lightly in the shoulder, ruffles another's hair. Ma Parnell gives them second helpings. Might my brother like horses and roast chicken with dumplings? Does he crinkle his nose when he laughs? And most important of all, does he know about me?

After the meal I offer to help Ma Parnell with the washing up. She refuses and motions to Corky and Dow. It's their turn.

"You come with Benny and me," Edana says.

Benny carries a lantern as we cross the yard, though I can see quite well by the moon. I still feel as if I'm dreaming, but inside the barn soft rustling and whickers greet us, along with the real scent of dried hay, and faintly, manure, though the barn looks very clean. Edana leads the way, stopping at each stall to rub a nose, hand over a carrot, pat a neck, or scratch between a pair of ears.

"Four of these are mine at the moment," Edana explains. "The gelding you saw previously outside, the stallion at the end, the mare and foal across the way. Two other mares are here to be bred to the stallion. We'll keep them a while yet. And of course, here's your donkey."

"I called him Dusty," Benny says, "cause I didn't know his real name."

"He hasn't one," I admit.

"A horse or donkey always has a name," Edana says. "That's even more important than people having names, right, boy?" She ruffles Benny's hair affectionately.

"No," he says stoutly. "Everything has a name, even boys."

"Sorry, Benny," Edana agrees immediately. "You're right, I shouldn't tease you when I know you don't like it."

For a while we watch the mare feeding her foal. The animal seems all skinny legs to me. It totters around the oversized stall and I wonder whether it's sickly or whether all young horses look like this.

"We'll put them both out in the pasture tomorrow." Edana turns to me. "If you stay, you'll learn a lot about horses. We can use another pair of hands right now."

It's something to think about because I have no idea really where to look for my father and brother and perhaps this town will be a good place to get information. They might even be living here. Still, I'll have to watch out for those two men.

Upstairs a lantern welcomes me and a small vase of heartsease, white and purple petals glowing in the light, sits on a trunk. Across the foot of the bed lies my brushed blanket. On a hook behind the door hang all my clothes, also clean, but still damp from being washed. I feel for the coins which remain where I hid them. My satchel sits on the floor. I stretch out on the bed.

"So what do you think?" Edana perches on a stool.

I am about to speak when the window rattles. "Is that the wind?"

She shakes her head. "No wind at all tonight." In smooth motion she rises, steps to the window and flings back the curtains. "Huh!" she exclaims. "There's a raven out there."

I jump up. "It's Mord."

Edana fumbles with the catch. A flutter of darkness and then Mord hops onto the bed. Edana looks at me with one eyebrow raised.

"Mord doesn't really belong to me the way, say a horse, belongs to you," I explain. "He's more of a friend who looks out for me."

"Horses don't belong to anyone either. They give us their friendship and allow us to ride them sometimes in return for food and care. Still, it's not uncommon for horses to be friends with humans. A raven now that's rare!"

"My, that is, we raised him from a fledgling. But speaking of food and care, how much do I owe you for the bath, the meal and the bed?"

"What?"

"You said I'd have to pay; I'd just like to know how much."

Edana shakes her head and grins. "I was teasing, though I meant what I said earlier about helping with the horses. Whatever it is that you're doing or wherever you're going, time with horses will stand you in good stead, believe me."

Karl and Karolina wouldn't have sent me to someone they didn't trust, but my first instinct is to be careful about how much I tell her. So I say that my mother has died and I've just found out that I have a father and brother somewhere in the south, perhaps in this town. I'm going to look for them. I have a relative taking care of things at home, and I want to send a message to her by Mord in the morning.

"So if you still want me I'd like to stay at least until Mord returns."

Edana nods and pats me on the shoulder. Then she asks me to describe my father and brother. I tell her what the man and boy I've seen in dreams look like. She says she has never seen them here, but that doesn't mean they aren't in the area.

In the morning first thing I write to Thea on a scrap of parchment: *Safe with friend of Karl's in Timberton. Will stay till I hear from you.*

I help Ma Parnell get breakfast, then insist on helping her wash up. After that Corky shows me how to curry the horses, where to get water and feed for them. It's a peaceful dead end street so I don't feel as if I'm in a town. I wonder how many people actually live here, and whether Edana knows them all. She is out in the fenced enclosure leading the gelding around with a young girl on its back. The mare and the foal meander in a far corner near a tree under Benny's watchful eye.

Dow joins me at the fence. "You stayin'?"

"For a while," I say. "To learn about horses."

He taps the rail of the fence with his fist. "She knows."

I suppose he means Edana and that she knows about horses, but he could equally mean that she knows about other things. How to take homeless boys and give them a place and a purpose, how to teach an awkward girl to ride, how to soothe a worn out donkey. Edana stops the gelding and the girl slides off. She gets a pat on the shoulder and so does the horse. The girl leaves and Edana brings the gelding over to Dow and me.

"Rowan," she says, "I see you've got your breeches on, want to take a turn? Dow can lead Angel."

I've never ridden a horse which is a lot bigger than a donkey, and I'd expected to have more time to get used to the idea, watch how other people do it. But Edana is standing right there and so is Dow. Both of them look at me expectantly.

"Angel?" I ask, to give myself more time. "I thought geldings were boy horses?"

"So?" Edana grins. "A boy can't be an angel?" She pats the horse's neck. "Come over here."

I climb over the fence. Dow follows taking the reins from Edana. I approach the horse which is as high as my shoulder, slowly.

"No," Dow says, "other side."

I glance at Edana. She nods. "Always mount from the left side of the horse. Let me get you a block of wood. Easier that way."

Dow demonstrates by putting his left foot in the stirrup, then swinging his right over. When he gets off, I step onto the block. My left foot goes in too far, poking Angel in the side. He squeals and starts walking, with me trying to either get my right leg over, or my left foot out, but Dow stops the horse.

"Again," he says.

This time I manage to mount, though I feel very high up and precarious. On the donkey I'd made do with a padded blanket and no stirrups, but it was a much shorter distance to fall. I want something to hang onto so reach for the horse's mane.

"No," Dow says, "pommel." He points to the bump projecting at the front of the saddle.

I grab hold. Edana leaves us to it. I want to call after her, but that would mean I have no confidence in Dow. In reality I have no confidence at all, haven't felt this useless and awkward for years. What if I fall off the horse and break a leg or an arm? The boy leads the horse slowly, and gradually I grow more at ease. Then Dow stops and gives me the reins, showing me how to hold them. They will be no help if I start to slip; I want to hang onto the pommel again, but Dow won't let me. Slowly we make a couple of circuits. Finally the boy halts the horse and helps me get down. My legs are trembling.

"Tomorrow," Dow says. I nod. "Come," he continues. "Barn."

I walk beside him as he leads Angel to his stall, then do my best to help and not get in the way as Dow removes the riding tack. He lets me curry the horse by myself, since he knows Corky showed me how. Edana arrives just as I'm finishing.

"How was it?"

"Odd," I say. "I kept expecting to slide off."

She laughs. "You did fine for a first time, though falls are part of riding."

***

When I can, I wander the streets of Timberton in hopes of seeing the man who might be my father. Beyond the main road that leads from one gate to the other lie many winding, narrow lanes and streets. Houses, stores, temples and other buildings I don't know the use of are packed together like twigs in a broom. Some structures lean sideways, others project over the street. I find myself hurrying, afraid that one building or another will collapse and bury me.

There are people everywhere, many walking or seated on doorsteps. Children play on cobblestones with not even a blade of grass to alleviate the deadness of stone and milled wood. Are there no gardens, I wonder?

I retreat to Edana's property. When I ask, she tells me that of course there are gardens and fields on the edge of town, and even in the centre, people grow vegetables and flowers behind their houses. If it weren't for the space around Edana's house and barn, I would have to run beyond the walls to the fields and trees so I could breathe. I wonder whether my life in the northern forest has spoiled me for any other place.

Still I make myself walk the streets every day or so for at least an hour or two, watching people. There are plenty of dark-haired men and many children. None has the appearance I expect of my father and brother. Thankfully, I see no sign of the two men who followed me on the road. Perhaps they've moved on.

One evening after the boys and Ma Parnell have gone to their rooms Edana and I sit in the kitchen drinking a tisane of rose hips. I gaze at the flame of the candle and remember another evening when I waited and fell asleep.

"What is it?" Edana asks.

"Mord. I thought he'd be back by now."

Edana gets up for hot water to replenish the pot. "What will you do if you can`t find your father and brother here?"

I put my head in my hands and stare into my cup. "I don't know," I sigh. "I don't know where to go from here."

"It's a huge land out there."

"I know they're somewhere in a southern city, but not how far or which one. Are there a lot of cities and towns?"

"Quite a few." She pauses. "You can stay here as long as you like, you know."

I raise my head. "Thank you, Edana. That means a lot to me, but I really do want to go and look for them."

"I have a friend who could have some insights," Edana says slowly.

"She's been away, just got back today."

I stand. "Is she good at finding people? Can we go see her now? Or is it too late?" I sit down again. "She'll probably be tired and maybe asleep."

Edana chuckles. "She's like an owl, likes the night." Then she frowns. "Perhaps I shouldn't have said anything. She's rather strange."

"Not all owls hunt only at night," I say, ignoring her other words. I'm willing to try anything. "Where I come from there are snowy owls, which hunt both day and night."

"I didn't know that. At any rate, Julina will still be awake."

"What are we waiting for then?"

Edana leads the way out, turning left at the main street and then left again. Soon we are in a maze of twisting narrow lanes. It's a good thing Edana has brought a lantern, for the cobbles under our feet are rough and sometimes heaps of refuse lie about. I'm having second thoughts about this night time walk. However, Edana soon stops in front of a house. There doesn't seem to be any light on inside or else the curtains are unusually thick. Edana doesn't knock on the door, rather she slips into a niche nearby, and I follow up a steep flight of wooden stairs that creak alarmingly. Perhaps Edana has decided I need an adventure to take my mind off my troubles and she is supplying all the atmosphere she can. We reach a small landing and an oddly carved door. The lantern flickers, throwing shadows that seem to cause the carvings of snakes and grotesque faces on the door to slither and writhe. Edana grabs a knocker shaped like a skull and thumps.

Chapter VI
Samel

I untangle myself from the tunic I have run into outside our front door, and raise my head. It's Papa.

"Samel! I was on my way to find you. "What have you been doing in your room? Trying to set fire to it?"

I push the fist still clutching the bracelet into my pocket. "What? Oh, never mind that. I need . . ."

Papa grabs my arm and pulls me into our house. "No!" he shouts. "Not never mind. You're going to sit there and tell me what's going on." He pushes me into a chair.

I jump up. "It's you who has to tell me!" I yell back. "Keeping secrets! Not telling me my mother is or was still alive! And my sister!"

He sinks into the chair I just left. "Your sister?" he whispers. "What do you know about her?"

The floor shifts under my feet. We stare at each other. Now that he's confirmed what I suspected, I don't want to speak again for fear of saying the wrong thing. Don't want explanations or evasions, just the truth. I don't say any of that. His face is pale as a full moon. He shakes his head, gestures at the table. There's a jug of water. I pour him a glass. He sips.

"Oh," he says finally in a thin, strangled voice, "what shall I do?"

"Tell me the truth," I answer immediately. "All of it. Now."

He takes another sip of water. "It's not a pretty story," he mumbles.

And then, slowly, he fills in details. I have a sister who is two years older than me. He hasn't seen her since she was three. He mentions the bracelets he and mother made their partnering vows with, then tells me how my sister and maybe I, too, demonstrated spellcraft abilities when a wolf came near us. It was after that Papa and my mother decided to separate. They were afraid our growing abilities might draw danger to us. I have a feeling he knows more about this than he is telling, but he hurries on to other things.

"It worries me that my bracelet has disappeared," Papa says. Where did it go?"

"Doesn't my sister worry you?" I snap. "If our mother is dead as you dreamt, what's happening to her? By the way what's my sister's name?"

"Rowan."

The word is a sob, and tears stream down his face. It hits me that Papa has been holding in a lot of pain and sadness. I see it now in his bowed head and hunched back. There are words I need to say. I know they will cause him more pain, but that can't be helped.

"You always said that we should take care of each other, you and I. Stick together through thick and thin."

"You were all I had left," he gulps.

"No!" I shout.

Pound my fist on the table. A glint of silver flashes as the bracelet falls out of the pocket where I have been clutching it. Clink and tinkle as it falls to the floor and rolls. I dive after it, but Papa has seen, too.

"Samel!" he bellows.

I don't let his yell stop me. We bash shoulders. Papa shoves me aside into the table leg. The table tips and falls with a crash, hitting Papa on the head. He yells. I slide along the floor, stretch out my hand. The bracelet rolls into it. I make a fist and shove it back into my pocket.

"I'm not all you had or have left," I say quietly. "What are we going to do about Rowan?"

"Samel," Papa says equally quietly, "give me back that bracelet."

"No," I say firmly. "It's left you, you said so yourself. It's mine now to use as I see fit. I'm going to use it to find my sister."

Papa shakes his head, "You don't know what you're saying. What you're doing." He holds out his hand. "Give. Me. Back. My. Bracelet."

"It rolled into my hand," I point out. "Isn't yours anymore."

I stand and begin to move backwards toward the door to the hall. Papa rises too. He is still bigger than I am, and a lot bulkier, but he doesn't come any farther. Just hunches there, looking at me sadly.

"Help me," I say. "I need you. We'll go get Rowan together."

His head bows. "She isn't there anymore," he mumbles.

"What? Where? Isn't where anymore?"

"Zarmine," his voice breaks. "Your mother and sister stayed in the house we found together."

I nod. "In a cottage, in a clearing in the woods."

"Yes, in the north." His head comes up. He stares at me. "How did you know that? I didn't tell you. Oh, you guessed when I told you about the wolf."

"No," I shake my head. "I might have, but I knew before. I've had a few visions of my own."

I decide not to mention Ali. She promised to keep my secrets, so I'll keep hers. Papa bends over, picks up the table and rights it. He gets a broom and sweeps up the broken crockery from the goblets and the pitcher. I watch him, my back against the door frame. I have no idea what he's going to do next, and I don't entirely trust him anymore.

"We've been doing a lot of breaking lately," Papa says as he pulls out a chair and sits.

I cross my arms and don't answer. I'm waiting to hear him say that he'll help me find my sister, wherever she is. Because I'm fairly certain he knows.

Papa sighs. "Samel, will you ever forgive me?"

"I don't know. Where's Rowan?" I remember the last thing I saw in the bracelet. "She's gone off somewhere on a donkey with a raven, hasn't she? Do you know where?"

A narrowing of Papa's eyes. "How do you know that?" He glances aside at the pocket where I'm still clutching the bracelet. "More visions? You have no idea how dangerous this is."

"Then help me," I beg, "if you know so much more than me. Help your son and your daughter. Where has she gone? Do you know? Would she try to find us? Of course she would! Papa, she'll be coming to find us if Mother died."

"Maybe. But how would she know? Unless Zarmine told her. I'm not sure that's a good thing. Besides, I don't know for certain that they remained in that cottage."

I work my way through this tangled mess of words. "So Rowan might not know where to find us, might not even know she's got a father and brother. If there's danger, as you say, she could be riding straight into it. Papa we have to find her!"

"This isn't a good idea," he mutters.

"You know something. Tell me!"

He stares at me. Taps his fingers on the table. "Timberton. That's where she might be."

"Where's that? And how do you . . . wait, the eagle. You sent the eagle to look for her! Why didn't you tell me?" I rush over and give him a hug. "I'm sorry. I should have known you wouldn't leave her alone. So we can pack up and go, right now, or maybe early tomorrow morning would be best." I straighten. "I can go get more food at the market and we should buy a couple of camels."

"Stop!" Papa exclaims. "Wait. Let me explain. Sit down."

I sink into a chair. Wait impatiently while Papa rubs his face, takes a deep breath.

"I did send an eagle to keep watch over Rowan after I had the dream. I thought it would be an unobtrusive way to find out what she was doing, if she needed anything. According to what I could understand from the eagle, there was a woman with her at the cottage." He holds up a hand as I'm about to speak. "Not your mother, if I've read the eagle correctly, but I'm not completely sure of that. Anyway the woman could be your mother's cousin, Thea her name was. The eagle let me know that Rowan left, as you say, on a donkey. The raven was with her, which made it more difficult for the eagle and he lost sight of them. Then the eagle found Rowan again in a town where the forest meets the grasslands. That's Timberton, northeast of here. I don't know what Rowan is doing or why she left home. And all of this depends on my interpretation of an eagle's communication."

"That's easy," I say, ignoring all the questions I have about how Papa can talk to eagles and why he never told me. "Of course, she's coming to find us. It's what I would do."

Papa sighs. "You could be right."

"So we go to this Timberton place to meet her. The eagle can guide us."

"I don't think we should rush to do anything. We need to think carefully before we act."

I ignore this. "Where's the eagle now? Can you call it again? And how on earth can you talk with an eagle?"

Papa sighs. "It's complicated. Sometimes if an eagle and a human meet early in life they maintain a bond and can get impressions from each other's minds."

"You're reading an eagle's mind? I'm surprised. You, who always cautioned me about hocus-pocus and folk medicine!"

"Let's not go into all that again," Papa says. "I suppose you'll give me no peace until you see the eagle for yourself."

Papa's pace through the streets is much too slow for my liking and I keep urging him to walk faster. He ignores me. I guess that's fair because I've not been taking any notice of his warnings. My experiences with the flute and bracelet, though unnerving at first, haven't been really frightening. I don't understand why Papa keeps talking about some great danger. True, I might have burned down the house, but that would have been due to my own carelessness. I go over everything he's told me and try to imagine my mother and father as young people, maybe not much older than Magenta. Newly partnered and then with small children. I can understand doing everything you can to protect your children. After all, I have Papa's example before me, and he always took good care of me. I try to picture my sister Rowan and me with a wolf nearby. If I'd been a parent I guess that would have scared me. Wouldn't I have wanted to leave the place where wolves could come so close to my children? Something doesn't make sense.

"Papa," I say, "tell me again about this light you saw when the wolf came. Could you tell where the light was coming from? Could it have been a reflection of the sun?"

"I'm tired of talking about this, Samel. I've told you what I know. Told you what we feared and what we did. It doesn't matter whether you like it or not, whether you understand it or not. What's done is done."

He speeds up and reaches the gate of the palace ahead of me. I run to catch up. It's not a very dignified way to arrive. The guard waves us through.

Papa knows even more short cuts than I do. To the right and through a hidden gate. Along a path between tangled rose bushes, red, white, pink and yellow blossoms under our feet. Into a short passage, then along a narrow man-made stream. One more gate and we're in the garden by the tower where he has a room.

He gestures to a bench. "Sit. Be quiet. I don't know whether the eagle will come or even where he might be. The last time I saw him was yesterday. I suggested he rest before going back to keep watch over Rowan. If we're lucky he's still in the vicinity."

I do as he tells me. Watch as Papa pulls a small wooden whistle out of his pocket. He puts it to his lips and blows. But there is no sound; I wonder if the whistle is broken. Papa waits then blows again. Still nothing. One more time.

"Your whistle is useless."

"No," he says, coming to sit beside me. "It's a special whistle. We can't hear it, but an Aquilan eagle can. If he's nearby, he'll come."

"So how long do we wait?"

"I think we'd have heard his answering call by now, so he must be too far away. Sorry, Samel, we'll have to try another day."

I stand and point. Papa looks.

"Do you see something?"

"No, but why not try at the north tower?"

Papa shrugs and leads the way out of this small courtyard garden through a different door than where we came in. A long passage lined with columns, then a larger courtyard with people moving here and there, horses coming in, men dismounting, and horses being led away. There is a lot more activity than I've ever seen around here. One of the men nods to Papa, another raises a hand. Others smile at me. We move across to a door with a guard, who stops us.

"What's going on?" Papa asks. "I haven't seen this many guards in one place in a long while."

"You haven't heard? That's good. We're trying to keep it quiet so as not to alarm the people of the city."

"I won't spread gossip," Papa assures him.

"Unfortunately it's not gossip, but wolves."

"What?" Papa goes rigid.

"Or not exactly wolves. We're not sure what they are. They look sort of like wolves, but twisted, with a paw like a hand, a leg with skin instead of fur, a head with distorted features." He shudders. "Nightmare stuff."

"You've seen one?" Papa has shifted so that his back is against a wall. His head is moving as if he's looking for a wolf, but that's silly, there wouldn't be any in here.

"Several, all dead," the guard nods. "Looked almost as if they'd been tortured." He glances at me. "Nothing to worry about, really," he adds. "We're keeping an extra sharp lookout, but no one's seen any live ones."

"Samel," Papa says, "maybe we should just go home."

"No! You heard him, nothing to worry about. I want to finish what we started."

The guard lets us through into a narrow passage. High above slit-like windows let in light. Soon the passage curves sharply and then there's a set of stairs. Another guard and door. I just want to be at the tower, but there's no way to speed this up. At last we reach the top of the wall where the tower looms above us, another two stories. The flag of Aquila, a golden eagle on a silver back ground, flies from the top. I've never been on this part of the wall before, nor this high up. To the south, west and east, the palace is laid out below us. Beyond that, Aquila stretches south and east to the river, which holds the city in a curve. To the west and north lies desert. Somewhere beyond that is my sister.

I search the sky, see nothing but blue sprinkled with white clouds. Papa tries his whistle again, three times. No eagle appears. Finally, I have to agree with Papa and admit that we aren't going to achieve anything today. He's scanning the countryside beyond the wall. Maybe looking for those wolf creatures, but there's nothing moving nearby.

Just as we're about to leave the wall, I turn to Papa. "Does Rowan have black hair? Like you?"

He stares at me. "More of your visions?" Shakes his head. "Sorry, I shouldn't take my anger and frustration out on you because none of this is your fault." He grips my shoulder. "Your sister has black hair like me, and grey eyes like your mother."

On the way home neither of us speaks; we've said it all before. I don't even feel angry anymore, just deflated, like the goat's bladder I saw some boys kicking in the street once. The bladder bounced up against the wall of a house and must have hit a rough spot. It was punctured and lost its form slowly. The boys left it lying there, a dirty sack. When we get back to our house it's time for the evening meal, but I can't eat. Without saying a word to Papa I go upstairs and lie on my bed. I hear him moving around downstairs. After a while he calls me, but I don't answer. It's quite dark in my room by now; I don't bother lighting any candles.

The bracelet – what have I done with it? I search my pockets. Find it, pull it out. Breathe a sigh of relief. Clutch the circlet tightly in my fist and fall asleep.

Chapter VII

Rowan

As Edana pushes on Julina's door it moves inwards, slowly and silently, raising hairs on the back of my neck. Faint illumination spills out and Edana gives me a nudge and a cluck, as if I'm a recalcitrant horse. We enter a tiny, dimly lit room that contains nothing except a dark curtain in front of us not quite meeting the floor, thus letting through light from the other room. The curtain brushes by me, soft, thick and dusty; my nose tickles and I'm having third and fourth thoughts. Edana is in front so her body obscures most of the room. There are a mixture of smells -- herbs and perfumes.

"Atmosphere is illusion," a deep voice drawls. "Illusion conceals . . . masks are useful . . . but can be penetrated."

Edana steps to the side and I see a huge figure dressed and hooded in scarlet. Candles throughout the room throw shadows over the face. Edana has brought me to the Fire Queen, and I don't know whether she's friend or foe. The figure steps forward and somehow down, then throws back the hood. A normal-sized woman with flowing black hair accented by a reddish streak smiles at me.

"I see you've brought a friend, Edana. Sit."

She points to a low table and multi-coloured cushions. The room is a riot of colour, shades of red and yellow, brown and black, blue, green, purple. Hangings, rugs, cushions, candles. I sink into softness.

"This is Rowan," Edana says. "Julina."

"How do you like my games, Rowan?"

She gestures around the room and at herself. That's when I notice the stool that she had been standing on when we entered. It was concealed by the length of her robe.

"Illusions for what reason?" I ask, not sure that I like this woman or this room.

She smiles, showing teeth. "Some expect this kind of thing of a soothsayer; it gives them confidence in what I tell them."

"Are you a soothsayer?"

She smiles again. "That's up to each person to decide. I assume you have a question."

"Is that the only reason for illusion?"

"There are many, including being able to hide your secrets from those who have no business knowing them."

Julina and I study each other. Her eyes are dark and deep as wells, shadowed at this moment by partially lowered lids. Her face is smooth and unlined, but I get a sense of age or timelessness. This woman is strange, but is her strangeness a mask? Several candles blaze up, flicker and subside. Shadows gather in the corners of the room. She opens her eyes so wide that a person could fall in and drown, or perhaps find water to drink.

"I have two questions," I say.

"Besides the ones you've already asked?" Julina laughs. "Are you willing to pay?"

I fumble with the pouch at my waist. "I have coin."

Julina waves that away. "From you I want no coin."

"What then?"

Edana speaks for the first time since we sat. "Be wary, Rowan. Julina is my friend, but even I don't trust her unreservedly. Whatever she asks, think carefully before you agree."

I want to demand why she's brought me here if she doesn't trust this woman, but at the same time, I'm curious and interested. What might Julina be able to tell me?

"Good advice," Julina nods. "Now, my price for your two questions."

"Wait," I say, "don't you want to hear the questions first? What if you can't answer them, will I still be required to pay?"

"No. I'll give you answers though you may not like them. Yes."

I digest this and she waits. "What's your price?" I ask finally.

"For the first question, a look at what you carry hidden in your pouch."

My hand goes to my belt. "Perhaps there are several hidden things," I reply. "Which is it you want to see?" I'm testing her, and she knows it because she raises one eyebrow.

"Silver," she says, "and larger than a coin."

I have to decide right now how much to trust Julina. Though maybe it's not about trust at all, but using whatever comes to hand in order to find my father and brother. I've already dared much by leaving home and going among strangers. This is just one more step along the way.

"You want to see it now?" I ask. "Before the question?"

Julina gestures toward my pouch.

I draw out the bracelet, let it lie in my palm. It glows in the candlelight. Julina leans forward, but doesn't touch it.

"Interesting," she says. She glances at me. "And what about the necklace you wear? Did you make it?"

"No, it was a present from my mother."

"I can't tell exactly what she did to the beads, whether it's how she marked them or what she polished them with, probably both. Also the way she wove the wool and leather. Small spellcraft, but effective. The sapphire gives protection while travelling."

My hand trembles as I touch the necklace. "Magic? My mother's gifts had to do with herbs and healing."

"Just that?" The words are quiet, but they pierce me like a knife. "Did she say anything when she gave you the necklace? Was it a special occasion?"

"My fifteenth birthday. She was always making grass weavings and hanging them in the trees around our cottage, said they were for luck and protection. I thought the necklace was similar." Did Mother give me this gift because she thought I would leave home soon? Perhaps she saw more than I realized.

Julina intertwines her fingers. "It is in a way." She shifts her eyes. "Let me look more closely at the bracelet."

I hold it out to her.

"Put in on the table," she says. She bends over still not touching it. "Ivy leaves."

"Is there special meaning to that?"

"Everlasting love is the meaning of ivy, also death because the vine can strangle. Most things have shades of dark and light within, as do people." She widens her eyes at me.

I don't like that look, so slip the bracelet quickly onto my wrist. It feels heavier than I remember. The edges of the leaves catch the glow of a nearby candle and flash back light. I close my other hand over it.

"How did you know," I ask, "that I carried this in my pouch?"

"Ah," Julina shrugs. "I'm no ordinary person. Put it away and tell me the question."

I tuck the bracelet into my pouch, take a deep breath. "I'm looking for my father and brother. I believe they're somewhere in the south country. Can you tell me where?"

"You have something that belonged to them or that they have touched?"

"Maybe."

I pull my pouch open again. Julina clears everything off the low table where we sit except for one candle. She spreads a white cloth over the dark wood. Gestures. I take out the black and red curls of hair and lay them on the cloth.

She points at the coarse red and the soft black curls. "Not these."

I put them back into my pouch, thinking they're probably Mother's and mine. Julina touches each of the other two briefly with a forefinger.

"Rowan, you and Edana move away, over there." She points to a low divan against the opposite wall. "I need space and quiet."

As she leans forward I see a flash of gold at her neck, a yellow orange stone on a thin cord of black. She strokes the stone, then cups her hands around the bits of hair – my father's and brother's if I'm right. Hopefully she isn't going to do something irrevocable like set them alight. Suddenly all the candles go out and we are plunged into darkness. Slowly a faint golden luminescence grows near the table, as if the stone around the woman's neck has caught light from some hidden place. Julina's pale face and her disembodied hands float in the dark. Is this merely more illusion, another of her tricks? I want to believe she can find answers for me. The light grows brighter and for an instant a face hovers there, the man I've seen before – in the fireplace at home, in a vision from the hill behind the cottage, in dreams. Light blazes like a lightning bolt and I close my eyes against its blinding flash. Darkness swallows everything.

"Rowan." Edana leans over me. "You fainted."

I'm lying full length on the divan with a pillow under my head. Edana's face whirls. I close my eyes again.

"Here." Julina's voice. "Take a little wine."

I open my eyes and with Edana's help manage to sit up. Julina hands me a silver goblet. I sip. The room looks much as it had earlier when we first entered. Candles are burning everywhere and the white cloth is gone from the table.

"Where's my pouch?" I find it at my waist and the four curls of hair, as well as the bracelet, inside. I face Julina. "Did you see anything?"

"Join me in a light meal," she says, not meeting my eyes. "Both of you. Bread and cheese and wine will revive you, Rowan. We'll talk then. After all, you still have one more question."

I'm not interested in food, but at the first bite, realize that I am, after all, ravenous, as if I've walked for half a day without eating. Edana nibbles at a piece of cheese and watches me with concern. Julina brings a bowl of purple plums and sits cross legged. She takes a plum and bites into it, her teeth white against the dusky skin. Juice runs down her fingers, and she licks them. I don't know why I'm watching her like this; it's almost as if she's done something to tie me to her, draw my attention constantly to her. I look for the golden stone, but it's hidden. I force myself to look away, at the loaf of bread.

"What was shown to me," Julina says, looking not at me, but at the wall behind me, "was a tall dark man together with a red-haired boy. The two of them walked along a crowded street lined with two and three story houses built of mud bricks. From their gestures I thought they argued, but this vision carried no sound. They walked for some time until they came to a great wall where a soldier let them in through a gate. Then they passed through gardens and more gates until they came to a stairway. They ascended to a walkway and stood looking out from the top of the wall. I saw the sun moving across the sky and knew that they looked north across a desert. On a tower to one side of the man, a flag fluttered. The design was a gold eagle on a silver background."

"Aquila!" Edana exclaims. "The city of the Lords of Ameer."

"Is that good or bad?" I ask.

"Neither. Or both." Julina shrugs

"My father and brother?"

"I can tell you no more than what the vision showed me when I held the hair in my hands."

Can it be as easy as this? What if Julina has made all this up. No, there's something about her that is mysterious and like Mother when she was concentrating on healing a difficult illness. So I accept that she saw what she says, but it may not have been my father and brother that she saw. I could go back and forth like this forever; it's time to take another chance.

"Aquila is where I need to go, then." I push back from the table.

"Rowan!" Edana puts a hand on my arm. "Think about this. Whereever your father and brother are, even if the vision was true, it's a long way, over grasslands, across a sea of sand. There will be difficulties and dangers in finding them. You should stay until you get better at riding."

"What about other travellers?" I ask. "Caravans and such? Maybe I could join one."

"Are you in a tearing hurry to leave us?" Edana asks, and her voice is sad.

"Twice seven days," Julina says. "I see you staying in Timberton for that long. Seven is a powerful number. Now what's your second question?"

"The second doesn't matter anymore if I leave tomorrow."

Edana shakes her head. "I thought you were going to wait for Mord to return? Have you forgotten about him?"

I'm about to answer when Julina snaps her fingers and all the candles go out. The room is dark as a cave without a moon when the stars are covered by clouds. A disk the size of my thumbnail appears and glows at the centre of the table. It grows gradually larger until finally I see a silver mask with holes for eyes, nose and mouth, but no one's face is behind the mask. It seems to me that darkness pours like liquid out of the holes. I rub my hands over my face, rub at my eyes. I wish I knew how she's doing all this.

A voice speaks. "Illusion has its uses. Ask your question."

"I . . . how . . . was going to ask," I stutter, "ask you to teach me some of your illusions or tricks, or whatever they are. For concealment," I mutter, "but if I leave tomorrow there won't be time."

"You've asked your question, you'll pay the price."

"But . . ."

Light blazes again from the candles. The mask has disappeared.

"I'll teach you as much as I can in two weeks," Julina promises, "and so will Edana. Meanwhile, I'll keep a watch on the City of Eagles; let you know if those two leave. No charge for that."

What can I do but agree? Much as I want to hurry off, I know it's foolish to go without proper preparation. I've been lucky and safe on my journey up to now, and it occurs to me that perhaps the necklace Mother made me may be responsible for that. If so, I have things to thank her for. She did take care of me all those years; I just wish she'd been more open.

Before we leave her rooms that night, Julina gives me advice that I really don't need. "Keep that bracelet out of sight," she says. "Don't show it to anyone else, and don't hold it in your hands too much."

That night my dreams are filled with a bright city – sun and white walls, narrow streets down which a red-haired boy runs. I try to call him, but my voice is muted and my feet are slow. I wake tired and with a headache.

***

Edana begins teaching me to jump low barriers on horseback. She also shows me how to ride around obstacles such as a series of posts set at intervals in the ground. A couple of days later she takes me out of the town to gallop through treed and rolling countryside, jumping over hedges, galloping through valleys, and racing over meadows. I have a few falls, though thankfully only bruises result, and can't really see how this will be useful. Edana insists that building muscles and agility is never a waste.

In between rides I help Ma Parnell in the kitchen. I learn that Edana is her adopted daughter. Ma Parnell and her now dead husband took in the girl when her parents died.

"My husband was a soldier," Ma Parnell says. "Edana was company when he had to be away. We never had any other children."

One afternoon, Edana picks one of the boys to work with me in the second-floor room of the barn, on unarmed combat. "My father taught me," she explains. "He thought that girls as well as boys should be able to protect themselves."

Edana teaches us how to escape from holds by using elbows, knees, feet, fingers. How to stamp on toes and kick knees as well as gouge at eyes. The boys don't like this much as it's mainly they who get the bruises, even with the extra padding that Edana makes all of us wear. To be fair, Edana always takes a turn, but it's rarely that I'm able to touch her.

Evenings I go alone to Julina's rooms. At my first visit without Edana, Julina talks about clothes and posture. How dirt and rags along with shuffling feet, downcast eyes, and a bent back can make a person virtually invisible. She drapes me in odd bits of ragged, dirty cloth. It seems a waste of time. I ask when she's going to teach me real things. She frowns and counsels patience.

"Patience is for people who have unlimited time," I snap. "That's not me."

"Rowan." She holds up a hand.

"You promised that you'd teach me some of your illusions, tricks, whatever they are. So give me more than a few shuffling steps."

"Discipline is part of the learning," she insists. "I'm the teacher, you're the student. So pay attention!"

"No!" I shout and I tear out of the place, nearly falling down the stairs in my haste.

I've bruised my knee, and limp. Because I've left the lantern behind I have to be careful or I might get lost. I move slowly down the narrow streets. A soldier of the town guard stops me and asks if I have a place to stay.

"There's a shelter for beggars," he says.

I nod, mumble that I have a place, and shuffle off. I can feel his eyes on my back and hope he doesn't follow me. I don't want Edana to get into trouble. After that, I keep to the shadows, though that makes it more difficult not to get lost. Finally I reach Edana's house. The door is unlocked and there's still a light in the kitchen. Ma Parnell gasps when I enter and Edana rises from her chair.

"It's me," I say quickly, "Rowan."

"Girl," Ma Parnell says, with a hand to her heart, "you gave me quite a start. Wearing those old rags over your clothes, your dirty face, I didn't know who you were for a moment."

"Good first lesson!" Edana adds with a chuckle.

I hang my head sheepishly. "Yes, I guess it works as Julina said it would."

The next evening when I tell Julina what happened with my disguise, and try to apologize for my disbelief at her methods and my impatience, she doesn't castigate me. Waves her hands, as if my words are smoke and invites me to sit down at the table. I do so, yawning.

"What's the matter," Julina says caustically. "Bored already?"

"Not been sleeping that well," I mumble through my hands.

She puts a finger under my chin and raises my head. Stares into my face, her eyes piercing. I shake her off, her touch and the scent of her fingers making me uncomfortable.

"Dreams?" she asks.

I nod. "About the city, or a city at any rate. I don't know if it's a real city I'm dreaming about."

Julina begins to pace the room so that candles flicker, throwing long shadows against the walls. I rub surreptitiously at my face, trying to erase her lingering scent and wishing I could identify it. Mother always said that the scent of herbs gave some indication of their use – mint soothing to the nose as well as the stomach, garlic sharp and antiseptic. Julina's smell makes me think of animals of the forest.

Finally, she stops pacing and sits across from me with a lit candle in her hand. She places it in the centre of the table. By passing one hand quickly over the flame she causes it to flare bright yellow so that I spring back for fear of getting burned.

"A pinch of powder cast on flames," she says, "and if you're quick no one realizes what you've done, but it can startle people, especially when it's cast into a larger fire. That gives you time to run away or conceal yourself. I'll give you some."

"Is everything you do a trick?"

Julina smiles. "No. Those dreams you're having, for instance. I think that you have some natural abilities of your own, things I can't or don't need to teach you. But perhaps being near me has acted as a catalyst for you. Do you know what that is?"

I shake my head.

"A substance that accelerates or slows down change in other substances, though in this case I think it's the former. Does it really matter whether what I do are tricks? If they're effective?"

She waits patiently for my answer. Trying to teach me how I ought to behave. I know I should say, no, it doesn't matter, but I'm feeling stubborn. Something about Julina makes me want to go contrary to whatever she expects. I want to see what she'll say or do if I don't respond. We stare at each other in silence. Finally Julina speaks, but gently, when I had expected a loud voice and more argument.

"Rowan, I understand that things haven't been easy for you. Much has happened in a short time, and it's a lot to take in, a lot to get over.

Anger and sadness along with other feelings are all jammed together inside you, like a ball of string that's snarled and knotted. It will take time and patience to untangle all those emotions."

"What if I don't want to take the time?" I snap. "What if I want to yell and scream and hit someone?"

"Who? There's no one to blame."

"Oh?" I spit out the words. "What about my father. Or my mother. One left and the other didn't tell me a couple of the most important things about my life."

"Rowan, children and parents commonly misunderstand each other. You're not unique in that. Just now your anger flared like the candle and you're the one who caused that to happen. So let me ask you, what are you concealing with that flame?"

I try to glare at her, but her face softens and blurs around the edges, and then my tears well, overflow and run down my cheeks. Julina brings me an orange silk handkerchief and I hold it in my hands, letting the tears run because it's too beautiful to blow my nose in. Julina shakes her head and brings me a white linen square instead. When I've dried my face she tosses me a pillow that smells faintly of lavender and roses.

"That's your mother," she says. "Or your father. Maybe both of them. Whoever you want."

I hold it in my hands, think of my mother's face, cold and still. She can't help me now. If the black-haired man is my father, what do I want to say to him? I shake my head, toss the pillow away.

"Rowan," Julina says, "you needed to cry and you may need to again. I'm here and so are Edana and Ma Parnell. Don't try to carry it all alone."

The words are meant to be comforting, but I'm angry. Julina's so calm, almost unfeeling. I wonder what she would do if something terrible happened to her. What if I tip over a candle and burn the place down? I shudder at the thought of flames, and flesh blistering. I don`t want to be the wicked Fire Queen. Julina probably thinks I'm feeling cold because she puts a shawl around my shoulders. Her hands brush against me and there's still that scent I don't like.

"Let me make you some mulled wine." Julina takes a jug from a shelf behind a hanging. From a lower cupboard, she removes a cast iron pot as well as a small brazier on a stand. She adds charcoal and lights it, mixes wine, honey and spices in the pot. She's deft and quick, no wasted motion. I breathe in the aroma, feel the taste on my tongue. Words I don't want but need to say are stuck in my throat, almost choking me. I cough.

"It's my fault," I whisper.

Julina sets a pottery goblet in front of me. "Drink," she directs.

I take a couple of sips. Warmth and sweetness loosen my tongue. "It's my fault Mother died that night."

I don't wait for her to respond, but let the words spill out like a pail of water over cobblestones. How I had wanted to leave home, travel on my own. Mother must have sensed it, known that I wanted to leave her. I had not warned Mother enough about the coming storm, insisting that she stay home. If only I had gone with her to help her find the goat I could have prevented her falling in the river. I should have done this or that, said one thing or another. Julina lets me talk until I run down.

"Think about what you've said, Rowan. Did you chase the goat away?" I shake my head. "Did you cause the storm?" Another shake. "Just because you wanted to leave home doesn't mean you're responsible for what happened to your mother. She might have slipped on the muddy path at any time, or a tree could have fallen and knocked her into the river." She sighs. "The bond between a mother and daughter is one of the most difficult. Often they are so alike that they irritate each other. Each is a separate person and yet they are of one flesh. What if your mother hadn't drowned that night, and you'd told her you wanted to leave. What do you imagine she would have said?"

A memory comes back to me. At the age of ten I had wanted to walk to the village alone and sell some eggs. I wouldn't tell Mother why, just that I wanted to do it. She might have guessed that I wanted to buy a present for her birthday instead of making a gift as I usually did, but she didn't ask for my reasons. She merely thought for a few minutes and then said yes, as long as I got there and back in daylight and took Mord, I could go.

"If I really wanted to go, she wouldn't have prevented me." She might have helped me pack, given me herbs to take. Sent me to friends who would have guided me along the way. Maybe she'd even have told me about my father and brother soon.

Julina pours more wine and I sip. Yawn.

"You'll have more times when you're sad or angry or want to rage at yourself or your parents. Keep your goal clearly in mind and those times will pass."

I barely take in her words. I'm so tired. Eyelids droop and my head follows. There is a soft cushion and a warm blanket. Someone is taking off my boots. My whole body is as relaxed as if it had soaked in a long hot bath. There's a taste of honey, cinnamon and wine in my mouth.

***

I'm in the forest again, walking through the trees, following something or someone, don't know who or what. I keep touching my necklace to give myself courage, and I'm worried because I can't remember where Mother's silver bracelet is. It seems to me that someone has just asked me a question, but who could that be? I can't remember the question. I stumble, put out a hand and a branch hits my face.

When I open my eyes I'm under a velvet patchwork quilt on a low bed in a small room draped with blue and green hangings. On my right a hexagonal window lets in what I take to be morning light. Braided rag rugs cover the floor. A small wooden chest holds an unlit candle, a pitcher of water and a goblet stand next to it. Just beyond the foot of the bed is a door and on a peg hang my clothes. Am I still in Julina's home, or has she transported me away, like a sorcerer in one of the old stories? I wouldn't put it past her; some new lesson no doubt. I'm almost certain she put a sleeping draught into my wine last night. The thing is, I've never noticed any sign of a door in the room where Julina always receives me. Of course, its walls were covered with hangings.

I lift the pitcher of water, sniff suspiciously, pour some into the goblet and taste carefully. It seems like normal water. Now that I know about the tisane Mother used to give me, I should be more careful what I drink, especially when given by a strange woman. I get up and open my pouch, find the bracelet and sigh in relief. After dressing, I try the door. It opens, but there's a brown curtain hanging over it. I push that aside and step through into the familiar room. She isn't there or at least I can't see her. Everything looks as usual. I wait, but Julina doesn't appear.

It's an opportunity. If she didn't want me to snoop, she shouldn't have left me alone. I pull aside hangings, poke into shelves, examine bottles and jugs, scrolls of parchment, sniff packets of herbs. Tucked behind a jar I find a small painting of a young girl and wonder who it is. She looks a little like Julina, though her hair is red rather than black. I feel a stab of sorrow, thinking of Mother's hair, though the girl doesn't look anything like Mother. I miss her right now, wish I could be a small girl, crawl into her lap, feel safe. I brush tears from my eyes, take a deep breath and get back to snooping. There are stacks of candles as well as the brazier. A cupboard holds bread and cheese, a basket is filled with nuts, another with plums. I decide not to eat anything here. Besides the door to the room I'd slept in and the door to the outside, I find no other doors. More illusion, I'm sure. Unless Julina slept in the main room last night and gave me her bedroom. Still I wouldn't be surprised if there is a secret door with a hidden catch. Finally, I gather my possessions and leave.

The morning is cool and cloudy with a hint of rain, so I pull my cloak tightly around me, leaving the hood down. The streets bustle with carts, horses, and people. My stomach rumbles as I pass a bakery where they are putting out long loaves of bread and round honey cakes. I find a copper in my pouch and buy one of the latter, eating it as I walk and licking the sweetness off my fingers. A small boy tugs at my cloak, his big eyes on the bit of cake left in my hand. I give him a copper and he hugs me round the waist before running off. Nearby two plump women stand in the middle of the street, arguing. They wave their arms and gesticulate so broadly that I can't get around them easily, and I decide to step back and wait. Just beyond, an inn-keeper sweeps dirt from his front door.

A man sticks his head out, says something to the innkeeper. I can't hear the words, but recognize the hooked nose. It's one of the men I saw on the road. Quickly I step into the shadow of a doorway. I hope he hasn't noticed me. There's nothing specific to indicate that this man is or has been looking for me, but I don't intend to take any chances. I turn back toward Julina's and take one of the crooked side streets until I'm sure I'm well past the inn. Cautiously I find my way back to the main street. Just in case the man or his partner is out and about, I pull the hood of my cloak over my head and keep it down. Finally I reached Edana's street and as I turn into it a dark flutter above my head startles me.

"Mord!" I stroke his feathers after he lands on my shoulder.

He croaks softly into my ear. I touch his leg and feel the parchment there, but don't try to read it now. As quickly as possible without actually running I reach Edana's house. Mord leaves my shoulder and flies up to the bedroom window. As I open the front door Ma Parnell comes out of the kitchen and smiles.

"I hope you weren't worried," I say. "I slept at Julina's last night."

"Oh, she sent word," Ma Parnell gives me a pat on the cheek. "I've saved you some breakfast, though. That Julina never rises before noon, so you'd have slim pickings at her place."

"I just need to go up to my room," I say. "I'll be down in a few minutes."

Thea's message reads: *All fine here. Twins walking and talking. Don't send Mord again. He was battered and very tired. Getting old or caught in a storm? All my love.*

I sink into the cushions on the bed, watching Mord hop out the window and fly to a nearby tree. He sits there and begins to preen his feathers, which are rather bedraggled. Thea's message is both heartening and worrying. I was about six and a half when we saved the raven after the nest had been knocked out of a tree by some predator and the parents disappeared. After that I spent great parts of every day finding bugs to feed the voracious appetite until I realized he would eat almost anything, including eggs, meat, and berries. How long do ravens live? Mother would have known. I don't want to lose Mord.

I miss Thea. Her short note just isn't enough, and I wish I'd spent more time with her and the twins, not left so precipitously. Though it had seemed the right thing to do at the time, I'm feeling uprooted. My emotions swing back and forth these days and I wish I had Mother's advice on herbs to settle them. If I don't find my father and brother, those three up north are the only family I have left. I close my eyes and sigh, not wanting to argue with myself anymore about what I should have done or not, what I could do in the future. Half asleep, I reach into the leather pouch at my belt and clutch Mother's bracelet for comfort, drift to the edge of sleep.

Mist surrounds me and I am both part of it and concealed by it. I look down on a small cottage. See chickens and two tiny boys. A woman comes out of the cottage; I want to descend, join her and the boys, but a wind roars out of nowhere, sweeps the mist away and me with it. I'm a raven blown over a forest, a horse galloping across grasslands, a gust of sand far above a desert. The song of a flute, high and sweet, then low and sad calls me and I follow. A man and a boy stand in a garden near a tall tower, the top of which is obscured by mist.

"So how long do we wait?" the boy asks.

"I think we'd have heard his scream by now. He must be too far away."

I don't understand what they're talking about. The mist swirls, thickens until I can no longer see anything and I struggle to reach them.

"Rowan! Wake up."

"What is it?"

Edana looms over my bed. "Ma Parnell was worried when you didn't come down to eat breakfast. It's almost lunch time. What's the matter with you?"

I shake my head. Too complicated to try and explain. Edana would probably think I was sickening for something. Maybe I am, for my head aches and pounds. No the pounding is coming from the window.

"Mord," I say. "Maybe he's hungry."

"So he's back." Edana lets him in and gives him grain from her pocket.

I remember what happened and clear my throat. I have to tell someone, need help to decide what to do. "I saw a man who might be following me."

She grabs my shoulder. "Where?"

"In the street near an inn. And that's not all," I add. "I think Julina may have drugged me last night. You told me not to trust her, I should have paid attention. Why did you take me to her in the first place?"

"Wait, wait," Edana says. "What about this man you saw?"

"I saw him first on the forest track with another man when I was on my way here. I'm sure they didn't see me then because I was hiding, and Mord warned me of their coming. I'd been told that strangers were asking about me in my village. This morning one of those men was at an inn on the main street."

Edana glares at me. "And you felt no need to tell me? What trouble are you in?"

I sigh. "It's complicated. Too long a story. I haven't done anything wrong."

"All right, first things first. Describe these men to me, and I'll have the boys find out as much as they can." She raises a hand as I start to speak. "Don't worry; they won't be obvious about it."

So I tell her what I remember about the man with the hooked nose, his companion and their horses. She asks a lot of questions about the horses, their colouring and size, and wants to know which inn I saw the man at. I don't know the name, but can describe its location well enough for Edana to identify. She tells me the horses might be a good starting point for the boys. They know most of the stable lads in the town.

"Now, about Julina, didn't I tell you not to trust her unreservedly? But if she did drug you it would have been for a purpose."

"Whose purpose, though? She hides behind layers, never revealing her true self. What if she's using me for some plan of her own or is involved with these men?"

Edana shifts to the foot of the bed. "Let me tell you a story." I shrug and she continues. "A few years ago I had a partner, a man. He was younger than I, handsome, funny, and a very good horseman. I trusted and loved him though Julina warned me to be careful. She said he was fickle, but I thought she was merely jealous because she didn't have a man of her own. Women generally liked him and he them. He was very good with the women who came here to learn riding, and we had to buy more horses to accommodate all the business. Many of the women flirted with him, but I thought it harmless. Sometimes he went off in the middle of the afternoon or stayed out late in the evening, saying it was business and I didn't question him about it. Julina came to see me one of the evenings he was away, which was very unusual because she likes to see people in her own place, where she can control things more easily. She said there was proof that my man was spending a lot of time with another woman. I accused her of jealously and meddling; we quarrelled, and she left. When I asked my man about where he'd spent the evening, he said that he'd been selling one of our horses. And indeed the next day a man came and closed the bargain, paying a very good price. Then a week or so later a boy brought me a written message from Julina. 'Please,' it said, 'forgive me. I need your help desperately. Come to my rooms at midnight. Don't tell anyone. I'll leave the door open for you.' I was still furious with her, wasn't going to go, but in the end I did."

Edana pauses, swallows, and shakes her head. "It still makes me angry to remember. I found the two of them together, my man and Julina, and there was no doubt what they were doing. I ran out, came home and got a horse. I rode most of the night, not sure where I was going, just needing to be moving. Finally I came home to find that my man had taken three of the horses and disappeared for good. Julina came to see me. She said that she had wooed him to show me conclusive proof of what he was. 'If he'd been true to you,' she said, 'he would have told me to go about my business and leave him alone. I had to do it. I'm sorry. I'll pay you for the horses he took.' Of course

I didn't let her do that. But I found out that he'd had several women on his string, and each of them thought he was going to run away with her."

"That's terrible," I declare, and wonder whether she told me this story because she suspects something similar about my father.

Edana shrugs. "Julina was right about that man. Anyway, she and I became friends again eventually, though I still don't like her methods sometimes. What I'm trying to say, is that whatever she does to or with you will be for your own good, whether you like it or not. Are you not learning things from her that could be useful?"

Reluctantly I nod. "She was kind to me last night when I felt guilty about my mother and sorry for myself. But then she gave me mulled wine that put me to sleep."

"That's nothing so very bad, is it?"

I sigh. "I don't know. I'm not sure I want to go back to her."

Edana leans forward and tugs on one of my feet. "Come have some food. Then you and I will go for a long ride. If those men are looking for you, getting out of the town might be just the thing. I'll send the boys off to ferret while we're away."

At lunch Ma Parnell gives me an extra helping of everything though I keep telling her I'm full. She reminds me of Mother a little, although Ma Parnell is plump and short and Mother was the opposite. I suppose it's that care-taking thing that mothers do. I don't need these kinds of memories right now and shove them away, watching the boys who, after Edana has explained what she wants them to do, are quite excited. Benny and Corky can't stop jabbering. Dow just nods and tucks into the food.

"You're to be careful," Edana cautions. "Remember no one is to suspect you're asking questions."

Benny glowers. "Course not! We're like seeds in the hay."

***

Beyond the town walls, wind in my hair, the horse moving to my direction, a race against Edana blows the last cobwebs out of my head. She yells encouragement. Angel and the stallion thunder across the ground. Gasping, I bring Angel to a halt on top of the small knoll we set as the finish point and wait. Edana gallops up laughing, just an instant behind me.

"Well ridden," she says.

"I think you let me win," I grin.

She gazes out across the grass-covered land that spreads to the south of us. A large bird circles lazily in the distance. I'm not sure what kind it is. It dives in a sudden rush that ends with a flurry in the grass. The bird carries a small body aloft in its talons.

"Hawk," Edana says, and turns to me. "I can't come with you to find your father and brother. I've got to look after my horses, and none of the boys would be much help to you, probably more of a nuisance."

"It doesn't matter," I say. "I'll be all right." Though I don't feel as confident as I sound.

Edana shakes her head. "I'd be betraying the trust Karl and Karolina put in me when they sent you here if I didn't do more to help you on your way."

"You've done plenty," I assure her.

"Still," she continues, "there are people I know who could be useful – a retired captain of guards, a former trader. I'll enquire discreetly," she emphasizes, "whether one of them is available and willing."

"Edana, if I wasn't sitting on a horse, I'd hug you."

"There is one other thing I can do. I've had contact with the people who live out there."

She waves at the seemingly empty land and I wonder what sort of life one could live there, out in the open without the shelter of trees. What sort of house would you build without wood? Did it rain enough for a good garden? The wind is pushing billows into the tall gold-green grasses, so that it makes me think of a huge sun drenched lake – very beautiful, but strange.

"Horses."

I glance around, but can't see any other than our own.

Edana laughs and shakes her head. "Sorry. I meant that I buy horses from out there now and then, and they've taught me a lot about handling and healing them."

"What are the people like?"

"Independent and self-sufficient. Live in tents and travel from place to place, hunting and gathering food. There's no guarantee that you'll find them even if you look, but I can give you a token that will smooth your way if you do encounter them."

Like everything in her house, Edana's bedroom is much more to my taste than Julina's rooms. No hangings and lots of wood – walls, floor, furniture. The bed is covered with a thick patchwork quilt and there's a rustic arm chair made of tree branches with plump pillows padding the bottom and back. A wooden trunk stands at the foot of the bed and another by the window. Clothes are strewn here and there, a pair of muddy sabots lies half hidden under the bed. Obviously Ma Parnell isn't allowed in very often.

At the window, dangling from a strip of leather is a twig, bent and tied into a circle. More leather and grass is woven into it like a spider's web. A white feather dangles from the lower edge.

"Where did you get that?" I exclaim. "It's similar to what my mother taught me to make, the good luck charms I mentioned to Julina."

Edana looks from the window to me and back again. "Grandmother gave it to me," she says. "A woman of the grassland people. I can give this to you and you can show it when you meet one of them. Grandmother said it would bring me good dreams and help them to come true. She gave it to me after my man left, when I bought a horse from her."

I shake my head. "You should keep it."

Edana runs her fingers through her short hair and scratches her head. "Perhaps your mother knew the grassland people?"

I fling my hands into the air. "The things my mother didn't tell me are as many as the leaves on the trees of a forest! She and my father travelled before I was born, so it could be. But Grandmother must have another name, otherwise how will I find or know her?"

Edana sits on the bed and gazes at the woven circle. "Her people all have secret names that are only shared with a few, because they believe names allow one to have power over others. However, they also have designations and common names for everyone to use. Grandmother is also called Wisdom."

I take the armchair. "They sound interesting."

"I wish I understood more about people, could figure out why they do what they do. At my age, I should be better at it than I am. I know horses and boys, not much else."

"Yes," I say, thinking of my mother and father.

"But then," Edana continues, "I look at that beautiful thing and think that if I picked it apart, there'd just be broken pieces, and I wonder if trying to understand people is like that."

"You're a maker, Edana, not a breaker." On impulse I lean forward. "Can I tell you the rest of my story? Would you listen and ask questions? It might help me sort things out."

Edana reaches out and takes my hands. "Julina is the one you should tell. She's much better at this kind of thing than I am."

I jerk my hands away. "No. Please listen."

And she does, as I tell her about my mother's death, Thea, my father's letter and the bracelet. At the end, she shakes her head.

"Tell it all to Julina. She sees more clearly than I do. Knows how to create and penetrate illusion. You need her."

Chapter VIII
Samel

Darkness – it must be night, but I'm not in bed. There are cobblestones under my feet and the looming walls of houses on either side. Perhaps I've gone sleep walking for the first time in my life. Everyone else seems to be home in their beds. Then I hear footsteps. I can see more clearly as my eyes adjust, and consider making my presence known, but that could startle and scare whoever's coming. I discern a shape, not very large, about Magenta's size. Might she be returning after a late evening with her husband to be? Why would he let her come home alone? Watching the figure approach, I realize that I'm not standing in my own street; in fact, this area is totally strange to me. I'll have to stop whoever's coming to ask where I am. I clear my throat, take one step out of the doorway. The person keeps coming, and I see the pale blur of a face with wisps of dark hair escaping from the hood of a green cloak. Grey eyes peer down the street. There's a look of Papa about her.

"Rowan?" I whisper.

And find myself sitting in bed. I've not been sleep walking after all, but dreaming. My right hand is cramped and sore. I've clutched the circlet so hard that its shape is pressed into my palm.

Faint snoring comes from Papa's bedroom. Quietly I get up and close my door. At my table I light a candle, lay the bracelet on the plate which is still there. Change my mind. Pick it up and slip it on my left wrist, stroke the circlet with the thumb of my other hand. It feels sticky. That's never happened before. I try to slip it off, but that's hard to do, as if the bracelet doesn't want to leave my hand. Finally I get it off and hold it up to my eye, following an impulse. It's like looking through a large keyhole at a candle flame. The flame flutters, flares and I blink.

The next moment when my eye is open and steady again, I see a room that doesn't look anything like mine. There are red, yellow, brown, black and blue tapestries on the walls, multi-coloured rugs on the floor, lots of cushions, many candles. The shapes of shadows are flung up against the tapestries. Darkness moves across the keyhole and then an eye is peering at me. It gives me shivers.

I pull the bracelet away from my face. Toss it on my bed, rub my eye. Across the room hangs a small mirror and in it I look the same as usual except for a reddish line around my right eye. I rub at it with one finger. It seems to be fading. The bracelet still lies on my bed. Thankfully it hasn't started my blanket on fire. When I pick it up it's only slightly warm.

I wonder whose room that was; I didn't like the feeling I got from the eye. Now that Papa knows I have the bracelet, I don't have to keep it secret from him any longer. I could slip it onto an ordinary piece of leather around my neck. But what if someone really is watching me? Maybe I should heed Papa's warnings. I tie the silver circlet into the sleeve of an old shirt. It should be safe in the bottom of the chest at the foot of my bed, under all my other clothes.

The shutters are still closed over my window though light seeps through the cracks. I throw the shutters wide. By the paleness of the sky it's barely dawn. A whistling man tramps down the street with a hoe over his shoulder. I look across the artists' courtyard; there's light in Ali's window. Just then her door opens, she looks directly at me and waves. I point down toward the front door of her house, make knocking motions. She starts across the courtyard. I dress quickly and think briefly about taking the bracelet with me. It would be interesting to see what happens when she paints with it near, but after what just happened I don't want to do that. Papa is still snoring so I sneak downstairs and reach the artists' front door as it opens.

Ali puts a finger to her lips. "They're all asleep."

Neither of us speaks as we move down the hall and across the courtyard. Ali eases open the door of her room, motions me inside. Several candles are alight. More has been added to the paintings on the walls.

In the scene of Aquila Papa and I are standing on the wall looking north. The eagle flag flies on the tower and there's an eagle above us. In the forest view there is now also a goat with two kids. The desert still has indistinct figures in the middle of a sand storm. I turn toward the wall with the mountain. One of the peaks has sprouted a cluster of towers.

"More dreams?" I say.

"Sometimes I get a whole bunch of bits and pieces. Other times, it's like a story."

"Tell me one of the stories." I pick the most familiar. "The one of me and Papa on the walls, for instance."

"Well," Ali says, "that one's the simplest. I see you and your papa walking through the palace, climbing stairs, and then you're on the wall. Your papa blows a whistle and both of you look north across the desert. Nothing much happens."

"And the eagle?" I ask. "Is it there all the time in the dream or does it come after Papa blows the whistle?"

Ali frowns and shakes her head. "I'm not sure. It might not be there at all. When I was painting it seemed right to have an eagle in the picture. After all eagles do guard our city."

I sit on the mattress, notice she hasn't made her bed yet. I remember that I didn't make mine either. It wouldn't be the first time so Papa won't be surprised.

"Ali, what do you know about the eagles?"

"The same as everyone, I guess. I'm sure you know it, too."

"Tell me anyway, as if I knew nothing."

She frowns again. "There's an old story that the first Lord, before he was a lord and before the city was built, saved an eagle and its nest. The Lord was looking for a tall tree to climb near the river to scan the land. He saw another man had already climbed the tree, had captured an eagle and was putting the eggs into a pouch. The Lord stopped the fellow, made him put the eggs back and released the eagle. Then he banished the man, who was a soldier in his army."

"I'm glad he did."

"Well, there's this other story that the man the Lord banished became a terrible and evil sorcerer, but as for the eagle, it was grateful and promised that she and her descendants would protect the city that the Lord planned to build. And that's what they've done."

"So the Lord could actually talk to the eagle."

Ali smiles. "It's an old story. They always have talking animals."

"Have you ever seen one of the eagles close up?" I ask casually.

She shakes her head. "Have you?"

"Once." I glance at the painting of Aquila. "They are really big."

"And fierce, I suppose."

"Not always." I turn back to Ali. "Have you heard any other stories about the eagles? That they are able to do special things for instance?"

"Besides talk?"

"I didn't say the eagles could talk, but what if someone learned how to talk to them?"

Ali looks thoughtful. "There are people who seem to understand animal behaviour easily."

"So there could be a person, people, who have a special bond with the eagles. Like the Captain of Eagles."

"You'd know more about all this than I do, Samel. You're the one who goes to the palace all the time. If you want to talk to the Captain of Eagles, ask your papa to introduce you." Ali taps my knee. "What's really going on?"

I reach into my shirt and pull out the eagle feather that I've been carrying with me ever since the day I saw Papa talking to the eagle.

"It's beautiful," she says. "How did you get it?"

"An eagle left it behind. Do you think it was all right for me to take it?"

Ali shrugs. "That's not the only thing bothering you is it? Has something else happened with the bracelet?"

So I tell her about my dream and the vision through a keyhole. About my talks with Papa, too. As usual, Ali doesn't interrupt. After I finish she thinks about what I've said. "It's like we're in a story," she says finally. "Exciting, don't you think?"

I groan. "It's confusing and upsetting. I discover that I've got a sister and I can't go and meet her. Why not? Because my father, who should be rushing off to find his daughter, says it's too dangerous for me. And the bracelet? I don't know that it's useful for this. So it brings wind or burns a hole in paper, or maybe causes visions. How does any of that help when I don't know how it works?"

"I bet your father does have a plan, just hasn't told you about it. Parents don't always explain things. You should know that by now."

A plan. I stand and glance wildly around the room at the paintings on the walls. "You haven't had any dreams of my father travelling have you?"

Ali shakes her head, but that doesn't reassure me. What if Papa does have a plan and it doesn't include me? I stuff the eagle feather back into my shirt, wrench open Ali's door, race across the courtyard and thunder down the hall, not caring if I wake the whole family. I've got to get home.

The main floor of the house is quiet, so I race up the stairs two at a time. Papa's room is empty, the bed unmade, as if he left in a hurry. I clatter back down.

Papa stands in the kitchen doorway scowling. "Morning," he mutters.

"Papa!" I grab him in a hug. "You haven't left."

He pushes me away. "It's too early to go to the palace and I haven't had breakfast yet." He grabs and shakes me. "Where have you been? I thought you'd taken it into your head to go and find your sister alone. I was contemplating calling the Lord's militia to look for you when you so noisily came home."

"I thought you'd left to go and find Rowan. Without me. Promise me you won't do that, please, whatever happens. Whatever you decide, promise not to leave without telling me."

He gives me a pat on the shoulder. "I'm not going anywhere. Get in here and have breakfast with me."

While we eat, we talk about Rowan and what we might do next. Papa says he'll stay home with me for the day; there's nothing urgent at the palace. I remind him that he should try finding his eagle again. Anyway, it's an afternoon I'm supposed to spend with Tamtan.

"All right then," Papa says. "The palace this afternoon for me, as long as you behave."

I wish he'd go sooner, but there's no sense arguing about it. Besides, there are things I want to ask him. Now is a good opportunity.

"Tell me about the danger you think is connected to the bracelet. I get the feeling you know more than you've been saying."

Papa glares at me, but I just look right back. Finally he sighs and shakes himself. "I suppose you have a right to know more." he says finally. "In the beginning neither your mother nor I thought of the bracelets as intrinsically bad. We knew that both of us had special abilities, and the bracelets seemed to make those stronger. As well, they could help us do some of the things you've discovered – making light and fire for instance. Later, we became convinced that doing these things had drawn unwanted attention from those who might want to use the powers for their own ends. Now," he reaches for his goblet of water, takes a sip, "what I haven't told you is that I left my own home as a young man because of a person who had harmed my family. Caused my father's death, in fact, though I could never discover whether it was an accident or on purpose. This person had abilities, too, and was always looking for ways to increase them, through sorcery and spellcraft, perhaps. I left home to escape him, and always worried that he'd find me."

"Who?"

I can tell Papa doesn't want to answer.

"A relative," he admits, finally.

"He might be behind the bracelet's power?"

"Perhaps." He shrugs. "Though as far as I know, he wasn't anywhere near us when we had the bracelets made. Anyway, for a time, I searched monasteries and old shops for scrolls and books about items of power – bracelets, rings, any kind of enchanted objects. Collected tales in taverns and inns. Your mother and I even considered moving back to your mother's town to see whether her grandparents still had their collection of books, but in the end we didn't. You know there have been stories of powerful rings from very ancient times. Good rings, evil rings, protective belts, enchanted swords, and other special objects. All these tales that I amassed didn't help me any. We found out for ourselves that our bracelets had the greatest effect as a pair, so we separated them. She kept hers, I kept mine. I thought that if my relative was involved, he would leave Zarmine alone."

"You tried to lure him to follow you?"

"Of course not!" he protests. "I had my small son with me, why would I put you in danger? I believed both bracelets were needed for the greatest power, and I never tried to use mine after your mother and I parted. I hoped whoever was interested lost track of us. Haven't we had a quiet life?" I nod. "If Zarmine is truly dead," he stops, sighs and shakes his head. "I have a hard time believing that I'll never see her again. Also, we don't know what happened to her bracelet."

"She might have given it to Rowan. Maybe she's using it to find us."

"That's what I'm afraid of. I know you want nothing more than to locate your sister, but I still believe there is danger for all of us in the use of the bracelets."

"But what else can we do?" I exclaim. "Are you telling me that it's best if I never try to find my sister? That we never ever meet? Maybe you want me to destroy the bracelet?"

Papa shakes his head. "We thought about that, but everything I'd read suggested that magical objects like this weren't easy to destroy. We were afraid of causing some kind of catastrophe." He sighs. "Perhaps you think your mother and me cruel and heartless, but we did it for the best. I already had the death of my father haunting me, couldn't bear to imagine the death of my children. We thought we had to keep you two children separated."

"And now?"

"We may have been wrong."

For a long time I sit and stare at the top of the table, study the knot holes, the whorls of the grain in the wood, crumbs from breakfast. I'm only thirteen, what do I know? Papa has a lot more experience of the world than I do. Then I remember what he always says when we play music.

"Let your heart lead," I whisper.

Papa looks at me sadly. "Yes, and your heart and mine don't agree in this. So what to do?"

I have no answer, so Papa suggests we clean house. The place can use it, and sometimes doing work with your hands allows your head to sort things out on its own. We still haven't come to a decision about what to do by the mid day meal. When it's time for us to go our separate ways for the afternoon, Papa gives me a crushing hug.

"Take care of yourself," he says. "I hope you won't leave the city without telling me."

It seems to me that he's certain I will go eventually, though I'm not so sure myself. Yes, I desperately want to meet my sister, though she could already be making her way here. I might miss her if I go looking, and I'm not ignoring Papa's worries, either. If there is some person wanting to use our abilities, to use us, we have to be careful. I know nothing of travelling in the world, don't even know how to ride a camel. I suppose I could go to meet my sister on foot, but I'm counting on persuading Papa and going with him. I would need his help anyway for money and supplies. How many days journey is it from Aquila to the north country? Papa probably knows, but there must be others who do as well. Perhaps I should try to find out as much as I can.

Chapter IX

Rowan

That evening when I enter Julina's rooms I think she must be away, for the lantern I carry casts the only light. I set it on the low table and look around. Would she leave the door open if she's not home? All seems normal, with candles ready, cushions and hangings, and the cold brazier. I hear a rustle of cloth against cloth. Hold my breath and stare into the dimness from where it seems the sound has come.

"You're getting better."

A small flame appears, then glows more brightly lighting Julina's face as she glides into the room. She comes from the left of where I remember the door to the bedroom. This time she is dressed in a long gown of midnight blue that covers everything except her head. Her hair is braided and coiled into a coronet.

"So?" she says, coming to stand near me. "Nothing to say?"

I let a very slight smile appear on my face, but still speak not a word. Our faces are quite close together and between the light from her candle and my lantern, I can see her plainly. She doesn't smile, but there are glints in her eyes. Then she laughs and sets her candle on the table.

"You're a good student, Rowan. You've learned to play some of my games. Sit."

I take the cushion opposite. Tonight there are lines in her face that I'm sure weren't there before. Does she have the ability to change her looks? Julina might be close to my mother's age, though there is no grey or white in her hair. On the other hand, when I first saw her, I thought she was Edana's contemporary.

"I wish I could trust you," I mutter.

Julina shakes her head. "Ah, trust is a delicate flower, and not always useful. You have a question, so ask."

"What about the price?"

She leans forward. "This time the information you give me will be the price."

"Why did you betray Edana?"

Julina flinches as if I've struck her. "That has nothing to do with you."

"What if that's my fee? You want information from me?" I tap the table. "Pay."

"Rowan." Julina spreads her hands. "I can help you. Why bring up things that have nothing to do with you, that are over and done with and that you don't understand?"

"No," I shake my head vigorously in emphasis. "All I want from you is a satisfactory answer, and then I'll go on with the rest."

Julina frowns, holds my eyes with hers, and sighs. "Perhaps I didn't see it as betrayal. I'd had much more experience with men than Edana and I thought she could benefit from that. Besides, he'd already broken faith with her in a multitude of ways, though she couldn't see it, wouldn't hear it. I did the only thing I thought might work."

"For her own good of course. Save me from friends like you."

She doesn't respond to that taunt. I continue to stare at her, aware that she has never claimed to be my friend, only that she could help. I wait for her next move.

"All right," she admits, "I did it for myself, too. Edana was my friend before she met him. Do you let your friends make mistakes that you know will cause devastation?"

I think of Lynx, and of Karolina's daughters. I can't imagine one of them in such a situation, don't think they would behave like that.

"I was afraid I'd lose her if I didn't get rid of him, and he was doing her no good. Better a quick sharp pain than prolonged agony."

"Self-interest. Hmm, sounds more honest."

Julina gestures, holding out an open palm. "Your turn."

That means she's not going to tell me anything more about her and Edana's man. I consider how much to tell, and what she's really getting out of this. Julina doesn't hurry me, just waits, calm and quiet. Finally I decide to begin with only a little information.

"Edana says I should tell you the bits and pieces that I left out of what I told you before."

The candle on the table and the one in my lantern are burning low so that I can't see her face clearly. After a few more moments of silence, Julina rises, fetches more candles and lights them. She also brings out a loaf of bread and a wedge of cheese.

Finally she sits opposite me again. "I'm willing to listen."

I eat a few bites and sip watered wine that Julina mixes in front of me. I taste no herbs or spices in any of it, but there are substances that don't leave a strong flavour.

"There's nothing added," she says, probably reading the expression on my face. "And the other night – I never meant to frighten you, only to give you a good night's rest."

I'm still not sure I believe her. "How do I know that it's safe for me to speak?"

Julina stands again. "I'll spread as much protection around this room and us as I can. In case there are listeners."

I watch her place lighted candles around the room, make passes in the air, light the brazier and place aromatic herbs on it. Has she deliberately misunderstood me, I wonder? It's not others I'm worried about right now, but the woman who is in this room with me. She lifts the golden gemstone out of her robe and holds it with shuttered eyes. Then she goes out and I hear her open and close, then lock the entrance door. Back in the room, she looks behind all the hangings. I wonder whether she can tell if things have been moved or disarranged, whether she knows that I snooped. She doesn't say anything though, and I'm not about to risk antagonizing her by confessing to a minor transgression. Finally she comes back to the table.

"We're as safe as we can be," Julina says.

"I'm worried someone may be following me," I say.

"What reason do you have for this?"

"I saw a man here who I'd also seen on the road, though I don't think he noticed me either time. It may be nothing, but I didn't like him or his companion. Edana is going to find out more."

"If someone is after you, there'll be a reason. Evil exists, people who want power for their own ends, those who hurt and take advantage of others. Some are minor tyrants; others are interested in gathering power. Not necessarily recruiting soldiers or building armies, but rather collecting knowledge and learning how to use it to manipulate people. Perhaps your mother and father encountered such a person."

Is she merely guessing or has she other means of finding out about me? "Do you have any thoughts about who it might be?"

Julina shrugs. "How could I when you've told me so little?"

No matter how wary I am of her, I have seen that she has abilities I can't dismiss. I'll go carefully and slowly. "Well," I say, "my father wrote a letter to my mother, and in it spoke of someone he obviously didn't trust: 'I wonder at times whether he brought us together.'"

"Did your father make any other reference to this 'he'?"

"No."

"Then it's not conclusive."

"If he exists, how do I fight this person?"

"Tell me more of your story first."

I plump up a couple of cushions and begin with the storm when Mother went out to fetch the goat. Julina has heard some of this before, but I try to fill in everything I can remember. She stops me now and then to ask a question or clarify a detail, but she doesn't offer any explanations or make any judgements. She wants to know whether anyone had seen strangers in the area before the storm, whether any of the animals behaved oddly. Not that I can remember I tell her; I don't mention Thea's abilities, my mother's fear of wolves, or tell her everything my father wrote. Perhaps she won't be able to help me as much if she doesn't know all the details, but I prefer to leave a few things private. Periodically I pause to sip wine, which Julina mixes with honey and water and warms on the brazier. When I mention the wolf in my father's letter, Julina questions me exhaustively, is disappointed that I have no memories of the incident myself. She sighs and tells me to go on.

"There was a fox later," I say, "that came to my camp in the forest."

She waves a hand. "Wild animals live in the woods. Often they are curious."

"It just sat there looking at me."

She clears her throat. "Did you see it again?"

"I'm not sure. Maybe. A shape in the woods."

"Keep on with your story."

"Can't you give me any idea what it's all about?" I ask impatiently.

She shakes her head. "Try not to rush to judgement when you lack information."

The night wears on and I have difficulty keeping my eyes open, but at last I come to the part in my tale where I arrived in Timberton.

Julina stretches until her joints crack. "I'm exhausted. You must be too. Can I offer you a bed?"

"I thought you were going to tell me what it all means."

"In the morning. I need time to reflect, to let the bits and pieces stew in my mind."

I giggle. "Like the ingredients for soup? If that's all it takes, I should make soup more often."

Julina tries to look stern, but her eyes smile. "Are you staying?"

I hesitate.

"If you prefer, I can walk with you back to Edana's."

I yawn. "No," I mumble. "I'll take the bed."

This time sleep doesn't come easily even though I'm very tired. My mind swirls with images that I want to hold in place and fit together, but the more I try, the more confused everything seems. Faces – my mother, Thea, Edana, Julina, a dark man and boy. Forests and grasslands, a high tower, a road that twists back and forth with some sort of animal moving along it. Then a great wind roars out of the west and sweeps everything away, me with it. I hear laughter booming, echoing in my head. Wake to rain on the roof, lightning and a crack of thunder.

"Rowan?" A soft voice. "Are you all right?"

Julina gleams just inside the door, a lit candle shining on the cream-coloured gown she wears. Her hair is tumbled about her shoulders. I can't tell whether I'm having a dream or a vision. She moves closer.

"Mord came. He was worried about you. So I sent him back to Edana with a message that you were here."

"Julina, do you know how long ravens live?"

Her teeth flash white. "I've heard of them living ten years or more if they aren't killed by hunters or other predators."

"Good." I close my eyes.

I stretch and smile in warm sun blazing in through the small window, feeling buoyant as if given the right puff of wind I could float like a feather. In the other room – a creak, a thump, then muttered words I can't quite make out, though it sounds like Julina's voice. I dress quickly.

"Do I smell food?" I poke my head out of the bedroom door.

Julina kneels on the floor, picking up a loaf of bread. She dusts it off and lays it on the table. A round of yellow cheese, like a small moon sits there. Also, a pot of what smells like gruel steams gently on the brazier.

"No harm done," Julina smiles at me. "I hope you slept well. Ma Parnell sent us breakfast, though it's actually mid-day."

I tear off a hunk of bread and cram it into my mouth. Julina hands me a knife.

"Here," she says, "there's butter and honey, too."

When I have dampened my hunger, I say, "Did you come into my room in the night?"

"Yes, there was a lot of thunder and I thought it might have startled you."

"I was having odd dreams and wasn't sure whether you were part of them or not."

"What dreams?" Her eyes are piercing.

"All mixed up about what I'd been telling you." I cut a piece of cheese and slather honey on a slice of bread. "Do you have any thoughts now that you've had time, anything specific that might help me find my father?"

Julina is at the brazier ladling gruel into a bowl. She holds it up to me, and I shake my head. I chew a few more bites while she settles herself at the table.

"Ideas, yes. Whether they'll help you find your father and brother, I don't know." She pauses to eat a spoonful. "I believe that the bracelets your parents had made functioned as a kind of focus; the way a piece of glass will concentrate sunlight and cause grass to burn if you hold it correctly. Perhaps the man who made them used wizardry in their creation or the metal itself holds power from the earth – that occurs now and then. Your parents sensed danger, some force they thought was interested in them for ill, so they tucked the bracelets away and found a quiet, isolated place to live. They discussed what had happened and tried to understand it. Unfortunately, we don't know what conclusions, if any, they came to because your father burned their notes. When you and your brother were born with both of your parents blood in each of you, perhaps there were surges of power."

"What power?" I interrupt. "Mother and I, we're healers. We know about herbs and things like that. Anyone can learn that, can't they?"

"Remember what your father saw when you and your brother were threatened by the wolf?"

I grimace. "A flash of light? It could have been anything. A reflection."

"And why did the wolf run away?"

"He smelled my father and mother? I don't know."

"Rowan, there are things about you that are exceptional besides your healing abilities. You're good with animals – Mord, the donkey, horses."

"Edana . . ."

"Yes, of course, she has a connection with horses, almost seems to be able to read their thoughts and they hers. That's fairly rare, but so is what you have."

"Mother taught me about herbs from an early age."

"She passed her gifts on to you. And you have a certain amount of protection because you've travelled quite a distance alone; you've found people to help you and avoided danger. The sapphire in your necklace can account for some of it, but perhaps not all."

"Why is your face like a thundercloud?"

"There's at least one other very plausible explanation for your luck."

"And it's not a good one, of course. Why am I not surprised?"

Julina sighs. "Don't get cranky now, we haven't time for it and I haven't the patience."

I spread my hands. "Just tell me."

"Your father wondered whether someone, though he didn't say who, planned for him and your mother to meet. What if that same person hoped for a child or children he could mould to his purpose? Kept watch, is now moving events toward his own ends? And if that's the case . . ."

"I'm probably walking straight into his hands by looking for my father and brother."

"This person also may be keeping you safe, watching and helping you until you reach your, or perhaps his, goal."

"How?" I ask.

Julina shrugs. "There are many ways."

I stare at her, but she's fiddling with a piece of bread and won't meet my eyes.

"What aren't you telling me? Am I walking into a trap? Is it meant for all my family? If someone is watching me, why don't they just take me, then my brother and bring us together?"

"Too many questions. But like I said, I think you do have some protections, even if you're not aware of them."

"I'm still going to look for my father, but I will just have to be even more careful." I sip water. "Could my father know that my mother is dead, that I'm coming to find him?"

"He may know nothing or everything and be waiting for you. It could be your father's power that's keeping you safe."

"But if that's true, why hasn't he come to meet me?"

"Rowan, I can only speculate."

"Go on."

She frowns. "Your father may not want to show his hand openly. He quite probably knows more than either you or I about all this. So, he's doing what he thinks is best. Don't forget, he's got your brother to take care of."

"We need somebody really brave," I mumble. "A fearless knight, like in the stories Mother used to read me. He would know what to do to save us all."

"My dear, don't you know that those knights started out as ordinary people who merely did what they had to?"

"All right, I wish I had a great horse and a wonderful sword then."

"I'd like to take another look at that bracelet of your mother's."

"You think it's like an enchanted sword?"

Julina doesn't answer; her eyes are partially hooded again.

I touch my pouch, reluctant to untie the strings.

"Silver," she says, "is in some traditions linked to the moon."

"I put the bracelet in moonlight once at home. It glowed, but nothing else happened."

I notice that sunlight is streaming in the window, laying a beam across the wooden surface of the table. Slowly I unwrap the circlet, lay it down. It sticks to my fingers. I move it slightly so it's directly in the light and the bracelet begins to shimmer. A small halo expands. I reach into that circle; it's cool, but tingles my skin. A sudden flare of light blazes into my eyes.

Julina slaps my hand away and throws a black cloth over the bracelet. "What did you think you were doing?"

I raise a shoulder. "Just wanted to see what would happen. Didn't you?"

She shakes her head at me. "What if you'd attracted something or someone? Maybe activated the bracelet and sent out a message."

"I'm tired of secrets. There are things my mother never had a chance to tell me. And what if my father lied to her? Suppose," I stop and swallow as the thought occurs to me, "suppose he had another woman somewhere the way Edana's man did? He could have played on my mother's worries and fears, convinced her they should separate."

"Rowan," she starts gently.

"No, don't," I interrupt. "Don't try to soothe me with lies."

"Think," she says, "they hid the bracelets away before you were born, though somehow you and your brother got hold of them once. Significant. Anyway, your parents had doubts about the smith who made them. Those are facts. You never saw your mother wear hers. There had to be reasons for that."

"You mean the smith was – what? A god or dragon in disguise?" I ask flippantly.

In an exasperated voice Julina says, "Stop trying to make light of this. Promise me you won't try to work with the bracelet by yourself again."

I look at the black cloth on the table, then at Julina. If I don't promise will she find some way to take the bracelet from me? That would not be a good thing, I feel sure. Equally, I don't believe that pretty silver circlet of leaves holds danger for me. On the contrary, what if it's what helped to protect me on my journey so far, perhaps along with the necklace?

"I'll be careful with the bracelet and keep it hidden."

"Good." She flattens a palm on the table. "Now, you've spent most of the day inside. Edana wouldn't approve. Get away, go riding, and rest there tonight."

***

Edana's house is empty of people, hollow and full of echoes, bringing back memories I don't want to deal with, so I wander out to the barn. The stallion snorts at me and stamps his feet. I take a couple of steps back. Edana has admitted that he can be unpredictable, but she prefers his independent spirit she says, and his touch of recklessness. I lean against the wall opposite the stall and touch the pouch at my waist. I supposed some would say I've been reckless, too. Slowly, I draw out the bracelet and slip it onto my wrist. The stallion snorts again, then pokes his head over the stall door and regards me.

I hold the bracelet up. "What do you think?" I ask. "Is it dangerous?"

He shakes his head and whinnies. I grin, leave him to his solitude. Outside I sit on the fence, watching the horses in the paddock. I wonder what Julina would say about what's just happened. Probably yell at me and tell me to put the bracelet away immediately. My donkey, Dusty, droops under a tree. He looks a lot better now; in fact, is getting fat and needs exercise. I'll suggest that Edana put him to work giving rides to children; she may as well make money from him to pay for his voracious appetite. Three horses stand nearby, nearly asleep on their feet. Angel, the liveliest of the bunch comes trotting over and sticks his nose in my lap.

"Sorry," I say, "no carrots." I reach to pat his nose and the bracelet slides out from under my sleeve.

Angel huffs as if in disgust and ambles away. I watch him, then take the bracelet off and put it away again, get down and wander off in the direction of the orchard. I'll find an apple or two and then the horses will come running. Yes, great excitement. I kick at a stone in the path; it flies up and arches over a bush.

"Ow!" A thatch of reddish hair appears out of the leaves, followed by a scowling face.

"Corky! I'm sorry. I was just . . ."

"Throwing stones for fun?" he snaps.

"No, I kicked it."

"Aim's not bad. Could do something with that maybe."

"I wasn't aiming at anything," I growl. Take a deep breath. "Sorry, guess I'm just cross."

Corky shuffles around the bush looking hopeful. He reminds me of Angel. I'm tempted to say that I have no food for him, but then I notice that he's holding a tangle of wood and leather.

"What's that?" I ask.

"Slingshot. It throws pebbles. You want to learn? The others are in town, so no one will notice your poor shots." He grins.

That does it. I'm going to show him that I can fling stones and aim them on purpose! We use the back of the barn as a target.

Corky explains, "Best because no windows to break and really huge so you can't totally miss."

He shows me a spot where the paint is gone, and suggests trying to hit that. He has no trouble. At first my pebbles go everywhere but to the spot, though at least most touch the side of the barn. A few fly wild and every time that happens, Corky runs for cover, snickering. I ignore him. Gradually I get the hang of it and once or twice I come within a hand span of what Corky calls the 'bull's eye.' It doesn't look anything like an eye to me.

Then, on an impulse, as Corky hunts for the last stone I flung at the wall, I reach into my pouch and slip the bracelet onto my wrist, pushing it up high where it can't be seen. It's as if my hands have taken on a life of their own. Smoothly, I fit a stone into the leather, pull back, aim and let go. The stone flies in an arc, hits the spot, dead centre. I grin and Corky stands with his mouth open. Then we hear voices.

Edana has news of the man I'd seen. We gather in a stuffy cramped room that Edana calls the parlour. I've never sat in there before, but Ma Parnell says she wants none of us underfoot as she cooks the evening meal.

"Both the men you described are staying at that inn," Edana confirms. "The innkeeper's a friend of mine; we had a beer and chatted. The boys have done their best hanging around the stable, but all in all, none of us found out much to help you. The men arrived the day before you did, which could mean they weren't following you at all or they knew where you were going. They have boasted about easy work that pays good coin, however, they haven't said who their employer is. From their speech and some of the accoutrements with the horses, we think they come from the northwest, near the mountains probably. They generally pay the innkeeper a few days in advance and have paid for two more days."

"Did they suspect you were asking questions?" I want to know.

Edana shakes her head. "All of us made sure they didn't see us, and the innkeeper will just assume I was curious about strangers, the way anyone might be. As for the stable lad, those two men hardly say a word to him."

"I don't like it," I say.

"They're cooling their heels for a reason," Benny says, "but we couldn't find out what."

Edana sends the boys out to look after the horses. When they've gone, she turns to me.

"I've found someone to guide you when you're ready. An old trader, who doesn't generally ride out anymore, but he's willing to go with you."

"Thank you! What's his fee?"

She shakes her head. "He owes me a favour. I said I'd supply his horse and equipment, as well as food and so on."

"Then it's you I should pay."

"Absolutely not. You owe me nothing, Rowan. In fact, I owe you for the work you've done around here."

"Hah! And I owe you for what you've taught me."

"Fine, so we're even."

"When can I meet him?" I ask.

"Tomorrow afternoon."

Later, in my room, I push up my right sleeve. It takes extra effort for me to move the bracelet and slide it down over my hand. It's left a red mark on my upper arm. The mark doesn't hurt, but it doesn't disappear when I rub at it. I hide the bracelet at the bottom of my pouch and tie the strings tightly.

***

Nesgor lives with his married daughter and I can see immediately why he might want to go on an excursion. The house is large, two-story, but besides the married couple and Nesgor, there are four children, three young boys and a girl. The noise of their shouts and running footsteps follows us through the house to the back room

"Close the door," growls a voice, and Edana complies, shutting out most of the noise.

The shape of a man is backlit by an open window. He looks lopsided though large and when he moves to a great carved chair, I see that he's missing his right arm below the elbow. I turn to Edana, who catches my look, and makes a small negative movement with her head.

"So," Nesgor continues, in the same growl, "this the young lady? Hey?"

"This is Rowan," Edana says.

"Sit. I don't like standing too long, and I don't like bending my neck to look up."

He points to a couple of folding stools, wood and leather. They look none too sturdy, but hold our weight and are surprisingly comfortable. The room is filled with strange bits and pieces – a painted wooden mask on one wall, a large bow on another, weapons, woven hangings, a couple of small rugs on the floor – the accumulation of a lifetime of travel.

"She doesn't approve of me," Nesgor says to Edana. He turns to me. "Hey? That's right isn't it?"

"Umm," I mumble, "you're not what I expected."

"I can still ride a horse, wield a sword." He points to a massive one hanging beside the narrow bed.

"And you know the route to Aquila," Edana adds.

"Like my own room. Know where everything is, notice if she tries to move it." He jerks his head toward the door.

"He's the best, Rowan," Edana says.

Nesgor heaves himself out of the chair. "Show you something. Might make you feel better about me."

I watch him struggle with the lid of a wooden chest. Wonder if I should go and help him. Probably not.

"There."

Nesgor holds out a tangle of leather harness and a club-like piece of wood. He sees that I don't know what it is. Grapples with it, fits it to the stump of his right arm.

"The harness goes over the back," he says. "It works. There's no fingers, but a sort of hand and I can tighten it to hold things, like reins. Though," he growls, "I don't really need it. Can manage perfectly well without. More for looks, really."

The wooden arm is smooth brown. A sort of claw forms the end, and as Nesgor demonstrates with his left hand, I see that he can indeed use the wooden limb to hold things. He heaves the sword off the wall, and I duck, though he isn't actually near me. It's just, I don't trust that claw. If it gives way the sword would go flying. I'm much happier when Nesgor puts the weapon down again.

"So, when are we leaving?" the old man asks.

I want to say that I haven't agreed to him coming with me, but Edana gets in first. "Soon. We'll let you know a day or two in advance."

When we're well away from the house, I grab Edana's arm. "Isn't there anyone else who could go with me? He's old and well, crippled."

She shakes her head. "Look beyond the surface. He has an immense amount of knowledge and whether you believe it or not, he can still handle a horse and a sword. Which is more than you can do!"

"I can handle a horse! You said I was doing really well."

"Just think about it. The other person I had thought of has been ill and can't travel."

That evening I return to Julina, in the hope that she will have more ideas about Mother's bracelet, that she has had some flash of insight. But the door is locked and she doesn't answer no matter how hard I knock. I kick at the door in disgust, but that merely gives me a sore toe.

When I get home, Edana shrugs philosophically. "She's always flitting here and there. Other people besides you need her services. She could be gone for the evening or for a few days."

"Why didn't she tell me yesterday?"

"Probably didn't know then that she would be away. Relax."

I don't know what to do with myself, so go upstairs and huddle at the window staring out at the new moon. I wonder whether I'm doing the right thing, especially now that Julina's gone and Edana's so-called guard doesn't seem very guard-like. If someone is truly working to get my father, brother and me together, and I refuse to go, will that mysterious person find a way to make my father come after me? That would be fine. I could stay here in Timberton and see what happens, but I don't like the thought of waiting. I suppose I should be thinking of plans to thwart anyone who might be after us, but it's hard to do when you have no idea what the danger consists of and when or how it might manifest itself. My head begins to ache and I press it against the cool glass.

Below in the yard, a small shadow slips along the fence and disappears behind a tree. An animal? I stare at the tree but nothing stirs. Out of the corner of my eye, I catch a flicker of movement coming closer to the house. I run out of my room and pound down the stairs nearly knocking down Ma Parnell, who is sweeping the hall.

"Rowan!" she exclaims. "What?"

I ignore her, race to the door and fling it open. A small form falls at my feet, scrambles up and clutches my legs. The light from the hall illuminates the face of a boy. Edana arrives to stand beside me.

"What is it?" she asks.

"Lady," the boy whispers, clutching harder, his eyes large and round.

Then I remember. "I gave you a coin."

He nods. "A thing to tell."

Edana pulls at my shoulder. "Take him into the kitchen. I'll lock the door."

The boy perches on a chair, watching Ma Parnell who is rummaging in a cupboard. His clothes are ragged, and his hands and bare feet, dirty. He smells of stale sweat and horses. Obviously no one has been taking proper care of him. Perhaps he sleeps in the dark corners of stables, and hears things that could be useful. I open my mouth to ask what he has to tell, but Ma Parnell thrusts herself in front of me.

"Bread and jam." She slides a plate onto the table.

The boy stares first at the plate, next at Ma Parnell, and then at me. I expect her to tell him to go wash his hands, but she just nods at him and points at the plate. The boy grabs the bread and wolfs it down. Edana enters as he's finishing. Ma Parnell puts a metal goblet of water in front of the boy and another piece of bread and jam. At a tip of the head from Edana, Ma Parnell slips out of the kitchen. Edana pulls up a chair. The boy ducks his head.

"He's shy," I whisper. "Could you leave the two of us?"

When we're alone, the boy reaches for the goblet and gulps water. He wipes his mouth with the back of a hand. Snatches the last slice of bread and takes a few more bites.

"So what do you have to tell me?" I ask quietly.

He swallows, still holding the bread. "Man at inn," he says. "Boys asking. I hear. Man and two other talk in dark about girl at horse lady's."

I clasp my hands in my lap, holding myself back from grabbing the boy and shaking the words out of him. Instead, I smile encouragingly, tell myself to be patient. He will tell me in his own way, at his own pace.

He finishes the bread, takes a sip of water. "Man say wait but other say no, go now. Hear coin clink."

"So," I say slowly, "you heard the man from the inn talking with two others at night. They mentioned me. He wanted to wait, but one of the others said they were to go now. And then you heard the sound of coins. Maybe they were getting paid."

The boy grins and nods vigorously. He may not have good speech of his own, but he can understand. I think for a moment.

"Have the men left the inn and the town?"

He shakes his head. "Next day."

"Tomorrow?"

Another vigorous nod.

"Good. Thank you."

Edana re-enters the kitchen. "We could give this boy more food if he likes," she says.

The boy smiles, so I get up and fetch a couple of currant and dried fruit pastries, specialties of Ma Parnell. Edana motions to me and I follow her out into the hall.

"I've seen him on the streets," she whispers. "Lives by his wits, sleeps in stables, begs or steals food. I'd like to give him a bath and bed. He might be skittish, like a horse not yet broken. Can you help me convince him to stay?"

"I could try, but why not get one of the boys to help?"

Edana fetches Dow, himself a quiet one, who takes the young boy, who says he's called Freki, under his wing. We leave them splashing in the tub.

I start to tell Edana everything Freki said, but she waves my words away. "I was listening at the door."

For a moment I'm annoyed, but push it away. "What do you think it means?"

"My guess is they were told to watch you, and now they've been paid. What we don't know is if they'll wait for you somewhere outside the town when you leave. That could cause problems. However, if the payment was the final settling up, we don't need to worry about them. We should be prepared for either eventuality. What concerns me now is that, from what the boy said, there's a third person."

"Who we know nothing about."

"Yes." Edana shakes her head. "I don't like it, Rowan. Even if Nesgor is with you, it could be three against two."

"So what shall I do?"

"Talk to Julina again as soon as she comes back. Maybe she can see something useful. Meantime, the boys and I, and Freki can try to find out more."

***

I'm woken in the night by the neighing of horses. A fragment of dream tugs at my mind – darkness with shadows moving. The rest of the dream is driven away by the clatter of feet on stairs, the slam of a door and shouts. I rush to the window. By the light of the moon I can see several people moving around near the barn. I run downstairs and encounter Ma Parnell wearing a loose nightgown and a frilled cap.

"It's all right," she says. "Edana and the boys will sort things."

"What happened?"

"Something disturbed the horses. They'll get to the bottom of it. Come to the kitchen and I'll make a tisane."

When Edana returns, she hasn't much to tell. The horses were spooked by something, but all that she and the boys found were a few tracks near the corral.

"Could be from a small dog or something similar," Edana says.

"I don't like it," I say.

"Nothing to do but go back to bed. The boys will keep an eye out."

***

The next evening as I prepare to visit Julina, nothing else has disturbed the horses, and little more has been discovered about the two men at the inn. By all accounts they left the town in the morning, riding north. That is a relief, for surely they won't try to double back through the forest and lie in wait for me. As for the person they'd been talking to, no one knows anything. No one except Freki overheard the conversation. No one else caught so much as a glimpse of a third stranger; none of the stable boys in the town took care of an extra horse. It's frustrating.

"So whoever it was," Edana muses, "he or she slipped in and out without passing the guards at the gate. In that case, we're dealing with someone really sneaky or incredibly good."

"That scares me," I put in.

"On the other hand," Edana continues, "he or she could have been masquerading as some ordinary traveller with legitimate business for some time. In that case our third person could still be here in the town."

I don't like that scenario any more than the others. "Julina had better be at home tonight," I growl, probably sounding like Nesgor.

Stamping as loudly as possible, I ascend the wooden steps. I'm just raising my hand to knock when she opens it. I scowl.

"I've heard," she says. "And I have a few things to tell you."

"Good," I snap, and follow her so closely that I almost tread on her heels. "It's about time."

She doesn't respond to that dig, but merely gestures to a heap of pillows near a low tripod of wood. A large silver bowl filled with water sits on the tripod. The room is lit only with candles. I plump myself down and wait impatiently as Julina closes and locks the door.

"This is a scrying bowl," she says. "The results are often ambiguous, so I've hesitated to try it with you."

"And now you've changed your mind?"

"I'll tell you how it works and you can decide for yourself whether you want to use it."

"Fine," I snap.

"The water comes from a stream and was collected on a night of the full moon. The tripod and this wand," she picks up a twig, "are of laurel wood."

"Do I need to know all this?" I interrupt. "Can't you just tell me how it works?"

"I wet the tip of the wand in the water, then draw it around the edge of the bowl. See the vibrations and ripples? That's what you look at and interpret."

"I just see ripples." I glare at her. "Is this all you have to tell me?"

Julina puts down the wand and sits. "Actually, I found out more about the two men from the inn. When they had breakfast this morning a friend of mine was cleaning windows. She said they were disgruntled, muttering about a job half done."

"So if they were watching me, they've been called off?"

"Yes, and there's confirmation from two other sources. Someone else followed the men unobtrusively in the street and overheard them talking. They said they were planning to head home toward Shale; that's a town on the edge of the northern mountains."

"Edana's information from the gate guards agrees with that." I sigh in relief. "So," I point, "why do we need the scrying bowl?"

"In a minute." Julina smiles. "I was also able to trace the silversmith."

"Who?"

"The one who made the bracelets."

"That's great! How did you manage it? What did he have to say?"

"Unfortunately I didn't actually find him. He'd left, but his neighbours in the town where he used to live said he'd always been an honest man."

"So what?" I snap. "That's not proof. And where did he disappear to and when?"

"He left a few years ago, but no one knew where he went."

"Great news," I say sarcastically. "Did you make all this up?"

Julina touches the bowl. "Do you want to talk about scrying?"

"Oh, why not."

"Remember the other person that was heard in conversation with the two men from the inn. Let's see if we can find out whether there's any danger for you from that quarter when you leave Timberton. It won't be easy. We need to focus on one question only to get a strong response."

I sigh. "What do I do?"

"First we decide on the question and clear our minds of everything else. While we're focused, you wet the wand, then draw it three times around the edge of the bowl. We'll both watch the patterns, try to see images or pictures. Each of us says whatever comes to mind at that moment. Do you understand?"

"Umhum," I mumble.

"Rowan, I'm trying to help you here. A little more enthusiasm?"

"Let's do it."

"The question is . . ."

"Will anyone pursue me out of Timberton."

"Good."

At first the patterns remind me of currents in the river the night Mother drowned. Light from the candles flashes on the water, causing small flares. After the last drawing of the wand, a candle flames up, water catches the light more strongly than before and shoots it into my eyes. I squeeze my eyes shut.

"Are you all right?" Julina asks.

I nod and wait. No specific pictures come to mind for me. I can't stop thinking of Mother, wondering what she would think of all this. It's her fault I'm here. Julina breaks into my thoughts and I open my eyes.

"One in the centre," she says in a quiet voice, "another off to the side, and just at the end there's someone else, or maybe two people, coming in."

"I didn't see anything but a bunch of ripples and a flash of light."

"It takes practice. The sense I got is that you, at the centre are alone at the beginning. Then at some point in your journey south there will be another person of significance crossing your path, though I can't tell if that person means you good or ill. However, your ripples go on afterwards, so that's positive. And then there's a new person or two, again, it's not clear, coming in near the end."

"Could that be my father and brother when I reach Aquila?"

"Perhaps."

"Maybe the person at the side is Nesgor."

"Who?"

"A friend of Edana's, an old trader. I guess I forgot to tell you. She arranged for him to go with me."

Julina frowns. "The ripples show you going on alone from here."

"Do you think someone or something will try to stop me or separate me from Nesgor?"

Julina taps the table. "As I said, the scrying bowl can be ambiguous. Though I have to say, caution is probably the best thing. You don't want curious people around you."

"I have no intention of telling Nesgor anything except that I'm going south to relatives." I move away from the bowl. "The other night you said that you were going to reflect on the bracelet and its possible power. What can you tell me about that?"

"The bracelet catches and manipulates light, maybe heat and flames, too, though we haven't seen that; your father wrote about cold fire. Although the bracelets were made not so long ago, I keep getting a sense of great age." She shakes her head. "Perhaps it's the smith who's old."

"I know most of this," I mutter. "Isn't there anything new?"

"A lot has been written about enchanted rings. There are also stories about magical cauldrons, spears and swords. Sometimes there's a curse associated with a ring, or a demon is said to live in it. People have used rings to enchant others or to see the future. Stories and speculation."

"Still nothing really useful for me."

"What's the matter with you tonight, Rowan? Nothing I say satisfies you."

"Oh, that's great, blame me. You the great seer can't tell what's wrong? How about foot dragging? Mumbo jumbo. Edana led me to expect great things of you, but you haven't helped very much at all."

Julina frowns. "Something's changed about you."

"Me!" I burst out, and clasp my arms around my body. I'm wearing long sleeves so that she can't see the faint mark of the bracelet on my arm. It's fading, but not completely gone yet. "You're the one who takes off without telling me and then comes back with hardly any new information or anything useful. Oh, but I'm forgetting, it's concealment and illusion that are important to you, right? And misdirection. What are you hiding from me? What have you found out and why don't you want to tell me?"

"It's complicated," she says. "Not everything in my life has to do with your affairs. But I am worried about you. It's as if you've been touched."

"Touched how?" I glare at her. "A touch of evil? Go ahead put it all on me."

"I'm not blaming you, I'm just concerned." She narrows her eyes. "You know," she says slowly, "perhaps I've not paid enough attention to your necklace."

"No!" I shout. "You're not fooling around with that." I stand up. "I've had enough."

Julina doesn't try to stop me.

***

The final evening of my stay in Timberton we gather in Edana's house for a farewell meal, and Julina is there as well, though I didn't ask her. I haven't spoken to her since my last visit, but Edana probably issued the invitation. Ma Parnell has outdone herself with four roast chickens, baked potatoes, mashed spiced turnips, mixed greens, fresh bread, and two large apple cakes. The boys all have third helpings of everything though the rest of us are more moderate. Julina has brought a barrel of wine.

As we are all sighing and patting our rounded stomachs, Julina says, "A toast to Rowan. May she achieve her dreams."

I duck my head, not knowing what to say. I'm still unable to trust her completely nor yet to see her as my enemy. Edana waters the boys' wine over their protests that they are old enough to drink it as is. I pour some water into my goblet, too. Dawn will come early and I don't want to sleep late or have a foggy head.

At the end of the toast, Ma Parnell points to a corner of the kitchen. Four bulging saddle bags lie there. "Food for your journey – unleavened flat bread, cheese, dried apples, salt and sugar, dried mint, dried meat, and a few other things."

I give Ma Parnell a hug. "Poor donkey, I mean Dusty. I don't know how he'll carry two bags and me. I may have to walk. Or put it all on Nesgor's horse."

"Ah," says Edana, "I have another gift for you, though it's too large to bring into the kitchen. I'm giving you Angel. Dusty can stay here and continue his rest."

I screech and leap into Edana's arms. "My very own horse!"

"And saddle," Dow says.

"With bridle," Benny adds.

"Not new, but we cleaned and fixed 'em," Corky finishes.

"Freki helped," the boy chimes in.

"They worked really hard," Edana grins. "So everything's better than new because it's soft and in good repair."

By this time I can't talk because my chest is tight, my throat almost closed and my eyes swimming with tears. Once again I have found friends who it will be very difficult to leave. I wonder what Mother would say if she could see me now. My life with her alone in the forest feels like a long time ago. I raise my glass and we drink to each other.

All, except Julina who of course likes to sleep late, get up the next morning to help me saddle Angel. Nesgor arrives on foot and Edana brings out a horse for him. The boys get him saddled and packed as well. I shiver in the early morning chill and am glad for my green cloak, which Ma Parnell cleaned and mended. When I'm mounted Edana ties a white feather to Angel's bridle, for luck, she says.

Corky pats the horse and slips me a sling shot. "I made it for you," he whispers.

We start off, Mord perched on the pommel of my saddle, Nesgor glowering. I hope he's not going to be in a bad mood the whole way. Angel's ears twitch when the raven flies down, but otherwise he remains calm. I ride partly twisted, waving at all of them standing in a row and waving back at me. My eyes prick, but I'm determined not to cry. When we reach the cross street, one last flurry of hands and I can't see them anymore. Nesgor coughs.

"Are you sick?" I ask.

"No," he growls. "Just early morning phlegm."

As the guards let us out of the southern gate the sun lifts free of the horizon, a gold disc. Above us curves sky, a bowl of pale blue. In the forest one usually sees only fragments of sky between the trees or in a clearing, never this huge emptiness where we seem to be the only moving things. I should be used to it after two weeks in Timberton, but feel exposed; eyes could be scrutinizing us, and yet, in this open land, it would be hard for a watcher to hide. Dew glitters on the grass and on the delicate webs of spiders, catching the early sun; it's as if sparkling jewels are scattered all around. A trail cuts through the jewels and across the grasslands.

Nesgor points with his chin. "Traders' Road, hey?"

Edana told me about this ancient trail made by the hooves of many horses and oxen, the wheels of carts, and the feet of people over years. It will take us in the direction of the City of Eagles. I turn once to look behind at the wooden walls of Timberton and the green smudge of the forest at both sides of the town. Of course, there's no sign of my friends, and thankfully no one following.

Angel trots, jouncing Mord, who croaks and bounces into the air, spreads his wings and circles close above me, calling all the while. He sounds sad and agitated, but I can see no hint of danger near, and Nesgor is riding without concern. Of course, Mord's eyes are much better than mine or the old man's and the raven has a higher vantage point.

"Mord," I call, "what is it?"

Nesgor snorts in derision, but I ignore him. I've explained to him that I'm taking my raven and that the bird will keep watch. I don't care whether he believes me or not. Mord flies down to sit on my shoulder, but the perch is too unsteady. Next, he hops to the pommel of my saddle and tries to put his head under my cloak. I pull on the reins and stop Angel.

"What are you doing now?" Nesgor shouts.

Mord wriggles until he is completely hidden, nothing but a green lump. I have never seen him behave like this. It worries me, but I don't know what to do about it.

"Oh, that's a wonderful bird you've got there," Nesgor taunts. "Sees through leather, hey? Keeps watch from inside your cloak?"

I ignore him. If he's going to be this annoying, I'd rather be alone. Cluck at Angel and he starts off again, tossing his head and snorting as if he can't understand what's the matter with us. It's a beautiful day he seems to be saying, why not enjoy it?

The sun begins to warm the land so I push the hood of my cloak down and pull out an old wide-brimmed hat that Ma Parnell gave me. Unfamiliar insects whirr about, a fly or two lands, then an orange and brown butterfly settles between Angel's ears and rides there. Around us the grasses ripple slightly in a light breeze. The land stretches out flatly in all directions; this, however, is an illusion created partly by long grass and distance. Now and then, the road descends through a dip or valley; a few of these are a mere wrinkle in the land, others are wide and filled with bushes and small trees. Anyone could be hiding there.

Nesgor rides sometimes beside me or behind. Occasionally he gallops ahead, and then he races back. He actually has a smile on his face most of the time and it occurs to me that he's happy to be out of his daughter's house and that small bedroom. I don't mind providing an excuse for him to go off on an adventure, but I hope that he's equal to the task. He's wearing his artificial arm, and because the harness and most of the arm is covered by clothing, it looks quite natural unless you peer closely at where a hand would be.

Near mid day we reach a valley with a narrow stream winding through it. Nesgor indicates that we should stop at the edge of a grove of trees. After dismounting I decide to unload everything from Angel, including the saddle and bridle.

"Hey, we're not camping for the night yet!" Nesgor exclaims.

"I know," I answer. "I'm going to give my horse a good rub down and let him drink and eat. He'll feel better for it. Want me to do your horse, too?"

He mutters and grumbles under his breath, but I notice that he's taken off his saddle bags. Removing a horse's tack isn't easy at the best of times, and it's going to be even harder with only one good hand. I can't insist that he let me do it, so I pretend not to notice his struggles. He gets everything off the horse, finally.

"Do caravan leaders rub down their own horses?" I ask, not looking at Nesgor.

He growls something I can't make out. Then, more loudly, "Hey you, rub down this horse."

When I'm done I spread food on a flat rock. Nesgor is resting his back against a tree. Mord, enticed by a few crumbs of cheese consents to come out into the open, but stays close to me. I don't know what I'm going to do if he keeps on like this. I'd intended to send him off with a message to Edana, but that may not be possible. When we're done eating I pack away the food and am getting ready to saddle the horses.

Nesgor stops me. "We've made good time," he says. "Let's take a longer rest."

I want to protest, but then it occurs to me that perhaps he's tired and sore, no longer accustomed to riding long distances. He stretches out in the shade of the trees, but I walk around peering into the distance. Mord's agitation continues to worry me, but I see no sign of pursuit. Soon Nesgor is snoring. Edana told me that the trade caravans take several days to cross the grasslands. It's hard to measure progress in this land with no clear signs that I can read. Nesgor seemed to have no problem finding the way, however, even when the track faded or was overgrown with grass. The sun warms me; my full stomach makes me sleepy. I sit down with my back against a tree. The horses crop grass contentedly. Mord crawls back under my cloak which is bundled by my side. A tiny insect lands on my wrist and I watch it with interest, until takes a nip of me.

"Ouch!" I squash it with a slap.

Angel raises his head and whinnies. Nesgor grunts and sits up, looks around.

"What's going on?" he asks.

"You're right," I say. "We should get moving again."

This time, I saddle both horses. Negor is pointedly studying the horizon. He walks a few paces and picks up a little dirt, lets it trickle through his fingers and watches how the wind blows it. All this might be important or he could just be pretending so that I think he's occupied with weighty matters while I do the physical labour. I don't care; I'm younger and stronger than he is. Once I we're mounted, Angel flicks his tail and responds to my heels by setting off at a gallop. I give a yell and bend low over his neck, throw a look behind. Nesgor has been caught by surprise and his horse is barely moving. I laugh to myself and urge Angel on.

By mid-afternoon however, both horses have slowed to a walk. Even horses like to take things easy now and then. I notice that Nesgor is fidgeting, rolling his shoulders and fiddling with his artificial arm.

"Everything all right?" I ask.

Not unexpectedly, Nesgor merely grunts and mumbles something unintelligible. I shrug, and we ride. I'm enjoying it though I'm sore and will probably be worse tonight, but I have some of my salve to rub in. Maybe that's what's bothering Nesgor; probably hasn't ridden for years and his bones are older than mine. I smile to myself. Let him grumble. The sun moves toward the western horizon. The horses trot along, manes and tails waving in the wind. Heat and the buzzing of insects, the motion of riding nearly put me into a doze.

"Blinking, blithering!"

Nesgor's shout almost precipitates me over my horse's neck. I pull Angel up, turn him around and trot back to where Nesgor is standing beside his horse. He's tugging at his shirt. Pulls it over his head, throws it on the ground. I can see how the harness for his arm straps around him.

"Help me get this blasted thing off!" he orders.

I dismount and approach him warily. He turns his back, so I can get at the buckles. I fumble with them as Nesgor stamps impatiently.

"Hold still!" I mutter. "Isn't there a better way to fasten or unfasten this?"

"No!" he retorts. "Now you know why I'd rather not wear it."

Finally, I get the harness off him. There are red marks and indentations. Nesgor grabs the harness and bundles it into one of his saddle bags.

"I have salve," I say. "It would probably help the soreness."

Nesgor shakes his head and pulls his shirt on. "I'm fine," he says. "Now that thing's off me, I'm fine."

When we start again I let him go ahead so I can watch in case he has trouble, but he manages reasonably well with one good arm and a stump on the other. I'm just not sure how much help he'd be if we were attacked by bandits. Though Edana did say she hadn't heard of any raids on caravans for a long time. I study the land carefully, can't see any other riders. They could be hiding in the next valley or behind that hill over there. We pass the hill without being attacked. My heart beats more quickly, but then as nothing happens, it calms.

We're riding in a westerly direction so I have a good view of the setting sun. At first the sky grows paler at the edge, and a few clouds gather. The sun touches them and bright spears of light bounce outwards. Orange red, like flames, colours the sky. Like a yellow ball, the sun is falling behind the edge of the world. Soon we'll be enclosed by darkness yet open to the sky and to whatever animals roam this land at night. It's a prospect that makes my breath quicken and my heart speed up.

"Nesgor!" I call. "When are we going to stop for the night?"

"Not yet!" he shouts back over his shoulder.

My stomach is making odd noises because I'm hungry. There's an outcrop of trees up ahead so maybe that's where we'll stop; Nesgor keeps moving. I'm tempted to halt here in the trees and see what the old man will do, but there's no water, so I follow him. My legs start to cramp and then my back begins to ache. The sun has sunk below the horizon and soon we won't be able to see where we're going.

"Whoa!" Nesgor shouts. "Where are you heading off to?"

I've ridden right past him without noticing. We're in a valley with a clump of trees and I can hear water gurgling. I heave a sigh of relief as I dismount.

"Fire first," Nesgor says. "Then we can see what we're doing."

The night air refreshes and the flames comfort. We soon have camp set up and I make a stew of dried meat. Nesgor says it's the best meal he's had in a long time. He sounds sincere and since he seems in a good mood, I ask him to tell me about his travels as a trader.

"Well," he begins, pulling out a pipe and tobacco, "there are many tales I could tell. Some would make your hair stand on end, others are funny, some sad, but every once in a while there's an incident that you just can't get out of your head. Hey?" He takes a few puffs, leans against his saddle bags.

I snuggle into my cloak. A fire and a story after supper, perfect.

"I was trading in a town near the mountains many years ago. Not a large town, but I'd heard of a stone cutter there who had a few nice gems for sale. Precious stones are always sellable and easy to transport. I was making my way to his shop when I chanced on a musical performance in the town square. Quite a crowd, and rather than trying to batter my way through, I decided to stop and listen. Found a stairway to climb so I could get a better view. One of the musicians was exceptionally good, had three different sizes of wooden flutes and was playing them in turns. A hot day, sun beating down, nary a breeze, so strolling beer and water sellers made good money. I'd just bought myself a cup when the music changed to deeper, fuller notes. A breeze sprang up."

He stops to suck on his pipe; I think he's just trying to drag out the suspense.

"I took a look and saw that the musician was playing a thick, long flute now. The breeze got stronger, causing women's shawls to whip around their heads; the sleeves of men's shirts flapped. The flute player continued to play, but was having a hard time standing straight. A little boy got blown over and rolled between people's feet. And then," Nesgor pauses to take another couple of puffs from his pipe, "the flute player stopped and so did the wind. Instantly, just like that."

The fire flickers so I can't see the expression on the old man's face clearly. Is he joking with me? I'm supposed to believe this actually happened?

"Is that all?" I say.

"That's it. The musicians packed up and people moved away. I'd have liked to see the young man play again, though. Just to see what would happen, hey?"

"You actually imagine he was making the wind blow with his flute playing?"

"The world's a queer place."

"And you saw this? It's not some story you made up or that someone else told you?"

"Believe it or not, as you wish," Nesgor growls. "I'm going to sleep."

He knocks out his pipe, wraps himself in a blanket, and starts to snore. I sit listening to the horses stamp and snuffle. Mord rests in a tree, head tucked under his wing. The fire crackles and flares. I stare at it, thinking of the flute player. The power to raise wind. I've seen a woman and two children transform from goat to human, so why shouldn't anything be possible? I pull my cloak more tightly around me; it's a very big sky and a huge land.

***

Ugh, early morning fog and damp blankets. Nesgor has already kicked dirt over the fire; he's growling and cursing to himself. I'd been hoping for a hot tisane, but now I'll have to content myself with cold bread and cheese. I saddle the horses while the old trader finishes packing our bags.

"Keep close," Nesgor says as we mount.

Sound is muffled and I feel as if I'm riding through thick wet blankets that leave moisture on my face, hair, clothes and on Angel. Mord huddles under my cloak. I can barely see the tail of Nesgor's horse ahead and so I speed up to keep him in sight. Although it isn't raining, wetness continues to seep out of the air, and I shiver despite my layers of clothes. I peer all around hoping for sun to break through. I hear the muffled sound of hooves, can't tell whether they're ahead or behind. Anything or anyone could be creeping up on us through this murk, like those men who followed me to Timberton. Still, they'd have to have better eyes than mine. That's when I realize that the old man and his horse have vanished. I hear a shout and so I nudge Angel. A large rock shows suddenly on the ground in front of us. The horse leaps over, knocking Mord askew and he flutters to the ground, disappears somewhere behind. I halt Angel and wait, listening. Can't hear anything at all now.

"Nesgor!" I shout. There's no answer. "Mord!"

A flutter of wings and the raven emerges out of the fog. His feathers are sticking out all over the place. As he lands on the neck of the horse, Angel snorts. I grab Mord and wrap him in my cloak. He snuggles in and makes a few crooning noises, that sound comforting, but I'm still worried.

"Nesgor!" I yell again. There is only the sound of my own breath and Angel's.

Chapter X

Samel

Tamtan wants me to work with the oldest apprentice today to tune and repair drums. I'm disappointed because I'd hoped to talk to the master drummer and find out what he knows about the lands round Aquila, ask whether he's ever travelled there. Instead I'm stuck in a corner, head down, scraping, tightening, gluing. Parts of the work are interesting, like making a drum come alive again, hearing it sound just right. Much of it is boring and repetitive. I remember how Tamtan makes a lesson out of everything, so I decide to think how what I'm doing could be like me and Rowan.

I suppose in a way our lives have become a broken drum. Sadly, the pieces aren't all in one place. I guess the first thing to decide is whether the drum is worth fixing at all, whether it's worth hunting for all the missing parts. Papa and I have been happy together here in Aquila and our life has been good. Maybe we're more like an orchestra that's split up. They'd remember what it had been like to play together. I don't even know what I'm missing, have no memory at all of my mother or sister. All I can do is think about Ali and her family, imagine what it'd be like to live with them. I know not all families are like theirs. One of Tamtan's apprentices often has bruises on his arms and I wonder whether his father hits him. Another hates his younger brother and says he breaks everything he touches. Rowan might not want to come find us at all.

Ali asked me a few days ago what I want. I actually know the answer to that question, have known it all along. Ever since I found out I had a sister I knew I'd want to meet her. I just don't know the best way to do it.

When I get home, there's a note from Papa. He's been and gone again. No sign of his eagle he writes, and he forgot that he has to play for the Lord's dinner tonight. It'll be late by the time he gets home. Don't wait up for him.

I rattle around the house, eat a snack, wander into Papa's room. He's taken the whole case of flutes, so I can't play. Back in my room I notice the two drums I made a long time ago in Tamtan's workshop. Start playing first one, then the other, beat out rhythms, lose myself in the sound of horses hooves on packed earth. I sway to the sound, close my eyes, seem to feel wind in my hair. Rowan, I whisper, Rowan, where are you? I am surrounded by the thunder of hooves, like a troop of the Lord's militia riding by. The earth shakes; the sky shivers.

A great crack and boom makes my eyes fly open, hands stop. It's dark both inside my room and outside. Cool air blows into the open window, a rushing of rain, then another clap of thunder. Have I brought this storm with my drumming? That's pretty far-fetched. The bracelet is still hidden underneath my clothes in the chest at the foot of my bed. A gust of wind throws a shower of rain into my face. I get up and close the shutters.

I hurry downstairs to build a fire in the kitchen brazier and warm my hands. Then I check all the rooms to make sure windows are closed and the front and back doors locked. I've never felt afraid staying alone in this house, but tonight I'm spooked. Can't settle in any one place, start at the least sound. My skin feels itchy and my mouth keeps drying out even though I sip water. At last I get so tired I can hardly keep my eyes open and have to go to bed. I pull the covers over my head which I haven't done since I was small.

***

When I creep out of bed in the morning, I'm happy to see Papa asleep in his. I open one of my shutters to a grey, cool day, decide to cook gruel with honey and cinnamon, and eat it by my window. Afterwards I work on copying music. Eventually I hear Papa stirring, and then he pokes his head in.

"How was the music and dinner?" I ask.

"Good food, appreciative audience. And you?"

"Fine," I say, deciding not to tell him about my drumming visions and my worries about Rowan.

He nods. "Something smells good."

"There's more in the pot downstairs."

The rest of the day is quiet; Papa works mostly on his music. He takes a break and we play together – he on his flutes and me on a drum. No breezes, no moving papers or dust. I wonder whether it's because the bracelet is upstairs in my room, too far away to affect things, or whether Papa has learned, consciously or unconsciously, to stop or mute the effects of the bracelet.

***

Several days of ordinary life pass. Papa and I are careful with each other and neither of us mentions Rowan or leaving Aquila, though I hope that he's making plans.

Tamtan puts me to work on a small drum that can be fastened to a belt. He says he's been planning to design a set of instruments for a one-man band, so a musician can travel and have everything he needs close at hand. I like that.

Xylea gives me a new piece to learn on the harp. It's called 'Desert Wind' and is quite complicated. She lends me one of the small hand harps to take home so I can practise. I'm very careful to concentrate on the notes only and not think about wind when I'm playing the piece. Even though the bracelet is still in my trunk, a slight breeze rises whenever I pluck the strings. I practise in my room with the door closed, when Papa is out.

I'm trying hard to understand what this ability is that I have. It seems to be stronger around music, with rhythm and beat. If I handle the bracelet and make pictures in my head, I can make things happen, feel things more strongly, imagine myself in other places. Music becomes a way for me to move beyond the ordinary. A way to connect to the winds, maybe to rain and thunder. Weather in general? I'm not sure of that. Ali can't do that with music, though she has special talents with paint, knows how to find the different shades of earth and stones to grind into colours, knows how to mix and use them. Also the ability to dream about things that have probably happened or things that might happen. I wonder whether Rowan has these kinds of talents. Does she dream of us, see us in visions?

At times the bracelet almost seems to play me, and I wonder if it's got the upper hand. The scariest thought is that someone else is doing the controlling. I understand what Papa means when he talks about danger. Flames can be dangerous if they get out of control, and yet, in a closed space they give heat, light, the ability to cook food.

Papa watches me when he thinks I don't notice; I wait for signs that he's making plans without me. The atmosphere in our house is like the air before a thunder storm. It can make the hair on the back of your neck rise. Not the most comfortable feeling.

Late one afternoon Papa comes bursting in the door shouting for me. Because the next day is laundry day and I have to have our bundle ready for the woman when she comes, I'm upstairs sorting through my clothes. I drop everything and rush down the stairs. Stumble and almost fall. Papa grabs me.

"Careful!"

I shake him off. "What is it? What were you shouting about?"

Papa grins. "The eagle came back."

My mouth opens, but I can't speak.

"She's in the grasslands," he says. "Rowan."

"Where's that? Is she coming to us?"

"North of the desert," Papa says.

I sit beside him. "Then we go and meet her. The eagle can lead us. Please?" I don't say another word. Have said them all before. If he says no again . . .

"The first thing we need to do," Papa says, "is buy a couple of camels."

"Yes!" I jump up, pound him on the back. "We're going!"

"We'll need supplies. Also maps and information."

"How long will it take us to get ready?" I ask, bouncing from one foot to the other. I can't seem to keep still.

"Three or four days." Suddenly Papa thumps his forehead. The Lord's anniversary! It's in seven days." He grabs for my hand, pulls me down beside him again. "I absolutely have to be here for that performance."

I take a deep breath. "All right, but we leave the day after. Yes?"

"We can do that," Papa nods. "That will give us plenty of time to get ready. Even with all the work and meetings and rehearsal for the anniversary."

"Seven days," I say thoughtfully. "What's first?"

"Tomorrow," Papa says, "we go to visit an old friend of mine, a trader. Retired now, but he rode the caravans north and south for many years. He'll have maps, information and probably know the best place to buy camels."

I wish we could start tonight, right now, in fact, but it's getting dark, and Papa's probably hungry. I don't care if I eat or sleep, not tonight. I'd much rather stay up and watch the moon rise and the stars appear, look north and wonder whether Rowan, my sister, is watching the same moon and stars. And whether her thoughts are about me.

Then it occurs to me that the eagle could be wrong or Papa might have misinterpreted. Before, he was more cautious about believing what he learned from the eagle. Maybe I've convinced him it's better to be doing something, to be moving.

Chapter XI

Rowan

I send the horse forward slowly through the mist. Can't tell if we're still following the road or not. Should I trust to Angel? After a while I decide to dismount. By bending low I can see where the grass has been worn away and flattened; the road is here. I listen, but can hear no sound of other hooves. Where is Nesgor? I lead Angel on, then stop. Can't decide whether it's better to wait for the fog to lift or to attempt to continue. Surely Nesgor will try to double back and find us, but when I do stop, the damp and inactivity make me shiver. After a while it seems that the fog is thinning ahead, at least I can see a patch of blue sky. I walk faster and soon find myself on a low hill with the grasslands below clear of fog ahead and empty. Thick fog still swirls behind.

I can't see any sign of Nesgor so I decide to stop here, hoping he'll find us, hoping that he's not gotten lost, or worse, fallen and hurt himself. The sun warms me, drying my damp hair and cloak; Angel crops grass contentedly, but Mord prefers to stay inside my cloak. I lean against a rock. Nesgor supposedly travelled this road often so surely he has encountered mist before and knows what to do. Unless someone else encountered him first – the men who followed me earlier. If they've got him, there's nothing for me to do except keep on going and hope to escape.

I'm about to mount Angel when a deep rumbling along with a shaking of the earth stops me. The sky remains blue with a few fluffy white clouds, nothing to make me think a storm is coming. When I look around, I see that the fog is gone behind, too, but there's still no sign of Nesgor. The shaking and the sound increase and in the west dust billows like smoke.

As the dust approaches it rises to reveal a river of reddish brown surging across the ground, a mass of bolting animals. I catch flashes of horned heads. Angel raises his nose and neighs loudly. I think I hear an answer from the mass below and look for Nesgor's horse. There are indeed horses among the huge horned cattle-like creatures and people with spears riding the horses, but I don't see Nesgor among them.

One of the riders urges his horse sideways to break free of the throng. I mount, unsure of his purpose, thinking to turn Angel away. The rider gallops toward me. His horse will have to climb the hill, so I can probably get away if I leave now. I have only moments to decide. I notice that his spear is sheathed at the side of the horse. Perhaps these are the people Edana mentioned, and they might help me. The rider reaches the base of the hill and the time to flee is past. He rides bare back, long black hair hanging in many narrow braids down his back. His chest is streaked with red and yellow.

He points. "That white feather," he shouts, "where did you get it?"

I look down at myself. No feathers, not even a bit of Mord sticking out.

"Your horse."

Then I remember Edana tying the feather to my bridle. It's still there.

"Edana," I yell back. "The horse woman from Timberton, she gave it to me." I wave backwards in the direction I think the town lies. "She bought horses from some of your people?"

He motions for me to come down from the ridge. Despite a nervous quiver in my stomach, I nudge Angel and he picks his way carefully down the stony trail. The thunder of hooves has quietened, with most of the huge brown animals gone, except that carcasses lie scattered here and there on flattened grass. People are working at the cutting up.

"Come with me," the rider says when I reach him.

The man wheels his horse, giving me no chance to ask whether he's seen Nesgor. I hesitate for a moment, then decide to take the opportunity for possible information, and follow. If Nesgor is nearby, he may come upon the people cutting up meat, and they can direct him to me. It's a fast ride and though Angel keeps up it's impossible to hold a conversation. We leave Traders' Road behind.

After some time we reach a valley with a stream running through it. Round tan-coloured tents are scattered near the spot where the stream widens into a small pond. I smell smoke and as we get closer, I see wooden racks near several fires, probably for drying the meat that will be arriving soon. A few people walk about, others squat at various tasks or stand talking. A couple of loose horses amble nearby and some kind of deer-like animal with horns stands beside a distant tent. Angel shies suddenly as a rabbit darts between his feet and I struggle to control him. Several children run to meet us.

The man swings off his horse and motions me to do the same. I hold my cloak with Mord still bundled in it as the man slips the rope off his horse and lets it go. The children have already stripped the saddle and reins off Angel. One sets my saddlebags on the ground, another slaps the horse's rump.

"Wait!" I shout, but then see that Angel has not run away as I feared.

"Don't worry," the man says, "the young ones will take care of him." He gestures to a nearby tent. "You go there."

The tents are of hide, perhaps from the large cattle I saw on the grasslands. Colourful designs are painted there – yellow circles like the sun or moon, brown animals, red, blue or grey birds, straight and jagged lines, spirals. The man approaches a spot where a flap is partially laced. I expect him to duck down and enter, but instead he scratches at the hide.

A voice calls, "Enter."

After the brightness of outdoors, I find it hard to see more than vague shapes and lumps, but once the man backs out, light comes in through the opening, and I realize, from another opening above. Two women sit across from me on grass mats. One has flowing white hair, the other black. I am about to ask if they know Edana, when the older one speaks.

"I've been expecting you, friend of Edana, who carries one of my feathers."

A shiver goes up my back, and words stick in my throat. I know the man who has brought me here hasn't said a word to them, so how do they know about Edana? I take a step back. The younger woman indicates a grass mat near me.

"Please, sit."

It's then I notice that the old woman's eyes are filmed with white and stare slightly to one side of me. I half turn to find the place where I entered, but the flap is closed and I can't see how it's fastened.

"Don't be afraid," I hear the younger woman say behind me.

Mord squawks and struggles out of the cloak I've dropped.

"A raven!" the young woman exclaims.

"Yes," the old woman says. "A black bird of the north. We don't often see them here, and they don't make friends with humans easily."

And you're not seeing it now, I want to say, but that would be rude. Too much has happened in too short a time so that I've nearly forgotten my manners. It seems to me that I walk in a dream and I keep expecting at any moment to wake up. Mord bends his head first to one side, then the other as if he is looking at the women with each of his eyes in turn, then struts across the dirt floor of the tent until he reaches the hand the old woman puts out toward him. His feathers are ruffled and she smoothes them, bending her head to mutter words I can't hear.

"He's been upset," the old woman says. She turns her face toward me. "He doesn't like the open spaces with so few trees to roost in. You shouldn't have taken him this far from home."

A huge breath goes out of me. So that's all it is! "I'm sorry, Mord,"

I say, "I didn't know."

"Now you do," the old woman states, "so you can send him back tonight. He won't mind it so much in the dark."

"Send Mord away? But he, I . . ." my voice stutters to a halt.

"You know it's the best thing."

There is no way I want to cause Mord any more distress, but do I believe what this old woman says or does she want to get rid of the raven for some purpose of her own? I straighten and stare at that tanned and wrinkled face. It's calm and seems kind; I like it better than Julina's face. No one says anything until the young woman who has been looking at me as hard as I have been staring at the old one, speaks.

"My mother no longer sees well with her eyes, but more easily through her spirit. In case you've been wondering."

It's a gentle rebuke and I can feel the heat of a blush on my face and hope that they don't notice it in the dimness. I consider apologising for my assumptions and rudeness, but the old one forestalls me.

"My daughter is going to take you to a place where you can get clean and refreshed. When the hunters return, we will feast."

"Call me Mirage," the other woman says.

"I'm Rowan."

"And this is Grandmother Wisdom. Leave your possessions here, they'll be quite safe."

So this is Edana's friend. Perhaps I will trust her a little. "A man was with me –Nesgor. We got separated. Can your people find him?"

The old woman closes her eyes. Slowly she shakes her head. "I don't see him, but I will send a message for the others to watch for him."

As I'm still thinking of the implications of Grandmother Wisdom's words, Mirage leads me away, taking me to the edge of the camp near the stream and a grove of trees where a small dirt-coloured dome stands. There's another, slightly larger, some distance away. As we get closer I see that it's a hut made of branches covered with mud. A fire burns nearby and rocks are piled in and round it. An empty bark basket sits on the ground.

"Have you done this before?"

I shake my head.

"First fill that basket with water," she says. "I'll put some of these rocks into the hut. Then we'll take our clothes off, go inside and pour water on the hot rocks. You'll sweat and get clean. Not only your body, but also your spirit. It's a good thing to do after a journey."

It reminds me of the baths I took at Edana's house – heat loosening tight muscles. I close my eyes and let the warmth soak in. Mirage chants about sun rising and setting, the circle of the day, the round of the seasons, and of life. It seems to me that the old woman's voice speaks out of the steam or the rocks, or even the earth.

"In this place dream and life are one. Let yourself melt into the steam, turn to water, flow with the rivers and rise with the rain. There is no fear or struggle. You are safe, held by the earth, cupped in her hands."

I float in mist and music, drums and voices, winds made visible, swirling in a dance. Thunder plays drums and rain sings. Dust and grass bow and whirl. Mist rises and it seems to me that if I can only penetrate that fog I'll be able to see Mother, speak to her and learn everything.

Sweat beads on my skin as if my body is weeping. I curl forward; wrap myself in my own arms as I wish Mother could still do. She cared for me once; surely she wanted good things for me, so how could she not tell me about my father, my brother? Why couldn't my parents protect us by staying together? Maybe I'll never understand, never learn the reasons.

The feather of a snowy owl floats down, brushing across my bare skin.

"Come back now." Mirage says; the rocks are cool, no longer steaming. I feel hollow and light enough to rise into the sky. When I try to stand, my legs have turned to cloth and won't hold me. "Easy," she says. "The heat takes a lot out of you. Carefully now."

She guides me to a large tent near the centre of the encampment. Cook fires burn all around it; the smell of roasting meat makes my mouth water and my stomach rumble. People crowd around, tending the food. I ask if anyone has seen Nesgor, but they all shake their heads. Mirage snags two sticks of meat. Most people smile at us and nod; one or two stare at me, and I think about what they see. I'm wearing old leather breeches and a tunic, not so different from many of the people here. My skin is paler, however and my dark hair is twisted into a tail rather than braided all over my head. Mirage nudges me and I take some meat. Children race here and there carrying small bows, sticks, dolls, or just chasing each other. I nibble carefully, trying not to burn my lips and tongue. As we walk closer to the tent, I see that the entrance flap is open and that many people are gathered inside, including Grandmother Wisdom.

"Go ahead," Mirage says. "They've been waiting for you."

"Aren't you coming?"

She shakes her head, gives me a nudge.

***

"Welcome back child of the north," Grandmother says, as I join the circle.

Mord is sitting on her left shoulder; he dips his head at me, and it feels good that he hasn't left me yet. I've never been in a small space with this many people before, am tongue-tied. It feels very ceremonial; people are wearing beads and feathers, pendants of horns, teeth, or claws, embroidered shirts and dresses. Though my body is clean, my own clothes are dusty and travel stained. I'm afraid of saying or doing the wrong things. A woman nearby tugs at my leather breeches so I understand that I should sit.

Softly, another woman begins to chant, meaningless sounds at first, but gradually I realize she is telling a story. As I listen, it reminds me of Lynx and his family, the tales he used to share with me.

Long ago," the woman says, "there was only dark and cold and all the animals huddled for warmth. Some stamped their feet or flapped their wings very rapidly, trying to create heat. Eagle scratched one leg against the other and when two of his talons scraped together, there was a spark that landed on one of Eagle's feathers. He released that feather and it lay there in the midst of the animals, smouldering slowly. Raven came close and blew so hard that the feather burst into flame and scorched him. By this time the other animals had had enough time to gather bits and pieces of discarded fur, feathers and the odd scrap of wood so they could keep the fire going. They were comfortable in the circle around the flames, though those farthest away still shivered now and then. Raven said, what if we carry this fire high up into the sky so it can light everything? The animals thought it a good idea, but no one wanted to get burned. Finally Raven grabbed a flaming branch in his beak and flew very high. In the process, he was more than a little scorched, in fact his feathers turned black. He let go of the fire and it stayed there in the sky, becoming a great circle of light."

The woman pauses and I think she is finished, wonder whether to clap. Everyone else stays quiet and one or two have their eyes closed.

The story teller clears her throat. "Animals learned long ago that working together can help all, but they forgot that lesson and so have many of the people." Then she bows her head to Mord, and so does everyone else. He bobs as if in acknowledgement. "Animals shared fire with people, but not everyone shares it so freely or uses it properly."

The Fire Queen story pops into my head and I wonder if these people know that tale. There is silence and as it lengthens, I glance around, wondering what we are waiting for. Everyone watches me. One person nods, another smiles. Gradually I realize it's my turn to speak.

There are many people here, and even if they are all friendly to me, at some time my story could get repeated to ears belonging to those who might wish me harm. I don't want to speak at all, but they've been kind to a stranger. I should reciprocate. So I say only that my mother has died and I'm journeying south to relatives. It's a long journey and I have need of friends along the way for shelter and food. I mention Edana and the gifts she has been given by them in the past, and the gifts she and her friends gave to me. Several people nod at her name. Finally I add that I hope they will let me stay the night and give me a few provisions to continue on my journey, for a lot of the food from Ma Parnell was on Nesgor's horse. I think about offering to pay, but I have a sense that this would be the wrong thing to say. All the time I'm speaking I look around the circle, but I always avoid Grandmother's face because I'm afraid that, despite her blindness, she'll see much more than I'm telling. When I finish, there are murmurs of sympathy and promises of dried meat and whatever else I require. A sudden burst of singing from outside stops the talk.

"It's time for the hunters' feast," one of the women says.

We emerge from the tent to dusk; fires send sparks, like tiny stars, into the sky. Mirage waits nearby and offers me a basket laden with plump dark berries. I grab a handful and fill my mouth, letting the juices run down my throat. I smile.

"Your lips are purple," she says. "You eat them just the way my daughter does."

"They're delicious. Is your daughter my age? Can I meet her?"

The woman's mouth turns down. "She's away just now."

Drums call and flutes join in; I watch as men, women and children wearing hide clothing decorated with colourful beads, shells and feathers, dance. The beat of the drum gets inside me, joins with my pulse, becomes the heartbeat, moving blood through arms and legs. People near me join hands, someone grasps mine, and we circle around the musicians.

I begin to feel very warm, especially around the waist. I let go of the hands on either side of me and back out of the circle. Find a spot some distance away, unfasten my pouch and unwrap the bracelet. It glows and seems to throb in my hand.

"Child?"

When I turn Grandmother is there within touching distance. I look around for Mirage or anyone else who might have brought the old woman to me, but no one else is near.

"How do you do it?" I ask. "How do you move without seeing, know where to go when there is no one to guide you?"

She reaches out a hand and grasps my free one. Chuckles. "I was near when you left the circle and could follow the wind of your progress, and the warmth that you now hold in your other hand. Come, take me to my tent."

I lead, though I'm sure she can probably find the way herself. Inside, Grandmother's tent is lit only slightly by moonlight filtering through spaces. She makes herself comfortable, then motions to the circle of stones in the centre. Wood is laid around a core of shavings.

"Place that bit of warmth you carry in the centre," she says. "Then take both my hands and close your eyes." When our hands are clasped, she says, "Picture one of the fires out there. See it clearly in your mind."

"I'm not like the Queen of Fire," I say. "Can't create flames out of nothing."

"Ah," she nods, "I've heard old stories about a woman who could control fire."

"She did wicked things."

"Perhaps. Do not be quick to judge. People do things for many reasons and others don't always understand, or even remember events in the same way. All I'm asking you to do is to light my small fire."

I take a deep breath and think of the fires outside, logs glowing, flames flickering. Try to remember the smell of them and the warmth. There is a muffled sort of snap. When I open my eyes, a flame curls in the shavings. I pull the bracelet out with two fingers – it's barely warm – and drop it on the ground. Its glow fades quickly.

"What is this? How? Grandmother, what can you tell me about my mother's bracelet?"

"Is that what it is?" she says. "I could sense only concentrated warmth that had the ability to grow or shrink. It seems to me to have something to do with love. That emotion can be very powerful."

"Love," I whisper. "It's not evil or dangerous?"

"Ah," the old woman shakes her head. "Love can be both dangerous and evil, just like fire can warm or burn us."

"How can love be evil?"

"You are perhaps too young, but have you ever known someone who is so consumed by desire either for a person or thing that they cannot see anything else? This sort of person will do whatever is necessary to possess their heart's desire, without regard for the people or things they might injure or destroy." She puts out a hand. "Are you able to give the bracelet to me for a few moments?"

I hand it over and she cups it in her hands, head up, staring into distance. I remember how Julina avoided touching it. It occurs to me that may be important and I consider asking Grandmother, but I don't want to interrupt. I begin to feel sleepy and take a few deep breaths to keep awake. After a time Grandmother gives the bracelet back.

"Great love is in it," she says, "but heartache also surrounds it."

"There's something I want to tell you."

Grandmother nods. "I know you didn't give us everything back there in the big tent. That was wise."

"Do you think it's safe here?"

Again that far away look comes into the old woman's face. "Yes," she says.

So I recount my father's story of what happened one night when he and my mother put on their bracelets under the light of a full moon. I've shared this part of the story with no one except Thea. I also tell Grandmother how my parents had hidden their bracelets away after that. Grandmother listens without interrupting. When I finish, she continues to sit without speaking. I keep quiet.

Finally she says, "Put more wood on."

I do as she asks.

"Your parents were afraid. I'm sure you can understand that. An unexplained event like that happening suddenly can alarm anyone, and sometimes, unfortunately, terror keeps us from taking the next step on the path of our life. I can't say if that's what happened to your mother and father; however, you are on your own journey. What I will tell you is not to be afraid of what that bracelet can do."

I sigh. "When I was small I never thought of my mother being afraid. She seemed to me brave and wonderful and all knowing. Now . . ."

"You know that she was as human and imperfect as any of us."

"But it still makes me angry to think of my father leaving."

"Perhaps they wanted only to protect you."

I almost add, and my brother, but stop the words before they get to my tongue. Grandmother is right to advise caution about saying too much. However, she has already seen more than anyone else, so maybe she can help me further.

"Grandmother," I say slowly, "you said that you don't see danger around the bracelet, but what about around me? That companion I had when I left Timberton, for instance. Fog came up and we lost each other. Is he all right? Am I a danger to other people?"

"Give me your hands again and close your eyes."

I stare at the shifting darkness behind my eyelids and listen to the crackling fire, like distant thunder. I seem to hear faint laughter and it makes me uncomfortable. Grandmother lets go of my hands suddenly. My eyes snap open. She is moving her head from side to side and shaking her hands as if trying to get rid of excess water.

"I see no evil in you," she says, "but there is a man. He wants you, plans for you to help him, though he is hiding his true intentions, hiding what he wants you to do. So do not trust him."

"Who?" I ask urgently. "Is it my father? Or someone else?"

She holds her face in her hands, covering her eyes. "I don't know. I can see no more."

"Oh," I sigh, "I wish it weren't so difficult."

"Listen," the old woman says, "a toddler takes only a few steps at first; she can't run or jump. It takes time to gain the skills for the next part of what she has to do."

"Mother used to say I needed to learn patience. Among all the other things she said I still had to learn."

Grandmother chuckles. "Don't forget we all have things to learn even at my advanced age."

"What about Nesgor, though? Did you see anything of him? He's old and has only one arm. I hope he's all right."

"I did see a figure riding fast toward Timberton. Perhaps he's gone for help to find you."

"He's not being pursued?"

She shakes her head. "Not that I could see. Now, let's call that raven from the top of the tent."

Mord flutters to the ground near my feet, then hops into my lap.

He rubs his head against my hand and I smooth his feathers. He's been a part of my life for so long that I can't bear the thought of sending him away and perhaps never seeing him again.

"It's for the best," Grandmother says quietly. "Take him outside and make him understand that he has to go."

"I'll write a note first."

In my saddle bags I rummage for parchment, pen and ink. Two notes, I decide – one to Edana telling her I'm fine, that Nesgor and I have separated, I've met Grandmother Wisdom, and am sending Mord because he doesn't like the open spaces. The second for Edana to send on to Thea, telling her briefly that I'm safe.

Outside the tent the night is cool and quiet except for the muted sounds of people talking some distance away. I stare into the sky and find the North Star that will point Mord's way, tie the notes to his legs. Whisper to him that he must be strong, that I want him to go to Edana. He croaks once and ducks his head. I lift him to the sky, throw him up. His wings beat and then he is gone into the dark. Something flutters through the air and lands at my feet – a black feather.

"Come," Grandmother says from the doorway of the tent. "You need to get a good night's rest if you're going to leave early in the morning."

I take a minute to tie the feather to my necklace before going inside. Furs make a soft bed. I'm feeling exhausted for a lot has happened to me this day, but I'm not yet ready to sleep.

"Grandmother," I say, "have you ever been in the north country?"

She smiles and nods. "My parents travelled there and I was actually born one winter night in a small cabin by a frozen lake."

"Perhaps they met relatives of my friend Lynx," I say. 'Your people here remind me a lot of Lynx's family."

"Ah," Grandmother says, "our northern cousins. We rarely see each other. Some consider that my people are traditional enemies of the northern people, but I know that we are kin."

"Lynx says all the animals are our cousins and we should treat them with respect, even when we need their meat or fur."

"He's a wise one, your friend." She touches my hand. "Now am I right in thinking that the raven gave you a gift?"

"He dropped a feather."

She nods. "You now have several objects of power. You've gathered them or they have chosen to attach themselves to you – a stone in your necklace, the bracelet, and now the raven feather. Also, the snowy owl feather put on your horse by Edana – it's one of mine, and I don't give them out often. Each has something to contribute. The necklace protects you while travelling, the feathers help with clear and far vision, the bracelet we are not completely sure about. Take care of these things and pay attention. They will all help you in your journey."

I want to ask more questions, but Grandmother has thrown some stuff on the fire that fills the tent with a sweet smell. I yawn and close my eyes, nestling into the furs and think of Mord winging his way by the light of the moon. Perhaps I will dream of him or other things, and the old woman might tell me what my dreams mean. Darkness, sleep, and peace float me away, as a puff of wind takes a feather.

Chapter XII
Samel

Ulgar, the man who might be able to help us organize our journey, lives in a tiny house a few streets away. Papa warns me as we walk that the old man is proud and independent. Though he's knotted and bent with age, he doesn't want to be pitied and likes to do for himself as much as possible. That doesn't mean he won't accept a gift, especially when he's being asked for help. So Papa carries a skin of spiced wine.

A boy lets us in, leads us through a kitchen and bedroom into a minuscule garden. The garden is crowded with plants – an olive tree, a small vegetable patch, a lemon tree, a few flowers. On a bench under the olive tree hunches a man. He and the tree are so similar that it takes me a minute to see them separately.

"Ulgar," Papa says, going forward, "it's good to see you."

The old man straightens slightly. Pale blue eyes under a thinning thatch of grey hair glance from Papa to me. A hand reaches out for the wine skin.

"Boy!" Ulgar roars. "Bring goblets."

Papa pulls me forward. "My son, Samel."

Ulgar grunts.

"How do you do?" I say, deciding to be very polite.

A surprised glance from Papa and a glower from Ulgar. The boy returns with a small table which he sets at the old man's side. Papa brings another bench from beside the door and sets it near the table. The boy brings goblets on a small tray. Ulgar waves him away, returns the wine skin to Papa who pours for us all, including about a finger's height for me. I always drink my wine watered and have never had this kind. The first swallow gets me coughing.

A grin from Ulgar. "Make a man of you." He downs half in one gulp.

Papa tops up the old man's goblet, hangs the wine skin from a branch, and glances around the yard. I want Papa to get right to business, but he's told me many times that there's a rhythm to this kind of talk, like a piece of music. Bees buzz around the flowers; there is a straw hive in the back corner. Butterflies flutter, a bird sings in the lemon tree.

"Peaceful," Papa says. "Relaxing."

Ulgar scowls. "Boring."

"Ah," Papa says, "not enough for you to do?"

"Not enough visitors. My friends have forgotten me."

Papa nods. "Everyone's busy, I suppose."

"Yes, I hear you're composing for the Lord's big party."

"I'm only one of several."

"Still, an honour." The old man drinks more wine.

"You've had your share of honours, Ulgar, in the past."

Papa pours more wine; the skin is half empty. I notice that he's hardly touched his own goblet. The old man cradles his in both hands.

"Not all of us have forgotten you," Papa says. "I, for one, need your aid."

"Ah," the old man nods. "So you soften me up with wine and compliments."

Papa laughs. "Can't put one over on you."

I wish they'd hurry up and get to the point, but I know there's more of the ritual to come. Papa has told me about rituals before.

It's the things people say and do to be polite; also to lead up slowly to something important. It's a way of feeling out the situation, Papa says. If the other person doesn't respond the way you expect, then you can stop in time, before you get to the main point and maybe ask a direct question and get refused, thereby losing prestige. I just hope that the old man will help us.

"My mind is still sharp enough," Ulgar says, "though my body can't move as quickly as it used to."

"It's your knowledge I need," Papa leans forward, "and your experience."

The old man puts down his goblet, turns a hand palm up, slides it toward Papa. "Explain."

"If a person wanted to go north across the desert, would there be maps?"

"Perhaps."

"And what about camels? Do you still know who's got the best ones at fair prices?"

A smile and a nod.

"Good," Papa says. "Samel and I want to travel north in a week or so. We'll need two camels and a well-drawn map."

Ulgar frowns at him. "Why not join a caravan? And find a guide to take care of details. Especially now that there have been those sightings of strange wolf bodies."

"You know about that? I thought the guards were keeping it quiet."

"I still have friends." Ulgar shrugs.

"The guards don't seem worried about the wolves; they were all dead, so we're going ahead with our plans," Papa says. "Our situation is delicate, to do with honour. I don't want to say too much, though I know I could trust you with my life. It's not entirely my story to tell, and you know what hot beds of gossip caravans are."

I sit very quietly, barely breathing because I know this is the important stuff. Papa is very good at this, I realize. He hasn't told an outright lie yet. He also hasn't given anything away.

"Hmm." Ulgar nods. "An experienced guide can be discreet."

"Perhaps," Papa says. "I haven't travelled for years and the only time I crossed the desert it was with a caravan. Still, I think it's best that as few people as possible actually know where we're going. However, if in your estimation, we couldn't do it alone with a proper map . . . or if there are no adequate maps available…"

"No good maps? Hump!" Ulgar draws himself up.

The old man fumbles for a cane and totters to his feet. Papa doesn't rush forward to help, but gets up slowly. I follow his lead, as Ulgar takes one careful step after another to his back door. The boy is there to hold it open.

In the bedroom Ulgar sinks into the single arm chair and gestures at the two of us to sit on the narrow bed. The old man mumbles something to the boy, who opens a large chest at the foot. Ulgar waves the boy away and pulls his chair close. The open lid of the chest hides what he is doing, perhaps on purpose. Papa isn't the only cautious one here. I hear the sounds of rummaging and then Ulgar slams the lid. He places a roll of parchment on top.

"Yarvan, come."

Papa kneels by the old man's side. They unroll the map together. It's cracked and dirty, well used. "Aquila," Ulgar says, "and the route through the desert to the north, with landmarks."

I scrunch over so I can get a clear look. I've never seen a map this detailed before. Can recognize the river drawn in blue to the south of the city. The desert to the north is sand-coloured as you might expect, and there's a dark line meandering through it that must be the trail. Along the dark lines are marks and bits of writing. I guess those are the land marks.

"Are you willing to lend me this?" Papa asks.

Ulgar rocks back and forth. Finally nods. Rolls the map up and hands it to Papa. "Now," the old man says, "the best place to buy your camels is a couple of streets away from the Sand Shrine."

Papa says, "I know the place."

"Say I sent you, and they will deal fairly." Ulgar taps his lips with a finger. "You're an old friend," he says, so quietly, he could be just talking to himself.

Papa doesn't speak. I try to stay as motionless as possible. If Ulgar is about to give us some secret piece of advice, I don't want to distract him. The old man rocks, mumbles a few words I can't catch.

"There's a thing," he says finally, "that we used to do before starting a journey. Some of the caravan guides or leaders still do it."

Again we wait. I wonder what it is about being old that makes you take so much time over things. It should be the opposite, it seems to me. When you know you have only a little time left in this life, why not try to do as much as possible? Speed should be the thing. Of course, I don't say anything.

"The Sand Shrine," the old man says. "Not many remember it or pray to its gods, but there's a reason for the name. Whatever gods once lived and perhaps still live in the desert, the Shrine was built to honour them, so before setting off on such a journey the custom was to go and make an offering." He looks hard at Papa and then at me. "I suggest you do that."

Papa nods. "Is there something special we give?"

"Food. And a prayer or two."

"Thank you, Ulgar," Papa says. "You've done us great service today. If I can return the favour, I'd be only too happy."

"Bring the map back safe," Ulgar says, "and come tell an old man of your adventures."

Chapter XIII

Rowan

When Mirage shakes me awake in the tent, I remember no dreams at all. Angel is saddled, packed, and standing outside along with another horse encumbered with only a rope. Several people have come to see me off.

Grandmother gives me a hug. "My daughter will take you back to your path. All our good wishes go with you."

Angel stamps and paws the ground wanting to be off. So many good-byes, so many people and places that I've left behind. I wonder whether I will ever see any of them again. The thought of going on alone makes a hollow in my stomach, though I recall it's what Julina predicted.

"No long faces today," Mirage says. "Clear sky, a light breeze. Perfect for a race!"

Her horse bounds away, and without waiting for me to give the signal, Angel follows. A cheer rises up behind us and I half turn to wave, then have to grab for the reins as Angel leaps over a low bush. Mirage has pulled far ahead. The sun is washing the east in pink and lavender. I give Angel an extra nudge with my heels and he gallops after the other horse. I'm expecting to see signs of the place where the hunt happened, was it only yesterday? When I catch up to Mirage, she reins in her horse.

"Those low hills?" She points. "You'll get there this evening. Once you cross them, you'll be close to the land of sand."

"I don't see Traders' Road."

"Just a little more riding and we'll reach it. I've taken you farther south than you were yesterday."

"I wish . . ." I hesitate.

"What is it?"

"Couldn't you go with me, at least part of the way down the road, maybe to the hills?"

Mirage shakes her head. "My mother says that you have to do this alone, but you may meet my daughter, Juniper, who is out there somewhere."

"Has she run away from home?"

"Only for a time," Mirage smiles. "Though I miss her dreadfully even so. Many of our young people spend time alone, fasting and waiting for a vision that will give them their adult path. You're doing something like that with your journey."

"Do you think so?"

"Yes," Mirage says emphatically. "If you see Juniper, give her my love."

Soon it's time for another good-bye. Traders' Road unwinds in front of me and wind chases clouds across the sky.

Mirage leans over to touch my shoulder. "Take care of yourself."

I'm riding off again into unknown dangers in the hope that I will find my father and brother, and that they will welcome me. How stupid is that? And yet I have to go, feel driven to look for them, have to try no matter what the result. Is this my own need, something my mother left with me, or a compulsion from another source? I shiver despite the warmth, and wish I still had Mord . Angel is very much here and full of energy, wanting to gallop, so I raise myself slightly and put my weight in the stirrups.

Eventually Angel slows as we reach a small valley with a spring and pool of water. Here we spend the heat of mid-day. The horse browses on grass, I lie in the shade of a bush; I know that I should probably move on quickly, get to my destination as soon as possible, but there's a slowness in my blood, a reluctance to move. The place is so peaceful that I sleep for a long time with no dreams that I remember. Maybe I'm worn out with thinking too much and travelling so far from home. Anyway, it's Angel's nudge that finally pulls me out of sleep's oblivion and by then the sun is close to the horizon. I hurry to get the horse saddled and packed. By nightfall I want to reach the hills that Mirage pointed out to me, but now I don't know if I will.

We cover lot of ground, but even so by the time the first stars appear in the sky there is still some distance to go to the base of the hills. Should I stop and make camp? Now that I'm closer I can see that the hills are not uniformly smooth and that the road winds in and around them. Probably there will be better shelter there than out here on the grasslands. I decide to keep going for as long as possible. I'll slow down on rougher ground, hope that Angel doesn't stumble or put a foot in a hole.

The sky darkens gradually. Flashing and glinting stars begin to appear, jewels on the dress of night. I wish there were someone besides a horse to share this with, someone to talk to. A barking howl pierces the quiet; others follow as if in response. Angel raises his head and snorts. In the north country I would have thought of wolves, but the sounds aren't quite the same. The cries are both lonely and frightening, almost human. Would a pack of wolves attack a single person on a horse? I should have asked Grandmother or Mirage what kinds of dangerous animals I might meet out here. Why do I always forget to ask the important questions? Despite the darkness and the difficulty of seeing the road clearly, I nudge Angel to speed up, because we're quite close to the base of the hills. I can see shadows low to the ground, running along on either side. If they're hungry, perhaps I can distract them with food. I fumble with the straps of a saddle bag and extricate a package of dried meat, drop it. A few of the animals stop, but the rest continue to follow me. I can't drop any more food, may need it myself.

Could I figure out how to use Mother's bracelet to scare the animals away? There might not be enough time, and what if I lose it? Then I remember Corky's gift, search my pouch for the slingshot and handful of pebbles he gave me. I tie the reins to the pommel of the saddle and grip Angel with my knees. The horse seems to sense what's needed for he slows. Carefully I load a pebble, take aim at one of the shadows and let fly. A yelp! I load another pebble; this one misses because the animals are turning away. I hold the slingshot tightly in one hand and take hold of the reins with the other. It's awkward, but I manage. As the ground slopes up I search for a sheltered spot to camp, a place where I can build a fire that will hold off potential predators.

A faint glow to my right suggests someone has a cabin here, or it might be Mirage's daughter. I ease the horse to a walk and turn him in the direction of the light. There is a faint path worn in the dirt. I hear the trickle of water over stones.

"Are you my spirit vision?" The voice comes out of darkness, making me twitch.

Angel's ears go forward. A human shape appears, holding a burning torch which illuminates a young woman dressed in leather, hair gathered loosely at the back of her neck.

"Juniper?"

"If you know my name, you must have come to help me."

"Sorry, I'm no spirit," I respond. "My name's Rowan. But I do have greetings and love from your mother and grandmother. And rather than giving you my help, you could give me yours; I need a place to spend the night."

The lean-to is made of a large piece of tanned hide, thatched grass, and a few branches. A small fire dances at the front. The path I've been following leads past this spot to a spring. Juniper helps me unsaddle Angel and tether him near a shallow pool. In the lean-to I offer to share my food, but the girl declines.

"I'm fasting to get closer to the dreaming world." As I hesitate with a piece of bread part way to my mouth, she adds, "Go ahead and eat, it won't bother me."

I munch as Juniper rearranges her bedding to make room. She

brings a bundle of grasses for a second bed. I give her my blanket and cloak to spread over them. She settles by the fire with me, and as flames light her face, I see that she resembles both her mother and grandmother. I wish I could have known at least one of my own grandmothers. The lack of family hits me the way it has now and then on my journey when I see others with more connections than I. I miss Thea and the twins in a flood of regret.

Juniper leans forward. "What is it? So much pain in your face. Can you tell me?"

"My mother drowned a few weeks ago. I've been travelling to find my father and brother, who I never knew about. Someone is tracking me, I think. That's the short version. "

She sits staring into the night. Tears glint on her cheeks and she is biting her lips. Perhaps I shouldn't have told her so abruptly, but I'm too tired to search for gentler words. After a time, she turns her face to me. "How can you keep going?"

"I was angry."

"And now?"

If I go deep enough there's still a smoulder of anger, but it's less than before. I look at the black sky, the tiny brightness of the stars and the greater one of the moon; they make the night beautiful rather than frightening. "I'm doing what I can to fix things."

She nods and turns back to gaze at our own small light in the darkness. I remember other flames and the visions I saw there. I ask, "Do you ever see things in flames?"

Juniper shakes her head. "Visions," she says slowly. "That's what I've been hoping for, but I haven't had any at all." Then she sighs. "Did my mother tell you why I came out here?"

"Only that among your people it's often done."

For a moment Juniper's face seems carved out of stone, polished and beautiful. Then it cracks as she laughs harshly. "Did she tell you about all the offers I had to partner? Five. And there might have been more if I'd stayed. I refused them all. 'What's wrong with you? What do you want?' they said. 'People partner,' they said. 'Why not you?' I had no answers."

"How old are you?"

"Sixteen summers."

"I'm fifteen," I say. "And if my mother had lived or if I hadn't left, the neighbour's son would have offered for me, and though I like him, I don't want to partner."

"Sisters under the skin, that's us."

I put out my right hand, palm up. She lays hers on top and we clasp, pale and dark. Her teeth flash in a smile. I grin back. Suddenly wide awake, blood pumping as if I've been racing, I decide to tell her everything. All my hopes and fears, who I've met on the journey, the gifts they gave me, what her grandmother told me. It takes a long time. Juniper adds wood to the fire periodically, to keep the coyotes away, she says. That's what was probably out there following me. When I finally finish, my voice hoarse, she lets out a long sigh.

"You're a good story teller, you know? I mean, it's all true, but the way you put it together, the words you choose. Not everyone has that skill."

"Um . . . I . . ." I stutter, "I never think about it much, I just do it. It's as if the words build up inside, all the things that have happened in the last few weeks, and then one day, like steam from a kettle, I have to let them out. I always feel better when I do."

"Hmm. My grandmother is amazing, too. I take my family for granted most times, but when you talk about her, I see her differently."

"Sometimes," I offer, "things or people that are familiar don't seem very special until we're away from them."

She yawns. "We'd better get some sleep."

"Wait," I say. "What I've told you. Don't you have any thoughts or advice?"

Slowly she shakes her head. "That's what my grandmother does, not me. Besides you seem to be doing fine. Are you continuing on in the morning or do you want to stay here a while?"

"I'd love to stay. There's never enough time to get to know people, but I also feel the need to keep moving."

We curl up on our makeshift beds. Stars sparkle above, a lone coyote howls. I can hear Angel snort and stamp now and then, and hope that he'll warn us if coyotes come too close.

***

Light creeps up from the horizon as the curtain of night lifts and three figures on horseback loom against the sky. They have the appearance of Grandmother, Mirage and Juniper. I blink and turn to look at the other bed. Juniper has just emerged from her fur to stretch. I sit up and glance back at the horizon – no one there. I rub my eyes.

"What is it?" she asks.

"I thought I saw you, your mother and grandmother. Must have been a dream."

"Before I went to sleep last night I thought of my grandmother. She's been there all my life, taking care of me, helping me, helping my mother, especially after my father died during a hunt." She shakes her head. "Tonight I dreamt that I walked into Grandmother's tent. She raised her head and said, 'I've been waiting for you.' So you see, Rowan, you were a kind of guide after all. You helped me to see that what I want is to learn to do the kinds of things Grandmother does. I'm going back today to ask her to teach me."

"Sounds right. Do you want to share some breakfast?"

As we eat, Juniper tells me what she knows of the land to the south and west where the traders' road will take me next. Much drier and more barren, though some animals do live there and she's heard that a few people wander through. There are strange formations, columns of sand and stone. She has never seen this herself, but has heard many tales.

"They say," Juniper explains in a hushed voice, "there are bones of great creatures lying partially exposed."

"Dragons, maybe?" I interrupt excitedly. "Like in the old stories."

Juniper shrugs. "Who can say? Not me, anyway. But if you keep travelling along the road you'll eventually come to hills of sand rippled like waves on the water. Sometimes there will be a few plants, a bush or two. Other times a stretch of grasses with a hill of sand sticking out. I've always wanted to see it."

"Why not come with me?"

She shakes her head. "I know my mother's waiting for me to come home, and I'm sure Grandmother is expecting me. This is your journey, not mine."

I sigh. "It's probably for the best. Anyone who's tried to travel with me hasn't lasted very long. Is there anything else I should know?"

"Take plenty of water. I'll give you one of my skins. There is water out there, but it's not always good. And be careful if it gets windy. Blowing sand will make it hard to see and you could lose your way."

We break camp together. She shows me how to leave the place so that there is little trace of anyone having disturbed the land.

"It's a sign of respect to the Great Mother who takes care of us," she says, "and also useful if you don't want people following you. Of course," she adds, "my people wouldn't be fooled. We know how to look for the smallest signs. A bent blade of grass, a few grains of ash, a blackened stone."

"I don't think anyone is following me anymore," I say. "Or if they are, they are so good, I haven't seen a single sign of them."

"I'll check," Juniper says.

She stands at the crest of the hill looking in all directions. Listening, she says, and smelling, but there's nothing unusual. Then she puts her ear to the ground in several different spots. She says she can feel vibrations of what are probably wild cattle passing a long way off, but again nothing that shouldn't be there.

At last we can't put it off any longer; it's time for each of us to go our separate way. We hug each other hard. Just as she is about to shoulder her pack, I put up a hand to stop her.

"Wait." I reach for Angel's bridle. "I want to give you something." I hold out the white feather.

"But this is one of Grandmother's," Juniper says. "If she gave it you should keep it."

"It came from her to Edana and then to me. I think it's meant to go to you now. Grandmother said it was for far and clear vision, so maybe it will connect you and me, help us find a way to keep in touch."

She takes it, and I mount my horse. I follow the road to the top of the hill, then turn. Juniper lopes off through the rippling grass leaving hardly any extra movement behind. Soon, I can't see her at all.

I keep staring at the last place I saw my new friend. She was so sure of herself, and knew who she wanted to become. I wish I had that kind of certainty. I'm following a dream that could become a nightmare or fade away and leave me with nothing.

"Rowan," I whisper to myself. "I'm Rowan."

A hawk screams in the distance. Who is Rowan it seems to say, only a speck in vast emptiness.

Angel saves me – impatient with standing, he trots down the hill. We cross a valley, then another range of hills; there's blue sky and white clouds, a slight breeze. My heart begins to lighten. Perhaps I will find the bones of a dragon, cross a desert, and reach the City of Eagles. And there will be my father and brother waiting for me, asking why it has taken me so long to find them. I laugh aloud at the thought. Three days? Four? A week perhaps. And so I ride that morning in a dream of what could be.

Chapter XIV

Samel

Papa decides to wait until next day to look at camels. He says 'look' not 'buy.' I don't know whether he's just being cautious or has had second thoughts about actually making the journey, however, I pretend not to notice. While Papa is at the palace that afternoon, I go to the market looking for compact and easy to carry food for a long trip. Cheese and bread are too heavy, but dried figs might be good. We'll need extra water skins. Dried meat would probably be all right, also nuts, and tea. I don't buy anything yet, but I've picked out the stalls where food looks best.

At first Papa doesn't want to take me along to the camel seller. He says it'll be tedious, and I'll get bored.

"I'm going on this trip, too," I say. "I want to be there to try out my camel."

In the end Papa relents and we head off together in the morning. It's still cool so we wear our over tunics and long trousers. The early sun lends a glow to pale mud-brick buildings. Some of the narrower streets are covered with archways and the light is quite dim there. Now and then we pass walled gardens where the branches of fig and other trees hang into the street. Papa takes a different route than Ali and I did, and so we come to the Street of Carpets. Shops display their colourful wares in front. If we were to enter and go into back rooms we would see the designers and weavers working there. Now and then a carpet seller nods at Papa and he bows back. I wonder if there's anything to the old tales about flying carpets.

Further on we pass one of the large stone cisterns that store water. Though we live near a river I know that in the past the city has experienced droughts. These cisterns have tall towers over them that catch wind to cool the water. I'm not sure exactly how they work, but Papa doesn't seem inclined to talk, so I don't ask. I have a hard time keeping up with his long steps because I want to see everything.

We hear them before we see them, though I don't know what the noise is at first –deep bellows with an occasional scream. Turn a corner and there are camels standing, kneeling, and walking about. A night-coloured man comes to meet us, and I notice his dagger and a scar on one cheek. To me he looks like a brigand, and I wonder whether he stole the camels. Papa exchanges greetings with him, mentions Ulgar, and introduces us. The man bows, and says his name is Mustafa. He leads us toward a couple of camels that are tethered nearby. One of them opens its mouth and groans loudly. I step back.

"You'll want males," Mustafa says. "They're cheaper." He grins, and bends to lift a foot. "I keep them in good condition, so they can walk far."

Papa goes cautiously closer. "Will they spit?" he asks.

The man laughs. "Maybe. But see how bright-eyed this one is? Alert. I won't sell you a sick camel. Ulgar is a friend."

One of the camels is smaller; I approach it slowly. It seems to be looking back at me and I stop, just in case it decides to spit or bellow at me, but nothing happens. I reach out a hand, touch the long neck. The camel steps toward me. I pet it some more.

"You like that one?" the man asks. "He likes you, too."

"We'll need saddles and bridles," Papa says.

"Have you ever ridden a camel?"

I shake my head, but Papa nods.

"Are you buying these for recreational riding? Why not take lessons before you decide to buy? Not that I mind selling to you, but as friends of Ulgar, I want to be honest with you. Camels are generally quite placid, but they can be hard to handle if you aren't used to them."

I want to see what Papa will say for I know nothing about camels. Papa travelled before I was born, though he's never talked about that until recently.

"I've ridden camels several times," Papa admits. "My son is new to it, but we'll manage."

The man shrugs. "Whatever you want. If you like these two, I'll let them go with saddles and bridles for a good price."

I pull at Papa's arm. "Could I talk to you first?"

We walk a few steps. The camel seller busies himself with his beasts.

"What is it?" Papa asks.

"We'll have to leave the camels, here, until we're ready to go, right? Can I come and take lessons?"

Papa looks at me thoughtfully. "That's not a bad idea. Let's see what Mustafa says."

We walk back together. "Would it be possible to buy the camels and leave them here for a week or so?" Papa asks.

"Certainly."

"And my son, Samel, he'd like to come learn to ride. Are you willing to do that? We could pay extra."

The man waves a hand. "For a little help with the camels, I'll give him free lessons."

***

When I return for my first lesson the next day, Mustafa makes introductions. "Your camel's name is Izmeer."

The camel kneels on the ground and in that position is about my height at the head. I feel as if I should do something, but what? Bow? Say hello?

"The first thing to do when getting ready to ride is to clean the camel's hide." He hands me a wooden rake. "Comb that all up and down his back and sides to make sure there's no dirt and twigs before we put the saddle on."

Izmeer seems to enjoy the raking, leaning up against me and rubbing his neck on the brush. I suppose it's like being scratched in your itchy spots and maybe taking a bath, too. Mustafa also shows me how to put a foot gently on the camel's knee so that he won't get up too soon. After that it gets more interesting. I learn how to put a u-shaped saddle on the hump and adjust it with special straps.

"If you're travelling for several days without much food or water," Mustafa says, "the hump will probably change shape. So you have to be able to adjust the saddle according to that."

I'm not sure what to do with the tangle of leather he hands me.

"You can't use a bit on a camel, the way you do on a horse," Mustafa explains. "Camels are cud chewing. That means they regurgitate any old time and chew whenever they want. A bit would cause problems so some camel riders use a nose peg. That can cause trouble. If you accidentally yank too hard on the reins and pull the peg out, it hurts and the camel will not be happy." I wince and he laughs. "An unhappy camel is bad for the rider; that's why I use a halter round the head and neck and fasten the reins to that."

Izmeer is ready, but am I? Mustafa is waiting, one foot gently on the camel's knee so it won't stand up unexpectedly. I put one leg over, sit down. Curl my legs around the font knob of the saddle the way Mustafa shows me. He hands me the reins, lifts his foot from Izmeer's knee.

"Up!" Mustafa says, and to me, "Lean back."

It's like nothing I've ever experienced before. First I'm thrown forward, but manage to keep my seat. Then I'm thrown backward. I still haven't fallen off and the camel is standing. Mustafa smiles. He leads Izmeer until I get the feel of it. Swaying from side to side turns out to be quite comfortable in its own way. At last Mustafa taps Izmeer on a front leg.

"Down."

I wonder how I'm supposed to do that tapping when I'm sitting way up here. Then Izmeer is swaying back and forth again as he goes down, and I have to hang on. It's odd when I get off and stand on the ground again. I feel so short. Mustafa claps me on the shoulder when I tell him.

"So, you liked your first camel ride?"

"It was . . . different."

Mustafa nods. "Take off his saddle and bridle while I watch. Then we'll tie him up and you can help me clean up the others. Be careful when you tie him; camels have very moveable lips and can untie simple knots."

I don't know whether Mustafa's just teasing or giving me a true warning, but I decide to believe him for now. It's not so easy to remove a saddle and bridle, even from a kneeling camel. Izmeer keeps swivelling his head to look at me. Now and then he groans or bellows. Every time it startles me because I'm still expecting him to spit. Things go well, though, and Mustafa gives me a nod. I slip a rope around Izmeer's neck and lead him to a post. Tie a double knot.

Then I help Mustafa rake the other camels. They all seem to enjoy it. We bring pails of water from a well to a large trough. All the loose camels rush forward as soon as the first pail is dumped. I can see the others' heads going down to work on the knots tying them. By the time we bring the second set of pails, a few more camels are at the trough. Izmeer is among them.

Mustafa laughs. "Looks like you'll have to learn to tie a better knot."

I watch the camels jostle and drink. "I thought they didn't need water all that much."

"Oh, they'll drink whenever they get the chance and usually a lot in one sitting. Survival instinct. They can also go for months without it if they have food that has moisture in it. A couple of weeks without water in really hot desert."

"You've got a fence here. Why do you tie some camels up and others not?"

"I train camels, sell and rent them so I want them to get used to all kinds of conditions and people. Out in the desert there's not much to tie a camel to."

"Where do you get your camels?" I ask.

Mustafa scowls at me and I wonder if I shouldn't have asked. It's really none of my business, but I always like to know things. Finally he decides to answer.

"I have a friend who breeds them. I buy from him. Also from other people if the camels are in good shape."

"They're quite interesting beasts, aren't they?" I say.

"If you see that, you're well on your way to becoming a camel rider." Mustafa grins.

The next days go quickly. Papa is getting ready for the anniversary concert, but he gives me money and tells me to go ahead, buy the provisions I've picked out. I have to spent time with Tamtan and Xylea performing my apprentice duties; the rest of the time I'm with the camels. I'm getting more used to them now and find it easy to mount and dismount. I also learn a couple of really good knots that Izmeer can't undo. Still, working with camels can be a challenge. I get stepped on, spit on, and narrowly avoid getting pooped on.

One afternoon I meet Ali in the street. She looks me up and down. Holds her nose. "What have you been doing?" she asks. "I haven't seen you for days."

"Camels," I say, and add, "It's a long story."

"I thought you were avoiding me."

"Why would I do that?"

Ali shrugs. "I don't know. That's what I wanted to ask you."

"Look," I say, "I don't want to talk in the street and I have to wash. Do you want to come in and wait?"

"I can't. Mère wants me to go and pick something up for her."

"What about after that? I have lots to tell you."

"I'll try." She wrinkles her nose. "You really smell. Make sure you wash well."

Papa won't be home until late, so I take my time cleaning up. I'm hungry and get out half a cold meat pie. I wonder if Ali has had more dreams and wants to tell me about them. Time passes and she doesn't come. Maybe she's angry with me. I tidy up the kitchen and am considering going to bed, when there's a knock on the door.

"Ali! I thought you weren't coming."

"I sneaked out," she says. "Just for a minute. What's happening?"

I tell her what Papa and I are planning. She nods. "It's what you want, isn't it?"

"Yes, it is. What about you? Have you had any more dreams?"

"Only one. You were in a sand storm. There seemed to be other people with you, but I couldn't see any of them clearly. What I could see, though, was that you had the bracelet around your neck, a small drum tied to your belt, and your father's soprano flute in its case over your shoulder."

"Come into the kitchen," I say. "Do you want anything to eat or drink?"

Ali shakes her head.

"Didn't you have a dream about a sandstorm before?" I ask. "At least I thought I saw that in your wall paintings."

She nods. "That dream was brief and vague. I couldn't tell who any of the people were. This time I saw you just as you're standing here now."

"Does that mean we shouldn't go? If we do, will we survive the storm?"

"Well, you'll have camels. I've heard that you just crouch down beside them in a storm and you'll be fine. Besides, you really want to go looking for your sister, don't you?"

"I guess your dream doesn't change anything. Except we'll be ready for a storm."

I put my finger on the table. Follow the grain of the wood as it curves and swirls. That's what sand might do, though it would be all around us, in our eyes and nose, making it hard to breathe.

"Camels can close their nostrils," I say.

Ali laughs. "Is that what you've been doing? Learning about camels?"

I smile. "It's interesting."

"I should get home. Don't stay away from us so long next time."

I get up and walk to the door with her. "Oh, are you going to the Lord's anniversary concert?"

"Of course. The whole family will be there. Mère and Père get special invitations to those kinds of things because of the work they've done for the Lord and the palace in the past. Magenta's intended is in the militia, so he'll be there for certain, though he may have to work."

"See you then, if not before."

Chapter XV

Rowan

After leaving Juniper I ride until mid day, take a brief rest and food, then continue on, dust puffing up from Angel's hooves. The land is dry and there's been no rain since I left Timberton. I hope that all will be well with the grasslands people.

At the top of a hill when I stop the horse for a breather, spread out before me is a huge irregular bowl of a valley that looks as if it has been chopped out of the earth by a mad giant with a hoe and a pick axe. Great columns of earth rise up, some coming to a point; others are crowned with a flat piece of earth or rock as if wearing hats. My eyes want to make sense of it, imagine the shape of an arm or leg, a pair of hands, a partially sculpted face, figures created by someone. Whether this place has been made on purpose or fashioned by chance through wind and water, it's no less astounding. The road leads down.

Strange pale greenish grey plants grow here and there. They have no stems, but rather flat, thick leaves with spines on them. Occasionally there is a bush and clumps of dry-looking grass. As we descend into the depths, the sun casts huge shadows from columns that seem to lean over me. People could easily be concealed here. I ride more and more slowly turning this way and that, until finally Angel stops. I get off and lead him into shade, pulling the reins down to drag on the ground so he won't stray.

"I've got to take a closer look," I whisper. "Stay quiet in case there are living creatures hiding here watching us."

I give Angel a handful of water and take a drink myself. A nearby tower is hard packed earth with small stones embedded. I pry a few out, but they are nothing special. Across the road a wide slanted shelf of dirt rises like a path along the side of a hill more than four times my height. Sun glints off something up high, more stones perhaps. I look around and listen, but hear and see no one. Still, I feel uneasy. The air is hot and heavy, causing sweat to break out all over my body. I need a place to see more clearly, so begin to climb.

Dirt slides under my feet. I reach for a rocky outcrop and pull myself up. Although I'm carrying nothing with me, I feel as if a heavy pack is strapped to my back and it's hard to take the next few steps. A rock loosens and rolls causing me to grab wildly at the next protrusion and I manage to hang on. The rock bounces down onto the road so that Angel snorts and moves away. I wipe sweat from my brow with the back of my hand, look down briefly and imagine falling, rolling, battered against earth and stones. From somewhere above comes the scream of a bird. I don't dare tip my head back and look for fear of sliding down after the dirt and rocks. The distance isn't far, but I can't risk twisting an ankle or injuring myself in a more serious way. At last I crouch at the summit. Slowly I straighten.

Rocks, dirt and pebbles spread around me. Not a place where I would want to live, and yet didn't Juniper say that people did live out here somewhere? I haven't even seen any animals recently. I poke at the dirt with the tip of my boot, dislodge a stone which rolls away from me. I follow it down a slight incline. Stop.

Before me unfolds a pattern of light tan with pale grey lines and curves, a language of bones – ribs, neck, head, and teeth. Spread out to one side is what looks like the shape of a large wing, much bigger than any bird I've ever seen. I have found my dragon. I want to shout and scream, wave my arms, but Angel might run away, terrified, and be lost in the halls of sand columns. And someone might hear; someone I don't want to alert.

Could this place have held a city? I see it in my imagination. Great structures of sun-baked mud, carved with intricate designs. Tall people walk about. Perhaps they had skills with water, knew how to find and collect it so they could grow gardens. Above in the sky, I imagine a dragon patrolling on guard. In stories there's some special power associated with dragon bones and teeth, though I can't remember what it is.

A faint cry comes again and I look into the pale blue sky. In the distance a large hawk or some other bird of prey circles, perhaps waiting for me or Angel to grow weak and helpless. There's no other sign of life. The sun beats down on my head and my throat feels as if I've swallowed a mouthful of sand. I glance into the valley where Angel crops at a small, pale clump of grass. Look back at the bones. Whatever was here, I have no certainties; I don't know what happened to this creature. Did it just lie down and die or was it wounded in a fight? What might it have looked like? I kneel and trace the bones along the back over the head down to the huge teeth. Imagine muscles and skin over bones, leathery green and gold hide, and brown scales.

Under my fingers lies a tooth the size of my middle finger, much whiter than the bones. I pick it up. It slips in my sweaty hands so I clutch and grab. The point of the tooth pierces flesh, draws blood. There's a rushing sound in my ears like water, or wings. The sun blazes along pale bone, hitting my head like the flat side of a sword. I close my eyes and curl into a ball, trying to shelter my head from the heat. If I open my eyes too soon the Queen of Fire might be standing over me with her sword of flame. Though perhaps she'd be friendly; I could use the company. I feel my necklace swing forward over my hands. Through half closed eyes I see Mord's feather touch the tooth, black on white. A cool shadow hides me and when I look up, I see that a cloud has covered the sun.

The tooth, now tipped with blood, lies in my hands. I notice that it has a small hole at the blunt end, perhaps worn by water or some burrowing insect. I should put it down, leave it here with the bones, but there's a voice in my mind that says, no, take it, it could be useful. I slip the leather lace over my head, untie it and add the tooth to the sapphire, wooden beads and Mord's feather.

Before I slide back down to the road, I take a good look all around. Still see no one, not even dust in the distance. If someone is following me, they are far away or well concealed. When I reach the bottom of the hill, Angel bobs his head, as if nodding in agreement that it's time to go. I give both of us another drink and then we head off down the road. With a good dig in the ribs from my heels Angel gallops, stirring up dust. I don't care if anyone or anything sees us, I want to move. Imagine myself riding under the eyes of a gigantic dragon as it soars, wings spread over the valley.

It's late afternoon and soon I'll have to find a place to spend the night, hopefully a place with water, a tree or two. Company would be nice. I've grown used to finding friendly people on my journey, but that doesn't seem likely on this stretch. It's very still and quiet except for the thump of Angel's hooves. Does land listen? Perhaps this land is waiting for something to happen, but I don't like that thought. The road winds in and out among the odd formations that are starting to look ominous to me. Here and there I think I can see more pale bits – bones or other things. I don't stop to look at them. A feeling steals over me, like fog seeping out of the ground in the morning. Death and emptiness, that's what this land is about. I am a small beetle crawling over it, the only moving thing. I had a family once, friends. Now all that's lost, gone forever. I am doomed to wander in this barren place for the rest of my life.

Clouds gather and darken. The sun shifts across the sky to the west. I welcome motion and change, the possibility of rain. But if it does rain, I need to find shelter. Juniper said this was a dry land, and it appears she was right because rain doesn't fall, though more clouds mass, and then comes wind. Bits of dirt and tiny stones fly into my face. Grit lodges in my nostrils and my mouth if I open it. Angel's head is down and he slows to a trudge. The dirt and wind are probably causing him pain. Ahead the road is rising because I can see the top of the valley and some green. With my knees, I urge Angel on; he obeys and trots. I lean over the horse's neck and pull my hat lower.

On the crest I stop to reconnoitre. Clumps of grass and shrubs are scattered about, also more of those odd spiny plants, and it isn't as dusty, even though the wind still blows.

Angel raises his head and whinnies, and so suddenly that I almost fall off, he starts to gallop. I cling to his mane, then grab the reins. The horse tears down the road as if something is after us, though when I manage a quick glance behind, there is nothing but flat land. The valley is no longer visible. Whatever is making Angel run must be ahead, so it's something he wants rather than fears. The road dips and I spy a clump of trees and a glint of water. When we reach the spot, I slide off and give Angel a couple of pats on the neck.

"You're smarter than I am."

He tosses his head and walks to the small water hole. While he drinks, I unsaddle him and remove the packs. There's a hollow near a tree with a circle of blackened stones, obviously a favourite camping spot. I find marks of tent pegs and bits of rubbish; not very tidy campers. I wonder if they are long gone or recent? Remembering what Juniper said about respecting the land, I clean up, dig a hole and bury the bits of leather, an old shoe, a few pieces of twisted metal. Then I brush and curry Angel. It's good to have things to do, a routine, because if I didn't I might spend too much time thinking.

The sun is close to the horizon and I relax for a moment, drinking in the rose, orange, and purple colours that bleed sideways and upward into the rest of the sky. I gather dead wood to make a fire. Heat water and add dried meat, crumbled bread and herbs. Angel stands nearby on three legs, shifting from one to the other while I eat. He doesn't often lie down and I guess this is the way he rests his feet. The first star blinks as I lean against a tree and sigh. If Juniper were with me she would surely have a story or two to tell or I could have asked questions about her growing up.

"Just me to talk to myself," I say out loud.

Angel snorts.

"Yes, I can talk to you, but you don't say anything in response."

The horse tosses his head. I smile and go back to contemplating the sky as more stars appear and a waning moon creeps over the horizon. The fire snaps, sending out a sweet smell so I wonder what sort of wood I'm burning. At home I would have known. I remember Thea and her twins and wonder what they are doing, probably asleep. I yearn to see them walk and talk, to feel Thea's hand stroking my hair. It has been a long day and I'm so far from home. All that has happened in the last weeks can't really have happened to me. Who am I, this girl sitting out here under a huge sky, with only a horse for company?

On the other side of the fire golden eyes glow. I straighten slowly peering across flames that dazzle eyesight. Ease to one side. The eyes move and a shadow shifts – red-brown body, shape of a plumed tail, paler face and muzzle. Sharp teeth in a grinning mouth.

"Hello, fox. Are you the one that I saw before?"

The animal raises its nose, flicks its tail and fades away into darkness. Angel hasn't made a sound. I wonder if that means my horse is petrified with fear or not in the least concerned. When I glance at him, I can't tell if he's asleep or not. I'm glad to know the fox is out there, another living creature nearby. Perhaps I should be afraid, but the other fox didn't harm me. I throw a few more pieces of wood on the fire, find my blanket, arrange one pack as a pillow and stretch out. Above me the sky is a dark curtain with stars like pin pricks, holes where light can come through. I close my eyes.

Open them on a dark place where, no matter how wide I stretch my eyelids, no light shows. This must be what total blindness is like. I bite my lips to stop a scream. Underneath my legs is hard stone. I feel around, but there isn't anything else within reach. The darkness is a thick blanket around me and I'm starting to have trouble breathing. It seems to me that I am in a vast chamber; I sense great space. Then in the distance, a spark of light. I sit up and stare. The spark grows as it comes closer. I don't want to see the hand that carries that light, the face behind the lantern. I throw up my hand to shield my eyes.

"Ouch!"

I have hit myself in the nose. A ray of sunlight lances through the branches and leaves of the tree under which I lie. Angel stands nearby, cropping grass; there is no other human or animal in my vicinity. I shiver and pull the blanket around my shoulders. Moisture beads its surface, and now that I look more closely, I see the morning dew on plants and the ground. Perhaps I dreamt the red fox last night and certainly the dark chamber. I haven't minded the dreams about my father and brother, but this last one I don't like at all and hope it's not a foretelling of what will happen to me.

Most of that day and the next passes in blessed monotony. Arid land, a couple of deep valleys with the strange formations, now and then a small water hole. The first of these Angel will not go near, and I don't blame him, for the water smells rotten and there is a crust of white all around the edge of the pool. The next is fine and then two more are crusted with white. I'm glad that I took the opportunity to top up my water skins when the water was drinkable.

The sun thrums like a drum on my head so I wear a hat all the time and light clothes that still cover my arms and legs because I don't want to get a sunburn. It's good I brought a cotton shirt and pants for they are much cooler in this weather than the leather breeches and long tunic I've worn for riding before. When I change clothes, I think of Edana, Ma Parnell and the boys. I wish I could talk to them, get Edana's practical advice. I'd even welcome a chat with Julina.

I scan above in the vain hope that Edana might have sent Mord with a return message for me, but of course she wouldn't do that, for I explained why I was sending him back. A few wisps of cloud scatter across the blue sky. Sweat drips into my eyes, stinging, and there's no breeze at all to cool the skin. Under Angel's feet insects rise and whirr about us for an instant, then fall back to earth. At least none of them are biting. I remember one of the stories in the leather book. It was about an angry god that had sent insects to eat all the crops, a punishment for some action or inaction of the god's people. Heat could be a punishment, too, and dust. I imagine what the gods of this place might look like – tall and sand coloured, leathery skin, harsh, dry voices. I clear my throat and the sound is loud and incongruous.

Ahead the road stretches straight to the horizon. I sigh at the monotony of it, then blink. Is that a shimmer of water, a huge blue lake stretching to either side? We continue on and the lake is still there, but it isn't getting any closer. Angel doesn't raise his head and snort or sniff; he doesn't gallop. I have heard of this. People imagine they see all kinds of things – water often, but also buildings sometimes, cities. It's like a vision, but more dangerous because it can lure you into a false sense of hope. I might urge Angel to gallop and we could ride and ride without ever reaching that lake, ride until Angel is exhausted and can go no further. I shake my head and rub my eyes, but water still lies ahead – enticing, deceptive, and dangerous. No, I won't look at it. Better to watch the road in front of the horse's feet. The sun's motion across the sky is imperceptible. The day feels interminable. I hope that eventually we will reach evening, sunset, darkness and cooler air.

I pull at the water skin hanging near my left knee, bring it up and squirt a stream of water into my mouth. Some drips down my chin and I rub it into my face, let some dribble over my wrists. Angel snorts and stops as he smells the water. I get down and give him some in my cupped hand. Pour a little down my neck, more to Angel, realize the skin is half empty. I check the other one. How can it be half empty, too? I haven't drunk from it at all. And then I feel the moisture at the bottom – a leak. Quickly I uncork the leaky skin and tip it to run into the sound one. I have to be careful for both have narrow mouths and we can't afford to lose any more water. Angel paws the ground as if impatient to be going, but I don't let him distract me. There is nothing more important at that moment than saving as much of our water as I can. After I finish I try to figure out how the leak might have happened. Had Juniper been my enemy after all and wanted me to fail? She could easily have poked a small hole in the water skin she gave me, but I don't believe that. There were sharp tree branches at the camp, stones on the ground where I left my packs. It could have happened anywhere. All I can do now is be careful and watch for water.

That's when I notice that the sun is hidden behind clouds. I stuff the damaged skin into a saddlebag, hang the good, full one carefully around my neck and climb back onto Angel. I hope it's going to rain. Even if we are caught in it I will welcome the wet, and Angel probably will too. He responds willingly to my urging and gallops down the road as if scenting a warm and cosy barn at the end of it.

No rain falls; instead wind begins to blow from the southwest, lightly at first, then more strongly. It picks up dirt and loose bits of plants, tiny stones. I stop Angel and get out my breeches and leather jacket. My skin needs all the protection I can give it. Unfortunately I can't do the same for Angel.

At first, it's not too bad, just uncomfortable. I can still see to follow the road. On my left a large pale mound looms out of the whirling dust. I wonder if it's another illusion or more of the strange packed earth formations. A gust of wind lifts a handful of sand up and flings it into my face. I close my eyes just in time. When I open them again, Angel has stopped head down, and I can see nothing but a curtain of sand closing us in. I slide off the horse's back, wrestle my cloak loose and drape it over both our heads. We huddle there, battered by wind, sand, and stones, protecting each other. I fall into a doze standing there leaning against Angel's neck.

I seem to hear the sound of great wings beating around me and a high, sighing singing, like a lullaby. My mind struggles with this to determine if it's good or bad, but my thoughts are sluggish as if pushing against a wind in my head. Finally I give it up and merely lean against whatever I'm leaning against and don't bother thinking at all.

A long time later the thing propping me up moves. I lose my balance and slide down into softness to find myself half buried in sand. The horse struggles and kicks until he is free again. I do the same. Above us is a clear night sky with stars and a bright quarter moon. Except for heaps of sand scattered over the road and around us, all sign of the storm is gone.

I check my remaining water bag; it's intact and full. I give both of us a drink. Then I pull on my cloak against the chill and begin to lead Angel forward. This is hard at first; both of us sink into the sand and I have to search carefully to find signs of the road. In the wash of moonlight I notice a post or bare tree trunk on the right. As I draw closer, I can make out a board with faint letters scratched on it. I trace the indentations with a finger. 'Tra er Roa' it reads.

I mount Angel as the going is easier now and we move carefully forward with many stops so that I can dismount and search the ground. More than once I wish that I had learned some of the lore of reading direction from the moon and stars. Or that I had Mord to guide me, or even that Nesgor still rode nearby. But I have to find the way alone, though the horse seems to have a sense of the right way to go. Perhaps he can smell the road, the lingering scent of all the feet and hooves that have followed it. We walk at least half the night, for the moon is just past its zenith when I see the unmistakable shape of trees ahead. At that point, I don't care whether there is water or not, just some kind of shelter where I can lie down and sleep. Angel, too has been walking slowly, head down. I unsaddle him, put down my packs, stretch out with them, and cover myself with my cloak.

"Good night, moon," I whisper just before I close my eyes. "Watch over us, please."

When I wake in the morning, I remember no dreams, and there are no creatures sitting and watching me, only Angel nudging my shoulder. I give him water. As he breakfasts on coarse grass I eat dried meat and stale bread. My provisions are running low, which worries me. With the food Grandmother Wisdom's people gave me I should have had plenty. Have I been travelling longer than I realize? Moving through dreams and visions? I consider turning back, going home, but what if the trails fade, and blowing dust obliterates the road? The land is equally empty in all directions. I may have to forage, though I can't make a meal of grass like a horse and I've seen no berries. There might be roots however, that I can dig and roast or cut up in a stew with a little of the meat. Tonight I decide will be soon enough to try that.

"Come, Angel," I say. "Another day of dull travelling; I feel as if we've been going forever. Are there still people out there somewhere I wonder? Will we ever see them again?"

I scan the sky and it's clear. That seems hopeful, though yesterday the storm crept up on me unawares. I resolve to be more watchful today.

Just beyond our campsite more hills of sand rise on either side of the road. They are attractive in their own way, rippled like water and coloured by the early morning sun. A patch of sand on one of the dunes shifts creating a pattern of light and dark. Then I gasp as the sinuous length of a snake winds its way over the ground. Angel must have seen it at the same moment, for he shies and gallops away. It takes time for me to slow and quiet him. At least the snake shows me there is meat of a sort if I become altogether desperate for food. Still, I hope that I won't have to resort to figuring out how to capture and cook a snake, especially since I don't know if they're poisonous. After that I look more closely at the vegetation and at the dunes. Here and there I discern tracks of small animals. Some of the plants have blossoms. I stop Angel when I think I see a wild rose bush. Indeed it is. Angel begins to munch on the flowers, seemingly immune to the thorns. I find a couple of handfuls of last year's rose hips, dry but still good. They'll make a useful addition to my evening meal. There is a variety of animal and plant life here. If other creatures can survive, I hope I can, too.

We reach a small grove of trees with a tiny spring bubbling out of the ground. There is a patch of lush grass and an obvious camp site with a flat rock that can be used as a table and several smaller ones for seats. I think of the caravans that must have stopped here and wish that I could have been part of one. Even though it's barely mid-day, I decide to stay at this spot and spend the night. Angel and I need the rest, I can top up our water skin in the morning, and meanwhile, I can search for plants, roots and berries to supplement my food supply.

Not too far away is another sand dune; my curiosity gets me up and moving. I have put on my coolest clothes again, wear my broad brimmed hat, and my boots. At the edge of the dune I stop, kneel down and sift sand through my fingers. It's fine as flour, sliding through my hands like water. On impulse I slip off my boots and socks, jump into the sand. My toes curl, dig in and I race up the side of the hill, sand sliding under me, but never causing me to lose my footing. When I reach the top I see that there are other dunes in the distance, some smaller others larger, but most surrounded by areas of grass and scrub. Down at the campsite, Angel is placidly sipping water at the spring. Farther on, the road curves around a large hill and in the distance beyond that it seems to me that I can see the faint outlines of mountains against the sky. Another trick of the light. I know that there are mountains to the west, but surely they are too far to see from here. A puff of dust in the distance glimpsed out of the corner of my eyes brings my gaze to ground level. I squint, trying to see what is causing the dust. Can't tell whether it's moving toward me or away. Finally I give up. The sun sinks toward the horizon. I contemplate the long slope of sand below me. Giggle, lie down and roll like a child, over and over, scattering sand until I reach the bottom with a thump that jars my teeth.

Back in the trees with Angel I rig a small lean-to. Now and then, I gaze to the west, but the clouds have shifted and no mountains show on the horizon. Neither can I see any sign of dust or creatures that might cause it. In any case, if someone or something is on the way toward me, I will know soon enough. I keep my sling shot close by, also a thick cudgel that I shape from a dead tree branch. Neither of these will offer me much protection from a pack of coyotes or a group of people bent on attack. Even one strong warrior could easily overcome me. However, I feel better making the preparations.

Chapter XVI

Samel

Nothing noteworthy happens in the days leading up to the Lord's concert. Papa is preoccupied, occasionally short tempered; that's not unusual when he's got an important project coming up. I keep out of his way and pay no attention when he snaps at me. He doesn't really mean it. Both of us have new clothes for the event – loose indigo trousers and white embroidered shirts. We wear black robes over that because it gets cool in the evening.

A crowd makes its way toward the palace and we join the river of people. Papa greets old friends here and there; I look for Ali and her family, but don't see them. The moon has just risen and the sky is still quite light, but torches and watch fires burn on the walls of the palace casting a warm glow over everything. The large main gate stands open, though there are several members of the militia there to check carefully that each person has an invitation.

More guards wait inside directing everyone along pathways and through passages toward a large courtyard. Here chairs have been set up in a semi circle around the area where the musicians will play. The Lord and his family will sit above in one of the balconies. Special guests also have a place on the balconies. Papa has to go and be with the musicians now, but one of the guards leads me upstairs. It feels odd to have this kind of honour, though I know it's because of Papa. Then I see Ali waving to my left.

"Excuse me," I say to the guard, "could I go and join my friends?"

He inclines his head and leads me to the spot; Ali makes room. Magenta is on the other side of her, then Mère, Ivoire and Père. Ivoire bounces and keeps scooting forward to lean over the balustrade. Mère pulls her back.

"I want to see," Ivoire grumbles. "Look at all the people and their fancy clothes."

Ali shrugs at me as if to say, what can you do? But I agree with Ivoire; it's exciting. Not only are there rich and well known people of Aquila, but space has also been reserved on the main floor for special, less well off guests. I recognize my favourite cheese seller from the market; he's brought his plump wife and little boy. Across the way in another balcony I notice Tamtan's oldest apprentice. Tamtan himself will be part of the concert orchestra. Xylea is playing as well. Here and there sit various officers and officials that I've encountered now and then around the palace. I look for the old man I got the drum from, but don't see him. There are lots of men with white hair and beards just as Papa said. A few people are arriving at the largest and most central balcony – minor princes, and cousins, uncles and aunts of the Lord and his wife.

Ivoire rushes forward to lean over again. Two men have entered the courtyard. One has long flowing black hair, warm brown skin, and is wearing a green robe richly embroidered with gold thread. I glance at the other man, take a second look. It's Mustafa, the camel seller, dressed in baggy purple trousers and an embroidered pink shirt. Ali nudges me.

"Look," she whispers, "the Captain of Eagles."

Coming up the stairs with an honour guard of two militia is a man wearing the eagle helmet of beaten silver and gold. Only the Captain of Eagles is allowed that privilege. In some situations he would have an actual live eagle perched on his shoulder, but eagles don't like crowds. A wide leather baldric crosses his chest from the left shoulder; this is where the eagle would dig in its talons. I remember the eagle that I saw with Papa that day and don't know how anyone could carry such a weight, but perhaps the Captain chooses one of the young ones. The Captain enters the main balcony and stands near the back.

"I used to want to be Captain of Eagles," Ali whispers.

"What? Girls can't . . ."

She stops me with a jab in the ribs. "Of course they can," she says. "Don't you remember the story of the eagle that the first Lord saved?"

"Yes, but there wasn't any captain in that story much less one who was a girl."

"Hah!" Ali breathes. "You don't remember. The Lord put one of his soldiers in charge of looking after the eagle's safety. I remember that eagle was female and didn't like any of the men. The story goes that she flew around the camp screaming until the Lord's young wife came out of her tent. The eagle landed at her feet and bowed. So the first Captain of Eagles was a woman."

"I don't remember that. Are you sure you didn't make it up?"

Ali scowls at me and is about to speak when a trumpet blares. Immediately everyone stops talking, and looks toward the main balcony, which is to our left. A trumpeter stands there. The trumpet sounds again and we all rise to our feet.

First the standard bearer carries in the flag, a gold eagle on a silver background. He walks to the opposite side of the balcony from the trumpeter. Next, a few officials enter – the Lord's soothsayer, his military advisor, and the civilian administrator. They all remain standing. The Lord's brother and his family take their places. Finally the Lord, his wife, and the prince arrive and sit down. The trumpeter blows once more and the rest of us take our seats. Everyone is still looking at the main balcony. The civilian administrator gets up and crosses to the balustrade.

"Welcome one and all." This concert marks the beginning of the special celebrations that will be held for the next three days in honour of Lord Davus and Lady Domitilla."

I tune out the administrator, looking at the crowd below, trying to see people I know. Though the sky has darkened, torchlight and firelight brightens the courtyard. There's the baker from the market with his family, and just down the row from them, my two least favourite apprentices from Tamtan's. I draw back, but they haven't noticed me. I glance around the balconies instead. To the right of us I catch a glimpse of a white beard, look again. Yes, it's the old man I met before. He nods at me then drifts behind a pillar. The administrator has finished speaking and Lady Domitilla rises.

She's no longer young and has let her hair go white, but people say the Lady is still beautiful. I can't see her face clearly from where I sit. Her back is straight and she moves gracefully to the balustrade. People begin clapping. She inclines her head and waits for the applause to stop.

"Thank you people of Aquila," she says in a well modulated voice.

I've heard that she was a singer many years ago, before she married the Lord. The training still shows. Papa says that when you're a musician you have to pay attention to all kinds of sound – voices as well as instruments – and so I do.

"Lord Davus and I are pleased to welcome you to this evening's concert. The finest musicians in our city are doing us the great honour of playing tonight."

More applause. Again the Lady waits until it has ended. I notice that Ivoire is fidgeting again. Mère puts an arm around her to hold her still. I'm feeling restless myself. I want to hear the music.

"I know that you will give them a warm welcome and your greatest attention. Let the music begin!"

Everyone claps and stamps as the Lady takes her seat, and I'm sure I can feel the balcony vibrating. I hope it's strong enough. Another burst of applause as a group of young men and women run into the centre of the courtyard. They take places in front of their drums. Tamtan walks in, bows to the Lord and Lady, then to everyone else.

Tamtan crosses to the big drum at the centre. I've seen this one up close and it's bigger than me. He takes the two sticks out of his belt and starts the rhythm. The other drummers follow. The sound seems to get right into my skin as well as ears and every other part of my body. I become one with the beat and the drums. Sometimes I close my eyes, but only for a few seconds because I like to see the motion of the drummers. They too are part of the beat, fused with the drums. I'm always impressed that they can drum so hard and so long, always moving. I know that I'll never be as good as they are on any drum because they live and breathe their music, practise many hours a day. Tamtan asked me once if I would like to join one of the troupes. I was honoured that he would even consider me, but knew that I didn't have the discipline to work so hard at one thing almost exclusively. I'm too interested in many things.

After the drummers have played several numbers a strolling harp player wanders among the audience. This gives time for the drums to be removed and a large harp to be put out. I recognize it from Xylea's store room.

The strolling player leaves as Xylea, in flowing robes of burnt sienna, arrives. The silence is almost absolute, only a small rustle here and there. Even Ivoire has stopped twitching. Xylea sits on a stool by the harp and all other movement stops in the courtyard. Harp music always reminds me of water – fountains, waterfalls, babbling brooks, rain. But Xylea weaves in other sounds, I don't know how – wind in trees, branches bending in a storm, a child's laughter, the cry of a baby. I close my eyes and float away on a raft full of people, all of us enchanted. When Xylea stops playing the silence continues for a moment before applause erupts.

The city administrator stands at the balustrade again. "There will be a short intermission. Vendors of food and drink will pass through. For anyone who needs wash room facilities, members of the militia will direct you."

"Amazing," Ali says. "Now I can't decide whether I want to be a drummer or a harp player."

"Too late," I say. "You should have started when you began to walk."

She shakes her head at me. "Samel, I was joking. You've gotten far too serious lately."

"Sorry. It's just that I'm around both Tamtan and Xylea a lot and I know how much their apprentices practise. Never mind the masters themselves. They've had a lifetime of playing."

"Hmm." Ali nods. "It's like my sisters and me. Mere says we were practically born with paint brushes in our hands."

"All good painters, though you're the best of the bunch."

"Not better than Père!"

"He's had more years than any of you." Watching Ali and her sisters, I can't help but think of Rowan. What would she make of this concert? Is she musical or does she paint or have some other thing she loves? I hope that soon I'll see her and can ask her all the questions in the world.

"Ali, Samel," says Mère, "do either of you want food?"

A vendor stands nearby. Ivoire is already chewing bits of cooked meat on a stick. Ali and I get a couple of sticks each. Then wine and water sellers come by. Mère has thoughtfully brought a couple of the family's wooden goblets, which we share. Also, a couple of cloths to wipe our greasy chins and hands.

Then the city administrator is back, tapping the balustrade with a stick that looks like one of the ones from Tamtan's drum troupe. "People of Aquila please take your seats again. The final performance of the evening is about to begin."

While everyone was busy concentrating on food and drink Xylea's harp and stool were moved to the side. Several more stools were brought in, also a small drum ensemble. Now Papa, Tamtan, Xylea and other musicians take their places. Papa has his flutes of course, and there is another flute player. As well, there are a couple of musicians with box zithers and trumpets.

Tamtan stands in front of the group and bows to the main balcony. "My Lord and Lady, this piece of music has been especially composed for the twenty-fifth anniversary of your wedding. May you have many more years of ruling together over the people of Aquila."

Music is like life in a way. There are different instruments just as there are different people. They all have their own voices and their own stories. When a group of people get together it's interesting to listen to the anecdotes they tell about their lives, some happy, others sad. This music makes me think of a bunch of really entertaining people at a party. They start off quietly enough, Papa with the soprano flute, just a little tune. Then the box zithers join in singing a duet, telling their story together. Tamtan adds a few notes from the drums, his comments on what has already been said. Xylea strokes the harp and everyone else listens, then chimes in, building on previous themes. And so it goes. Absorbing, humorous at times. Now happy, then sad.

I look around and see that Ali is listening with her eyes closed and her chin in her hand. Maybe she's seeing pictures that she'll paint later. Magenta has her eyes closed too, and she's gently swaying to the music. Ivoire has crept up to the balustrade and is leaning on it. Mère and Père are holding hands. It occurs to me that the music could be like a couple's life, might be telling the story of the Lord and Lady's marriage.

I sigh deeply. Wonder whether I'll ever be able to play as well as Papa or compose music like this. Is that what I want to do? I always thought that I would grow up to be a musician of some kind, that's what all my training has been. Finding out that I have a sister has changed things; the most important thing for me now is to find Rowan. After that I might be able to think about the rest of my life.

The music draws to a close, and ends with a rousing, triumphal movement that all the instruments join in. The musicians stand, bend in thanks. The Lord and Lady come to the balustrade and stand, clapping. The crowd rises to its feet, cheering, clapping, stamping. The musicians bow again. They are smiling.

"Whew!" Ali jabs me in the ribs. "No one will forget that in a hurry! It makes me want to go home and paint."

Chapter XVII

Rowan

Angel neighs and at that moment I spy a rider approaching from the west. Clutching the cudgel in one hand and the sling shot in the other, I wait. Then, remembering that I have something much better for protection, I drop the slingshot and fumble with the ties of my belt pouch, reach for Mother's bracelet. The horse is black as are the clothing and accoutrements of the rider. As they draw near, I see that both figures are overlain with a fine powdering of dust as if they've ridden hard for some distance. The rider raises a hand in greeting. This does not look like the beginnings of an attack, so I relax my grip on the cudgel and tuck the bracelet out of sight.

"Greetings!" the stranger calls.

By now I can distinguish a slim build and shoulder length reddish-brown hair. "Good day to you," I respond.

The stranger's horse stops a short distance from me. A wide smile, white teeth, a tanned face; it's the face of a woman. She swings easily from her horse, bows slightly to me. There's something odd about her eyes.

"May I share your camping spot for a night?"

I spread my hands. "It doesn't belong particularly to me."

She laughs, and steps closer, widening her eyes and I see that they are brown flecked with gold. "Of course not," she says. "But I was being polite."

"Please," I say charmed by her looks and manner and happy to see another woman out here. "I'd welcome the company."

"It's been a long and dusty ride. My horse will be glad of a rest, some food and water."

"Plenty for all. Can I help you unsaddle?" I take a couple of steps forward.

Her horse blows, showing teeth and backs up.

"He's skittish," she apologizes. "Doesn't let strangers touch him."

"I'll just get out of your way, then."

She smiles her thanks and leads her horse to the other end of the grove of trees where she tethers him and begins to unsaddle. I putter around, not wanting to seem inquisitive or nosy, but I manage to sneak a glance or two. Tooled and carved saddle and bridle with silver inlays, plump filled saddle bags, a sword in a black leather scabbard. This woman does not look like a casual traveller; in fact, despite finding her interesting, I should remember that she could be dangerous so I will remain alert.

The sun is sinking and I'm hungry. I gather branches, smaller bits and pieces, get out a pot, fill it with water and set it on the stones. My flints are still in my pack and I am rummaging for them when I hear a clearing of throat.

"Can I start the fire for you? I've got my tinderbox handy." She's standing nearby, right hand on her hip, left holding the box.

"Thank you."

"Varonne."

"I beg your pardon?"

"My name."

"Ah!" I smile. "I'm Rowan."

"Good, now we've met."

She bends to light the fire, and her movements seem familiar. Have I seen this woman before, perhaps on the streets of Timberton?

She straightens. "Will you allow me to share some of my food with you?"

"Of course! I have dried meat and herbs that will make a stew, but otherwise, I'm low on supplies."

Varonne returns to her saddle pouches and comes back with a string bag. "A few potatoes and carrots."

"Excellent! You can't have been travelling long if you've still got such stuff."

She shrugs. "I ride fast."

"Do you know the roads and trails of this country?"

"Adequately."

I cut up the vegetables and add them to the water. Toss in salt, stir, put the lid on. Varonne watches, not offering to help, hands on hips. She's keeping her distance, like her horse.

"Have you ever been in Timberton?" I ask.

She shakes her head. "That's a town on the edge of the forest? Is that where you're from?"

"Hmm," I respond. "Have you come a long way?"

"Fairly far."

"It's just that I haven't seen any other people," I say, "and I know it's a traders' road."

A shrug. "Not as much travel as usual this year. Listen, I'd better give my horse a good brushing."

She turns and I watch her lazy amble, notice the way her eyes shift under half-lowered lids, and her head moves as she scans not only the area around us, but also the sky. Obviously she has a knowledge of this place I will never have, possibly senses dangers I am too ignorant to be aware of. I can't decide whether to trust her or not. If I had to choose I would say that she reminds me more of Julina than of Edana. She takes good care of her horse, though, works hard at getting the dust out of his coat. Untangles mane and tail, taking it slow. Recalling how I have poured out my life story to Edana and others, I decide to be more sparing with my words this time. Still, Varonne is a woman, and on this journey of mine, women have often been helpers and guides. I add a handful of dried meat, a sprinkle of thyme and parsley to the stew.

A bird screams; Varonne spins, scanning the sky.

"There." I point to the south. "Is it a hawk?"

"Perhaps."

'Nothing to worry about?"

Her face is blank, but then she smiles. "I think we're safe for the night."

I nod, stirring the stew.

"Smells good," she says, easing herself onto a nearby rock.

"Should be ready soon if you want to get your bowl and spoon. I have only my own, but you could eat out of the pot in a pinch."

"No need for that. I have utensils."

All the time we're eating I wonder about Varonne. She seemed so friendly at first, but now she's become much quieter. I want to know what she knows about this land and what I might expect in my travels. I'm also curious about Varonne herself. What weapons has she mastered? Has she fought in battle, killed someone? The person sitting across from me sipping stew could be a real hero, a woman who has destroyed monsters and saved people. If I ask will she help me, dare I tell her about myself? I try not to look at her too much, but she must sense my interest, because when she puts down her bowl, she glowers at me. Then the frown is cracked by a smile.

"I suppose your curiosity is natural," she says.

The heat of a flush rises in my face. I duck my head and concentrate on scraping the last of the stew out of my bowl. Varonne doesn't say anything more, and finally I raise my head again. She's still looking at me.

"What do you want to know?" she says.

"Umm, I ah you, that is, the country, I was wondering how much farther this land stretches. The dry part that is."

"The country." She glances around. "To the southwest, in the direction you're heading, it's three days hard riding until you reach the lands of the Lords of Ameer, but even then you'll ride through desert until you get to Aquila. If you want to go in another direction, there's a fork in the road about half a day from here. Follow that and it will take you to the mountains in about seven days. It all depends on where you're going."

"Oh. Yes, of course." She is waiting for me to tell her. Instead, I ask boldly, "Where have you come from?"

An infinitesimal shrug of one shoulder. "Here and there."

"It must be fascinating to travel all the time, seeing different lands and people."

Her look is shrewd. "You should know. Haven't you been doing the same?"

"Only for a short time, not like you. That is, I don't know, but you have the look of someone who travels constantly."

"I guard caravans now and then," she says, offering this snippet of information with a hand gesture, an open palm toward me, indicating that it's my turn.

"There were no caravans available when I started out, so I couldn't join one. I suppose it would have been better, safer, if I'd travelled with others."

Again that tiniest of shrugs. "Have you had much trouble?"

A long ululating cry pierces the evening, and I jerk, dropping my bowl.

"Other than wild animals," she grins. "It's only a coyote. They're generally harmless to people."

"Not always," I say. "A pack of them chased me a few days ago."

"Oh?" She isn't looking at me now, rather scanning the deepening shadows around us, as the sun disappears behind the horizon. "Perhaps we should build up the fire."

"But you have a sword!" I exclaim. "Surely you're not frightened of a coyote or two?"

She stands. "A bow and arrows, too. No, I'm not frightened, though it never hurts to be prepared."

I watch her circle our camp muttering to herself. Is she looking for animal tracks? Surely the horses will give some indication if coyotes or other dangerous beasts come close. I leave her to whatever she is doing and clear up from our meal. Then I arrange my bed in the lean-to.

"Turning in already?"Varonne says, coming up behind me. She gestures to the sky. "The stars are just coming out and the moon hasn't risen yet."

"Are the stars the same everywhere?" I ask. "Do they have different names in different places?" I point toward the north. "Where I come from we call that group Mother Bear."

"Night and it's time for stories?" she says sarcastically, it seems to me. "My people call it the King's War Chariot. But you must have encountered others in your travels. Didn't you ever talk about the stars before?" She perches on a rock across from me.

"And that over there is her cub," I continue, stubbornly.

"Or the Prince's Chariot. And nearby is the Dragon."

"Where?" I peer into the sky.

"Wait until it gets darker," she laughs. "Then we can tell stories all night."

I yawn. "Have you ever seen a real dragon? Or even its bones? Maybe you've killed one."

She is silent for so long that I wonder if she's dozed off and I am half asleep myself when she says, very quietly. "Have you seen a dragon's bones?"

Her words pull me awake; it's my slight befuddlement that saves me from blurting too much. "Dragon? Where would I see a dragon?"

"There are stories," she says lazily, "that dragons lived here once, but they died out. Somewhere in this land ancient bones lie hidden. Whoever finds dragon bones will find potent strength."

"Really?" I yawn to give myself time to think. Should I tell her? There is something about her tone of voice, however, that I don't like. "Have you ever found any?"

"No," she mutters. "Though not for lack of searching. Lately I've had a feeling that I'm very close."

My hand clutches for the tooth hidden beneath my shirt, but turn the movement into a scratch of my nose instead. "So that's what you're doing out here?"

"And you?" She snaps out suddenly. "What are you doing?"

"I'm on a journey. To visit relatives."

"Alone? Have you no friends? Other relations? People who care about you? Worry about you?"

The back of my neck prickles. The prickles move down my arms. "That's a lot of questions," I say, and rise. "I think we need more wood. It's getting very dark."

She doesn't follow, but lets me fumble alone in the shadows. Beware of people asking too many questions. Did I start this by asking too much of Varonne or has she been looking for me all this time? She arrived from the wrong direction to be following, though if she does know this part of the land thoroughly, she could have been riding cross country. There is really not much I can do at this moment. If I wait until she's asleep and try to sneak away in the night, she'll likely hear. Someone like her would sleep always with one ear cocked and an eye half open. That picture in my mind makes me giggle, but I disguise it with a cough. I want advice, a friend to talk to. Once again I realize I've been a fool to set off on this journey by myself, have just been lucky; so many things could have gone wrong. On the other hand, I might be seeing shadows where there aren't any. Varonne could be the guide I need. Just because she asks questions and doesn't answer many might mean merely that she is cautious as befits a warrior who travels alone.

Each of my friends in turn comes to mind, and I imagine what they'd say to me. I can hear their voices in my head –

Thea: *Come home, Rowan, we're waiting for you.*

Edana: *Your horse can usually save you if you give it a chance.*

Julina: *Remember illusion can be your friend or enemy.*

Juniper: *Jump on your horse and ride like the wind!*

Mirage: *Be careful.*

Grandmother Wisdom: *One step at a time. This is your journey to take. You will do what needs doing.*

I wait behind a tree with an armful of wood and stare across at Varonne. She's turned slightly so that I can't see her face. In trees nearby her horse makes a dark shadow. Angel is tethered close to where I stand, but the ground here is littered with bits of wood and other plant debris. I am not skilled enough to sneak anywhere so I walk forward and deposit my armload of wood by the fire.

"An exchange," I say. "I'll tell you where I'm from and where I'm going if you tell me the same."

A shrug of one shoulder. "Why not."

"I'm from the north and left there when my mother died. I'm going down to Aquila to visit some relatives."

"My home is in the mountains to the west. I'm footloose and fancy free, and also without a mother."

"I'm sorry," I respond, wondering if this is truth or merely a way to create empathy between us. "I know how hard that can be."

"It was a long time ago."

There's something in her voice – pain, anger, or both – that makes me think she hasn't gotten over it. I wonder how long it takes. Clear my throat. "No particular destination?"

"Not at the moment."

I study Varonne's face again, those strange eyes that seem cold now, though maybe it's sadness. I want to say something comforting, but I'm sure she wouldn't welcome sympathy, would probably see it as weakness. I wonder whether she's from the same part of the mountains as Thea and my mother. Since I don't know the name of that city, I can't ask Varonne.

I yawn. "I'm going to sleep."

A short nod. "I'll stay by the fire."

Tucked in my lean-to I can neither see nor hear Varonne. Is she moving around the camp, creeping about to do me harm? Stop it I tell myself and yawn again. I hear a hawk's scream, but that's silly, they don't hunt at night. Owls do, at least some owls. Big eyes, heads able to turn almost completely around. Long wings spread out, gliding silently over the land.

Chapter XVIII

Samel

The next day Papa stays home to rest. I don't have any apprentice work to do because Tamtan and Xylea are recuperating as well. I tell Papa I'm ready to go find Rowan any time. He hems and haws, but finally says we could go in a couple of days.

"We'll wait until the Lord and Lady's anniversary celebrations are over," Papa says. "It would be rude to leave while they are still going on."

I remind him of Ulgar's suggestion that we visit the Sand Shrine. "What about tomorrow afternoon? We could see Mustafa afterwards and tell him when we'll need the camels."

Papa agrees.

After lunch the following day I'm in my room putting on my new clothes again. It seems fitting to dress up to go and see a god or goddess.

From downstairs, I hear Papa. "Samel! I'm ready to go. What are you doing?"

I find the bracelet in my trunk and slip it onto a piece of leather around my neck. On impulse I tie on the feather the eagle left behind that day at the palace. My shirt hides everything. The miniature drum I made is lying next to my bed so I pick it up, tie it to my belt. Music might incline the gods to be favourable to us. I go to the head of the stairs.

"Papa, could we take your soprano flute?"

He comes out of the kitchen carrying a small bundle. "I've got bread and cheese for an offering," he says. He glances at the drum on my belt. "You think they'd like music as well?"

I nod. Papa shrugs. I take that for agreement and run into his room to get the flute in its bag.

In the streets, musicians wander through the crowd playing small harps, flutes and drums. Food vendors with temporary stalls set up here and there call out their wares. Children yell or scream. People laugh and talk. It's hard to move quickly. I'd forgotten there's a performance of acrobats later this afternoon at the outdoor amphitheatre, so I guess people are out early, getting ready and celebrating. Maybe Papa and I will finish our business in time to go to the performance. I stick close to him as he uses shoulders and elbows to make his way. Because the Sand Shrine is in the opposite direction from the amphitheatre, there are fewer people as we get closer to our destination. Papa has brought a water skin and I'm glad. The sun beats down on us making me sweat.

"What's the story of the Shrine?" I ask as we walk under the cracked arch at the entrance.

"All I know is that there used to be walls around it and more buildings, but most of that has crumbled to dust. I've heard it said that the shrine was here when the first Lord of Ameer came to build his city."

"I wonder if the caretaker could tell us more?"

Papa just shrugs as we walk along the winding dirt path outlined with stones. When Ali and I came we ran across the grounds to the right where the olive grove stands, and avoided the shrine itself. I don't see any other people at all. The only complete building left standing looks like a smooth hill of sand pocked with dark holes. There's an arched doorway in the middle. As we get closer I see that the building is of mud bricks, pitted and worn with age. Some bricks are missing altogether and it gives the building a precarious air, as if it's going to collapse any minute.

"I don't want to go in there," I say.

Papa stops. "This was your idea."

"I know, but now . . ."

A figure dressed in white is moving in the darkness of the doorway. At first I think it's the old man from the palace, though why he'd be here, I don't know. As the person comes closer I realize that it is a different old man, totally bald.

"Greetings to you," he says. "The Spirit of the Shrine is pleased you've come. Enter."

Papa gives me a nudge. The man turns and Papa follows, looking back at me. Slowly I move my feet forward. It's much cooler inside than out, and very dark. If it weren't for the moving blotch of white just ahead, I wouldn't know where to go, but gradually my eyes adjust. I notice that light does enter here and there through the holes left by missing bricks. I relax; if I don't like it I can easily find my way back out. We walk for quite a while and this surprises me because the building didn't look that large from the outside.

"We're walking in circles," Papa whispers to me, as if he knows what I'm thinking. "Or a spiral into the centre probably. It's an ancient sacred form."

"Hush," the caretaker says. "Compose your minds to meet the Shrine Spirit."

A final turn and the light is so bright after the semi darkness that I'm temporarily blinded. We've entered a circular open space with a large hole in the roof. The sun blazes down on us and onto a low sort of table. The old man stands beside it.

"Leave your offerings here. Say your prayers. I'll return at the proper time." He slips away.

Papa and I step forward. He places the wrapped bread and cheese on the table. Whispers to me, "That's probably going to be the old caretaker's supper."

I snort a laugh, quickly suppress it. "Do you suppose there really is a spirit of the shrine?"

"We're here, so we may as well act as if it's true."

With all that light pouring down, I feel dizzy. Papa pulls out his flute, nods at me and begins to play. I give my drum a tap. The tune Papa plays isn't one I recognize, but we often improvise together so it's not hard for me to follow his lead.

As we play I see sand in the desert, sliding across sand. Sun beats on my head. The heat spreads down my body, centres at my chest, at the bracelet. I throw a quick glance at Papa, but he has his eyes closed and is swaying to the music. I tap the drum again speeding up the beat. Papa follows on the flute. A puff of sand rises in front of the altar, whirls around it and is gone. Another, larger puff of sand billows, picks up more sand and swirls between me and Papa. The thin wall of sand grows thicker as I watch. My throat is dry. How can this be happening with Papa here? I thought he had a way to stop the bracelet from working. I stop drumming, but the wind doesn't stop. It's keening now, and I think I can almost distinguish words. I can hardly hear the notes of the flute.

"Papa!" I yell. "Stop playing!"

I race toward the wall of sand, and through it, grab Papa's shoulder. He turns to me, takes the flute from his lips.

"What's happening?" he says.

"I don't know!"

We stand in a vortex of stinging sand that obscures everything around us. I can barely see Papa. Both of us put away our instruments, but the wind doesn't die down. I'm shaking as Papa tries to move us toward an invisible door. The wind holds us back. A gust whips our clothes about and I can hardly stay upright. My feet leave the ground.

Papa's hand grabs and tightens on mine. "Hold on!" he yells.

Chapter XIX

Rowan

I'm in that state between waking and sleeping when you're still aware of things around, but dreams are tugging at your mind. Through my eyelids I can see a glow of light, faint as if from a candle or two, almost as if I'm back in Julina's bedroom and she's bending over me. There's a tug on my belt and a soft curse.

I sit up. Varonne is crouched not far away. She has the fingers of one hand in her mouth.

"What is it?" I ask.

She drops her hand. "Snake," she says.

"What!" I leap up, scattering blanket and cloak, nearly cracking my head on one of the poles of my lean-to. "Where?"

"No, it's all right." Varonne stands more slowly than I did. "I thought I saw a snake crawl toward you, but it must have been a shadow cast by the fire. Sorry I woke you."

I search the ground carefully; see no mark of a snake or any other animal. The horses are quiet. Varonne has curled up in her cloak and seems to have fallen asleep. I turn my back on her and examine my pouch; it's intact. I think she may have been trying to get into it. Was she looking specifically for the bracelet or did she just want to steal my money? I don't like this. I put a few pieces of wood on the fire, rearrange my blanket and cloak, lie down. I'm going to rest, but plan to stay awake.

From a height I view a battle: not one with armies, soldiers or warriors, but two wild creatures in a duel of sorts. A great white-headed eagle, legs and claws extended, swoops over a red fox. The fox rises on its hind legs, mouth open, teeth glittering. Blood already marks fur and feathers. A whirl of red, white and brown motion. Then the fox lies panting on the ground, while the eagle hunches a distance away, one wing extended. If I can get closer and grab a stick, I'll chase them away from each other, but I'm held motionless. Again the eagle attacks and the fox retaliates. More blood spatters.

"No!" I shout.

I come awake to the first light of dawn illuminating the campsite. Angel stamps and nickers softly. Of Varonne and her horse, there is no sign. I rub my eyes, shake my head. Was all of yesterday late afternoon and evening a dream? No fox sits watching me, and there is no eagle in the sky or anywhere that I can see. I wrestle myself free of my bed and stand up, shiver and grab my cloak to pull around my shoulders, continuing a scan of the surroundings. Cold mornings and blistering hot days – an odd climate.

"So where are they?" I ask rhetorically, as I stand by Angel, stroking his nose.

"Where's who?"

I spin. Varonne, leading her horse, moves along the edge of the dune just across the road. She is wearing a black leather helm, also a breast plate of overlapping leather scales. A sword hangs at her side and a bow over her shoulder.

"Are you leaving?" I ask.

"No, having a look around."

As she steps forward and ties her horse to a tree, I notice that she is limping. "Was there trouble? Are you hurt?"

"My horse shied at a snake and I fell off," she says. "Nothing to worry about."

"A lot of snakes about lately," I say. "I was just going to make breakfast."

She nods in response.

We are back to minimal talk; maybe Varonne isn't a morning person. I blow dirt off the flat rock and put out dried meat, a small piece of stale bread and two wizened apples. Varonne fiddles with her saddle bags, then brings a chunk of cheese and half a loaf of bread.

"Is there any town or village close by where I might get more food?" I ask as she sits.

"Nothing until a day out of Aquila."

"And from here it's more than three days to the City of Eagles?"

She nods, then asks, "Have you enough food?"

'I can manage on two meals a day instead of three."

"If you're not delayed by a sandstorm or other problems."

"Like what?"

"I've heard of raids occasionally on caravans. There are landless, lordless men out here who live by violence. Alone, you'd be even more vulnerable than a caravan."

"But I've seen no sign of any people other than you, up to now."

"You've been lucky, then."

I stare at her. Too lucky perhaps. I look around wildly, half expecting to see raiders creeping up on us. Is she telling me the truth or a lie?

Varonne holds out a palm. "Sorry if I've scared you. You're so young, you shouldn't be out here by yourself without adequate protection." She taps her fingers on the flat rock where the remains of our breakfast are scattered. "Look, I don't want to push you into anything you might not want to do, but I could travel with you. If you'd like."

There are no answers in the scrub around me. No response from the sand dune or the road. No one is there to help me make up my mind. Just this woman who I don't entirely trust. But what choices do I have?

"Yes," I say, "all right. We'll ride together."

We clean up, kill the fire, get the horses ready. It's still early. If we ride hard until dark and don't run into any problems we might make it more than half way to the lands of Ameer. Perhaps by the afternoon of the second day, whether Varonne continues on with me or not, I can reach the village she spoke of. My back is to Varonne as I adjust Angel's girth. I reach into my pouch and briefly touch the circlet of leaves. Help me, I whisper in my mind. The bracelet warms briefly against my fingers.

"Ready?" Varonne is mounted; her horse stamps, impatient to be gone.

I swing into my saddle, nod once and nudge Angel hard with my heels. He jumps into a gallop, tearing down the road as if a pack of coyotes are after us. Varonne is left in our dust, and I hear her shouting behind me, though I can't make out the words. I grin and bend low over Angel's neck.

"Go, Angel, go!" I yell into his ears. "As fast as you can!"

Drumbeat of hooves and my heart thumps as hair whips around my face. I don't know how hard and long Angel can run, but I realize that I've never really tested him before even when we ran from the coyotes. He is giving me his absolute best and it's more than enough to keep ahead of Varonne with her black horse. Let raiders come. We'll outrun them too. Whenever I glance around there is no one except Varonne, and she isn't catching up any time soon. Scrub grass, bushes, and the occasional dune flash by, landscape as usual. The sun blazes brightly and the sky lies blue and clear above. A perfect day for a ride. I whoop and holler to celebrate, and Angel takes it for encouragement, puts on another burst of speed.

"Take it easy, boy," I mutter, "don't hurt yourself."

Angel slows to a more reasonable pace, and whenever I look, Varonne is well behind. The road descends into a small valley with a tiny stream running through it. I give Angel a quick breather and a drink. For myself, a wizened apple and a moment to fill the water skin, then off we go again. When the sun is close to its zenith I notice a tall post in the distance. This must be the place where the road forks if Varonne told me the truth. At the same moment I see dust clouds rolling along toward us from the west. Wind and sand! And there is no shelter to be had. I throw a glance behind and gasp, for

Varonne has almost caught up.

Then the sandstorm is upon us, grit in my eyes, nose and mouth. Angel stops. I slide off and huddle against him, hoping that Varonne will have to stop, too. No one could see in this. The wind howls like a crazed monster, sand whirls, abrading exposed skin. It seems to me that I can hear a voice chanting or is it merely my ears putting words to the howling?

"Wind blow, sand swirl!" The voice becomes louder and more clear. "Lift and carry, bear them to me!"

I raise my head and try to peer through the sand. See shapes dimly – horse and rider, and two more figures. One of them calls out, words I can't discern in the howling noise. Someone lunges at me, feels for my arm, clasps my right hand. A young face close to mine, with gold-flecked eyes. I try to pull away. The wind is tugging at me, too, loosening my hold on Angel. My feet leave the ground.

"No!" I shout, but wind and sand swallow my voice.

I try to grasp for my bracelet with my left hand, but it flails uselessly in the turmoil. My head whirls along with the wind; I grow dizzy and disoriented. Am I really flying through the air? I attempt to look down and around. Sand blows into my eyes, my nose. I can't see, can't catch my breath. Can't

Here Be Dragons

Chapter XX

Rowan

Wind whirls a blast of abrasive sand into my face, then there's silence. I open gritty eyes; still can't see, for thick mist has taken the sand's place. Shivers shake my body, rattle my teeth as I rub my face. Because feet and hands find no solid surfaces, I must still be suspended in air, although I can't feel motion. I'm glad mist is hiding the truth – how far up am I? This feels like real sorcery, greater than anything Julina ever did. It's so quiet that I wonder if I've gone deaf.

My stomach lurches as I drop suddenly, then stop. A sour taste invades my mouth so I swallow, hoping to avoid throwing up. My hair flutters, floats up from my head. I swallow several more times. Another quick drop and my feet hit hard. I stagger, fall to my knees, grunt in pain. Can't see through the mist.

"I was on my way! Why did you do this?" The voice is loud and angry. Varonne?

A deeper voice answers, "It looked as if she was getting away. Now, let's welcome our guests."

The mist swirls and thins. Sunlight blazes into my eyes and I blink away tears. Shapes of stone walls and towers loom. I lurch to my feet. Four other people stand in a courtyard – a white-haired, slightly stooped old man wearing a fur trimmed grey cloak, the back of a black-haired man in dark robes, a red-haired boy in a white shirt and baggy blue pants whose face is turned away, and Varonne.

Someone gasps, then shouts, "You!"

"Ah, my dear Samel," the old man says, "We haven't seen each other since the Lord's concert."

My breath stops at my brother's name. I step toward the boy with hair like Mother's. He pays no attention to me, but stretches a hand toward the black-haired man.

"Papa! Are you all right?"

"How do you know this man, Samel?" the dark-haired man asks gruffly.

I'm stunned to silence and immobility. Have I really been united with my father and brother? If Varonne knew who I was why not tell me?

"Let me make the introductions," Varonne chimes in.

"Yes, daughter, do," the old man says.

"A family gathering," Varonne bows, then says each of our names. "Greetings, cousins."

"What!" I swivel from one to another, then turn back to Varonne. "You're related, too?"

Samel and his father step forward in unison. "Rowan?" They say my name as if it's the first word of a song, their voices harmonizing.

My fingers flutter at my side as the two stop an arms' length away. A daughter should reach for her father, a brother for his sister, but we are strangers to each other, though both their faces are familiar from dreams and visions. Their eye-colour is gold-flecked brown – like Varonne's. Am I dreaming or is all this real? And if it is real, why should I trust any of them? I step back.

The man looks hurt, but the boy nods; perhaps he too feels confused. He pokes an elbow in Varonne's direction. "A friend of yours?"

"She came to me in the desert. And who's he?"

"An old man who lived in the Lord's palace at Aquila."

"Illusion," the old man says dryly, then adds, "You know all about illusion, don't you Rowan, my dear?"

"What does he mean?" Samel whispers. "Why does he speak as if he knows you?"

My head spins, perhaps from the wind, maybe because I'm reminded of Julina. Could that woman be involved in this? Have helped to bring me to this place? There are too many coincidences. My knees feel watery and my heart beats rapidly, but I manage to straighten my back.

"What do you want?" I glare at the old man. "Who are you, really and why have you brought us here?"

"Weren't you listening?" He shakes his head. "Too much like your father." He points at Varonne. "My daughter." Then at the robed man. "My nephew, Yarvan."

"So, Papa, you do know him," Samel says.

Yarvan puts an arm around Samel's shoulders. "I wish I didn't, wish I'd paid more attention when you mentioned the old man at the palace." He shakes his head. "I tried to keep us away from here."

"Will someone please explain what's going on?" I snap.

"Enough!" the old man thunders. "You're all here because I wanted it. I planned it, I made it happen. I've been watching all of you for years waiting for exactly the right time, for moon and stars to be aligned, for ages to be right, for events to fall into my hands. I have great patience." He smiles at Yarvan. "I was the wolf, of course." Points at Varonne and nods at me. "She was the fox. We have abilities of shape changing and enchantment, spellcraft. Did you think you'd escape me? No, don't speak."

It wasn't a coincidence that Varonne found me in the desert. It's as if while gathering herbs I noticed a poisonous weed among the plants. I want to yank Varonne's hair, yell at the old man and Yarvan. Samel is the only one I'm feeling in the least friendly toward. His face is red and he's frowning. A tightness in my throat makes it impossible to speak.

"We don't need to be enemies," the old man says. "For those of you who don't know, my name is Hrashak, Lord of this bastion and the mountains around it." He flicks his fingers and my throat loosens.

The old man bows slightly, then spreads his hands. "Welcome."

Samel snorts and I shoot a frown at him. Maybe we should try not to antagonize the old man until we find out more about him; he seems quite powerful. Samel appears to understand because he gives a small nod.

Yarvan holds out a hand to me, palm up. "Whatever your plans, Hrashak, these children have no part in them. Let them go, send them home. Your business is with me."

Hrashak throws back his head and laughter echoes around the courtyard. When he stops there is no hint of a smile on his face. "Don't act like more of a fool than you are, Yarvan. I'd hardly call them children. I think they're old enough to speak for themselves, to make their own decisions."

Yarvan opens his mouth. Harashak flicks his fingers and Yarvan is mute, but that doesn't stop him. He takes a run at Hrashak, hands outstretched. Varonne pulls her sword and steps into Yarvan's path.

"No, Varonne!" I shout. "He's unarmed."

Hrashak waves Varonne away. As soon as she steps to the side, Yarvan is on the move again, until the old man speaks a few unintelligible words. Yarvan freezes like a statue, though his face is still mobile. He glowers.

Samel rushes forward in turn, but stops near Yarvan. "What have you done to him? Why can't I get closer? Let him go, now!"

"Or what?" Hrashak takes a step toward Samel.

Instantly I move between them; it's like a reflex to protect my brother. Despite his stoop, Hrashak is a little taller than I and his eyes glitter. My bones feel as if they might turn to liquid at any moment and I wonder if he's doing that. The old one throws back his head and laughs again. The laughter cascades over me like ice water. I want to clap hands to ears, curl up and cower. A warm hand slips into mine.

"I'm with you," Samel whispers, "and so's Papa, even if he can't move right now."

My impulse is to refuse Samel's help. He's my younger brother, after all, and I've just found him. An older sister should be a protector.

Still, Samel isn't a child and he's nearly as tall as I; maybe together we can get out of this. I squeeze his hand.

"Tell us what you want," I say to Hrashak. "Perhaps if you treat us well, we'll help you."

Now Yarvan's glower is turned on me, but I ignore it. After all, he and Mother probably set this whole thing in motion many years ago, so at least some of it is his fault. I'm not going to let him or anyone else make decisions for me anymore. I wait with my brother quiet beside me. Varonne stands nearby, sword sheathed, arms crossed.

Hrashak smiles. "Good," he says. "At least one of you is sensible. I can reciprocate. This conversation will go better indoors over food." Loudly, he calls, "Guards!"

Four tall men in leather armour carrying unsheathed swords arrive and surround us. Hrashak murmurs under his breath and Yarvan can move again. He doesn't speak, but continues to throw black looks at everyone. Hrashak leads the way inside. It's dark so that I have trouble seeing. Our footsteps echo along a stone passage.

Chapter XXI

Samel

As my eyes adjust to the dimness I notice that my sister has slipped close to Varonne. My sister! It's amazing. I move forward to hear a whisper.

"Aren't you ashamed?" Rowan says softly. "We're your relatives, family. Why treat us like this? We could be friends."

Varonne shrugs one shoulder as if trying to get rid of a flying insect that has settled there. She doesn't turn or answer. I study the woman's profile. It's stern and unyielding.

"Remember the desert?" Rowan prods. "You helped me."

"Only on my father's orders," Varonne tosses out of the side of her mouth.

"Do you always do everything that your father tells you to? Even the best of parents can be annoying. Don't you ever stand up for yourself? No one's right all the time, not even parents."

Varonne is frowning now, but whether it's because she's thinking over what Rowan has said or just angry, is impossible to know. As I wait for Rowan to say something more, to try to push Varonne to some action, the guards close up behind and the moment is lost.

I fall into step beside my sister. We are related and yet haven't seen each other since we were tiny. I think about nudging her shoulder as if accidentally, but refrain. Don't know how she will react; don't want to start off wrong with her. I remember the way Ali and her sisters touch and scuffle, chatter and tease each other. Rowan doesn't look very friendly right now, but I have to know.

"Mother," I whisper, "is she . . .?"

Rowan grabs my hand, squeezes it and nods once. She's looking straight ahead. I squeeze back. I couldn't speak past the lump in my throat even if I found the right words. I guess I was hoping that Papa's dream was wrong. Now I know that I'll never see my mother. Before I really have time to take this in, Varonne stops and I let go of Rowan's hand.

We've reached a door where a barrage of delicious smells hits. Inside a table is filled with dishes of hot and cold meat, breads, cheese, fruit, plates and goblets. A guard pushes me forward. Hrashak sits at the head of the table, Varonne at the foot. Two of the guards guide Papa to a chair on one length of the table and sit to either side of him. Rowan and I, separated by a guard, are seated opposite. There are only spoons by our plates. That's going to make it awkward to eat some things, though I can hardly keep from grabbing one of every dish in sight. My stomach rumbles.

"I've taken a few elementary precautions," Harashak says. "No sharp objects. Meat, cheese and bread are already cut for you. Feel free to eat with your fingers. There are napkins for wiping afterwards."

"Do you think this will soften us?" Yarvan sneers. "What if we refuse to eat?"

"Your children are practically drooling with hunger."

I stop the hand reaching for a piece of bread, and Rowan, who had bent toward a plate of cheese, leans back in her chair, clasps her hands in her lap and clamps her lips together. I wonder whether Mother looked like this sometimes.

Papa glares at Harashak, then grimaces at Rowan and me. "Go ahead, eat. We need to keep up our strength."

"Very wise," Hrashak nods.

He reaches for a chunk of cheese and a slice of bread. I snatch a slice of meat with one hand, flip it onto bread, and grab an apple. Rowan watches as Papa studies the table and chooses three figs. Rowan reaches for a piece of cheese. Varonne nibbles at a handful of nuts. None of the guards eat anything.

"Well," Harshak says, "this is the way it should be. All friends together."

He looks sideways at Varonne who stops eating immediately. Harshak tips his head slightly. Papa stares with narrowed eyes at his uncle.

"What do you want?" Papa says. "Tell us now!"

"Why did you run away from home, nephew? There was a place for you here, there still is, for you and your children, too. It's a large fortress, plenty of room for all of us, even with all my soldiers. We could have a good life, though you do like to run away from responsibilities don't you?"

What is the old man is up to now? Rowan has stopped eating as well. I'm aware of the bracelet lying warm against my chest, wonder if it could help me. I hope Hrashak is not aware of the circlet or its capability. Does Rowan have our mother's?

"You know why I left, Uncle. My father . . ." Papa shakes his head and throws two untouched figs unto the plate in front of him. "Just tell me what you want."

Hrashak doesn't answer right away. Papa and the old man are taking their time getting to the heart of the matter. Playing the overture before reaching the themes of the music.

"As you no doubt know, your children have special abilities," Hrashak says finally. "Just as you do, and just as that woman did."

"Our mother," Rowan says. "Her name was Zarmine." She is scowling at Papa as she speaks.

It occurs to me that our mother may have said bad things about Papa to Rowan. Probably Papa hasn't told me everything that happened when we left the north, split up our family. There are so many questions, so much I need to find out. Rowan and I can ask Papa, but our mother is beyond questioning. I'm thinking of Mère, how she scolds her daughters sometimes, comforts them at others, ignores them now and then. So much I've missed. But Hrashak is speaking and I need to pay attention.

"None of you have taken real advantage of your abilities. Perhaps you aren't fully aware of what you can do, or maybe you're afraid. Well, I can help. Caution is wise, but I've studied hard and long, read old scrolls, put my own gifts to various tests."

"You're wasting time," Papa interrupts. "I won't help you."

He's trying to get Hrashak angry. Papa explained once that anger can be a tool to get what you want, but if you let it control you it might cloud your judgement and you could make mistakes.

The old man isn't getting caught so easily. He smiles. "If you hadn't run away you would have seen what I wanted." He pauses. "The might and weapons to conquer Aquila."

"What?" I can't believe he's serious.

"The City of Eagles?" Rowan says.

"My rightful inheritance," Hrashak nods.

Now it's Papa who begins to laugh, throwing back his head, tears running down his face.

Hrashak waits for Papa to stop and when he doesn't, the old man thumps on the table. "Enough!" he bellows. "You think it's humorous that I've been thwarted of my rights time after time?"

"Aquila?" Papa snorts. "How can you possibly think that's your inheritance?"

"It doesn't matter, you don't need to know. You're not a part of this any longer. You gave up your rights when you ran away. It's your children I need to speak to." Hrashak nods down the table. "Rowan, Samel . . ."

"No!" Papa shouts. Leaps from his seat, knocks his chair over, causing guards on either side to jump up and grab him by the arms. "You will NOT involve my children in this, Hrashak. I forbid it!"

Is this real anger? I wish I knew for sure what Papa is trying to do so that I could help. It's all bewildering and I'm tired of listening to an old man rant. I need a chance to talk privately with Papa and Rowan.

"When can we go home?"

The moment the words come out of my mouth I realize that I sound like a small boy. To hide my embarrassment, I frown at Papa who is standing between two guards. Papa slumps and shakes his head.

"He's right, though," Rowan gets up, more slowly than Papa did. She glares at Hrashak. "You have no good justification for keeping us here."

"And the Lord of Aquila will be looking for us," I add, "with his militia." I hope that's true though how will they know where to look?

"Enough!" Hrashak shouts. He rises to his feet and raises his arms.

Darkness descends, like a curtain falling across a window.

Chapter XXII

Rowan

Underneath my back is a hard, cold and lumpy surface. There is no sound. My stomach roils and my head spins as I sit up and open my eyes on darkness. Clamp them shut again, rub them, then widen them once more in an attempt to capture whatever light there is. Still the same view of nothing, like a thick blanket around me. If only I could wake lying in front of the fire at the cottage with Mother walking in the door, have this all be a dream. I taste blood, feel pain, realize I've bitten my lip. The darkness doesn't go away. They say that if you feel pain and don't wake up it can't be a dream. We've been captured by an evil wizard and there's no knight in shining armour riding to the rescue.

A groan. That sound didn't come from my mouth, so one or more of the others could be here as well, or some other prisoner.

"Hello?" My voice is faint in vast emptiness.

"Anyone there?"

It's what I intended to say next but someone else has spoken. I grope around. Nothing but rough stone and dirt under my fingers.

"Yes," I say. "I'm here. But I can't see anything."

"Wait," the voice responds.

For a while nothing changes except I hear a few grunts and the odd curse. I consider offering to help. The voice didn't sound that far away, but it wouldn't be easy to find each other in the dark and there might be holes and obstacles.

"Ah! Got it. Now," the voice continues, "picture light. A candle flame maybe. Concentrate."

I want to ask why, and is that you, Samel? It would take too long to speak all the questions I have. So I think of a candle, try to imagine the flame bright, steady. It's surprisingly difficult staring into darkness trying to picture a candle burning. I close my eyes to make it easier. Decide to choose one of the candles in Julina's room, a thick red one with an extra large flame. If I still have her pouch . . . I fumble and find it at my belt . . . I could take a pinch of that powder Julina gave me and throw it on the candle to make it flare up so we could see in the dark.

"Ouch!"

The word is a duet, two voices shouting it out at almost the same moment. My eyes fly open as I jerk my fingers away from the bracelet which I touched while investigating my pouch. The glowing bracelet drops onto the stone floor with a clang, flaring up into silver fire that is mirrored by another flame just a short distance away.

"Should have let go of the bracelet before picturing fire." Samel's gold-flecked eyes stare at me.

I shake my head. "Am I dreaming again? I saw you in dreams so many times. This light, the bracelets, are you doing that?"

"You saw me in dreams, too?" Samel grins. "And Papa? Did you see him?" His grin turns to a frown as he looks around. "Where is he?"

We are in a large stone-floored and stone-walled room. I can't see any doors or windows, though the bracelets have created only a small circle of illumination. I shiver, teeth chattering. Wrap arms around myself, but that doesn't make me any warmer. I try holding my hands near the bracelet.

"Weird, isn't it?" Samel says. "The flames I mean. Sort of hot and cold at the same time."

"I wonder where we are?"

"In a dungeon?"

I rub the base of my neck. "My back aches as if I've been lying on rocks for hours, and my head is thick, like I've been drinking poppy seed elixir."

"Or as if we've come in during the middle of a piece of music and we're supposed to play, but no one's given us the score."

"I don't know what you're talking about."

"It's a tangle, like a messy knot." Samel bites his lip, takes a deep breath. "Is our mother really dead?"

I feel tears prickling. I've not cried much about Mother, but now, thinking about this boy, my brother who probably can't remember his mother who drowned, it all just rushes over me. I rub my eyes.

"I'm sorry."

I gulp. "You're sorry?" Rage surges, making me want to leap up and start pounding and kicking against the stone walls. I push it down – useless. "They started it! Our mother and father, when they had the bracelets made."

Samel shakes his head. "No, before that, Hrashak. He wants to be Lord of Aquila."

"Do you think he really meant that?" I remember Grandmother Wisdom telling me of a man who wanted something from me, and not to trust him. "He may want something else entirely."

Samel shakes his head. "I don't care what he wants. I want to know all about you."

In bits and pieces, crying a little now and then, we tell each other what we know, moving gradually closer, nudging the glowing bracelets forward with our feet, so that finally we sit an arm's length apart, the two lights between. I study my brother's face, see our mother there, despite the unusual eye colour. Nose and chin are the same and a way of tilting the head when asking a question. Maybe I have characteristics of our father. Will we make the same mistakes our parents did?

As if in answer to my unspoken thoughts, Samel says, "You look like Papa, you know? The way you frown.Your hair and ears."

"So, where do you suppose our father is and what is Hrashak doing to him? Mother kept me in the dark about so many things. Was Papa (the word feels awkward in my mouth) any better with you?"

"Sis, you ask a lot of questions," Samel says. "Reminds me of me."

Water wells in my eyes. Samel puts out a hand. "Why are you crying again?"

I shake my head, tears flying. "Sis. No one ever called me that before. Brother."

Samel sucks in air. "Yes, it's different when someone says it to you." He stands and stretches. "I wonder if anyone in Aquila realizes we're gone?" he muses. "I've lost track of time."

"No one would miss me yet. I was travelling alone in the desert. Trying to reach you and him."

"The caretaker at the shrine will have seen we're gone, but he might think we just walked out, unless he was in on Hrashak's plot." Samel rubs at his eyes. "People at the Lord's palace will realize eventually that Papa is missing. Tamtan and Xylea will notice I haven't come. Ali will wonder where I am."

I wonder who all these people are, but don't ask. "We should try to explore. There's got to be a door or window somewhere and maybe we can use the bracelets to open the locks."

"Except how do we carry the bracelets while they're flaming?"

We find a couple of loose flat stones on which we can support the circlets. Then we locate a wall and follow it around. At one spot there's a glow on the wall near Samel's shoulder. He puts out a finger to touch a shiny black stone. It pries easily out of the wall and falls into his hand.

"Obsidian," Samel says. "I saw some once in the market and I know the Lord's Militia has arrowheads made of it."

"Does it have magical properties? The sapphire Mother put on my necklace is supposed to protect travellers, though it doesn't seem to be working anymore."

Samel stares at the stone~~, but nothing happens so he shrugs and~~ pockets it. "Let's keep looking for a way out."

The room is at least twice as large as Mother's and my whole cottage, but it has no windows and not a single door.

"There could be a secret door," Samel says. "Like the one in Ali's room." He begins pressing a hand against various parts of the wall.

"It's no use," I say eventually. "We're prisoners."

"Tell me something I don't know."

I sit with my back against a wall. "I wonder why he's put us here."

"Trying to wear us down, or to get Papa to do what he wants, whatever that is. I don't see how he expects us to help him conquer Aquila." He sinks to the floor beside me.

I contemplate the twin lights in front of us. There should be something we can do, some way to use the bracelets. "How well do you understand your bracelet?"

"What do you mean?"

"Well, take herbs, for example. They come from different parts of plants. You can use roots, leaves and stems, blossoms, fruit. Some plant parts are poisonous if taken in large quantities or certain parts are more efficacious than others. Learning to be a healer involves knowing which part of a plant to use and when to pick it. Also whether to use it fresh or dry, whether to make a poultice, a tisane or prepare it in some other way."

"I don't understand any of that," Samel says. "Though when you're learning to play a musical instrument, a harp for instance, you have to think about the tension of the strings, where to place your fingers, all the technical stuff. Still if you don't have a feel for music, don't have it inside you, the flow of it, the life of it, then the playing lacks spirit and fails to move people."

I nod slowly. "I think those are the kinds of things we need to know. For instance, these bracelets are made of silver. A metal smelted from the earth, but worked by a man, with skill and knowledge into a pleasing form. There's got to be a way to use that knowledge." I nudge one of the bracelets with a foot.

"What are you doing?"

"Trying to imagine the bracelet melting into the stones of the floor. It was part of the earth once, maybe it can move through earth."

Samel knocks my foot away. "No! It might fall totally out of our reach."

I lean over to stare at the circlets. "Does it look to you as if there's a slight dip in the floor?"

"I can't tell. Maybe."

"Too slow then, or I just don't know how to do it. Is there anything else that comes to mind?"

"They're circles."

"With ivy leaves that can strangle or be allowed to climb freely in sunshine. Though Julina told me silver is a metal of the moon."

"Who's Julina?"

"A woman who helped me, I think."

"You're not sure?"

"She was a strange one."

"So did you mean there are contrasts, opposites maybe in the bracelets? Does that help us in some way?"

"Just continuing to think out loud. Mother and Father had the bracelets made for each other. They did this to us, to themselves. Why couldn't they have worked together, faced their fears, met the danger as a unit?"

Samel clears his throat, shifts against the stone wall. "You sound really angry with both of them, but we can't know what it was like. We were only little. They did what they thought was best."

"I'm not convinced. How can you love your children and split them up?"

"Papa told me they had the bracelets made because it was a custom of Mother's people, a way to show their love and connection to each other and their families."

"So? Custom has reason, too, even if people have forgotten the why. You're trying to say they had grounds to separate us? "

He shrugs.

"Love and connection," I muse. "Maybe it's that power Hrashak wants. Even though Varonne is his daughter, I think she fears rather than loves him. But how does that help us? How could that help him become ruler of Aquila?"

"If enough people love and follow you, you might be able to conquer a city," Samel says. "Others might be so afraid of your charisma and power that they'll do whatever you want."

"Soldiers you mean? He needs us to help build his army? How would the bracelets do that?"

"Maybe they focus love or power in a way that can affect people?"

"Yes." I nod slowly. "But I think he's been trying to use them at a distance ever since Mother and Father found each other. And the bracelets somehow prevented that. Why didn't he just come and get the bracelets before our parents separated? He said he came as a wolf when we were children, but he couldn't come near us. So it's not that easy."

"Wolves," says Samel slowly. "There were stories of strange wolves around the City of Aquila for a while. I wonder if that was Hrashak trying to attack." He shakes his head. "It didn't work though. The wolves all died, though I never saw the bodies. Maybe he needed the bracelets together and closer to him. He couldn't get the bracelets so he found a way to bring us? Maybe it's taken him a while to figure this out?"

"I refuse to be used. All right, so there's no knight in shining armour on a white horse, but together maybe you and I can manipulate these bracelets to find a way out of here."

"He's made a mistake, then." Samel grins.

"How do you mean?"

"Not taking the bracelets away from us right at the beginning, unless, even here, there's some spells binding them, stopping him from just taking them."

"Yes. He may be older and have the abilities of sorcery, but we're not stupid. Look at what we've been able to do so far." I gesture at the shining flames.

"That's nice, but what I'd really like to do is to be able to look out. If only there was a window . . ." Samel's voice gets very quiet and he grabs one of the bracelets. "Ouch!" Drops it again. He sucks his fingers. "I just remembered . . ."

"Wait!" I hold up a hand. "What if he's watching us? Or listening? What if that's why he's put us here."

"So we'll figure out how to use the bracelets and then he'll know and that will help him take them from us?"

"Maybe."

"We can't let that happen!" Samel stamps on the floor.

I reach for the cord that holds the hat Ma Parnell gave me. Pull it over my head and hold the hat high with both hands. "This is an illusion Julina talked about, but I haven't tried before. Imagine this hat hovering above and growing large enough to cover both of us."

Samel doesn't ask why, just nods and closes his eyes. I decide to do the same. After all, it was easier to picture a candle with my eyes shut. In my mind I see the hat float away from my fingers. There's a warm spot in the hollow at the front of my neck. I touch the sapphire, resist the temptation to open my eyes, and think of the protection of the stone growing to encompass the hat and expanding, like the bud of a flower unfurling. A huge sunflower that looks like a hat, and is as large as an eagle.

"That wasn't my thought," I open my eyes.

Samel grins. "The eagle? That was mine. I thought it was better than a sunflower. Fiercer." He points up. "Protection is what you were aiming at, right?"

The hat hovers over us, large enough to shield both our heads.

"Did we just read each other's thoughts?" I ask.

Samel shrugs. "I think we shared visions or dreams before."

I turn my gaze to the hat. It has a slightly menacing tilt. I smile at Samel. "I'm hoping the hat will conceal our thoughts, even from someone who can read minds."

"I have another thing we could do," Samel says. "Once I looked through my bracelet and it seemed as if I could see into another room. If we can make a hat expand, what about the bracelets?"

"Shall we use yours?"

Samel puts a hand near one bracelet. "I'm not sure if this one's mine and Papa's. Would it matter if we pick the wrong one?"

"They know us."

My brother reaches for one of the circlets, which slides away. He picks up the other, and its light dims. My bracelet lies on the floor, still blazing brightly. Samel holds the bracelet close to his face, staring into it.

"Should I do anything?" I ask softly.

"Maybe just concentrate on creating an opening, like a window in the air."

Nothing happens for a while. My eyes begin to itch; I try not to blink, then can't help doing it. When I look again the circle of silver has expanded to twice its normal size.

"I wish you'd tell me more of your plans!"

The voice is Varonne's, I'm sure of that. I grab Samel's arm, put a finger to my lips. The bracelet doesn't appear to be growing any larger.

"All in good time," Hrashak says. "I've been thwarted too many times to tell anyone the details prematurely now."

Samel has moved closer to the bracelet and is peering into it. I tighten my hand on his arm. He nods and mouths, "I don't think they can see us."

"You mean my mother, don't you?" says Varonne. "You thought she'd help and then she betrayed you."

"The past is done. It's the present we have to deal with."

"I still don't understand why you've taken it so slow. Why didn't you grab the bracelets long ago? Even if you didn't know how to use them at first, you could have figured it out over time."

"It's not as simple as that. The bracelets were joined to Zarmine and Yarvan by strong spellcraft. I tried to take them, but was thwarted. When the couple separated and stopped wearing the bracelets, I wasn't sure for a while if they'd destroyed them or not. I had to proceed cautiously. Now it appears the silver has chosen new hosts."

"So why not just take the bracelets since you've got the two children?"

I snort, then clap a hand over my mouth.

"What was that?" Hrashak asks. "Did you hear a noise? Is someone listening at the door?"

Samel quickly slips the bracelet under his tunic and wraps it tightly in the cloth. I hold my breath. Samel shakes his head. "I think it's all right now," he whispers. "The bracelet feels normal again."

"Sorry, couldn't help the snort. I'm not a child."

"Neither am I," Samel responds. "But if they think that, they've underestimated us and that's a good thing. So what are we going to do next?"

"Sounds as if the bracelets give us some protection. Hrashak can't just take them from us whenever he wants. He's got to persuade or pressure us to help him."

"We've got to get out of here," Samel says. "Find Papa. He'll know what to do."

"Maybe. If they haven't got him locked up somewhere we can't get at him. If he's willing to help."

"Of course, he'll help!" Samel insists. "He wants to get out of here as much as we do."

"Hmm." I get an idea. "Can you control where the bracelet will open to? And can you make the opening bigger?"

"I can try. You think we could get them large enough for us to fit through?"

"Let's hold the bracelets, one each and hold hands. That means letting the light go out. I don't want to burn myself. Take my other hand. Think of darkness."

Two hands reach for two silver circlets. My fingers touch cool metal. Light disappears. My fingers feel thick, as if there's another force working against us. I grip my bracelet tightly, hope Samel is doing the same. A bump and clang. I tug, but my bracelet seems to be pulling in the opposite direction. The two circlets have joined, like links in a silver chain. Through each of them comes a glimpse of candlelight.

"Think larger," I whisper.

Gradually the circles expand. The width of two hands, then large enough to put a head through. Samel glances at me. I peer into light, can't make out any walls or people. Maybe we've found a gateway to the outside. I nod and we push forward. What will happen when we have to let go of each other and the bracelets? A twisting sensation and a sudden whirling in the head. We fall, no longer holding hands. As my knees touch a rug, it occurs to me that the hat has been left behind.

A dry voice says, "Well done."

Hrashak and Yarvan stand together in a small, round room, with stone walls and floor. For a moment I wonder if they've joined forces, but then notice that Yarvan is grimacing as if in pain. What has the old man been doing to him? A window shows night sky, so it's been several hours or perhaps longer since we first arrived at this castle. Opposite the window, a door gapes slightly ajar and I glimpse the shape of another person standing just beyond the doorway.

Hrashak smiles, though his eyes are cold. "Did you think to get away? Leave your father behind? This castle has my protections to prevent people leaving unless I allow it."

I see out of the corner of my eye that I'm wearing the bracelet now, on my left wrist. Shaking my sleeve down over my hand, I glance sideways at Samel. He's got his on as well. I hope the old man hasn't noticed.

"Papa?" Samel says. "Are you all right?" Yarvan doesn't move or speak.

Hrashak shakes his head. "He's being uncooperative again. I've immobilized and silenced him temporarily." He holds up a hand to stop us moving forward. "Your father is unharmed. Now, I know that you each have one of your parents' bracelets and that you've found out more about them. I think there's a great deal more to learn. With my help you could do and have almost anything you want." He nods at Samel. "What about owning a string of camels? You could send a caravan across the desert, travel with them if you like. And you, Rowan, could buy as many horses for your friend Edana as you wish. Both of you could be rich, famous, admired."

"And what if," I say slowly, "we want none of that?"

"Then tell me what you do want."

"To go home," Samel says. "Rowan, Papa and me. To be left alone."

"My dear boy," Hrashak says, "I know you're more intelligent than that. The arcane arts draw envy and greed so you have to learn how to protect yourself. Even at home you wouldn't be left in peace. If I agreed to let you go others who are interested in what you have would find you eventually." He grimaces and I wonder if that's intended for a smile. "You can't hide your lights, neither in northern forests nor in southern cities, neither in the dark of night or in the blazing light of the sun. That's what your parents didn't understand. I believe both of you are smarter. And I can help protect you."

I touch Samel's arm. "We need time to think about this, to talk about it."

Hrashak regards me with narrowed eyes. I try to keep my face neutral and my mind blank. I hope that Samel is doing the same, but I don't want to look away in case the old man interprets that as fear. Finally Hrashak nods once.

"Daughter!" calls the old man. Varonne walks into the room. "We'll leave them, let them consider the pros and cons of cooperation. Just don't take too long about it," he says, brushing past me. I recoil from the swish of his robes against my hands. A sudden flare of burn on my left wrist makes me gasp, but I clamp my teeth on further sounds. Varonne follows the old man. In the doorway, Hrashak turns and flicks his fingers at Yarvan. Then the door slams shut with a boom.

Samel rushes toward it, and when it won't open, he seeks the window. "We're in a tower, really high up. And I can see mountains."

"No escape."

Samel whirls, leaps across the room, skidding on a loose rug, just in time to steady his father, who slumps in his arms. "Help me!" Samel flings the words at me.

Together we half carry, half drag our father to the divan under the window. The light of the moon falls across his pale face. He breathes shallowly and winces every now and then.

"What is it, Papa?" Samel asks. "Where do you hurt?"

I nudge Samel aside. "Let me see. Remember, I know about hurts and healing." I fumble with my belt pouch as Yarvan bites his lips and shakes his head.

"Can you chew? I'll give you poppy seeds that will ease whatever pain you have, and make you sleep."

"No," he whispers, "no sleep yet."

For the moment, I don't think of this man as my father, don't consider what he did or didn't do to me. He is a person in pain and in need. I move my hands over his body in the stroking motions Mother taught me, never quite touching him. Gradually his face loses its pinched look and even his limbs relax. He begins to breathe more easily and deeply. Samel settles to the floor at the foot of the divan. I wonder if he's thinking of using the bracelets to try and get to Aquila. It's one thing to use the circlets to go from one room of a fortress to another. But across country? Besides, maybe Hrashak wasn't lying about the power of his protections.

I sigh, sinking to the floor near Samel. "He should be better now."

"I am," Yarvan says without opening his eyes. "Thank you."

I touch Samel's hand and point around the room. Samel nods and we get up and begin to quietly explore our prison. There are blankets in a chest, so I spread one over Yarvan. He grasps my hand briefly, and then as if the effort is too much, lets go. Samel finds a niche in the stone wall with a jug of water and a loaf of bread.

"Would these be safe?"

I smell them both, then hold my bracelet over them. "They're probably all right. If anything was wrong with them I think the bracelet would have heated. That's what happened to mine when he walked too close."

"Hrashak." The word is almost a croak.

We turn.

"You shouldn't be sitting up," Samel says.

"Don't treat me like a decrepit old fool, even if I am one." Yarvan puts out a hand to me. "Greetings daughter."

I hesitate for a moment; shake away the tears that prickle my eyes and take the hand. "Father," I whisper.

"I'm sorry," he says. "Your mother is truly gone, isn`t she?"

I nod.

"I know now that we should never have separated our two children."

"I was terribly angry with both of you," I admit.

"And now?"

"I'm not sure. I don't think we have time for anger at the moment, and the past is over and done with. I have to come to terms with that. There are things I wish I could have asked Mother, said to her, but," I squeeze his hand, "we have to deal with the present, need to find a way to get out of here."

"Did you hear that Samel, my son?" He raises his voice. "My daughter has wisdom beyond her years."

Samel comes closer and punches him gently in the shoulder. "Of course she does. She takes after me."

"Listen," Father says quietly, "I don't know how much time we have and whether he's listening. I need to tell you a few things."

"Samel and I have already shared what we know."

"There are things I didn't tell him." He motions both of us closer to the divan. "When my grandfather died, Hrashak thought he should get the bastion and the lands around it because he was the eldest son, but Grandfather promised all that to my father, in front of witnesses. He gave Hraskak a hunting lodge and some land deeper in the mountains. That seemed to satisfy my uncle, but what none of us realized until later, is that he found something in the mountains, a source of sorcery I think, and he began to brood on what he saw as the injustice of being disinherited. He made plans and my father died."

"You mean," Samel interrupts, "he was the one who killed your father?"

Father shrugs. "I never had proof, was barely in my twentieth year and no match for him. He manipulated people, treated me like a simpleton, seemed to convince everyone that I could never rule here after my father's death."

"And so you left," I nod. "It makes sense. He might have killed you."

Father shakes his head. "I didn't leave right away because I wanted to find proof that Hrashak had murdered my father. I found nothing. In the meantime he found himself a wife."

"Varonne's mother?" I ask.

"I suppose so, though I wasn't here for the birth. The woman frightened me more than Hrashak did because she seemed to see inside my mind. That's when I left. It was probably cowardly, but I don't regret leaving, because eventually I met your mother."

"What happened to Varonne's mother?"

"I don't know. It doesn't seem as if she's here."

"But you never really got away from him!" Samel bursts out. "He said he's been watching us! In Aquila."

"How could I know? I'd never have stayed there with you if I'd suspected he was there. You know I wanted to keep you safe. Your mother and I wanted to keep both of you safe."

"But it didn't work!" I start to pace. "I told you to let the past be, but if you insist on bringing it up, let me tell you a few things."

"Uh, oh," Samel mumbles.

I ignore him. "Mother lied to me by omission. About you and Samel, about her own life, about her cousin Thea. Imagine what it felt like when she died, to find all that out. Samel says you dreamt her death. Why didn't you send me a message? I could have used your support."

Father groans. "What can I do to make it up to you?"

"I don't know. Maybe there's nothing you can do."

"You haven't really forgiven us, have you?"

I shrug. My feelings are mixed.

"What are we going to do about Hrashak, though?" Samel asks. "We can't trust him. He said Papa was unharmed, but he's not."

"I'm fine," Father insists. "Just achy and short of breath."

"Of course we can't trust the old man, but we need time," I says. "For Father to feel better, for us to make plans."

"He's probably listening to everything we say," Father warns.

"We'll have to face him sooner or later," I say.

"Do you think I'm going to stand by and let him hurt either one of you?"

"You'll have no choice," I say coldly.

"In case you haven't noticed," Samel adds more kindly, "we're not so little anymore."

I yawn and mumble, "Too tired to think."

"We all need rest for clear heads. Samel, see if there are any more blankets in that chest."

"But Papa, we can't sleep now!" Samel turns from one to the other. "Rowan, we've got to make plans!"

"No," Father insists, "we'll rest."

Samel fidgets. "What if they come and separate us? Or move us? Shouldn't we at least take turns keeping watch?"

"Not a bad idea." I rub my eyes. "As long as someone other than me takes first turn."

"I'll do it." Samel stomps to the wooden chest.

He flings back the lid. Pulls out more blankets and a thick quilt. I fold the quilt into a mattress and wrap myself in a blanket, lie down and close my eyes. I hear Samel snort in disgust.

"She's been travelling a long time," comes Father's voice. "Tiredness hits you all of a sudden like that sometimes."

"Yeah, yeah," Samel mutters. "Go to sleep."

Chapter XXIII

Samel

The moon has moved across the sky and no longer shines directly in at the window, though it still gives enough light that I can see part of the courtyard below, a piece of wall and a section of moat. Beyond that are crags and rocks, and mountain peaks, some covered with snow. From what I know of the geography of the land I believe that we're somewhere to the west of Aquila. Most probably somewhat north as well. It's interesting to know, but doesn't help figure out how to get away from here, or how to fight against Hrashak. Still, if this is the fortress where Papa spent the first twenty or so years of his life, he ought to have useful knowledge. Secret passages, for example.

When I turn I see that both Papa and Rowan are asleep. The sound of breathing and snoring is very relaxing, making me want to lie down and close my eyes. I scrub at my face and rub my eyes. Glance at the bracelet on my left wrist.

"Neither Rowan nor I will surrender," I whisper.

Maybe the bracelet can help me find a way out while everyone else is asleep. I move to the niche that held the bread and water. Turn my back to the rest of the room and take off the circlet. Hold it with both hands.

"Grow. Show me my bedroom at home."

But no matter how hard or long I stare and concentrate, nothing happens except that the bracelet gets slightly warmer. So escape isn't going to be that easy. The barriers Hrashak talked about may be around this room as well as around the whole castle. I slip the bangle back onto my wrist. To stay awake, I wander through the room, press against stones, try to manipulate parts of the chest, poke at the niche. When I get to the door I push against it and to my surprise, it opens.

I'm about to turn and call Papa and Rowan when Varonne sticks her head in. "My father wants you," she whispers.

"Just me?"

She nods. "Come."

"Why? What does he want with me?"

"If you help him he might let you all go."

I throw another glance behind; both sleep soundly. I slip out the door and watch as Varonne locks it again. If I could get that key . . .

She puts it into a pouch at her belt, gestures. "Down the stairs."

Varonne leads me to a small room on the next floor. The old man is sitting in a carved wooden chair that looks like a throne. He waves to another, smaller chair. I sit as Varonne leaves and closes the door. For several moments Hrashak says nothing. I hold my tongue also. Probably should be afraid, but I remember Hrashak as the innocuous old man at the palace in Aquila. Let him see that this boy is not easily manipulated.

"So," Hrashak says finally, "how's Tamtan?"

I wave a hand in dismissal. How am I to know when Tamtan is such a long way from here? This is all part of the game and I'm not playing. The old man taps a finger on the arm of his chair. Perhaps he's annoyed. Good.

"You're an excellent musician, I hear."

Again I let the words go unanswered. Besides, they're an exaggeration. I know that I'm good, but still have a lot to learn and a long way to go before I can be called excellent. Flattery will not work. I feel like yelling at the old man to get to the point, but am not going to. Instead I breathe slowly and deeply.

Hrashak sighs. "I can see you're going to make things difficult for me young Samel. Very well. I'll tell you why I brought you here without any more of the preliminaries used in polite society. You're obviously in no mood to be courteous this evening. Perhaps you're too tired." He pauses.

This time I have to bite my tongue to stop a retort. "Talk about courtesy!" I want to growl. "Taking people against their will and keeping them prisoner is a whole lot worse than a refusal to talk." I don't open my mouth, though I can taste blood.

A quick smile flits across Hrashak's face. It never reaches his eyes, however. Cold eyes. Why didn't I notice those eyes in Aquila?

"Well, my boy, I'm sorry to be keeping you and your family here, but I need your help and I didn't think your father would give it if I asked politely. He's never liked me for some reason."

"You killed his father," I spit out. "My grandfather."

"Ah, so that's the lie he told you." Hrashak shakes his head. "Probably couldn't face his own guilt."

"Whatever you're trying to say, I know it's not true."

"Oh, I feel for him. I did my best, but I couldn't save my brother."

I realize that I've gotten drawn into conversation against my will. I'm not going to do that again.

Hrashak smiles briefly, but the smile never reaches his eyes. "I'll tell you what really happened. It was on a ride into the mountains after a light snowfall, and the trail was slippery. Your grandfather tumbled off his horse, was injured. By the time we got him back to the bastion, he'd fallen into in a coma. I used all the skill I had, but it wasn't enough."

I frown, can't help asking, "That's all? There's no more to the story?"

"Your father raged at me, wanted to know why I hadn't done more, accused me of killing him." Hrashak grimaces. "He was distraught, I understood that. Felt guilty because it had been his idea to go riding."

I stare at the old man. Is he telling the truth? I'll wait and hear

Papa's version before making up my mind.

"It was a sad and difficult time. I don't think your father ever got over it, but that's no reason for you to refuse your help to me, is it?" He leans forward. "Samel, I can give you so much, guide you in the use of the bracelets, show you things you could never imagine."

On impulse, I push back my left sleeve to expose the silver bracelet. Stretch out my arm and point at Hrashak. The old man shrinks back for an instant, then as nothing more happens, sits up straight again.

I smile. "So show me."

Hrashak shakes his head. "It's not that easy."

"Of course not." I pull the sleeve back down.

"Wait!" The old man stretches out a hand. "Don't put it away yet."

"Suggest something now. If you really want to help me, tell me one thing I can do here and now to test my bracelet."

Hrashak looks around the room as if searching for something to practise sorcery on. I wait, wondering if the old man is trying to make me impatient, so that I'll lose my temper. Better act as relaxed as possible. I lean back in the chair, put my right hand in my pocket. Touch the stone I placed there in the dungeon. It warms in my fingers and the bracelet on my left wrist begins to warm as well.

Hrashak jerks in his chair. "What are you doing?"

"Nothing."

"All right." The old man studies me for a while. "What do you think of Varonne?"

"Your daughter? I barely know her."

"She's good looking, don't you think? Looks a little like your mother."

What is the old man up to now? I shrug. "I don't remember my mother."

"She's a little older than you. Varonne, I mean, but she likes you."

A shiver slithers down my back. Is Hrashak trying to make a match? It's ridiculous. "Besides we're cousins." This slips out, and I clamp my lips.

"Oh, Varonne doesn't mind that." The old man smiles. "Think

about it, get to know her."

I shake my head. "I don't trust either of you."

The old man stands. "You could be in more comfortable rooms. I can move you and your father and sister to a suite of rooms with soft beds, rich clothes. All you need to do is pledge to help me, and get to know your cousin."

I cover the bracelet. "I said I don't trust you." I take a step toward the door. "Varonne, are you out there? I want to go back."

There is silence for several moments. Then Hrashak calls, "Varonne!" The door opens.

Varonne leads the way quickly. I study the lines of her back, wonder if she knows everything her father is trying to do. After she leaves me in the room, I just watch Papa and Rowan sleeping. Did the old man actually expect to win me over? If not, what was his purpose, particularly with all that stuff about Varonne? To sow doubt probably or perhaps he hoped that as the youngest I'd give in before the others. At least Papa hasn't tried to make a match between me and some girl. What would Rowan think of my meeting with Hrashak?

I notice the lump of Rowan's belt pouch under the blanket. She took some seeds from there to help with Papa's pain. What else might she have? That reminds me of my own belt. The small drum is still tied to it. What about Papa's flute? Just before the sandstorm, he was playing it. Quietly, I walk around the room looking everywhere. No flute. It might have been lost during the storm, or Hrashnak, knowing Papa's abilities probably took it away. It will have to be the drum then. And if the old man is watching or listening, he'll see that I'm not under his thumb.

I stand by the window gazing at the clear sky where stars twinkle; they can't help. It's a calm night, no breeze at all. I tap the drum very quietly. Once, twice. A third time. Is that a swirl of dust on the stone windowsill? I speed up the tempo. Dust drifts over the sill and onto the floor, twisting and turning around my feet.

"What are you doing?" Papa throws off his covers.

After I still the drum, dust settles to lie inertly on the floor and on the toes of my sandals. "Making music. Sorry to wake you. I was trying to be quiet."

"Samel, this isn't a game!" Papa whispers fiercely. "We're in real danger."

"Tell me something I don't know. What are we going to do about it?" I throw back. "Sleep some more?"

"I dreamt." Papa props his forehead on his hand. "About your mother."

More dreams and visions. None of the previous ones have prevented us ending up here – prisoners. Maybe Hraskak sent all the dreams, even Ali's with the intention of bringing us here. Still, I want to hear about the mother I can't remember.

"What was Mother doing in the dream?" Rowan clasps her arms round her knees. "Did she say anything?"

"She was always more reluctant than I to separate her children, you know," Papa says. "I suppose I've been feeling guilty that I ended up convincing her."

"I'm not sure I believe that," Rowan interjects.

"Why?" I speak before Papa can.

"I lived with her longer than any of you, know her best, I think. She could be very persuasive and she wasn't above using herbs to make you forget things."

Papa frowns. "Are you trying to say that she manipulated me?"

"We'll never know," Rowan shrugs, "but consider that you aren't solely to blame for this mess."

I tap out a riff on my drum. I want to hear as much as possible about Mother, good and bad. Xylea has told me often that people are complicated, and I rather like the thought of a mother who could be devious.

"Are you saying, Papa, in your roundabout way, that there was nothing useful in your dream?"

He shakes his head. "I was just remembering, Samel." He sighs. "In the dream, she merely stood there," he points to the centre of the room, "smiling at me. Didn't say a word."

"Useless," Rowan mutters.

Papa is still staring. "The way her lips quirked reminded me of the first time we put on the bracelets, that ring of silver fire they gave off. She took my hand and said, "What if we step into the light."

"We haven't tried that, Rowan." I take a step toward my sister

She gets slowly to her feet. "Do you think it might get us farther than just enlarging the bracelets and crawling through?"

"It's worth trying."

Papa glances from one to the other. "What's going on?"

"Come here, Father, with us. Samel and I are going to try and recreate that circle of fire."

"But . . ."

"No arguments, Papa." I take Rowan's left hand. Hold out my other to papa. "Hurry."

Papa joins the circle. I glance at Rowan, she nods, and we touch wrists, making the bracelets chime. A faint glow emanates, encircling our joined hands, then growing larger as it moves up our arms, to shoulders and heads.

"Is that what it was like?" Rowan whispers.

Papa shakes his head. "No, much brighter and larger."

I stamp a foot. "What's wrong, then?"

"Wait," Rowan says.

Very slowly the silver glow expands to surround all three of us, but it's still quite pale. I look at Rowan and she nods, understanding what I want. We move forward, pulling Papa with us, stepping into and through the light. There's a slight tingle, but nothing else. We huddle in the centre of the round room looking at each other in disappointment. Finally let go of hands and the light dies.

'Moonlight?" Papa suggests. "The moon shone on your mother and me."

I groan. "We should have tried this earlier when the moon was beaming in through the window."

Rowan goes to look. "The moon is gone. It's almost dawn." She turns back to us. "You should get some sleep, Samel. Before Hrashak comes back."

"He's already been back," I say. "Or rather it was Varonne who came to take me to him."

"What!" Papa grabs my shoulder. "You went to him alone? What happened?" He studies me, looking for changes, probably.

I shake off Papa's hand.

Rowan is staring at me, too. "What did he do to you, Samel?"

"Tried to get me on his side. Told me a story about how grandfather died. He acted weird, asked me how I liked Varonne."

Rowan glances at Papa, then back at me. She reaches out a hand, but doesn't touch either one of us. The three of us stand like that for several moments, and then Rowan takes a step toward me as if to convince herself I'm still the same brother as before. Papa seems paralysed by thoughts that he can't express. Rowan has just opened her mouth to speak when there's the sound of bolts being drawn back at the door, and the scratching of a key in the lock.

Chapter XXIV

Rowan

Varonne swaggers into the room and takes a stance with hands on hips, one of them near the sword she still wears in its black scabbard. She glances quickly around to see where we are, as if we'd try to attack her without weapons.

"Hrashak wants to see Rowan. Alone."

"No!" Father lunges forward.

Varonne draws her sword. "Stand back."

Samel crosses to my side. "Why?"

Varonne flicks her sword. "Move back, you've had your turn. He wants to speak to Rowan."

"It's all right." I move my hands out to motion Varonne back. "I'll go."

"No," Father says again, but more quietly this time.

The sword points at Father's neck, then moves toward Samel. "You have no choice. I have an armed escort waiting just outside the door, so there's no point trying anything foolish."

"Father," I say "Samel, I'm going." I move toward the door.

Varonne pushes me out, follows quickly, shuts and locks the door. There is pounding and shouting from the other side, which we ignore. Varonne leads the way and four guards fall behind. The narrow staircase winds around and down. It seems to me that it gets darker the farther we go even though there are narrow slits in the walls here and there to let in daylight. We pass a landing and come to a hallway. Several doors line it, but all are closed. As we move along the hall I watch carefully in hopes of seeing a way out or finding an opportunity to make use of later – a moment of inattention or the possibility for a diversion, though I won't try to escape without Samel and Father.

"Varonne," I say quietly, "you could help us."

She shakes her head without looking at me. "He's my father. The only family I've got left."

"I'm family, too."

We've reach the top of another staircase, this one broad and straight. Below stand more guards and there's no sign of an outside door. Varonne shakes her head again as she guides us along another hallway, this one lined with suits of armour and weapons on the walls. I wonder how tightly some of those swords are fastened. Could I leap up and wrest one free? Varonne would probably knock it out of my hands before I had a chance to do anything. We stop in front of a tapestry, which Varonne pushes aside to reveal another door.

I wonder why Hrashak keeps meeting us in different rooms. Is he showing us the size of the castle to discourage escape, or does he merely want to keep us off balance? This one is a small room with one large wooden chair and several smaller ones around the walls. There's a low table with two pitchers, several metal goblets, and a small carved wooden casket. It reminds me of the one Mother used for the bracelet and letter from Father. Hrashak emerges from behind a wall hanging, and I'm reminded of Julina. The old man takes the large chair while Varonne stands by the door, hands on hips near sword and knife.

Hrashak motions. "Sit!"

"Why?" I raise my left arm slightly to let the sleeve all back and reveal the bracelet.

The old man shakes his head. "You're so much alike, you and your brother."

"What do you mean?"

"He attempted to threaten me exactly the same way." Hrashak smiles. "But it's an empty threat, isn't it my dear? Neither of you really understands those silver bangles and you won't without my help."

I open my mouth to retort, then clamp my lips. He might just be probing for the information I almost blurted out. If he's been watching us, he probably knows much of what we can do with the bracelets, but I'm not going to take the chance of giving anything away.

"Your brother is very young, but I'm hoping that you will show more maturity."

I still don't respond.

The old man smiles. "He doesn't really notice girls or young women yet, does he?"

"What?" I lean forward. "What have you been doing or saying to him?"

Hrashak shakes his head. "I can help, you know," he says softly. "Tell things your mother neglected."

"What can you know about my mother?"

"She loved to travel. Enjoyed new places and people."

"And yet she settled in a small village, moved to a cottage in the forest."

Hrashak rises and moves forward. I back to the wall. The old man goes to the table and pours a goblet of ruby liquid. He raises the pitcher. "Wine for you? Or water?" Indicating the other jug.

I shake my head. "Tell me what you meant about Samel."

The old man seats himself again, takes a sip. "We were just chatting. It became obvious to me that he's very young and I decided that you were the one I needed to speak to. I have a daughter too, as you know. Your mother did much for her children. Parents often do such things for their offspring."

I snort, come forward and take a chair near Varonne. I stay some distance from Hrashak, however. "So you're doing all this for your daughter?"

"Of course."

"And have you asked your daughter if she wants this? Does she approve?"

Hrashak thumps the goblet on the arm of his chair so that wine splashes out. "Your mother lied to you, drugged you, neglected to nurture your talents!"

"You don't have to shout. I know all that. But I thought you were trying to show me how well my mother planned for me and my brother. So tell me what you've planned for your daughter."

"Your father wasn't any better. What loyalty do you owe parents like that? None!"

"I owe you even less. You spied on me, stole me away from my search, and imprisoned me."

"For your own good, you stupid girl! Don't you see that I can help you? Show you how to use that bracelet and help you reach your full abilities?"

I shiver, though the room is warm. Once again the old man has reminded me of Julina. If the two of them plotted this whole thing . . . I've got to find out more. Clear my throat. "What's in the casket?"

"Ah, you appreciate beautiful things." He lifts the lid to show me a jewelled necklace and earrings – rubies? They make me think of huge drops of solidified blood. "Would you like to try this on?" The rubies drip from his hands.

So he's trying to win me over with presents. Surely he doesn't think . . . I shake my head.

"You could have a good life here." Hrashak puts the jewels away. "The castle is large, you could have rooms of your own to decorate as you wish. I have only a few servants, but could hire more." He smiles. "Give yourself a chance to know me."

I shiver. Is he truly suggesting a partnership between us, man and woman? If I wasn't interested in a young man like Medwyn, I'm certainly not going to join with an old and devious one. I should think of soft words, make him think I might consider his suggestions, but I can't. I feel like vomiting.

I stand. "No."

Hrashak throws his goblet into a corner. "Varonne, go fetch more wine, and honey cakes from the kitchen."

"It won't make any difference," I say when the door has closed on my cousin.

"I needed her out of the way for a while. My daughter isn't privy to all my plans."

I almost say, "I know," but swallow the words. The old man doesn't need to know what Samel and I overheard earlier.

"Sit, be comfortable, Rowan."

"I won't be comfortable until you release us."

Hrashak shrugs. "Be like that. Still, your stubbornness is one of the things I admire about you. I've had to be determined, too, in my life, or I'd never have achieve anything. What would you like to achieve, Rowan? I can help." He smiles.

I lean against the wall. Does he really think he can persuade me? Has Varonne been such a dutiful daughter that he thinks he knows how any girl's mind works?

"Well?"

I can tell he's growing impatient. I smile.

He takes that for encouragement. Nods. "Yes, my dear, I can help you to gain your greatest wish. So you don't want to partner with an old man like me. Understandable, though I could give you power you've probably not even dreamed of. But if there's a young man, in the northern woods perhaps who you've always wanted, I can help you get him."

"Oh, uncle," I say, "you are so far off the mark that I could laugh. There's nothing you can give me that I want except freedom."

He glowers and opens his mouth to speak or perhaps to shout when the door opens on Varonne. "Daughter," Hrashak says, "take her back, bring them all to the purple room."

When Varonne opens the door to the tower room, Samel and Father rush forward. "Rowan, are you all right?"

I nod. "Just a little queasy."

"Hrashak wants to see all of you," Varonne says.

"If he wants to eat me for breakfast," Samel says insolently, "he's going to have to come get me himself."

I laugh and even Father snorts. Varonne scowls. The scowl gives her face an inhuman expression. As if she had a snout and longer teeth. I close my eyes briefly and shake my head. Not enough sleep or else the bracelet is giving me visions again.

"I'd like nothing better than to chop you up for my father's breakfast," Varonne says to Samel, "but he wants you alive. So, unless you'd like me to call the guards to tie you up and roll you down several flights of stairs, I'd advise you to behave."

My legs are tired and I wonder if all this up and down is part of Hrashak's plan to wear us out, lower our resistance to him. I won't let it make any difference. Samel nudges me, Father touches my shoulder. We move out.

At a door surrounded by guards, Varonne stops, opens it and motions to one of the guards. She nods at me. "You go next, then another guard, then Samel with a guard. Then Yarvan. I'll follow at the end."

"What about the last guard?" I ask impudently, as if it were any of my business, though it has surprised me how many guards are assigned to us. Perhaps Hrashak fears what we can do, and that thought lifts my spirits, even if I'm not sure what we should or could do to seriously oppose him.

"He'll stay out here."

Hrashak is standing by a low table loaded with food and cushions around it.

"Trying to ape the eating customs of the Lords of Aquila?" Father sneers.

Hrashak scowls. "We're not going to eat yet. Not unless you all cooperate."

The soldiers arrange themselves around the walls. The old man leads the way across the room to another faded tapestry that he pushes aside to reveal a narrow door. He selects a key from the bunch at his waist and turns it in the lock. Two guards usher the three of us in and Varonne follows, shutting the door and leaving the guards outside.

We three move slowly, will show resistance with our smallest actions. Hrashak wants our help, and so he can't kill or harm us too severely, at least not yet. Father sits first, Samel and I take chairs on either side. None of us say anything, look at the old man and wait.

The old man smiles and bows slightly. "The game is underway. Actually it was begun long ago." He leans back in his chair. "I wasn't going to tell you this story, but after much thought, I've changed my mind. Perhaps you'll be more amenable when you understand what's at stake. Feel free to have wine or water. Daughter, pour me a goblet so our relations may see there's nothing harmful in it."

Varonne crosses to the table, pours. She carries the goblet to her father. He takes it and waves her away. She returns to the door.

"It began with my mother." Hrashak takes a sip. "She died before you were born, Yarvan, and she was beautiful. Golden-haired and golden-eyed. There's a portrait of her in the great hall here. I'm sure you remember that. We can show the children later."

"We're not children!" Samel bursts out.

"Tsk, tsk. Hrashak waves a finger. "I thought you were wiser than to lose your temper like that, Samel. I saw wisdom in you at the palace. Do you remember?"

Samel merely glowers. Hrashak smiles again. I take a deep breath and let it out very slowly. I'm determined to keep calm.

"My mother, Bella," Hrashak resumes, "who came here as a young woman, your grandfather's first wife, Yarvan. What you may not know is that she was from Aquila." Hrashak takes another sip from his goblet. "In fact, she was a daughter of the Lord at that time, Lord Boz."

"Hrashak, this may be riveting to you," Father says, "but I'm not particularly interested in ancient history at the moment. I'd rather discuss the present and the immediate future."

"Patience!" the old man barks. "Or I'll send you back to that tower room without food."

Father stands immediately. Samel and I follow a heartbeat later. Varonne moves directly in front of the door.

The old man shakes his head and chuckles. He waves a hand. "Relax, Varonne. The rest of you, sit down."

Father doesn't move. Neither do Samel or I.

Hrashak sighs. "Have it your way, but you'll get tired of standing. To resume, Lord Boz had a son who was meant to succeed him and that son died. The next in line should have been the sons of his daughter. The only son, me." Hrashak puts down his goblet and rises, lifting his hands to the ceiling. "I was meant to be Lord of Aquila!"

Samel raises his eyebrows. Father shakes his head slightly. Hrashak doesn't notice this exchange, but Varonne frowns at them and puts one hand on her sword hilt. Samel lowers his eyebrows and tries to look attentive and interested.

"And so I shall be," Hrashak continues as he lowers his arms. "And you," he points at Samel and me, "will help. And then our whole family will be the first family of the City of Eagles. I promise you that. We will have power no one else ever dreamed of."

"How can two young people help you?" Father asks. "You have far more conjuring abilities than either of them. Why not show compassion and let us go?"

"It's true I have knowledge," Hrashak says. "I have abilities of illusion and some control of wind and sand and stone. I've worked hard and learned much, but it's not enough! With the help of the bracelets, I could do a great deal more!"

Father is still standing. "Why not make your own?" he asks. "I can even direct you to the silversmith who made ours."

Hrashak stamps his foot. "Do you imagine I haven't tried?" he thunders. "That silversmith has disappeared. I tried others, but there's been failure after failure! I suspect someone has been working against me. That's why I finally had to bring you all here. I want your son and daughter to work with me and the bracelets to master fire, earth, water and air."

Father sinks into a chair and rubs his forehead as if he can't believe what he's been hearing. I feel as if I've fallen asleep and am living in a dream. It all seems too strange and impossible. I miss Mother's common sense. Someone has to tell Hrashak how ridiculous he is.

"You're living in an illusion," I say "It's as if you imagine yourself as some character in the old stories, but it's all make-believe. So what if

Samel and I can do tricks with the bracelets, and you can call wind to create a sandstorm strong enough to lift and bring us here? You expect us few to go against a whole city?"

Samel jumps in. "A city with a militia and eagles to defend it. Strong walls, and more than five thousand people."

"I have many soldiers and there are ways to get more."

Father snorts. "Why haven't you attacked Aquila already, then?"

"Timing is everything," Hrashak says softly, eyes half hooded. "So you're not even going to consider my offer?"

"No!" Samel and I exclaim together.

Hrashak stands very slowly. I have the sense that he is growing as he moves, the way a shadow will loom in candlelight. Illusion, I remind myself. No need to let the old man's tricks frighten me.

"We'll see," Hrashak says softly.

He opens his eyes wide and light seems to flash from them at Father. Father clutches his head and collapses, groaning to the floor. I try to leap forward to help, but am held fast by invisible bonds. Samel struggles in the same way, on the other side.

"Stop it!" I shout.

Hrashak chuckles. "Make believe you say? Well, whatever it is, it has its uses, doesn't it, my sweet Rowan? Even without the bracelets, I have enough spellcraft to hold you all immobile." Hrashak begins to pace back and forth in front of us. "It doesn't have to be like this! You could be living comfortably, soft beds, fine clothes, good food, riches. For only a few hours of your time given to me each day." He stops directly in front of me and holds my gaze with his own. "Consider it. Reflect. Talk it over with your father and brother. Convince them. Because I can cause a lot of suffering if you refuse."

Hrashak makes a motion with his hand, and Father groans, cradling one arm with the other. He glares at Hrashak and Samel struggles harder than ever to no avail. I close my eyes and concentrate, feel my left wrist get warm. Surreptitiously, I try to wiggle the fingers of that hand and after a moment, am successful. I feel equal warmth at the necklace. If I concentrate hard enough I might be able to break free of the paralysis, but I'm not ready to reveal that to Hrashak because I've got to figure out the best way to use my knowledge and the powers of the bracelet and necklace. I open my eyes.

"That's enough for now." Hrashak flicks his wrist to release us. He motions to Varonne. "Get the guards and take these fools back to the tower. Let them think on what I've said."

Samel helps Father up, then reaches a hand to me. I shake my head and move slowly, as if my body is still affected by Hrashak's enchantment. Varonne waits for us by the door. Samel glares at her as we pass, but she ignores him. I wonder what is going through Varonne's head. Does she approve of what her father does? Perhaps she is frightened of him, too much under his thumb. Might she be persuaded to help us?

Chapter XXV
Samel

In the tower room I help Papa to the divan. Varonne leaves, bolting the door.

"Was all that true, the things he told us? About being heir to Aquila?" I ask. "And if he is, aren't you, too?"

"Oh, his mother was from there," Papa says. "Father told me about her childhood in the City of Eagles. To me it was just a nice story, but it must have been much more real to Hrashak. When she died my grandfather married again and that was my father's mother. I don't think Hrashak ever forgave his father for remarrying and having another son. I also remember my father telling me that when they were both boys, Hrashak always had to be the winner – in games, in cliff climbing, and their studies. He was obsessive and ruthless about winning, and I suppose that's what Grandfather saw that made him choose my father to rule here."

"So what are we going to do?" I ask.

Papa shrugs. "We'll just give him the bracelets, be rid of them forever. I don't think he can truly defeat Aquila."

"Never!" I shout. "What if you're wrong?"

At almost the same moment, Rowan says, more quietly, "I doubt that will work."

Papa and I both stare at her.

"I mean," she adds, "even if Samel and I wanted to give up the bracelets, I don't think Hrashak can touch them. At least not without our consent. If he could, wouldn't he have taken them from us when we first arrived?"

"Hmm," Papa muses. "So you'll have to consent to give them to him."

"I think you're right, Rowan." I ignore Papa's words. "At first I thought it was just that he let us keep them, to see what we could do, what abilities we had. When he sent for me, I showed him my bracelet and asked him to suggest ways I could test it. We were alone in the room. He could have overpowered me and taken it." I pause, consider mentioning the black stone, wonder if Hrashak is listening. I raise my voice, "Hrashak didn't. Nor did he give me any suggestions. In fact, he looked frightened for a moment before he masked his face again."

Rowan nods. "That doesn't surprise me. He didn't attempt to take mine when he had me alone. Just tried to tell me things about Mother I already knew, and tempt me with jewels. He wanted to undermine my loyalty." She raises her head and says loudly to the ceiling, "But it didn't work." Then more quietly, "At any rate, he's kept his distance from those bracelets from the beginning."

"If he's listening, should we be speaking openly about this?" Papa suggests.

"He knows it already," Rowan says.

"I'm not giving him my bracelet," I insist. "And I'm not helping him."

"Not even if he hurts you?" Papa's voice is quiet. "I don't think he's shown his full range of sorcery to us yet."

"It's not Samel and me that he's going to hurt," Rowan says. "So far all he's done is kept us from going to our father's aid. It's you, Father, who's been attacked."

Papa shrugs it off. "Nothing serious."

"But there was pain."

"Only a little. Soon forgotten."

"It would make more sense to hurt us so we'd be afraid of pain and help him," I say.

"If he threatened to seriously injure Father, might you not do what he asked?"

"Do you think that's what he'll do?" I turn to Papa. "Would he kill you?"

"Don't worry about me, son, I'll take care of myself."

"The reason," Rowan interjects, "that he hasn't hurt Samel and me is that he can't as long as we're wearing the bracelets. Since he can't take them from us, we're relatively safe."

"What do you mean relatively?" I ask. "Either the bracelets protect us or they don't."

Rowan grimaces. "I don't think Hrashak can lay hands on us, but he could order someone else to kill us, though I'm not sure that would work. Or he could cause this tower to collapse and the stones might crush us."

There is a slight rumble and the floor shivers.

"Don't give him ideas!" I say loudly. "Besides if he hurts or kills us, he definitely won't have our help or the bracelets."

The room is at peace.

"But what if he starts on Father again?"

"I said don't worry about me!"

"I won't let him hurt you!" I insist. "I'll do things. And he'll be sorry."

"We should all rest and think," Rowan says. "Maybe we'll come up with a better plan than merely doing things." Rowan shakes her head as Papa and I both open their mouths to speak. She points at the window and mouths, "Moon. Tonight. We wait for moonlight." We nod very slightly.

If Hrashak is watching, all he sees are three people resting. Once in a while we talk about inconsequential things. Rowan and I compare childhoods. One of us drinks water now and then. Our stomachs rumble, but no food is delivered. We try not to talk about eating and regular meals, but I wonder how long Hrashak intends to leave us without food. As the day wanes we lie down and wrap blankets around themselves, then close our eyes. All of us plan to stay awake. I'm thinking about my bracelet and how it came to me, as if it chose me. That's both scary and satisfying. If the bracelets haven't gone over to Hrashak by now, they probably never will.

After a while, I find myself walking along a path through the desert. How did I get here? I'm wearing the bracelet on my left wrist, the eagle feather around my neck, and carrying the black stone in my right hand. The extreme heat has me drenched in sweat. I wish I hadn't lost my head scarf and that my water skin hadn't sprung a leak. Perhaps I can use the bracelet, the feather, and the stone somehow to find shade and water, though Papa wouldn't like it. There are specks in front of my eyes and I'm feeling faint. One of the specks is high up in the clear blue sky, growing larger and larger. Maybe I'll be swallowed by a speck and then at least I'll be cooler. There's a scream as a huge eagle lands in front of me.

Chapter XXVI

Rowan

I see Mord flying at great speed from place to place, dropping feathers. I want to call to him, tell him to stop before he loses all his pinions and can't fly anymore. I don't want to see him plummet to earth, but my voice is gone so all I can do is watch. Thea holds her twins by the hands. Edana and the boys wave at Mord. Then it's night and Mord flies over the grasslands to Grandmother Wisdom's tent, where three women sit staring into a fire. Suddenly I find myself on a hill with a great stone at my back. A storm rages with thunder and lightning, rain pouring down. I'm wet and cold. A bolt of lightning hurtles toward me, but I'm unable to move. I wait for the thunderbolt to hit me, but it crackles past and strikes the rock instead. I feel the shock of it through the soles of my feet and in a concussion of air that knocks me to my knees. When I raise my head to look at the rock I see that it's burning like a great torch. Light flashes from my left wrist and the bracelet shimmers, reflecting the fire.

I wake to find that the deep darkness of night has lessened, and the moon has crossed the night sky so that its rays enter the small window. I blink a few times, surprised to see only my father and brother in the room, the dreams were so vivid. I reach over to nudge my brother. Samel mutters and turns over. I shake him.

"What?" He sits.

I put a finger to my lips and touch his wrist with the bracelet on it. Samel nods. We move quietly together to the divan. Father stirs, then opens his eyes. He looks at us and smiles. Together we walk towards the centre of the room where moonlight pools on the stone floor. I give my right hand to Father, the left to Samel. I'm improvising, doing what feels right. This may not work, but it's the best idea so far. I hope that Hrashak and Varonne are asleep, that they won`t see what`s happening until it`s too late.

We form a circle. Samel moves so that moonlight falls directly on his bracelet. I do the same. It happens so gradually that for a few moments I notice nothing at all. Then I feel warmth around my wrist and the bracelet glows. Samel's bracelet shines as well.

"Close your eyes and imagine light growing around us," I whisper. "Nothing can penetrate it. Once we have the circle, imagine a room of your house in Aquila. If you see it clearly perhaps we can get there."

I picture circles of silver light rotating round from the bracelets, vines of pale ivy intertwining, enclosing and protecting us. I remember Grandmother Wisdom speaking of the power of love, and think of my parents pledging loyalty to each other, then devotion to their children. I know what it is to love a brother, to want to take care of him, to protect him. We are united as a family, as well as connected to many friends. Like strands of bright hair lifted by wind, the light turns and twists, looping and braiding itself into a cage of brightness.

A splintering crash sends eyelids up.

"Illusion!" Hrashak screams, striding into the room through the broken door. "That's all this is and I will break it!"

The old man stands in front of our rings of rotating light, waving his arms, but nothing happens. Varonne tramps behind, her sword at the ready. As she passes the window, moonlight flares along her sword, and she stumbles, then rights herself.

"Here!" Hrashak shouts. "Cut into one of the strands of light."

Varonne brings the weapon down. Silver smashes against silver.

My body shakes with the shock of contact. "Hold on!" I shout. "Keep thinking of light and fire and love."

Now Hrashak has Varonne's knife and both of them wield their weapons. Hrashak mutters words that I can't understand. Some kind of incantation perhaps, and one of the strands of lights disappears, another dims. I don't know if we can hold out. Samel pulls his right hand out of Father's.

"No!" I shout. "Don't let go!"

But many circles of light remain and continue to rotate, holding Hrashak and Varonne at bay as Samel starts to beat the small drum that hangs at his belt. He whispers over and over, words that sound like 'Tamtan' and 'Xylea.' Soon the thrum of another drum joins with Samel's, a deep boom boom that vibrates the floor. The rush of a harp comes in, the sound of wind raising the hair on my head. I think of all the people who have helped me on this journey, reach up to touch Mord's feather and the sapphire on my necklace. I feel the presence of friends, can see them in my mind nodding to us, reaching out their hands to help.

The whole room resounds with drumming and the cascade of a harp. Walls vibrate; it's as if the tower itself has become a musical instrument. Varonne and the old man sway and stumble, shift to keep their feet. Hrashak's shout of rage batters against the light, and shadows coalesce around his body, then flow outward. More of the strands around us dim and I wonder whether anything can save us. I don't know what to do, and hope that Father and Samel are still trying to see a room of their house so we can go there, but all the noise and commotion is probably distracting them. Father starts to hum in time with Samel's drumming. The remaining circles of light speed up even more.

The shadows around Hrashak grow and swell, looming over us. It's as if I'm standing at the joining of two great rivers, one black as pitch, the other pale as moonlight. Currents surge and beat against each other, rise up past my knees, shaking my stance. I can't keep going much longer, and what will happen then?

Above the rushing sound of water or wind, the humming of Father and the beat of Samel's drum, I hear a distant voice calling, "Hold on!" Don't know who it is.

I hear the croak of a raven and the shriek of an eagle. Samel's drum becomes my heartbeat, the heartbeats of friends, and Father's hum is the sound of breathing. Colours appear in the silver river, rise up and surround us, strengthening the light – flickers and flames of magenta, alizarine blue, ivory. Sparks fly so that Hrashak and Varonne have to duck and draw back.

"It's all illusion!" Hrashak screams. "I'll master it and you, or I'll kill you all just the way I killed your mother!"

A sudden silence falls as Samel's hands still on his drum and Father stops humming. I sway with shock, then rage explodes inside my chest. This is the man who cut short Mother's life and purpose; it wasn't my fault that she died. I'm not angry with Mother anymore, nor with Father. All my rage is focused on the old man in front of me. There isn't room in my body to hold this fury; I feel it blaze out of my eyes, run down my arms. I draw silver fire from my own and Samel's bracelets to feed that rage. My brother raises a hand with the black stone between his fingers. I remember the image of the stone torch burning on the hilltop. Then I feel the necklace that Mother made for me, heat around my neck.

I tear the necklace off, scattering beads and Mord's black feather; all burst into flame as they fly at Hrashak. I shout, "No one ever loved you! You don't know what love is! Even the bracelets refuse you. You can't conquer anyone."

Hrashak moves his hands and the knife he holds catches more moonlight which bounces off the blade and turns the beads to black ashes before they can strike him. He laughs wildly. "Who needs love?"

Varonne has moved back to stand against a wall, her sword pointing to the floor. She is staring at her father, eyes wide, mouth open. Her face is sun bleached bone. The power that I've drawn from the bracelets has dimmed the rings of light around the three of us. Hrashak, noticing this, screams at his daughter to bring up her sword. Varonne does nothing.

I feel a piece of necklace still pressing against my hand. It's the tooth of the dragon that I found, curved and sharp. I imagine the dragon opening its mouth and belching fire. I am the dragon, am the roaring flame. I touch the tooth to my bracelet and both flare with cold light. Hrashak is moving forward, his knife cutting through one of the rotating rings of colour when a dragon called Rowan sends the tooth flying straight as an arrow to Hrashak's heart.

He collapses with a scream, thrashes for a moment and is still. Varonne drops her sword with a clatter and runs out of the tower room door. Her footsteps thump and echo down the stairs, receding, dying away to nothing.

I am suddenly enclosed in a great bubble of silence, staring at a dead man on a floor. This is a nightmare and I want to wake up, but can't move. Someone shakes me, calls my name. All I have to do is open my eyes and I'll be safe at home, in bed, but my eyes are already open and no matter how many times I close and open them again, I still see the man that I killed. How can that be? He was the killer, not I. There is the presence of a second person beside me, but I can't turn my head. Perhaps I've become a statue of stone and will never be able to move again.

"Daughter," says a voice.

"Sister," pleads another.

Then someone comes into view with a blanket and puts it over the dead man. I begin to tremble, my legs shake. There is a hand holding mine, pulling me away. An arm comes around my shoulders, another hand turns my chin. I see a kind, sad face, gold-flecked eyes filled with tears.

"Oh, my daughter," a voice says.

"We can go now," another adds, someone pulls at my hand. "Let's leave this place."

Epilogue

Samel

He watches his sister, snatches glances at her even when Ali captures his attention. It's not that he doesn't want to talk to Ali. He needs to tell her everything, hear what she has to say, see if she can make paintings of it. Her images have helped him to make sense of things in the past, to see what he needs to do. But Samel has seen Papa's frown, the tentative way he touches his daughter, so different from the rough hugs and thumps he gives Samel. Of course, Rowan is a girl, but it's not just that. His sister makes him think of a harp string tuned too tightly, so that its tone is off key. And he keeps waiting for the snap.

At least she isn't lying rigidly at his feet or spending most of her time sleeping. He shivers as the memory of those last moments in the tower comes back. For an instant there, he'd thought Hrashak had killed his sister. Papa explained that it was probably shock, Rowan's mind reacting to what she'd had to do.

"But he deserved it and she was protecting us," Samel had protested. "Like a hero from one of the old stories."

Papa had shushed him. "It will take time for her to realize and accept that. It's no small thing to kill another person."

Samel wonders how Papa knows this, but he doesn't ask. Lately Rowan has been taking an interest in seeing Aquila, though she has been quiet and rather shy around the friends they have introduced her to. Papa says it will take more time, in fact, he wondered if this party at the artists' house might be overwhelming for Rowan. Too many people at once, too much noise and activity.

There's so much good in Aquila, so much he wants to show his sister. He wants to get to know her, but she doesn't seem very interested. Rowan has just gone to sit by the fig tree. She has closed her eyes and looks relaxed. Samel turns back to Ali, who has started to tell a joke. He hopes that his sister will be all right.

Rowan

Sun warmth soaks into Rowan's back like a comforting cloak across her shoulders. She's sitting near a fig tree and her eyes are closed, but she can tell what's happening around her by the sounds. Samel and Ali laugh as water plays in a fountain. Yarvan chats with Mère and Père nearby, and a door has just closed.

When Rowan opens her eyes on the scene in the courtyard people are gathered in groups as she had thought, except for Magenta, who has gone into the house, and Ivoire who isn't anywhere to be seen. It seems to Rowan that she's looking at the view through the wrong end of a far-seeing glass. There's distance between her and everyone else, just as there has been since that day in the tower.

A cloud slides across the sun, briefly darkening the bright scene, causing Rowan to shiver. She shivers often these days, as if she carries a permanent chill within. It's her fault that Hrashak is dead; she killed her father's uncle, became the Queen of Fire, the destroyer. Now she wonders how the Queen came to do the things she did. The stories never told of the Queen's childhood, what happened to her when she was young. Rowan remembers that Grandmother Wisdom said that even seemingly evil people had reasons for what they did.

Rowan doesn't remember the journey here to Aquila. Father says she fell into a sleep or trance and neither one of them could rouse her. Apparently they travelled by horses, wagon, and camels because Samel couldn't get the bracelets to work on his own. Samel likes to recall and talk about the journey, the scenery and the animals he saw, while Rowan barely listens.

Father says over and over that she did what she had to in order to save them. She knows he's trying to convince her and maybe he's right, but she can't accept it. If only he'd stop talking about it. There should have been another way, otherwise how could she condemn Hrashak? She shouldn't have lost her temper. Given more time she might have convinced Varonne to help them escape. Perhaps they should have pretended to help Hrashak, tried to gain his trust. They'd acted like billy goats, all of them, butting heads, giving no ground.

In her wildest imaginings she never saw herself killing another person, couldn't have envisioned the circumstances that made it happen. Yet she did it so easily with barely a thought, instinct taking over, the way she saw an eagle dive for a fish in the river just yesterday. That's what spooks her, how quickly it happened. Maybe Hrashak killed his brother and Rowan's mother just as effortlessly. She doesn't want to be like him, but doesn't having his death on her hands make them the same?

It could even be her fault that Hrashak killed her mother. If he was watching them all that time, what if he'd seen into her heart, known that she was growing annoyed with Zarmine, and he discerned Rowan's plans to leave. Perhaps he saw her mother's death as a way to grant a wish. Rowan shudders despite the warmth of the sun.

She used to think, if only the Queen of Fire could be made to see the good side of her capabilities things would turn out differently. Now she knows that sometimes events happen before a person has time to blink. Perhaps that happened to the Queen, and she didn't have time to change before the sea god's son destroyed her.

Rowan glances at Samel. He's just stuck his head into the fountain and come up dripping. She can't picture herself ever hurting him in any way, but how can she trust herself? Yarvan says not to worry about it, that she's more like Zarmine than anyone else, that her mother brought her up well and that she's a good person. He doesn't seem to see the dark side of his wife, the way she could manipulate people, and twist events to her own advantage. Though her father has been good to her, Rowan wonders if he has a shadow side, too.

Suddenly she's back in that horrible night of the storm. Cold, wet, lost. Everything might have been different if Rowan had gone with her mother to look for Thea. Would Hrashak have found another way? At least it might have given her mother time to tell Rowan about her father and brother, about the bracelets. She has imagined so many different ways the story could have gone, but she can't go back and change a thing.

People chatter and laugh. Sunlight glints on the cascading water of the fountain, a bird chirps nearby. Life goes on all around her, her own lungs breathe. Though her heart still beats, it feels like a weight in her chest.

In the distance she notices a speck in the sky. It might be an eagle. There were black birds wheeling around Hrashak's fortress that day. She looked out of the window and saw them, thought for a moment that Mord had come with friends, but the birds were too small to be ravens. Swifts Yarvan calls them. Nothing ominous he says, just regular birds that lived in the mountains. Her father doesn't know that at that moment she would have welcomed a flock of black birds come to take her away.

Mord is with Thea now, in the north. A message came a few days ago via eagle. The great birds, she has found out, make as good messengers as ravens. It seems that all her friends, relations, and animals are well. Angel found his way to Grandmother Wisdom's people, and even Nesgor made it safely back to Timberton.

Thinking of all of them and of her former life is like recalling a story she read long ago. She can't remember the ending. Did they live happily ever after?

For Varonne at least, there has been a somewhat of agreeable turn of events. Julina was actually Varonne's mother. In retrospect, Rowan is not surprised. It explains some of her ambivalent feelings about Varonne in the desert. Rowan doesn't know any details of Julina's life with Hrashak or why the woman left her daughter with him, but Yarvan said the two women have reunited. One mother lost, another found.

Rowan wonders if Julina knew all the time, playing her games of illusion in Timberton, that Hrashak was the danger Rowan and her family faced. Certainly the woman knew more than she told. It was too late then to save Rowan and Samel's mother, but Julina might have saved Hrashak. Though probably she didn't want to; she had left him after all, or been driven away by him. At least Julina could have been more forthcoming with Rowan, helped her prepare for the meeting with Hrashak, given her guidance in how to handle him and thus avoid murder. On the other hand, perhaps Rowan was the tool Julina needed to take revenge on her husband. Rowan bites her lip, tastes blood. Julina always did and probably always will keep secrets, just like Zarmine.

Yarvan has said that the horror of Hrashak's death will fade eventually, though it's good not to forget it entirely. "Remember the past," he said. "Learn from it."

At this moment all Rowan wants to do is turn the last page of the story. Close the book and lock it in a trunk, think about other things. It's hard to do.

Her father has promised that in a week or so, after Magenta's wedding, the three of them will join a caravan and travel north. She'll be able to see the grassland people again, her friends in Timberton, Karl and Karolina and their family, then Thea and the twins. Maybe even Lynx and his relations. It worries her that she has trouble remembering the details of faces, the characteristics of voices. What if none of them recognize her when they meet?

Samel has hardly been able to stop talking about the upcoming journey. Rowan watches her brother play a short piece on the flute that Yarvan gave him. She glances at her father, who is smiling. She envies them their closeness. Though they always try to include her in everything they do, the three of them don't feel like a real family yet, to her. Give it time, Yarvan has told her. They've been gentle with her and patient with her nightmares. At least she isn't having as many as she did at first. For several days she didn't want to go to sleep at all. The room next to the kitchen that they've converted to a bedroom for her felt too large, though she's grown more used to it. And it's not so strange anymore to wake in a two storey house with a noisy street outside, but Aquila doesn't feel like home.

She doesn't know where home is at this point, though it should be wherever her father and brother are. After all, she undertook this whole journey to find them. The thought of going back to live permanently at the cottage doesn't appeal either. Life has gotten more complicated instead of less. Finding her father and brother hasn't answered the questions, just raised more.

What, she wonders, does her father expect her to learn from the past? Not to lose your temper, perhaps. Not to keep important secrets from your children. And don't expect the world to stay the same from one day to the next. This is a comforting thought. If things change, then perhaps she won't feel this way forever.

Samel doesn't appear to be as affected by their recent experiences. At least Rowan hasn't caught him brooding. However, he has been rather frenetic in his wish to show her all the people and places he loves in Aquila, and he never stops chattering. Like one of the northern squirrels. Maybe he shows his feelings differently. Because they're alike in some ways doesn't mean they are identical.

Anyway, Samel is right in his pride of this city. It's an amazing place; like a colourful tapestry, woven on a background of rich threads and many colours. A city out of legend, with fierce-looking traders bringing exotic goods on camel caravans from dangerous corners of the world. People of all hues and costumes. A great palace with gardens, fountains and streams watering trees, flowers and fruits. Clamouring markets, festivals, performances and musical events.

Some days it's hard to grasp that not so many weeks ago she hadn't seen any of this, was a simple girl of the north woods. Then she still had a mother, but had no idea she had a father and brother, too. Some things are lost, others found.

Like the bracelets. Neither she nor Samel have attempted to use them since that day in Hrashak's bastion, though both are still wearing them. Hrashak was right that they can't ignore whatever it is the bracelets can do the way their parents did. At this moment Rowan understands why they might have wanted to. Interesting how she has more empathy for her mother and father now. Yarvan would say she's growing up. Rowan sighs and the leaves of the fig tree rustle above her.

"Hey," Ivoire whispers, "want to climb up here with me? The branches are strong and it's a good place to hide, watch what's going on. Especially when you don't feel like being with a lot of people. My family can be a little much sometimes. Quick! No one's watching right now."

Rowan climbs into the green to join Ivoire. They smile at each other, perching like two over-large birds. It's cooler here and Rowan can see over the walls of the house into the city. To the north is the Lord's palace with the eagle flag flying. Beyond that lies the desert, which Rowan can't see from this spot. Samel says she'll have to learn to ride a camel in the next few days. He thinks she'll like it, but she's not sure. On all sides are many houses and gardens, streets full of people. She tries to imagine what would have happened if Hrashak had attacked the city with his guards and with enchantment. What if his transformed wolves had lived to enter the city? Yarvan says the Lords of Ameer have a great many soldiers of their own, the Lords' Militia. So there would have been war and devastation – houses knocked down, burned perhaps, people left homeless, in fear and pain. Samel's friends might have been hurt. This pretty young girl in the tree would have been crying. Rowan is certain that Hrashak's way was wrong, and that thought offers some comfort.

Ivoire hands Rowan a fig. Sweet juice flows down Rowan's chin, seeds crunch between her teeth. She remembers the taste of the berries that Mirage gave her. That was just before the drumming and dancing. After that Grandmother came and took Rowan to her tent. A phrase of the old woman's comes back to Rowan: sometimes terror keeps us from taking the next step on the path of our life. Ivoire leans precariously from her branch to hand Rowan a grubby handkerchief to wipe away the fig juice. She is surrounded by people who keep giving her gifts. How can she not respond?

Hrashak had so much less than she does – no wife or brother, no friends. Merely soldiers who obeyed his commands, a daughter who feared him. Rowan can almost feel sorry for the man, but he did have choices. Just as Rowan decided to find her family rather than staying home, wallowing in sorrow and self pity, Hrashak could have decided to be a kind and wise ruler of the lands he already held instead of looking for ways to conquer others. Rowan sighs.

Ivoire takes the handkerchief from her. Looks at it and grimaces. "Sorry, I think I used this as a paint rag. But don't worry; you haven't any paint on your face."

"I didn't sigh because of that," Rowan shakes her head. It's too long and complicated to try and explain to the girl. "Anyway, thanks."

Ivoire has turned to study Magenta, who is standing in the doorway of the house talking to Mère. "Soon she'll be married," Ivoire says. "I wonder when they'll have a baby. That will make me an aunt." She grins at Rowan. "Think I'll be a good one?"

Rowan nods.

Babies and toddlers have to learn how to crawl and walk. Rowan remembers how hard it was for Thea's boys. They fell down a lot, but they kept getting up. Perhaps, just like those toddlers, it's time for her to start taking a few new steps.

There's a whole land out there to be explored, if she wants to see it. On the other hand, there isn't any rush. She could just stay here in the tree with Ivoire, pretend to be a little girl instead of the age she is, which is almost the age of Magenta, who is getting married. At least Rowan knows that marriage is not what she herself wants right now. Rather, it's pleasant to let the wind blow through her hair while birds sing a lullaby. She wonders what it might be like to go to sleep in a tree.

In the garden below Père has lit a brazier. He and Yarvan are getting ready to grill meat. Fire can be used for good purposes, too. Magenta and Mère have brought dishes of vegetables and fruit to the table. Ali and Samel are carrying jugs of water, juice and wine from the house.

"Ivoire!" Mere shouts. "Where are you? I need your help."

Ivoire puts a finger to her lips and shakes her head, grinning at Rowan. Now Samel is calling for his sister. There aren't that many places in the yard or the house where anyone could hide, but no one has come to the fig tree yet. The smells from the table and brazier are very enticing, and Rowan's stomach rumbles in anticipation.

Soon she'll have to act her age again, take up responsibilities, spend time learning about the bracelets and other things. But not today. Together the two girls in the tree watch as the others call and pretend to search for them.

Regine Haensel lives in Saskatoon, Saskatchewan, Canada. Her short stories and nonfiction have appeared previously in magazines and anthologies, and been broadcast on CBC radio. She has won several Saskatchewan Writers' Guild Short Manuscript Awards. Her first book, a collection of short stories, The Other Place, was published in 2012.

Made in the USA
Charleston, SC
25 February 2014